# HEIR *to* THORN & FLAME

# HEIR *to* THORN & FLAME

BEN ALDERSON

SECOND SKY

Published by Second Sky in 2023

An imprint of Storyfire Ltd.
Carmelite House
50 Victoria Embankment
London EC4Y 0DZ

www.secondskybooks.com

ISBN: 978-1-83790-691-8
eBook ISBN: 978-1-83790-690-1

*Harry, without you this book would never exist. Fictional men are great, but you, my love, are the best.*

# PART ONE

## THE FALSE SON

# CHAPTER 1

There were countless reasons why the library was my favourite room in the Gathrax manor; the portraits of long dead mages weren't one of them. The manor was a maze of rooms, ballrooms with elaborate chandeliers, and dining halls larger than most homes in the town. Of them all, the library warmed my soul. It was a place of comfort and escape. If Dame—the Lead of the Gathrax's army of servants—had not been assisting me, I might have slipped a book into my jacket to take home for later enjoyment.

I stared at the painting before me. It was one of many adorning the walls in the library, but certainly the biggest, taking up an entire wall by itself. The unnamed artist had colourfully depicted the Heart Oak, bathed in furious black flame.

'In all of your twenty-five years, Maximus Oaken, that darn painting hasn't changed,' Dame chortled, her voice rasped with age. 'If you want to finish up early, get back to dusting.'

I glanced over my shoulder as the ancient woman poked

her head around a stack of shelves, the spectacles on the end
of her nose enlarging her colourless eyes. 'I'm in no rush,' I
replied. 'Dancing isn't exactly high on the list of things I
enjoy.'

'Well.' Dame waved an oiled cloth at me in dismissal. 'I
bloody enjoy dancing, so get to it. These old bones deserve to
rattle tonight.'

Dame always had a way of making me laugh. With a
dramatic wink, her magnified eye was as comical as her grin.

'Dryads help you,' I called out, disappearing around a
stretch of shelves, each double stacked with old tomes. 'Rattling bones doesn't sound as enticing as you think.'

'Don't knock it until you try it, love.'

For such a stern-looking woman, Dame certainly looked
out for me, more so than her other members of staff. It was
likely because she's known me from such a young age. Like
the other children unfortunate enough to be born within the
servants' quarters, I was put to work by the age of six. Dame
had kept her eye out for me since.

I called it favouritism; she called it pity.

Plucking the cloth from my belt, and retrieving the vial of
oil from my pocket, I left the painting behind, although the
image was always deep in my mind. My nose itched as the
scent of ancient novels and dust struck me. Time, and lack of
use, blended into a pleasant smell. The stale air carried the
echo of countless stories. Over the years, I had read many of
them, though servants weren't allowed to so much as touch
the Gathraxs's collection of tomes. King Gathrax preferred his
servants to lack education; he believed an absence of knowledge would keep us controllable, which in some cases was
true. It never stopped me from *borrowing* a book or four.

It wasn't stealing if I put it back. But it was a risk, and one
worth taking.

Aldian was built on the back of stories. There were myths of dragons and dryads, phoenix kings who dwelled on thrones of fire, and the nymphs who once lived within the waterways of this world. I knew these tales as I knew the lines on my palm. Many were historic imaginings of Aldian's history, full of accurate accounts. Others were exaggerated, made up to reflect the world in the way the author deemed necessary.

One fact all the stories had in common was magic. And I loathed it. With every fibre of my being, I hated Magic.

Magic was to blame for the state of the world. A world where some thrive in wealth and others drown just trying to survive. Everyone else seemed to celebrate magic's memory, but I was never more thankful for something disappearing—burned away from our history when the source of the southern mages' power was destroyed.

I moved through the library, dusting the dark-stained shelves, passing the countless books I had read. Out of the hundreds I'd devoured, there were likely thousands more I had yet to open. Some might think it depressing, that I had a lifetime of serving ahead of me; I couldn't help but imagine just how many more of King Gathrax's books I would take, absorb and return without them ever realising. It was those small acts of defiance that kept me going.

The day slipped away quickly, as it always did in this room. Beyond the crimson-stained-glass windows, the skies darkened. I was bathed in the ruling colour of Gathrax: *red*.

'Have you not finished yet?' Dame shuffled around the wall of shelves towards me, fingertips stained orange from the cleaning oil. As always, her enlarged eyes surveyed my work. It was common for Dame to smile, which made reading her emotions a task in itself. Unless when she outright frowned, which she did at that very moment.

'How long's a piece of string?' I retorted.

'Maximus, the festival starts in just shy of an hour and you've not touched even half of your portion of the room.'

'It won't take me long,' I said, brushing off her displeased glare with a flick of my dust-coated cloth. 'Go. Leave me to finish in peace.'

'Are you dismissing me, boy?'

For all the years I had known Dame, she always looked the same. Long snow-white hair pinned up in a neat bun, the same apron wrapped around her aged frame, marked from years of grease, grime and muck.

'I'd never dismiss you,' I said, moving towards the large oak doors. 'It is merely a suggestion. The sooner you leave me, the quicker I will be finished.'

Dame clicked her tongue across her teeth, sizing me up with both hands on her rounded hips. 'One day, and one day soon, someone is going to smack that sarcastic look right off you.'

I raised a hand and rubbed the phantom ache at Dame's threat. 'And ruin such a pretty face?'

She rolled her eyes and moved for the door. 'Insufferable, you are.'

'I love you too,' I replied.

I swept my hand towards the now open door, encouraging her to leave. Dame passed me, mumbling something beneath her breath. I knew from the tone alone she was smiling.

'What would you have me tell your parents if you don't show up?' Dame asked.

'If you see them, tell them not to wait,' I said, proving to Dame something she already had figured out. I had no intention of joining in on the evening's festivities. With the library to myself, and King Gathrax and his family far from the manor, I had an entire night of fictional adventure ahead of me.

'If I see them, I shall tell them their son is a menace and lacks the ability to follow a command,' Dame replied, brushing her liver-spotted hand down her apron.

'Oh, you *know* me well.'

Dame popped her hip, leaning on one leg whilst she surveyed me. 'Perhaps you could trade those fictional men for one made of flesh and bone.'

I brought my fingers to my mouth and mocked a gag. 'Dryads, why would I do that?'

My sarcasm didn't go unnoticed. Dame's mouth cracked into a grin, her eyes narrowing as she fought the urge to laugh. 'At my old age, and experience, I could list off many reasons why flesh is better than paper, but I wouldn't want to embarrass you.'

As much as I enjoyed the concept of wasting my evening flirting, it wouldn't have served me come morning. News spread like wildfire through the manor, and I knew better than to have heads turning on me.

'Here,' I said, turning to the shelf behind me. My eyes traced the shelves, searching for a book I had recently read. Its cover was leatherbound and plain, no hint of the knee-buckling smut that made up most of the pages. 'Take this and then you'll discover why I prefer my men made from ink and parchment.'

Dame took the book, a cheeky glint illuminated by her thick glasses. 'I have already read it.'

Heat flooded my cheeks. 'You have.'

'Did you not hear what I said about age and experience?'

'You win,' I said, hands raised in surrender at my sides.

Dame rolled her eyes, again. 'Get the job done and I will see you at the Green, Master Oaken. I don't know how many more excuses I can conjure for you if Julian comes looking.'

Julian. Just the mention of him soured the saliva on my tongue.

'As if Julian will miss out on the Dance of the Dryads. That pompous prick loves the opportunity for attention,' I replied.

Julian Gathrax—the eldest child and next in the line to rule the Kingdom—was a sinister monster. For years, he had made his intentions with me clear. Even without admitting the extent of it to Dame, or my parents, the mere mention of him made me uneasy. But I was right about one thing. Julian would not be home tonight. Not with the opportunity of so much attention, which was something he needed as desperately as a fish needs water.

I could tell from Dame's expression that she was not as convinced on the matter as I was. 'I'm wasting my breath with you.'

I shrugged. 'Can you blame me for thirsting for escape?'

'I don't, but I do think it sensible you restrict yourself to dreaming in the fringes of sleep.' Dame slipped between the oak doors, all without taking her eyes off me. 'For punishment leaves no scars during a dream. I cannot say the same for the hand of the Gathrax heir if he comes looking.'

What Dame suggested was true. But I hadn't the heart to tell her Julian's slap never left a lingering mark. At least one that would not fade quickly. I would know, I had experienced enough of them.

I raised a hand to my heart as the corner of my mouth lifted into a smirk. 'You'll regret making me join you tonight when I come looking for a dance.'

'With me?' Dame almost choked on her rasped laugh.

'Trust me, I could rattle those bones like no other.'

One sharp slap to my upper arm, Dame's ancient face broke into the brightest of smiles. 'Did I mention you are insufferable, Maximus?'

I leaned into the door, slowly closing it. 'Did I mention I love you?'

Dame left, but a knot of unease had settled in my stomach. This was the power Julian Gathrax had over me. The mere mention of him made my skin itch and my chest tighten.

# CHAPTER 2

I slipped around the shelves, writing desks and mountainous cabinets, dabbing the brown cloth in the vial of diluted oil. I rubbed it across the oak shelves until they glistened. I moved quickly, losing myself deeper into the library. The sooner I was finished, the sooner I could kick my boots up and lose myself in some romance between star-crossed lovers.

There was a sense of identity to this place, and it warmed me better than any burning fire. So many histories of those who came before me.

History was something I would never have. I lived the life of a ghost. My existence would leave no mark on the map of this world. I was merely a nameless servant, moving from room to room, and completing the same tasks day to day. Unlike the many whose stories sat around me, I'd never have a life worth writing about.

Ghosts were beings of shadow, not parchment and quill.

The thought once bothered me. But now, with age, it didn't. Never had I heard my mother complain about her duties. Even after busy days minding King Gathrax's youngest children, when she'd return home with arms black and blue with bruises, she always found something to enjoy.

It was the same with my father. He worked tirelessly on the estate's endless grounds and would often return home exhausted. Especially during the winter months, he would fall asleep before raising a morsel of food to his mouth. And yet, he never made comment about how bad our lives were.

As I always did, I left cleaning the portraits to last. Pulling up a stool, I reached up and dragged mounds of the grime from the tops of the frames. Holding back a sneeze, I cleared as much as I could reach and watched it fall to the dark cedar floor like a sprinkling of fresh snow.

The painting before me was of a rounded man, cheeks as red as the jacket he wore, which was bursting at the seams. Some long-dead relative of the Gathrax family tree. There had been enough of them. He faced the painter, his hand raised until the telltale sign of his magic was on display.

Scarred across the man's palm was his mage-mark. Three interconnecting circles of puckered skin, threaded by two crossing lines that sliced through the scars. It was a sign of power, a mark that set those with magic apart from those without it.

A mark that had not been seen since the Heart Oak was destroyed by the North.

A mage-mark.

My arms ached by the time I reached the final portrait. A familiar shiver coursed up my spine as I took in the depiction mere inches from my face. My legs wobbled slightly as I reached to clean the glass protecting it. Across the canvas, scripted in a gold-leaf paint, was the title of the art.

*End of Red.*

Most of the image was painted with dull earth-tone

colours, except for the angry splashes of crimson cutting across a man, slain among a circle of his enemies.

Mage Damian Gathrax, the last mage to fall in the War of the Wood, stared back at me with all-seeing eyes. His wand lay snapped at his side, and blood pooled beneath him. Looking on from the shadows of trees was the masked army of the North. They were no more than phantoms lacking details.

A floorboard creaked somewhere behind me. I gasped, startled. Before I could laugh it off, a voice called out from the shadows.

'I thought I would find you here, *Max.*'

Blood drained from my face. I turned around to locate the speaker and lost my footing on the stool. It tilted beneath me, and suddenly I was falling. The herringbone floor raced up to greet me. I landed, heavily, in a lump with the echo of smashed glass at my side.

Slightly winded, I looked up to find Julian Gathrax. He knelt before me. 'Oh dear, allow me to help you.'

Julian held his hand outstretched towards me, fingers wiggling as they waited for me to take them. Which I didn't. I pushed myself from the floor, nicking my palm on a broken piece of glass. Recoiling with a hiss, the shallow cut stung, coated in spilled oil.

'Your grace, forgive me, I didn't hear you come in.' I lowered my gaze, but not before I caught the disappointment on his face.

'And what exactly are you apologising for this time… *Maximus?*' My name sounded vile on his tongue. He dragged it out, hissing as it came to an end.

I glanced up at him, with an unwavering gaze.

Julian had leaned himself up against the shelf, taut arms folded across his chest. His jacket was the shade of a ripened blood orange, the shirt beneath it white and full like the feathers of a proud bird. He was taller than me, only by a few inches, but I knew just how those few inches could make such a difference. Like his father, Julian's hair was the colour of autumn leaves, another sign of his powerful heritage. That, and the same sharp nose of his great-grandfather, Mage Damian Gathrax, whose picture towered behind me.

He was a strange type of handsome; the type that set me at unease.

'Is there something I can help you with, Julian?' I asked, unsure of what else to say.

'Don't act coy with me, Max. I think you know exactly what it is I want. Have I not made it obvious?' Julian stepped towards me, boots crunching glass. I couldn't move back even if I wanted to. I knew better than to make Julian think I was refusing him. It never ended well if I did.

'You have,' I replied. 'But have I not made my answer equally as obvious?'

Julian recoiled, eyes widening.

'I dislike your tone.' His grin cut wider across his face, his thin lips almost disappearing into his pale skin. 'Perhaps a lesson in manners, or a simple reminder as to why you belong to me, and thus, should do as I please?'

'That,' I said, clutching my bleeding hand, 'won't be necessary.'

As if Julian could smell my wound, his gaze dropped to it.

'Oh gosh, you have hurt yourself.' He faked surprised concern, hand reaching for my own. 'I will kiss it better.'

I pulled away, but he was quicker. Julian snatched my hand in his, not bothering to be gentle. His touch was icy, firm. I winced as his nails scratched my warm skin. This close to him, his scent smothered anything else. A tidal wave of lavender and mint cascaded over me, building with each inhale.

Julian smelled of wealth—of power.

He raised my palm to his mouth; his gaze immobilised me. As did the sickening press of his parted lips and the slight tickle of his tongue, which spread across my calloused palm.

I opened my mouth to say something, but my breath hitched in my throat.

'Better?' he asked, lowering my hand from his mouth, refusing to let it go.

'Please,' I began, voice shaking with anger more than fear.

'Please, what?' Julian's grip tightened as he felt my attempt to tug away from him.

'Let *fucking* go.'

Julian's eyes widened. 'What a tongue you have on you, Maximus. I like it, but I want to hear you ask me nicely.'

'*Please*, let me fucking go.'

His gaze narrowed. 'Do you believe me to be kind, like my father?' Julian leaned in, the smell of his warm breath offensive.

'I think you *could* be kind,' I lied.

'Ah,' Julian exhaled, shaking his head until a strand of red hair cascaded over his azure eyes. 'You are right. Maximus. It has been hard not to think of you these days. And when you refuse me, it hurts.'

'I really should go before my parents wonder where I am.'

A shadow crossed over Julian's angular face. His sharp brow furrowed; his smile straightened into a long, pale line. Before my eyes, his calm demeanour melted, revealing something darker beneath it. 'I am not finished—*we* are not finished. That is why you are here, isn't it, because you waited for me. You knew I would come looking for you.'

'No, Julian,' I said, knowing what was to happen next. 'That isn't what this is.'

'*No, Julian!*' He mocked, voice forced high and eyes rolling into his hairline. 'Max, do not spoil this moment.'

Julian released my hand, allowing me to step away until the portrait was pressed into my back. Its presence reminded me I had nowhere to go.

'I shall have you, Max. This chase you keep up will come to its end soon, perhaps tonight. Do you know the life I could give you? The status, power—the wealth. Stop resisting, stop fighting it and give in.'

Disgust coiled through me. 'And my answer, as it has been before, is no.' I forced as much confidence into my reply.

Although this man frightened some part of me, there was another part of me that longed to strike him. I could do it; I had no doubt in my ability to run him through. He was reed-thin and tall. I might not have been riddled with muscle, but my compact height could overpower him.

It was the consequences that kept me in line. It was not only my life at risk if I defied the Gathrax family; it was my parents' well-being. And I would do anything to keep them safe.

'Have a good evening—'

'Would you like to see what my father has gifted me?'

I shook my head, rising and trying to walk past him, only to be stopped as Julian moved his body in my way. 'Julian, let me leave.'

'It seems you do need reminding that I own you.'

Julian slipped his hand towards his belt, all without removing his gaze from me. Slowly, he withdrew something from it.

The blade gripped in his fist caught the fading light of the room. 'Beautiful, isn't she? The handle was crafted from the antlers of a fully grown stag, the very one I slaughtered during last year's hunt. Father had it made for me. Do you like it?'

I caught my distorted reflection in the blade as Julian

twirled it before my face. Wide, green eyes, unblinking. Frightened.

'I do prefer you speechless,' Julian purred. 'Now, give me your arm.'

'Why?' The word broke out of me, half-gasp and half-sob.

Julian sounded almost bored as he replied. 'Do not make me ask again.'

Refusing him was my only option.

Julian flashed his teeth, grunted and then lunged for me. There was no running. I jerked back and slammed my head into the wall. The moment of disorientation worked in Julian's favour, as he pulled my dirtied work-shirt up and exposed the skin of my forearm. Julian snaked the blade up, the tip pressed into my wrist until the skin beneath turned white.

'Scream,' he spat, inches from my face, 'no one will come to find you. And when they do, they will think it was your clumsiness that caused my mark.' His eyes flicked to the broken vial by our feet.

'You don't need to do this.' Anger sparked deep within, a rush of emotion warming my frozen body. I pulled back from him as much as his hold allowed.

Julian's taunting laugh echoed back at me. Squinting his eyes, he lifted the blade and looked down the sharp edge at me. 'I own you; you are mine.'

'Fuck... you.'

'Finally, you are coming round to the idea then.' Julian winked and my revulsion reached new heights.

The air shifted as he thrust the blade forward. Without thinking, I pulled my arm back, palm spread, and slammed it into the side of his face.

The slap silenced the room. Julian gasped as he turned away from me, his hand pressed against his cheek.

It took three heavy breaths for the realisation of what I had done to catch up with me. Through tear-filled eyes, Julian glared at me, spit lining his slack mouth. I had never seen him speechless. But, when he removed his hand from his cheek to reveal the red mark of my handprint, I could see why.

'You will pay for that—'

I shot forward, fuelled by the same foolish desperation that made me hit the King's son, and attacked him again. With every ounce of strength, I pushed hard into Julian's narrow chest with both hands. It was all I needed for him to fall backwards, arms failing. The thump of his reed-thin body smacking into the floor was followed by the clink of his dagger as it clattered into the shadows of the room.

I allowed myself a moment of confusion.

Then I ran.

# CHAPTER 3

It was early evening and Gathrax manor was empty—its residents and serving staff far away in town, enjoying the festivities. Which meant no one witnessed me running through empty corridors and rooms, nor heard Julian Gathrax scream with deranged fury behind me.

'I will gut you! Run, run as fast as you can. Oh, I love the *hunt.*'

Julian's taunting shouts chorused through me. It fuelled me to keep running, even though I had no sense of where to go.

Arms pumping at my sides, and heart thundering in my chest, the manor's interior passed in a blur. Soon enough, I was outside. With the first breath of fresh, autumn air, my adrenaline drained away from me. I was left only with the dread of my actions and the song of crunching twigs and leaves beneath my boots.

My breath fogged before me as I bolted through the connecting gardens of the manor, towards the shadow of Galloway Forest. Each biting inhale scored down my throat, burning my lungs. I fought the urge to look behind me and see just how close Julian was. I had to focus.

*Just keep running*—the muscles in my legs screamed, my arms felt weak as unset jelly—I kept my pace and forged ahead.

Deep in the corner of my mind, where the panic didn't reach, I was thankful for the years of tireless work. That, as well as my long legs and narrow build, helped me soar through stone courtyards, rose gardens and the lines of mani-cured bushes cut into shapes of bears, deer and swans.

'Do you think I will not catch you?' Julian panted after me. 'I'm going… to carve my name… into you. Then you will remember, you are mine.'

His voice drew closer the further from the manor I got, the dull thudding of his chase only an earshot away. Julian's threats came out rushed, breathless. He was unfit. A life of easy treatment had a negative effect on his body, but regard-less he was gaining on me. Not because he was faster, but because I was faltering—unsure where to go.

Up ahead, a line of tall trees signalled the beginning of dense woodland. Among the impenetrable darkness, if there was anywhere I could hide from Julian, it was in the Galloway Forest. It began at the back of the Gathrax estate and lasted for hundreds of miles until breaking in the North.

Branches clawed at my arms and face as I passed the sentinel line of trees. I risked a glance over my shoulder, the wood swallowing what little light the night offered. I couldn't see him, but the sound of Julian's heavy steps was close behind.

Panic seized me, sinking its talons of dread into my consciousness where it refused to let go. Julian would never forgive me for this. Not this time, because I had fought back. The deeper I lost myself, fumbling blindly over root and through thick walls of oak, cedar and yew trees, the more I couldn't ignore the outcome.

Perhaps, if I stopped and turned myself over to Julian, his punishment would be swift. I could beg him not to tell his father. If I gave him what he wanted, then maybe we both could forget about this.

As Julian shouted out again, breathless and deranged, I knew that option had long passed. 'I am going to slice my name into you, so you never forget. Never. Forget. You are... mine.'

*Beatrice.* My friend's name came to me in a flash, so sudden it almost distracted me from the giant trunk of a fallen tree. Just in time, I placed my hands on the rough bark and vaulted over it. Wind ripped past my ears. *Go to Beatrice.* Surely, she could help. But then, in my mind's eye, I saw what would happen to her when Julian found me.

'No.' I wheezed, speaking aloud to myself. 'Keep *fucking* running.'

I slowed, not because I wanted to, but because my body began to tire. Running and cleaning a manor were perhaps two different things. The dark body of the forest absorbed all sound beside my heavy breathing and the taunting laugh of Julian Gathrax.

*You deserve this,* I told myself. *Just get it over with, so you can go home.*

As I faced the dark wood, I scolded myself for my actions. My father always warned me my defiance would one day scorn me, and here I was. What did I expect? That I'd just run and run, and Julian would simply forget this by tomorrow? No. Julian would never drop this. Not until he got what he desired. It was how Julian's family had brought him up. Spoiled and arrogant, all the Gathrax children got whatever they wished for. I just so happened to catch the attention of the one with the darkest of desires.

I pushed as much power into my legs just to keep ahead, but his singsong voice grew closer.

'Maximus.' My name sounded grotesque as Julian sang out behind me. 'My Maximus. Run little… rabbit. Run.'

Even in his breathy, weak shout, the intention behind it was still clear.

My skin crawled as he repeated the nursery rhyme. It was a song I'd not heard for years. My mother used to sing it to me.

'Run… run. Rabbit, run.'

Distracted by his calls, my foot smashed into something firm. I cried out, choking with the pain exploding from my ankle.

I lost my footing, falling forward. My face took the brunt of the hit. Agony ripped through my neck and spread across my shoulders. Pushing the aching down, I rolled over, leaves and dirt getting into my mouth and eyes as I twisted across the forest bed. I stopped when my back slammed into the base of a tree. The force snatched my breath. I blinked and watched stars dance in the dark.

Suddenly, a heaviness weighed down over me.

'Got you, my little rabbit.'

Julian straddled my waist, pinning me with his legs whilst gripping my throat with his free hand. Nails pinched into my neck, slicing crescent moons into my flesh.

'I'm sorry,' I wheezed, grasping his wrist desperately. 'I'm sorry, I'm sorry.'

I hated to beg, but with his hand grasping my throat and the flash of his dagger in his free hand, there was no other option but to show him I was no threat.

'Scream for me,' Julian sneered, eyes wide. The way he

regarded me revealed a dark hunger—a want that turned man to monster. 'I told you, didn't I? I told you I would catch you, and I have. You are mine.'

I gathered saliva in my mouth, and, with a great force, I spat at him. Julian didn't so much as flinch as the glob of phlegm splattered across his cheek. Instead, he grinned wildly as it dribbled slowly down his face.

'Is this the respect you show me, your king?'

In the dark, I barely made out his red-flushed grin. Yet the minimal light seemed to illuminate his gaze and the malicious intent burning in his eyes.

'You're not my king,' I said, half growling and half weeping with panic. 'Your father is, not you!'

Julian's fingers tightened, silencing me. 'But I will be, Maximus, one day it will all be mine. I am not my father, *I* am much worse.'

'Help me...' I forced out with the little air I had left. Although, it was not Julian I pleaded with. Not exactly. I wished for the wood to fight back, just as it did in the stories I had left behind in the library. It was once said that spirits— dryads of old myth—roamed the darkened wood in search for souls to claim.

But I found no comfort in spirits and forgotten creatures of the wood, they would not help me. I was alone. I daren't close my eyes for fear of an old memory resurfacing. One I had fought hard to bury.

*Heavy weight over my thighs.*

*Long fingers bruising my wrists.*

'There are so many things I would like to do to... with you. I just need to decide where to start,' Julian whispered, flashing the dagger before me. I longed to cry out, but this far into the wood no one would hear me, and his fingers ensured breathing was near impossible. He wanted me to scream, he enjoyed it. Refusing him that reaction was my last form of revolt.

Julian's gaze traced up and down my body. He mumbled to himself, mouth parted and tongue trailing his lower lip. Then, before I could so much as blink to block out the horror, Julian swiped his blade at my chest.

Through material, the sharp end sliced skin. I waited for the pain, but it was warmth that answered. I attempted to look down to see the damage, but Julian held me in place.

'This is what you want, isn't it?' I no longer cared to watch him. Besides the tingling across my chest, and the horror gripping my mind, discomfort became a friend. 'You want me to hurt you. You like it, I see that now.'

Suddenly, his hand was removed from my throat. I took my chance and inhaled deeply, only to still when the kiss of his blade pressed into my skin.

'Will anyone even notice if you died, Maximus?' Julian asked. 'Not that it would matter if they did. No one will care to punish me for killing someone as worthless as you.'

I thought of my parents as the blade pressed further into my skin. Would they be waiting for me in the Green, wondering what had kept me? I conjured images of them, finding out their only child was bleeding out in the forest with nothing but the spirits of old to provide him comfort.

*This is not how I'm going to die.* The thought was hot and sudden.

One last time, I tried to plead with the madman atop me. 'Let me go, Julian. I know you want me, and I should never have refused you for so long. Please, take me. Have me—'

'Finally,' he hissed, eyes rolling as though my words had touched a pleasure spot. 'Except, what if I no longer care to have you? I like the worms on the end of my hook to wriggle, but your refusal of me is far from off-putting.'

'Then let me go, prove to me you are kind. I swear I won't say anything.'

Julian sighed. 'Obedience suits you, Maximus. Now, if you care to see tomorrow, then I suggest you keep still.'

Julian's bright eyes glanced towards my stomach where my shirt had ridden up during our tussle. His tongue trailed his lower lip, his eyes wide and unblinking. He lifted the blade from my throat, and a rush of hope flooded through me.

'This… this is the perfect place,' he said, finger tickling around my navel. 'No one will see the mark I leave you. It will make it special. Our special place, our secret. Just for you and me.'

'Yes,' I repeated. 'Our secret.'

Julian's spare hand reached awkwardly for my tunic. The chill of night brushed across my exposed stomach as he lifted it up. I cringed at the brush of his knuckles.

He was completely focused on my body, devouring me with his starving eyes. He didn't notice as I moved my hand across the forest bed beside me. My fingers crawled across the foliage, searching for something to use against him. I brushed over twigs and dried leaves, across stones and pinecones.

Julian hummed as he studied my stomach. I was his rabbit; he was my fox.

My heart stopped as my middle finger brushed over a large shape. Julian was too busy wiping my blood from his blade and didn't see me drag my weapon into my hand. I couldn't see it, but my touch told me it was nothing more than a branch of sorts. It felt right against my palm, promising me salvation. It was weightless and balanced, and my fingers wrapped perfectly around its base.

Not once had I dropped my stare from Julian. First in fear, now in calculation. It was all too familiar… searching blindly for something to protect myself with. This time would be different. No one would come running into my room to save me. I had to save myself.

'I hope you cry out for me again,' Julian said, finally breaking his gaze from my stomach. 'It will sound beautiful so deep in the woods.'

I bit down into my lower lip, already refusing to speak, let alone scream. There would be no awarding Julian what he desired, not as he balanced the tip of the dagger over my stomach and twisted it by the hilt.

'Wait…' I spluttered as the tip broke skin. 'That will—'

'Kill you? I know. Unless you are blessed with luck.'

In that moment, I knew Julian was never going to let me live. Servants had whispered about Julian's twisted enjoyments. When he was a child, he'd been known to trap small animals, cutting into their bodies. Once I had even been sent to his rooms to clean up the mess of his disembowelments— rats, mice and birds left scattered in pieces across his bedroom floor.

That was what I was to him. Just another one of his little animals.

I brought my weapon up before Julian could so much as blink. I jerked myself upwards. Julian didn't have enough time to make a sound as I lifted my weapon with as much might as I could summon.

Time stilled for a strange, prolonged moment.

When it crashed back into reality, a bright and scalding fire spread across my palm and up my arm. It was as if a star exploded within my bones. The sensation lit me from the inside, melting flesh and boiling my marrow. I pinched my eyes closed just as a bolt of striking-blue light lit up the short space between us, blinding the world entirely.

Julian's face, twisted in horror, was etched in the dark of my mind. One moment he was on me, the next he was gone, dragged into the dark beneath a conjured force. Air pushed my chestnut hair from my face and snatched the breath from my lungs.

Then it all disappeared. Gone, as suddenly as it arrived.

A tidal wave of darkness crashed over the scene, leaving impenetrable silence in its wake. I sat still, heart pounding in my ears, trying to understand what had happened. The peace that engulfed me lasted a moment, before the pain in my arm registered through the fog. I yelled out in sudden agony, dropping the twig onto my lap. Clutching my arm to my chest, my hand spasmed in boiling torture. Where I expected fire to cover my hand, there was nothing. But the feeling was pure, fiery and undeniable torment. It stole my breath. The skin seemed to sizzle as the smell of burned flesh infiltrated my nose. My palm throbbed as though my heart slammed beneath it.

I pried my hand open and held it close to my eyes. Squinting through the dark, I looked at the wound I knew with certainty would stare back at me.

Except, this should be impossible. A trick of my mind, it must have been.

Even in the dark, the mark was as clear as the waning moon in the sky. Three silvered circles, each overlapping one another. Through them were two sharp lines meeting in an X. It was hard to make out the finer details, but within the silver-scarred circles, I saw other marks. Smaller symbols I was all too familiar with but should never have seen on myself. I had seen them many times before. Almost every day since I could remember.

I stood, dazed. Shaking breaths racked my chest; the smell of my charred flesh invaded me. I doubled over, close to vomiting.

Then I saw it. The branch, discarded on the forest bed beside my feet.

My knees ached as I bent down to pick it up. As the cold wood met my boiling palm, all the details I had refused to remember until then came flooding back.

'Julian?' I called out his name, but I couldn't see him, not as my eyes scanned the immediate forest around me.

Dread clawed down my spine as I quickly determined that Julian had run away. I had hurt him, and he had fled. Likely to get help. Should I run before Julian returned? Should I take myself back to the estate before he got there, or find my parents at the festival? All those questions battered my mind as I stood in the cold forest, the stick gripped tight in my searing hand.

'Shit, shit, shit.' I turned around in circles, panicked.

The urge to just run without stopping was overwhelming. But I waded through the shadowed patch of wood, unwilling to look at my palm and the truth that waited on it. If I ignored it, it would not be real.

I couldn't find Julian anywhere. There was no sign of his ruby-toned jacket, or his lanky, sinister frame. Although I believed otherwise, I tried to convince myself he had run away. It was the better of the options. Lost in a maze of towering trees and darkness, there was no knowing the way home. It was better to think he was unconscious or hurt than on his way back to me.

Though, if Julian didn't kill me, his father, King Gathrax, would.

'Julian?' I called out again, hoping to hear his wretched voice reply.

There was no response.

I stepped further into the shadows. The only noise, besides my raspy breaths, was the slow drip of what sounded to be water. The louder it got, the more it taunted me. Something splashed onto the crown of my head. I shot up my hand to feel my hairline, only to find that my fingers came back wet and warm. I searched for the source, when another splash hit my cheek, close enough to my mouth that the taste leaked inside.

Iron burst across my tongue, knotting my stomach in disgust.

Then I looked up and found him. Julian had never fled. He had not run away, because he had no chance to.

In the pale light from the rising moon, I found his corpse.

Julian dangled within the tree before me, a large branch protruding through his stomach. The single beam of moonlight reflected off the crimson droplets as they fell in quick succession. I couldn't move, not before another splash hit my chin and dribbled down my neck.

Across his chest, his jacket and shirt had been charred, as was the skin that lingered beneath. Smoke slithered skywards as blood dribbled down his spoiled torso, falling over me like rain.

I stumbled back, losing my footing until I scrambled backwards across the uneven ground. The stick still tight in my hand; I wouldn't let go. I *couldn't*.

It took a moment for my gaze to focus and my heart to fix its irregular beat. Then I screamed. I cried out into the night, just as Julian wanted, until it felt as though a hundred knives sliced out from my chest. All the while, I didn't take my eyes off his corpse.

Julian's neck was bent at an awkward angle, his mouth wide open. His arms and legs dangled in the air, the branch through his stomach the only thing keeping him in the tree.

I attempted to scream again, but I vomited instead; I gagged until nothing but forced air came out and the acid bile burned my throat.

I kept my gaze locked on Julian, pleading, *begging*, for him to wake up.

*You did this. You've killed him.*

Peering back at my palm, I studied the mark across it in the new light. As clear as morning bells, I knew what it meant.

I had murdered Julian Gathrax, and—more horrific—I had a mage-mark.

# CHAPTER 4

The dead used to be left in the shadows of the forest. It was said the dryads would then claim the bodies, dragging them into the pits of the earth, or encasing them within trees. It was because of those old stories that I left Julian's corpse lodged in the tree, hanging like a puppet on a string. Lifeless and limp. Dead, because of me. I feared if I touched him, the forest spirits would feel threatened. Julian belonged to them now.

I sprinted back to Gathrax manor. The muscles in my legs burned as the cold winds wiped at my face. There was an urgency to create as much distance between the body and myself.

'You... killed him,' I mumbled, breathless as horror sunk its talons into me. True—riling fear blinded my vision with tears—I had killed someone. Not only someone, but the son of the King. The prince. The heir to the Gathrax estate. As was the colour of his Kingdom, my hands were stained red. Except, no blood covered them. If I looked down, I would find them void of gore but cursed with the silvered scars of a mage-mark.

*Run little rabbit, run.* Julian's taunting song echoed in my whirling mind.

*If you didn't kill him, he would've killed you.*

Time was a fragmented concept. Reality slipped through my fingers—the world stayed eerily quiet as I left the embrace of the wood. Even the owls refused to cry out their evening song, there was not the usual chatter of humans who filled the estate. There were only the winds as they screamed my crime and the waning moon above that had been the only witness.

Gathrax manor watched me too. In the dark wash of the night, the countless windows were lit from within. I slowed to a fast walk, breathless, as the manor regarded me—a face of stone watching me, grinning and all-knowing. I sensed its judgement, deep in my bones, as I moved into the glow of its fire-lit windows. I was covered in vomit, my shirt stained with blood from the wound across my chest. In my hand, I gripped the branch—no, the wand—as though my life depended on it. If anyone were to see me, one look, and all would have been revealed. The rough bark pinched into my scarred palm, reminding me it was very much real.

I couldn't contemplate what it meant, to hold a wand and be marked across my palm. There was no denying the truth of the matter, but I was no mage. I couldn't be.

*Are you not?*

It was impossible to focus on one thought for more than a short moment before another, more overwhelming one, took precedence. It had been years since the era of wands and magic. Since the death of the last mage—Damian Gathrax—there had not been another. Mages only retrieved wands from the Heart Oak, which had been destroyed in obsidian fires that had burned for months. It was the North who destroyed the Heart Oak, severing the ties to magic for the Southern ruling families. Yet here I was, holding a wand that I had plucked from the forest bed hundreds of miles from the very location the Heart Oak once stood.

Although the four Southern families still ruled in the shadow of their ancestors, the only known living mage was far beyond the Galloway Forest, leagues North.

Peeling back my stiffened fingers, I studied the mark on my palm. Puckered, angry, red. It was no different to the mutilation from a fresh burn.

I knew, without a doubt, I would be killed for this. Which led me to another concern, one far greater than my sake. My parents. They would suffer the same punishment.

*Find them.* The thought was hot coals, urging me on. *Get them far away from here.*

I dodged the pools of light that spilled from the windows. Keeping within the shadows of the grand walls, I circled the expansive grounds towards my home, which was no more than a glorified room stacked and built around others. The serving staff of the Gathrax family lived within a cramped dwelling in the far eastern corners of their land. A place out of sight of the King, yet close enough for his benefit if required.

I forced my anxiety into the pit of my stomach. There would be no one to see me because the night of the Dance of the Dryads was an annual excuse for freedom for the serving members of the Gathrax estate. Only I had been foolish enough not to grasp the chance and enjoy myself.

It seemed only a moment passed, and I was back in the burrows of my home. I closed the door behind me, pressed my back to it and slid helplessly to the floor. Time was a strange concept when gripped in horror.

'What have I done...' As the question broke out of me, a heart-breaking sob followed. Although there was no one to answer, the persistent inner voice infected me with its presence.

I should have joined the festivities, just as Dame said. If I had, this would never have happened. I could've been dancing around the bonfire, enjoying myself, untouched by murder.

Sobs shook my ribs. All the while, I never dropped the wand. No matter how far I lost myself, it stayed firmly gripped in my hand.

My palm tingled as I focused on the fireless hearth. By the time I looked back to the wand in my hand, a plan had formed. It was only a small spark of an idea, but that was all it took to dry my eyes and push me up from the floor.

In a trance, I changed into a fresh set of clothes. I dressed in black leather trousers and a loose white shirt. For my birth date this past year, my parents had gifted me a moss-green jacket, which mother had made from the worn velvet of one of her old work dresses. It fit me perfectly. Threading the brass buttons together, I closed the jacket over my chest, hoping the shallow cut wouldn't bleed through. Once I was clothed, I splashed handfuls of chilled water over my face to wash away the vomit and dirt. Every movement I made was detached, as though someone moved my body by pulling strings.

Even when I had to lay the wand upon my bed to change, its presence lingered in the tingling across my palm. It was as though it called to me. Sang to me.

And I couldn't help but wonder, would it scream when the fire devoured it? Would *I* feel its pain?

* * *

'Well, don't you look *lovely*,' Beatrice Hawthorn called from the shadowed doorway of the blacksmith's workshop. 'All dressed up for the big night. I must say, your mother did a number on that jacket. Do you think she would make me one to match?'

I found her, my one and only friend, without truly thinking about it. My destination was the Green, to my parents, so I could get them away from the Gathrax boundaries. But, with my mind on the wand and my crime, I came to a stop in the glow of the town's smithery.

As predictable as ever, Beatrice would never have joined in with the Dance of the Dryads. She, like me, was not one for dancing and pageantry.

'As if you care about clothes,' I replied, trying to force some semblance of our usual banter in my tone. If Beatrice caught wind something was wrong, she would not give up until she rooted it out. And for her sake, I couldn't put her in danger of being in the know.

Embers cast a glow over her face—highlighting the smudges of kohl across her cheek. Beatrice was a striking woman, in both appearance and posture. She stood over six foot, with a broad frame built for the hammer and anvil. Her tawny skin glowed with warmth, complimenting her bright gold eyes.

'Well, I might care,' Beatrice said. 'A nice dress for Yule would be ideal.'

If my mind was not gripped in anxiety, I might have laughed at that. For Beatrice never wore dresses. A flash of concern flooded across her eyes, enforced by the furrowing of thick brows. 'I thought you were going to skip tonight?'

'I contemplated it,' I said, hands clasped behind my back. The wand warmed against my skin where it lay hidden in the band of my trousers. I fought the urge to tell her everything.

'You just couldn't resist the chance to dance with some handsome men.'

I smiled, but it failed to reach my eyes. 'Yes, something like that.'

'The men in those stories you read are starting to bore you then.' Beatrice laughed, turning her attention back to the anvil before her. 'Whatever the book you told me of last time—the one with a hundred pages of debauchery—finally enticed you to chase something more tangible.'

'Have you been talking to Dame?' I replied, wringing my hands behind my back.

'No. But I did speak with your mother earlier, only briefly because she was with the twins. Poor Deborah, I would've thought King Gathrax could've found it in his stone-cold heart to give her the night off.'

I almost choked at the mention of the King and my mother. The overwhelming urge to shout and tell her everything overcame me.

'Something the matter?' Beatrice's gaze narrowed as it swept over me once again. 'You're too quiet.'

I shook myself, trying to focus on the moment and not the way my heart thundered in my chest. 'Mother never gets a night off. Not when the little devils are involved.'

'Likely because she is the only woman in the Gathrax boundaries who is strong enough to survive them.' Beatrice spat on the ground at her boots, unbothered to conceal her dislike for the youngest children of the Gathrax family.

*Their* only *children. Remember, you killed their firstborn.*

'What about you?' I rushed out. 'Here you stand with greased hands and smudges across your cheeks. Do you not want for a night off?'

'Uncle doesn't care what I do,' Beatrice replied. 'It is my choice not to go, as it is every year.'

Beatrice and her uncle were not family by blood, as she had told me years ago, but by choice. He was a man too old to raise the hammer, so he'd drafted young Beatrice into being his apprentice, which was simply a cheap way of giving a title to the person who did most of the work.

Beatrice slung the hammer around as though it weighed the same as a broom, when, in reality, I likely couldn't have held it up for longer than a minute.

'Come with me?' I couldn't stop the question from slipping out.

Beatrice surveyed me with her bright eyes. One dark brow raised. 'Max, get real. Do you really think I am going to be spending my only evening off surrounded by painful sonnets and off-beat dances? I'll leave the flamboyancy to you, friend.'

'Please.' My voice cracked, garnering her full attention.

Beatrice looked me over, truly looked at me as though drinking in every detail. My cheeks warmed beneath her stare; the spreading of crimson overwhelmed my neck. I tugged at the collar of my jacket and glimpsed my mage-marked palm. Quickly, I thrust it behind my back, but not without Beatrice noticing my haste.

'Seriously, what is up with you?' she asked, running a hand into her thick mane of dark brown hair.

It was in that moment I knew why I had come here. It was to say goodbye. And the realisation nearly broke me.

'Nothing,' I said, but even I could hear how pathetic my attempted lie sounded. 'I just wanted to come and see you.'

'Well, don't I feel special, but, sorry, Max. I am not your type, and you are not mine either.'

I stepped in close, unsure how to broach my farewell without telling her it was a farewell. In that moment, I had no idea where I was to go, although I knew it had to be far from this place. Between the other three Kingdoms in the South, there would be a place to hide, a place to carve a new life.

A new place to call home.

'You wound me with your words,' I said, faking a sob.

'And *you* look like you've had a fight with the dryads themselves. Don't think I have ever seen you so unkept before. Whatever will the boys think when they see you?' With a thick, calloused finger, she pointed to my brown curls. I lifted my unmarked hand, keeping the other glued behind me, and found the root of her concern. A single leaf had entrapped itself within my hair.

'Yes, something like that,' I muttered, trying to look everywhere but her inquisitive glare.

'Well, the costume suits you,' Beatrice said, screwing her mouth up as she heaved the hammer from one shoulder to the other.

'Costume?' My mind spun. 'Yes, my costume.' My shoulders sagged at the helpful reminder, and I let loose a shuddered breath. It was not uncommon for those who dwelled within the borders of the Gathrax estate to smudge their skin with leaves and bark for the Dance of Dryads. It was the civilians' way of respecting the forgotten spirits of the forest on the single night of the year when we honoured them.

'I thought I'd join in for once,' I lied, holding her stare so she didn't notice.

'Not to offend you, but you could have made more of an effort. One leaf?'

I grinned, looking towards the distant clatter of music and noise. The Green was only a short walk away. Even from here, I could feel the thumping beat of music through the cobbled street. If I looked towards the line of trees that surrounded the Green, I may have even caught flashes of light from the bonfire in its centre.

'Well, are you going to enjoy yourself or stand here gawking at me all night?' Beatrice smudged a hand over her brow, leaving a streak of grease across it. 'Some of us want to get a head start before tomorrow's market. If I can get a few more pieces finished, uncle and I might have a better chance at surviving the coming winter.'

'Always one for planning,' I replied meekly, my gaze wandering in the estate's direction.

'Well, rumours are spreading that King Gathrax will not be giving out as much coin as last year—Max, seriously, who are you waiting for?' Beatrice followed my gaze to where it was pinned on Galloway Forest.

'No one,' I said, turning back to face her so quickly my neck clicked.

'Wait, don't tell me you have left a lover in there? Is that why you look so distracted?'

'No.' My throat croaked the response. 'Bea, you are busy, and I need to find my parents. I just wanted to come and say…'

'Say what?' Beatrice stepped towards me.

'Have a good evening—'

'What are you not telling me?' A single brow peaked above her golden eyes.

It was there, the pleading of my guilt, lingering on the tip of my tongue. I couldn't stand to hold her stare any more, for the risk of speaking it aloud and endangering her with the knowledge of my crime. Giving into another selfish need, I threw my arms around Beatrice and held her. A small and surprised gasp burst out of her. I expected her to pull away, but she didn't. It took a moment, but Beatrice returned my embrace.

'You can talk to me.'

I shook my head, rested my chin on her shoulder and stared into the glowing ambers of the forge behind her. 'I know.'

'Then tell me.'

'I can't,' I said. 'Trust me, Beatrice, it is best you don't know.'

The sigh she expelled told me Beatrice knew, without a doubt, that I was hiding something. And if she moved her hands down, she would've discovered the lump of wood in the band at the back of my trousers, exposing everything.

I pulled away before she had the chance. 'I should go.'

'At least try and look less, I don't know—'

'Guilty?' I answered for her.

She nodded, a wrinkle forming between her brows. 'Max, whatever has happened, I can help.'

It was breaking me, knowing this was the last time I was to see my friend. But the pain inside, the agony, was well-deserved. I was a murderer. If Beatrice knew, she would not have looked at me with such concern and sympathy. If she knew what I had done, what I am...

'Tell me I will see you after the hunt, with a bottle of cheap wine in hand,' she said. Beatrice was always my rock, even when there were times her eyes suggested secrets in her past of which she never spoke.

'Stay safe,' I replied, knowing that my words were answer enough. I turned to leave, unable to watch her any more.

Beatrice didn't call after me as I left her, but she did watch.

Head down, I forged on, Beatrice's gaze burning holes into the back of my head. Each step was hard, and it didn't ease when I heard the powerful slams of Beatrice's hammer against the anvil. The heavy thuds joined the screeching autumn winds, pushing me on as they continued their ballad.

*Murderer*. The word brushed all around me. *Murderer*.

I focused ahead, preparing myself to enter the belly of the beast. A lot was riding on finding my parents and convincing them to leave this life behind. I would have to tell them what I did—the thought of that made me sick.

So did the knowledge of what I had to do with the wand in my possession.

Fire flickered in the periphery; a tower of flames built in a pyre in the centre of the Green.

As though sensing what I was to do, the wand haunted my mind with its presence. *If you destroy me, who else will protect you?*

# CHAPTER 5

With each step towards the Green, the louder the music became. It shook the very air. The vibrations of beating drums and thundering feet echoed through the soles of my boots.

The street was covered in trodden mud. Hundreds of townsfolk would have walked this very path hours before, each adorned in clothes of green and earthen tones. A gaggle of painted faces with skin covered in foliage. I could see them through the skeletons of the trees. The mountainous bonfire boiled with flames of gold, red and yellow, and they danced around blaze. From early evening till morning, the festivities would continue. It would only stop when the fire dwindled naturally, just like the obsidian flames that destroyed the Heart Oak had all those years ago.

With each shuddered breath the smoke filled my lungs. The smell brought a sense of nostalgia for just a moment of relief. Old chairs and tables helped to fuel the bonfire. Most of the furniture was from the manor, for Queen Remi Gathrax enjoyed wasting the Kingdom's money on replacing her interior every year. Instead of donating the items to those who needed it, she preferred to watch it burn from her seat on the dais in the centre of the Green.

But furniture was not the only thing to be thrown into the crimson flames.

I drew the wand from my belt, no longer needing to hide it. It would be one of many offerings thrown into the fire, so no one would suspect mine was any different.

Each family would craft a stick or branch, call it a wand, and provide it as an offering. Wands carved from fallen sticks, salvaged from the forest, would be decorated then discarded as a sacrifice.

From the outlines of people who moved around me, the offerings had yet to be thrown in.

Rid myself of the wand, find my parents, and then run.

*Run little rabbit. Run. Run. Run.*

A trickle of cold dribbled down my neck. It wasn't the growing heat from the bonfire that caused me to sweat. It was the desperate urge to rid myself from the weapon of murder.

*'Why does King Gathrax not throw an offering into the fire?'* I had asked my mother once. The memory was distant, but the physical feeling of her soft hand holding mine was not.

*'In their eyes, the Gathrax family have sacrificed enough. Whereas we throw made-up offerings into the flames, King Gathrax and his heirs will never know what it is like to wield magic. Their loss outweighs ours.'*

Even though Mother's words made sense, I never understood. The Gathrax family were wealthy beyond belief; careless and driven by mad privilege, the largest of the four Southern Kingdoms. As was Mage Gathrax, the devil who founded the estate. His family lived within his shadow, draining taxes to keep their control afloat. Yes, they didn't have access to magic, but that didn't take away from their power or control.

Heat flashed across my skin. The sweet scent of popping corn hit me with a single inhale. These sensations would have normally conjured excitement. Now, I only dreaded being under the watchful gaze of my rulers. The father and mother of the boy I had just murdered. The family I had torn apart.

I studied the wand under the orange glow of fire. Still the same. I didn't know what I expected to see every time I glanced at it. Perhaps a sign that it truly was nothing but useless. I didn't feel magic inside of me. Beside the thrumming of my marked palm, and the burden of guilt and panic, there was no ounce of proof I held any power.

*I must rid myself of it.* The thought was as intense as the sudden tickling on my hand. *You will be my sacrifice tonight. No one will know. No one will know.*

Slipping through the wall of guarding pine trees, I joined the fray of people that awaited me. Swaying bodies moved like the rush of a river. Arms waving and reaching. Cries and screams of delight, chorused with the popping of wood in the bonfire only yards ahead.

The Dance of the Dryads had begun.

I tried to pass through the wall of green-smudged faces as they moved clockwise around the bonfire. Some people wore wooden masks, imitating the dreaded army of the North. Others were covered in painted symbols, emerald leaves and springs of dried cherry blossom, imitating the long-lost dryads.

I recognised many faces beneath the paint. Gill, the cook from the Gathrax estate and her daughter, Mary. Dame was sat on the outskirts, bathed in the blaze whilst she stomped her feet and called out in tune with the music. Many of the staff from the estate enjoyed their evening of freedom.

Waiting to join the dance were others dressed in darker colours. They were not pretending to be the dryads, or the

masked army of the North. These dancers were dragons.
Creatures that haunted the stories of Aldian's past. The crowd
booed as the dancers joined in, they hissed and mocked the
dragons, because rich or poor, no one liked the creatures.
They were monsters of ice and wind. Beasts believed to have
been born when the earth first moved and the mountains
cracked in two.

It was on the backs of dragons that the masked armies of
the North flew over the Galloway Forest and destroyed the
Southern mages. It had been many years since the creatures
last flew through Southern skies, but their memory was as
fresh as the blood they had spilled in their wake. Once
haunting the skies above, they now only filled children's
stories and their parents' nightmares.

These costumes were pathetic attempts to create the image
of something terrifying. Smashed plates lined wooden masks
to resemble teeth. Ice blue eyes were painted in a rush.
Ripped, muddied sheets draped over outstretched arms like
wings.

I searched desperately for a sign of my parents. Instead, my
eyes fell upon the very people I should've run leagues from.
Behind the crowd, sitting in a line, the Gathrax family
watched on. There were five grand chairs set in a row, each
covered in red-velvet cushions and wood stained with gold
leaf. Four chairs were occupied. One was empty.

One missing. One dead.

*I killed him.*

A presence that haunted in the depths of my mind shivered. *Yes, you did.*

The heat of the fire intensified, and my skin broke out in
gooseflesh. All eight eyes were on me as I fumbled through the
crowd. The Gathrax family were dressed in their estate colour
of red, not knowing their son dripped his crimson gore across

the forest bed not far from this very spot. *Did they know? Could they sense what had become of Julian?*

King Gathrax was robed in a blood-red suit with gold-rope stitching and round coral buttons. His wife and queen, Remi Gathrax, sat beside him with her hands in her lap. Her dress was large and hideous, surrounding her like raised dough. The crimson shoulders were so large they over-whelmed her thin, pointed face. Her expression pinched with misery, eyes shifting over the crowd—Julian's name whispered across her painted lips.

I slipped into the shadows of the podium quickly, glimpsing the Gathrax twins. The two girls were nine years younger than Julian. Except, now they were the eldest children in the Gathrax family.

Away from their probing gaze, I continued my hunt for my parents. They would be close. Being the twins' minder, my mother never left their sight or side for long. Which meant father would be close too, because when Mother was with the devils, he hovered near her, ever the guardian of our family.

I didn't blame him for his worry. We had all seen the twins pinch and hurt her countless times, both girls as twisted and vile as the other. Each only adding to my desire to protect my family, to one day escape from this place and live free from the control of the four estates. A dream that was now forced upon me.

*Find them. Discard the wand. Leave before daylight.*

That was the only plan I had. The gaps would have to be filled in as we went.

My heart sank as I finally found my father. He leaned against the wall of a vendor, whose stall was overspilling with salted potatoes on skewers. In the shadows, he was looking towards the podium with a look of pure disdain.

As if he sensed my presence, he tore his focus from the

ruling family and levelled it on me. I stopped dead in my tracks. Even at twenty-five years of age, my father had the ability to make me feel like an infant with one look.

And right then, he looked seriously pissed.

'Maximus.' My name worked out of his gruff throat, rumbling with the deep base of his voice. 'You best have a good enough excuse as to where you've been!'

His expression was thunderous and as red as King Gathrax's suit. But that didn't deter me from melting into his arms. Father had a long, unkept beard that usually was stained a dark brown from the hours of work in the estate's many gardens. His hands were never smooth, not in the entirety of my life.

It was on the tip of my tongue to tell him. Instead, I forced out a single word.

'Sorry,' I whispered, the apology breaking out of me in a rasped cry.

'As you should be. Your mother has been out of her mind; you know not to worry her when she is with the devils.' His voice was muffled as I pressed my ear into his chest. 'She has enough on her plate and doesn't need you adding to it.'

Devils, a nickname my father always used when referring to the twins. It was not their appearance, both sweet with heart-shaped faces, ocean-blue eyes and fire-red hair captured in tight ringed curls. It was their personalities. All teeth and nail, wails and demands.

I pulled away from his hold, glancing to his flushed face. 'Where is she?'

Urgency raced through my veins.

'Running around like a blue-ass fly,' he replied.

I scanned the bustling crowds again, but it was near impossible to make anything out. Bodies moved around us. A sea of flesh. I couldn't spy her natural chestnut braids and doe-wide eyes. My eyes. Green as sea-glass and vivid as Galloway Forest in the peak of summer. She was nowhere near the twins, who fussed with one another on their over-sized chairs, nor was she lingering in the shadows of the podium.

Father tugged at my arm, moving us away from prying ears.

'The twins demanded a toffee apple,' he replied, voice dulled. 'She went to get them one a moment ago, but she has yet to return. Let's hope they hurt their teeth on them.'

The last part he muttered beneath the noise of the crowds.

Father was a towering man. His height was unmatched by anyone else who worked on the estate. Eyes blue-grey, the colour of a stormy sky. Sunkissed no matter the season.

Physically we were not similar, not with my light, brown curls and nose littered with freckles, but what I shared with my father was our outlooks on life. We viewed the world as though danger lurked in every shadow—which it did.

'… with Julian missing, she has been forced to entertain the twins longer than usual.'

'Missing?' My throat dried, making speech difficult.

'Likely off terrorising some poor soul. Nor do I care to find out. That spoiled shit will be floundering off doing his thing.'

I forced a laugh only to hide the sickness that clamped across my stomach. 'Can we just find mother? I need to talk to—'

'I can't remember the last time you brought an offering,' he interrupted.

The blood drained from my entire body as my father moved his attention to the wand gripped in my hand. He didn't seem to notice the tension; my knuckles paled beneath my grip on the wand.

'The dance is almost up, and your poor mother is on duty until the twins are in bed. Until then we have time to kill. Starting with discarding your offering in the fire, like the good old days.'

My breath hitched as I peered at the wand in my hand. Of course, it was the reason I was here, to destroy the wand. But why did hearing it from him make me wish to scream with refusal?

The crowd erupted in cheers. Heavy beats of the drum called for the end of the dance. Father turned sharp, mimicking the crowd's attention, and guided me by the shoulders. I followed his gaze, resting upon the face of our employer.

King Gathrax stood from his seat and clapped slowly. All eyes were on him. The dancing had stopped, the music had silenced. I was left with nothing but the crackling flames of the bonfire and the torturous winds.

*Murderer*, they sang. *Mage*.

'Tonight, we mourn the memory of my family's sacrifice,' King Gathrax called out, his voice clear as the entire crowd stilled into silence. A river of auburn hair laid over his narrowed shoulders, thin and dull, the ginger strands leaving his scalp white and visible in places, balding more as the years went on. King Gathrax ran a finger over his smoothed, vein-marked jaw as he surveyed the crowd, searching much like his wife, who still sat poised beside him.

He was searching for Julian. He had to be.

'Just as the black flames of the North destroyed the Heart Oak, take up your offerings and throw them into this blaze. May we never forget what *we* lost. May we always remember the price paid for the freedom we now grasp and may it never perish.'

The surrounding crowd watched on, but it was the movement behind him that stole my attention. A flash of chestnut curls, bright forest-green eyes.

'Mother,' I breathed, lifting a finger and pointing towards her. 'She's there.'

Her round, calm face was unreadable as she pandered to the twins. She handed them each a toffee apple; they snatched it from her without thanks. I could not hear her from this distance, but I watched her lips move as she spoke to them.

'As I said she would be,' my father muttered over his shoulder.

'We need to get her,' I replied, keeping my face forward. I took a step as the surrounding crowd surged to life. Like a wave they captured us, dragging us in the opposite direction. Father laughed as I looked frantically for a way out of the crowd. But it soon became clear the direction we were driven towards.

A line had begun to form ahead of the bonfire. I pushed and shoved at the people around me, fighting to break away from the line. In the bustle, I lost sight of Mother.

'What's gotten into you, Maximus?' Father's use of my full name was admonishment. He tripped on the back of my feet as he tried to steady me, conjuring a hiss of annoyance that blended in with the bonfire raging ahead.

'You need to let me go,' I said, but it wasn't me speaking. It was the voice, the one that twisted deep inside of me.

'Calm down.' A firm hand was now planted on my shoulder. 'We will find your mother as soon as we're done with your offering.'

Clutching the wand to my chest, the wood seemed to shiver.

The fire spat as false wands were thrown into the wild flames. The overwhelming urge to turn and run built within me.

*You will not destroy me.*

'I can't do this.'

My legs and arms turned to stone. I wanted to rid myself of the wand and whatever presence lingered within it. But in the same breath, I didn't.

'Can't do what?' Father asked, flashes of the bonfire casting shadows over his face.

My fist tightened around the wand until the wood pinched into my newly scarred skin. With each offering discarded into the fire, the crowd's cheers lifted, reaching a new crescendo. My feet moved without my control, stopping only when I stood before the flames.

I squinted against the heat, tongues of flame licking towards me. It was as though the fire sensed what I held in my hand.

'Throw it in.'

'I—I can't.'

*You won't.*

'You're causing a scene—'

There was a muttering of annoyance as I held up the line behind me. Eyes bore into me, countless, as though the entire Green watched on.

'—throw the damn thing in.'

My heart lifted into my throat. I raised the wand before me, looking at its smooth surface and pointed tip.

*You are the murderer.* I sent my awareness within the wand. *You killed Julian, not me.*

*No, no.* It sang back, filling my mind with its pressure. *We did.*

In a blink, the weight of the wand was yanked from my fist. I hardly had time to register as father took it. A feral sense to claim it overcame me. I clawed at my father's arm, my face contorted in fiery desperation. 'Give it back!'

Father drew himself away from me, shocked that I had attacked him. He murmured something, cocked his arm back, and threw my wand before I had another chance to fight him.

Time stopped as the wood left his hand and sailed into the waiting flames.

As the reaching tongues engulfed my wand, a stab of agony shot through my body. Despair split my face in a breathless cry, but it seemed I made no sound.

I watched the place in which it had disappeared. Father tugged at me to move, but all I could focus on was the flames. His grip faltered. A new, raw instinct within me took over. Without him holding me back, I lunged, outstretched arm reaching straight into the blaze.

Thunder clapped in the sky above. It sang my name. No, it was not the sky that cried for me. It was another. The scream burst across the panicked crowds. Somewhere in the depths of my mind, I registered who it belonged to.

*Mother.*

A cold sensation crawled up my arm as the fire engulfed it. My mind shut off from the pain. Then, as the wand found my fingers, the world exploded in light just as it had in the forest with Julian. I was thrown back beneath its force, as the blinding light engulfed the festival and everyone within it.

# CHAPTER 6

'Maximus Oaken.' A soft voice called from beyond the veil of darkness. It was featherlight and gentle, yet beheld the power to draw me from the shackles of a dreamscape. My name had never sounded so beautiful. It was a ballad. Between the dulcet tones, and the gentle touch brushing intricate circles over my forehead, there was nothing encouraging me to open my eyes. I didn't want to ruin the moment.

'My son, I need you to wake up.'

Through the dream of fire and blood, a face solidified.

'Get up,' the voice became urgent and pleading. 'Please!'

Sleep expelled me with not-so-caring hands. Like a newborn, taking its first breath, I gulped in a lungful of air as I bolted up in the bed. I came to, blinded by a burst of light, as the cool touch of hands caressed my face.

'Careful. I have got you.'

The world around me was blurred, but the outline of the figure before me was the first to solidify.

'Mother?' I asked as though not believing, my voice rasped and sore. But there she sat before me, lips parted and green eyes wet with recent tears. I blinked, straining against the sudden brightness that haloed around her frame. Our home had never seen so much daylight.

'I have got you. I'm here.' She embraced me before I could contemplate this strange place. Pressing my face into her wild hair, she smothered me. It was the vice-like grip of a desperate mother, which only added to the dread coiling in my stomach.

'Where is Father?' I choked out. The memory of the fire exploded behind my closed eyes.

'He is going to be fine. We are all going to be okay, but... for that you need to listen.'

Mother stumbled over her words, as if lying.

Words failed me. When I pulled back, the room no longer mattered. I stared endlessly at her, trying to discern Father's well-being. The bright light exposed every mark upon her. Every pore, every line of age. Worst of all, it did nothing to hide how her skin had lost its colouring, and her eyes were only bright compared to the dark circles beneath them.

'Did I... did I hurt him?'

She looked away, unable to hold my gaze. 'No.'

Another lie.

The dark circles were not the only sign that something was wrong. Her familiar chestnut curls were not in their usual braids, but down across her shoulders like dark, wild waves of water. Her fingers shook violently on her lap.

I shifted, trying to sit up, but stopped as discomfort in every limb and bone made itself known. Mother raised her hands and hushed. 'Maximus, more than ever before, I'm going to need you to stay calm.'

My mind was a storm of the events from the bonfire. My arm, the one I had reached into the fire, was not burned. I glanced down at it, where it rested on my lap, marvelling at the fresh skin. There was no charred flesh. My freckles were there, as they always had been. It was strange, how reliving one's trauma made the details around them less important. Only when I turned my hand over the bedsheets did I realise the colour of them.

Red silk upon a crimson comforter.

'Your father is safe, for now. We do not have long together, so I'm going to need you to listen carefully to me, Maximus—'

I was aware my mother was speaking, but it seemed my mind didn't care. Not when I finally took in the room, the bed, which didn't belong to me. Because this was not our home.

Noise filtered in the distance, snatching her attention from me. I peered over her shoulder, finally making sense of the room. Julian's room. The bed, three times the size of my own, rested in the far corner of the grand chamber, engulfed in papered walls and rich furnishings, which dripped in gold-leaf decoration. I should have known from how comfortable the bed was, with its down feather pillows and the thick blanket.

Panicked, I attempted to swing my legs from the bed. I met resistance as my ankle pulled hard on something beneath the duvet. A sharp clink of metal sounded by my feet.

'Why are we here...' I shook violently, both my voice and body trembling as though caught in a storm. Mother reached out, a single tear escaping from her swollen eyes.

I kicked at the duvet, exposing thick iron cuffs. They weighed heavy around my ankle, rubbing the skin raw. In my struggle and desperation, I had knocked the tankard of water from Mother's hand, which now seeped into the red carpet beneath her feet. Red. Gathrax red. The same carpet I had brushed and washed over and over. Julian's carpet.

'Maximus.' I cringed against her sharp commanding tone. 'There is no good to come from struggling against this. You need to listen to me... please.'

My mind was a maelstrom. 'I killed him,' I said, glaring

into my mother. She didn't wince at my revelation. She showed no sign of shock. 'Julian. I killed him.'

Mother leaned in, grasping my face with both her hands. It was the only thing keeping me from looking anywhere else but her. 'The wheels of motion are turning and gone is the time for action. Soon, you'll face a choice. One I have done my absolute best to shield you from.'

More noises sounded beyond Julian's door. Deep voices rattled through the walls, urging my mother to speak quicker.

'We need to get away from here,' I said, hoping for some reprieve from the guilt that devoured me.

'No, we are not going anywhere. It was only ever a matter of time before this happened...' Her gaze was lost in thought. 'Your father and I were fools to believe we could keep you safe.'

Everything stilled.

'Safe from what?' My question came out in a harsh croak.

'Your truth.'

Mother lifted my hand; unbothered by the damp palm and shaking fingers. She turned it, palm faced upwards, and pried my fingers away to reveal the mark beneath.

'You're a mage, Maximus.'

Hearing her say it broke me. 'I don't want it...'

'*They* already see you as a threat, but this mark will keep you safe. Maximus, you are going to need your wits about you. I don't know what *he* has planned for you, my darling, but you must be prepared for anything. Do you understand?'

Her gentle touch traced the scar upon my palm. The angry mark had healed since I last looked upon it.

'King Gathrax will... He will kill me for what I've done.'

'No, he will not harm you.' She spoke with complete confidence.

'I deserve it,' I said, allowing the tears to fall freely over my cheeks.

'I'm so sorry. This, all of this, is my doing.' My mother shook her head, pinching her doe-like eyes closed.

The overwhelming smell of the bonfire clogged my nose and lingered on my skin. Even Mother smelled like ash and burned wood as she drew me back into her arms.

'Your amplifier. How long have you been hiding it?'

*Amplifier?* 'I don't know what you mean.'

'I should have sent you away, but I had hoped...' She swallowed her words, talking more to herself than me as the voices and noise beyond the room reached a new high. Mother looked behind her once again, face pinched in worry. Even her hold on me tightened, to the point of discomfort.

'The North may not kill you, but you will receive punishment. For what I have done.' Deep-set lines burrowed across her forehead.

'Tell me what to do,' I urged, wishing to draw her attention back to me, but the sense of urgency was growing. 'Please, help me.'

When she looked back at me, the whites of her eyes had stained a Gathrax red. 'Promise me, Maximus, you will play along. Do as they say until you are no longer on Southern soil. The moment you get the chance to leave, take it, no matter what.'

The door handle rattled behind us.

'Promise me, Maximus, I need to hear you say it.'

'But—'

'I love you.'

The door flew open, smashing against the wall with such force the room shuddered. A wave of bodies streamed in, so fast they were a blur. With their entrance came chaos.

Mother jumped from her perch on the bed and placed her

back to me. It all happened so quickly. I was helpless to do anything as the men raced towards her.

She didn't fight, didn't resist. I begged for her to do something, but she fell to her knees with a crack, allowing the many hands to grasp her. A wave of anger crest over me, burying everything else. 'Take your hands off her!'

No one responded to me, they acted like I wasn't even here.

'Deborah Oaken,' a familiar voice drawled, 'I should have known.'

King Gathrax walked slowly into Julian's room. The sunlight hardly reached him as he seethed out of the shadows from the hallway beyond. He was a statue of disdain. Shoulders curved, back hunched, his hands were perfectly held before him.

'You took my son, Jonathan,' Mother snarled, stoic in the grasp of the King's guards. 'You couldn't keep me from him, even if you tried.'

King Gathrax's calm face broke into a smile. It lasted only a moment before he sprang forward. Three long strides and he reached her; palm raised. The slap echoed across Julian's room.

Mother made no sound as she hit the ground.

I cried out, pulling hard against the manacle until my skin broke beneath it. 'Stop it!'

He didn't. King Gathrax brought his hand down on her, time after time, smiling as though he enjoyed every moment.

'Please,' I broke, pleading, voice shattering as my fury faded to desperation.

I pulled at my chains hard, iron scratching the bed post.

King Gathrax's guards stood and watched as he rained down his attacks. I looked between them, begging for someone to stop him. No one listened, no one dared look at me. By the time he finally stopped, my heart had synchronised with each slam of his fist, each clap of his palm.

Breathless and red-faced, King Gathrax straightened himself, looking at his hand with an expression of excitement. He stroked down his thinning hair and flattened it back in place, steadying his breathing. Dishevelled, he cleared the dribble from his mouth before wiping it down his shirt. It left a red smear; from his broken knuckles or my mother's broken skin, I wasn't sure.

'Remove her,' King Gathrax said plainly, causing the guards to spring into action. 'Then report back to me when you locate the person who allowed her access into this room, followed by the guard who allowed it. They will share equal punishment.'

'Mother?' I rasped. 'Mother, look at me.'

She didn't raise her head, no matter how I pleaded. Her hair had fallen over her face, concealing the damage left by the King's hand. As one, the guards lifted her from the floor without an ounce of compassion. I couldn't take my eyes off her. Only when they dragged her towards the door did her head loll to the side. A sob broke out of me when I caught a flash of blood, tracing down her shattered nose, staining her parted mouth crimson.

'Forgive me,' King Gathrax said, when the room had emptied. Silence pulled taut between us, broken only by my heavy breaths and his slow-paced steps towards me. In all my years, I'd never shared a single word with King Gathrax. Now I was captured like a rabbit in a trap. 'I was carried away. That was certainly not the introduction I was hoping to greet you with. But means must.'

My fear quickly dissolved into abhorrence as I drew my eyes back to him. As though my snarl impressed him, King Gathrax released a slow rumbling laugh.

'If you lay a finger on her,' I spat, my threat failing me.

He placed a ringed hand above his heart. His long face pulled a shocked expression. 'If I was you, I would think carefully of how you speak to me. Considering…'

'I'll destroy you…' The threat came from the deepest, most feral part of me.

It didn't deter King Gathrax, who continued to stalk to the bed, a bejewelled finger trailing the sheets until he came to the spot my mother had not long left. Her mark still indented on the bedsheets.

'I am just a man, as you know or will come to realise. Deborah has worked closely with my family since that fateful day she turned up to my home with a screaming brat in her arms, searching for housing and a job. It pains me to hurt her, but you see I do not like being lied to, nor deceived, and I gather the impression your mother has done enough of both to last a lifetime.'

There were no words, not as I lost myself in the wide, bright eyes of the man before me.

'Speechless?' King Gathrax asked. 'I admit, I am lost for words as well. It is not every day you discover the impossible, concealed in your home. Now, mage, care to tell me where my heir is?'

As he spoke, spittle linked on his thin lips. With him sitting before me, I could smell the familiar scent of lavender and mint. Julian's scent. It repulsed me.

I swallowed, blades slicing down my throat. This man had caused me agony in those moments passed. So much so, I longed for him to feel the same.

'Dead,' I answered him, hoping the revelation pained him deeply.

'Oh, I gathered that much. Allow me to reiterate. *Where* is he?'

The lack of reaction scared me more than anything else. I searched his eyes for pain, but there was no emotion there.

'I...'

King Gathrax's hand shot out and gripped my wrist. Long, thin fingers pinched my skin. He was cold to the touch, not an ounce of comfort in his soft hands. Hands that had not seen a day of work in his entire life.

'Speak fast, boy. Each moment I am here prevents me from stopping those men from acting out their own desires against Deborah. There is no knowing what they are doing to her, and they will only stop when I tell them. So, if you care for her safety, you would do well to answer me.'

Just as he finished speaking, a scream registered far within the estate.

'Galloway Forest,' I shouted, practically screamed it.

King Gathrax smiled down at me. 'Good. It is a start. Now, enlighten me. What would the North be doing, sending someone as pathetic as you, to spy on me?'

My shocked silence at his accusation was enough of an answer for the King to continue. Perhaps King Gathrax saw the confusion in my eyes because he moved on.

'Perplexing.' His smile vanished. 'And your wand. Where did you get it?'

'I found it.'

I tried to scream at him through my unwavering gaze. To tell him I spoke the truth, no matter how unbelievable it sounded aloud. I willed him to believe me.

'Found it?' King Gathrax threw his head back and barked a laugh. In the gaping hole of his mouth, I spied countless rotten teeth caped with silver fillings. His scent did little to conceal the bad odour of his breath.

'Remember, your parents' well-being currently rests on

how honest you are being with me. Do you truly expect me to believe you simply *found it?*'

'I swear,' I said, afraid to blink. 'I'm not lying.'

'Interesting. You know, as well as I, it has been over sixty years since the Heart Oak was destroyed. Yet you expect me to believe you simply found a wand in the forest?' He leaned in close until his face was inches from mine. A wave of stale breath fogged over me.

King Gathrax reached into his long sleeve and produced something from it. My breath faltered as my eyes settled on the length of wood.

*My wand.*

It was unmarked, not a single burn on it. It looked like it never had been thrown into the fire.

'It has been many years since my bloodline has touched one of these. My grandfather, Mage Gathrax the Red, was the last ever to wield this smooth wood and its magic affinity. And now, a lowborn like you just stumbles across one in my forest? *My* land. I do not believe it.'

I watched as he twisted my wand in his fingers, devouring it with keen, lustful eyes. It was a surprise when he didn't trace his tongue over his lip. I wanted nothing more than to look away, but the territorial burning in the pit of my stomach bubbled. I bit down on my lip to stop myself from shouting.

*Give it to me.*

'It would have been simple if I could just take it from you. But you have linked yourself with its power already, as the mark on your palm confirms. This is no better to me than simple kindling.' King Gathrax tore his gaze from the wand and rested it back on me. 'Except even that would not work, for this wand cannot be destroyed by mundane fire, as you recently discovered.'

'I don't want it,' I said through gritted teeth. It was a lie.

Inside, knowing someone else touched it, I was feral. Protective. As though I would lash out at any moment and tear it from his vile hands.

'I believe you,' King Gathrax said. 'However, that is no longer an option, is it?'

'You can have it. Take it… I didn't mean for any of this.'

*Another lie.*

'You are mage-marked, the wand has been linked to you indefinitely. It belongs to you…' His bright eyes flickered with terror, if only for a moment. 'But you, boy, belong to me.'

The corners of his lips, dried with white spit, lifted into a smile that cut his face into a mask of horror.

'This is what shall happen if you wish for the safety of your parents, you will do well to listen to my words carefully and heed them. From this morning onwards, you are no longer Maximus Oaken. You are mine. And you will help restore my family's name to its highest peak. For the first time since the War of the Wood, the Gathrax name has the chance to repay those Northern dogs with the very destruction they had gifted us. We will finally get our revenge. It will be my name that is put in the history books, and *you* shall be my guarantor.'

Jonathan Gathrax didn't stop smiling as he continued his grand speech.

'And, in time, with your cooperation, you will come to benefit from the change in tide.'

In a blink, he slipped the wand back into his sleeve, and I glimpsed the leather holder wrapped around his forearm. I had only ever seen them in the glass cases that filled the many rooms of this estate. Like sheaths for swords, or a quiver for arrows, this kept the wand of a mage close.

I leaned forward just as it slipped from view, desperate to eradicate the distance between us.

'Let us discuss the matter of Julian.' King Gathrax's tone deepened. 'Your first task is to take me to him.'

'It was dark, and I wasn't—I was only trying to protect myself. I didn't mean for him to die.'

'That child would have only made a mockery of my Kingdom.' King Gathrax bolted forward, stopping mere inches from my face. 'His behaviour granted him an early death. His mother may not understand that yet, but I do. He was nothing but a problem, a problem now solved.'

There was no anger in the King's eyes. No hate. His blue gaze seemed to glow with other hints of emotion: excitement, wonder, pride. How could a father not want to seek revenge on the person who murdered his own flesh and blood?

'Whatever punishment awaits me, please don't involve my parents. This is my doing, not theirs.'

King Gathrax laughed slowly. 'As long as you comply with what I ask of you, your parents will not be harmed. In truth, I should thank them. They have provided me with a miracle. Riddle me this,' King Gathrax continued, lips slicing like a wound across his face, stretching from ear to ear. 'What is better than an heir?'

I couldn't answer him. The deranged joy that lit his eyes kept me silent.

'A mage.' He answered for me, throwing his head back, the lump in his throat protruding uncomfortably as he cackled. When he reached out for me, it was not to strike me but place a caring hand over the top of my head. His hand moved slowly, back and forth across my crown, rings catching in my curls and tugging slightly at my scalp.

'Welcome to the family, my *son*.'

# CHAPTER 7

Five members of the Gathrax's serving staff waited at the end of the bed, each face as familiar to me as the next. They'd flooded into the room, all the while, not a single one glanced my way.

As with the guards, the maids pretended as though I was not there, not chained to the bed or pleading for their help. They simply stood there, eyes down and silent, hands clasped together before them.

At first glance, I thought the eldest of the line was Dame. Perhaps it was my desperation that confused me, but when I looked harder, it was Gill, the cook. I couldn't figure what she was doing here. I passed my gaze from her, wrinkles carved into her skin and back hunched over her round frame, to the three younger women who stood around her. Their names escaped me, but I knew without a doubt I recognised them. In total, the Gathrax estate hired hundreds of serving staff, the Kingdom wouldn't run without them. It was impossible to know them all, but something silent tied us all together. The need to survive. Which was exactly the impression that oozed from them all as they awaited command.

'Gill,' I said, as I continued my fight against the chains. 'Help me.'

The only sign she heard me was the subtle flinch as I called her name. Lost to my anxieties, I shouted out again. 'Look at me, just look at me!'

I threw my eyes over them, begging someone to just see me. It was a strange desire. I reached the end of the line to find a man I didn't recognise. He lifted his chin up and looked at me through thick lashes. I settled my attention on him, breath hitching, just as he raised his head enough to train his eyes on me. His wide amber eyes were like jewels across his angular face. His skin was a russet brown, hair short and curled close to his scalp. There was something in his stare, the way his lips pursed, jaw clenched, that screamed *pity*.

'Help,' I pleaded, lips trembling violently.

To my surprise, he didn't look away, but nor did he answer me.

'*Julian*,' King Gathrax snapped. It took a moment to understand he spoke to me. He used his dead son's name whilst glaring at me with the biggest and proudest of smiles. 'For the sake of everyone in this room, stop your fussing. It isn't how my son would act, is it?'

There was a test in his question. It was as real as the iron around my ankle.

'I'm *not* your son,' I hissed, spit flying from my cracked lips.

The King's face dropped into one of disappointment. 'It would seem we have our work cut out for us.'

My eyes shot between the line of servants and King Gathrax, searching. No one looked shocked when the King spoke again, using that same name, the name that didn't belong to me. 'Julian, these kind people are going to help with this little issue we have stumbled across, and I trust you will behave whilst I am absent. You remember what may happen if I hear you are… resisting.'

My parents—he threatened them as though this was all a game to him. Perhaps it was. I nodded; it was all I could do. The fear in the room was palpable, and not entirely conjured by me. The maids shook with it, all but the man, who still had not looked away from me.

The natural light in the room had dulled. Beyond the red-glass windows, clouds thrummed through the sky, rain lashing from them. A chill had settled over Julian's room. It seeped through the thick stone walls, infecting its way into every inch of my skin. My head ached; my stomach longed for food, but I knew I would vomit if a morsel passed my lips.

'My son,' King Gathrax began, facing Gill with wide, suggestive eyes, 'is in shock. See that what I ask of you is completed efficiently.'

There was trepidation in the way Gill levelled her gaze to her King, and in the tremble of her voice. 'He is in good hands, sire.'

'Oh, I do hope he is,' he replied, predatory grin widening.

King Gathrax regarded me a final time. He spared me a single word before he swept as suddenly from the room as he had appeared. '*Behave.*'

Silence bathed the bedchamber, making the click of the door sound monumental. A long pause followed.

'You heard our King,' Gill spoke up, clapping her hands. Each of the servants jumped, all except the young man. He stayed still and silent, poised.

'Simion,' Gill snapped. 'See that… Julian here is freed.'

*Simion.* It was not a name I recognised. He only took his gaze from me as Gill withdrew a brass key from her belt and handed it to him.

With the key in hand, he paced towards the end of the bed —not once removing his eyes from me. A cold breeze filtered beneath the duvet as he lifted it and reached beneath. His hands, warm yet tough, reached for my ankle to hold me still. A slip of a cry escaped me as he inserted the key into the padlock. One quick turn and the metal imprisonment was free from my skin. Simion's knuckles brushed the ache left by the manacle as he carefully unclasped it, lifting it from view.

I wiggled my foot, testing out the skin. It was red raw, but nothing serious. It would heal, in time. The freedom of air brushing against the skin was a blessing.

'One of you fetch me a damp cloth and some whisky,' Gill said, only no one moved. Her face pinched into a punishing scowl, and she barked. 'Stop your standing around and get to it.'

The three women shot into action. One moved with haste, dashing beneath the arched doorway into Julian's bathing chamber. They each seemed to know exactly what task they had to complete. There was something orchestrated about their movements.

'Here,' Gill said, eyes full of sorrow, as one of the maid's provided what she asked for. 'The whisky may help ease some tension.'

Whilst one maid held a damp cloth to my ankle, Gill lifted a small bottle of spirits to my lips. It was one of Julian's, stashed away in his rooms for those long nights of dismembering creatures.

'My parents…' I began but was silenced by the kiss of the bottle to my lips.

'Don't,' Gill hissed, sorrow turning to warning. She shot her eyes to the door at our backs, shoulders relaxing only when she saw it was still closed. 'Don't mention them.'

The alcohol burned at first, the taste scorching up my nose

and filling my lungs. Displeasure melted quickly into the feeling of warmth that spread across my chest and through my mind. Relaxing enough for me to take in a full, deep breath.

'That is better,' Gill said, brushing a gentle hand across my forehead. Her touch was motherly and familiar but was ruined by the way she looked at me.

'Gill, please,' I began, the burn of alcohol giving me a moment of renewed bravery.

The patter of rushed feet distracted Gill. I got the impression she was thankful for the interruption from my plea. Although the servant answered my question for me as she spoke.

'Julian's bath will be drawn shortly.'

Perhaps it was the burn of alcohol, or my deep-rooted exhaustion, but I looked her dead in the eyes, noticing her flinch with a misplaced fear. 'That is *not* my name.'

'It is now,' Gill chimed in quickly, lowering her hand to my mouth and covering it before I could say another word. 'Now, quiet. No more of that talk. Simion, help me get *Julian* into the bath, he'll need a good scrub… and then some.'

Gill knew my name. My real name. She had known me for years, and her husband worked in the gardens with my father. Yet she refused to call me by it. In fact, the way she said Julian's name was poignant. It was a warning.

Across the room, Simion fussed with the hearth, which glowed with a newly lit fire. The iron poker clattered to the floor as he discarded it, got to his feet and walked towards me.

I cowered beneath his gaze, as delicate as cracked glass.

'Can you walk?' he asked, deep voice soft as velvet, 'or would you prefer if I carried you?'

A cold shiver raced down my spine. I kicked my free legs over the bed and stood. The room swayed for a moment. I blinked as my mind tilted, stilled only when warm hands found my arms and held firm. When I opened my eyes, it was to find Simion inches before my face. His dark brows were burrowed over his narrowed eyes, and, for a moment, I recognised concern before he steeled his face and it vanished.

'Steady,' Simion whispered. 'I've got you.'

I was thankful he held me up. My exhaustion seemed misplaced. It was not the same as if I had run for miles or worked tirelessly for a day straight. No. This feeling that lingered in the very pit of my stomach was a longing ache. It drained the strength from my body, as though it reached for something it could not grasp.

It was the wand. *My* wand. It called out to me, pulling at my soul as though it was a shard forcefully torn from it.

Simion didn't ask if I needed help again because he continued to hold me.

Through a tiled archway, the bathing chamber was fogged with heavy steam and incense. The golden-clawed tub sat beneath a sash window. Its surface shone from when I'd last scrubbed it, catching the light of late afternoon. The young maid struggled to carry the hot water from the hearth, dripping across the stone floor as she did so. The warmth slammed over me, threatening to suffocate me from the inside out.

'Undress,' another maid said, as she withdrew her hand from the water.

The sudden weight of many eyes upon me grew heavy. Mouth agape, I stared at the crowd that formed around me. Heat flooded my cheeks, pinching them red. Then I looked to Simion, his all-knowing eyes, and felt somewhat reassured.

'Do as she asked, *Maximus*,' Simion encouraged, his voice merely a whisper.

My knees almost gave out at the use of my name. My real

name. No one seemed to notice he had used it, but I did. It gave me some sense of normality.

'What are we waiting for?' Gill snapped, entering the room behind us, the steam passing around her stout frame like water around a rock. 'It is nothing we have not seen before.'

Simion released me, forcing me to find my footing alone. I followed him with my eyes, watching as he was the only one to turn his back on me, affording me privacy.

'Julian, now.' There it was again, the fear in Gill's eyes. It was enough for me to move into action. With shaking yet firm hands, I pulled the clothes from my body and discarded them in a heap on the floor beside me. Covering what little modesty I had left, I took small steps towards the tub.

Steam seeped off my very skin as I slipped back beneath the water, hoping the mounds of bubbles would keep my pride intact. I allowed myself a moment as the warmth hugged my body, morphing from discomfort to pleasure. The water in our home was never this hot. Always cold, lukewarm at best. Our hearth hadn't the room for large cauldrons to heat.

Simion strode forward, his eyes fixed on me once again. Everything about his movements showed confidence. I kept my attention on him until he was out of view behind me, my skin prickling in response to his proximity. Then there were hands. Warm, gentle; they dipped into the water behind me, sloshing it across my back.

'What are you doing?'

He didn't answer me with words. Instead, Simion pulled the soaked sponge from the shallows of the tub and rubbed it across my shoulders, down the ridge of my spine. Beneath his touch, calm flooded over me. It was as if I took a clear, deep breath for the first time. The anxiety within my stomach didn't fade completely, but it simmered into a faint ember.

No one spoke a word as I was washed. I sat up in the tub,

knees hugged to my chest, whilst a stranger offered me comfort. Only when he was done did I sink deeper into the water in hopes no one would notice the gooseflesh that spread across my skin.

The other maids soon joined in. They filled jugs of water and tipped it above my head until it cascaded over my face. My hair clung to my neck and covered my eyes. I didn't care to unblock my vision from the brown strands.

Once they had finished, I was acutely aware of the scent that seeped from my skin. One deep inhale, and my stomach spasmed. Lavender and mint.

In the distraction, I had not noticed the lack of pressure on my back. Intrigued, and fighting down nausea, I searched for Simion among the steam-filled chamber.

He was not there. Only Gill, and the three younger maids remained.

* * *

Sat upon a cushioned chair, I watched clumps of brown curls fall around me like snow. Strands littered my shoulders and lap, itching across my damp skin. Every now and then I would wince against the sudden snip of the blades so close to my ears. The hair scattered the chequered stone floor until one maid took a long broom and swept it away. I kept my eyes pinned to the floor, unable to watch the shake of the young maid's hand as she cut my hair. I gasped as pain nicked at the tip of my left ear. My hand shot up, fingertips wet when they returned, blossomed with crimson blood.

'Forgive me, Julian,' the young maid murmured, breathless with panic. 'I didn't mean to—'

'What have you done, foolish girl!' Gill shouted, snatching the scissors and cleaning the dribble of blood off on her apron. 'If King Gathrax knows you have harmed him…'

I wanted to scream my name at them. *Maximus, Maximus,* repeatedly it filled my head. King Gathrax's warning to behave chimed like tower bells in my mind.

No one spoke it again, not since Simion left. With the departure of the stranger, the storm of dark emotions returned with full force.

The prodding and pulling didn't stop until dusk settled beyond the window. Light drained from the rooms, only replaced by the amber glow of the fire from the hearth Simion had lit.

A maid stood me up before a gilded mirror. Regardless of the numbing shock that encompassed me, I was unable to tear my eyes from my reflection.

'It is the best we can do,' Gill said from where she hoovered just beyond my shoulder.

Someone I didn't recognise gazed back at me, sharing only the haunted look in our eyes. My eyes were the same, green as the canopy of a forest, but everything else had been changed.

My hair had been cut short, swept over to the side and plastered down with a thick paste. The colour had been altered by a slathering of cream rubbed into my scalp after the bath. My skin had screamed from the sting of chemicals as it sapped my brown tones, lightening it to a vivid orange.

I hadn't known what this was all for, until I drank in the reflection.

Gill had allowed me to dress myself. The jacket she had provided, although slightly too small for my frame, made my shoulders square and wide with the hidden padding in the seams. My posture looked stronger, for I had become an illusion draped in finery. The shirt beneath scratched at my skin.

And the trousers. They hugged my legs. Deep crimson with two stripes of white down the seams.

'You haven't said a word,' Gill said, encouraging me out of my silence.

I looked at the maid's reflection, dread strangling my throat. 'What would you have me say?'

Bile sloshed in my stomach as I stared at the person they'd made me into. A vision of Julian Gathrax.

Gill shrugged, shadows beneath her eyes from the long day of working me into this lie. They'd woven it, like spiders and silk; Gill and her maids had crafted an illusion, a vision of horror. I turned on my heel to face her. 'I'm not him. I'm not Julian.'

I shouted; control of my emotions ebbed away from me as my entire body buzzed with the need to scream. The tension inside vied for release and I afforded it. The glass shattered beneath the force of my knuckles, skin tearing. 'Do you hear me; I am not Julian. You can't do this, you can't!'

My shoulders heaved with every shuddering breath. I fisted my hands to still the shaking as I waited for her to snap back at me.

'Stop,' Gill pleaded, wide-eyed and pale. Sweat glistened her brow, the maids around her whimpering as though I'd struck them and not the mirror.

'No!' I screamed, blood seeping down my wrist.

'Please, you must, for us you must… Julian—'

'My name is Maximus Oaken, and you know it. Say it, I want to hear you say it.'

The door was thrown open, the hinges screeching as it announced a new arrival. Wide-eyed, breathless, I turned my attention, half expecting to find Simion returned.

But it was not Simion.

'Your name is Julian Gathrax.' King Gathrax slipped into

the room, staring at me like a cat at cream. 'You are my son; you are my heir.'

'No,' I replied through gritted teeth, my fury ebbing out of my grasp.

'What is your name?' the King asked, testing.

This was a trick. The warmth of the fire barely reached me as I was pinned beneath his stare.

'You know my name; they all know my name. You can't take it away from me.'

Disappointment drew down his cracked lips. 'It would seem you are in need of a reminder as to my warning.'

King Gathrax clapped his hands, and his guards flooded into the room. Gill and the three remaining servants hadn't the chance to fight back as they were each taken by careless hands.

'What're you doing?' I asked, unable to look away as each of the maids had a knife lifted and pressed to the soft skin of their necks.

'Reminding you what happens when you disobey me,' King Gathrax said, as his guards forced the four servants into a line before me, much like when I had first seen them in the room. 'You seem to think I am not a man of my word, which would be correct. I am a king of my word. What I say is true, always. My promises are as binding as my warning. You will come to comply, but I see you are in need of some encouragement.'

The hearth danced shadows across his gaunt face. They elongated Jonathan's monstrous smile. 'Thank the dryads our family colour is red. It makes removing unwanted stains less of a problem.'

'Don't—' The word was barely out of me as the blades drew across necks, sharp and sudden. I blinked as flesh parted and a fountain of gore burst free, stifling screams and leaving wet gasps in their wake.

Pain jarred through my knees as I fell to the ground. I tried to scream, but the horror silenced me. All I could do was watch as blood poured down the front of each of them, spilling into puddles across the red-woven carpet at their feet.

King Gathrax was right, it was impossible to discern the blood from the carpet, it melted into the material. Red on red.

Gill was the last to die. It seemed the man holding her knew little of how to murder because she spluttered and struggled like a fish out of water until the light finally drained from her eyes. With a thud, each of the dead was thrown forward where they landed face-first before me.

King Gathrax knelt at my side, wiry arm wrapped around my shoulders. 'Let it be a reminder of what may become of your parents if you act out again.'

I couldn't speak, couldn't form words. All I could do was look at the bodies, begging for them each to open their eyes and get up.

They didn't.

King Gathrax clicked his tongue over his crooked teeth and hissed, so close his cracked lips brushed against my ear. 'Now tell me, what is your name?'

I inhaled, unable to draw my eyes from the spreading of crimson.

'Say it.' King Gathrax tightened his grip on my upper arm. The pinch of his nails through the jacket seemed to draw me out of the trance as he asked the question again. 'What is your name?'

'Julian.' The scene before me blurred through tears as I choked on the word. 'My name is Julian Gathrax.'

# CHAPTER 8

The air stung at my face. It nipped at my ears and burned the end of my nose a bright red. Each inhale was painful as I dragged in the air through clenched teeth. Most believed autumn to be beautiful with its jewel-toned leaves and misty mornings; but those without the money to light their own hearths understood the truth. Autumn was a trickster, luring one into a false sense of safety with its beauty, only to strike with a deadly chill.

The polished, leather boots did little to protect me from the wet ground. Julian's shoes were not designed for traversing rough terrain. Each step allowed moisture to leak inside, freezing my toes and making the woollen socks beneath sodden. Regardless of it all, I was thankful to be away from Julian's room and the memory of death that haunted it.

I tried to busy myself with thinking of anything but the murder of the servants. Even as I walked ahead, with the silent party of two following behind me, I could still hear Gill's last gasped breath. In the dark of my mind, I witnessed the bodies being rolled up in the carpet they had fallen upon and dragged from the room by the guards. No one noticed the single smudge of dark crimson blood that was left on the flagstones beneath the carpet. No one cleaned it up. When night had fallen and I had pushed the armchair against the door, I found the cloth Gill had washed across my forehead, and I cleared the gore with it. Then I found the small bottle of whisky and finished it entirely.

I wouldn't have slept without the aid of alcohol, even if I suffered greatly for it now.

'I will do anything to hold up this illusion, boy, anything.' It was the first thing King Gathrax had said to me when he arrived in the room that morning. 'We can either work together, or you can continue working against me. The choice is yours.'

As if the deaths of those four women did not haunt me into submission enough, the threat he held against my parents kept me answering his question, over and over.

But then there was Simion—he survived. I allowed myself a moment of relief at the knowledge. The memory of him was always there, distracting me just when I thought I would drown in the guilt of killing the servants.

Because I did kill them, by refusing King Gathrax the name he wished to hear.

*My name is Julian. My name is Julian.*

The King's threat had buried deep in my mind. From his actions, it was clear that he meant what he said. He truly would do anything to hold this illusion in place.

So, on I trod, moving over thick roots and around clusters of trees, in search for the first death I had caused. Julian. Although Gill and the three servants did not die by my hand, they died because of me.

A single tear of sweat ran down my temple, leaving a nasty shiver in its wake. I dared reach up and clear it because every one of my movements were being scrutinised by King Gathrax.

If I didn't find Julian, I knew what King Gathrax would do next. Jonathan's eyes burned holes into the back of my head, his trusted advisor following suit.

Silas Graham was an old man. Tall and weathered. I knew him well, although had been lucky enough not to be in his line of sight, until now. He wore a pin of folded red cloth to show his allegiance to Kingdom, to the King. It was not only his unwanted touch you had to escape, but his gaze. One eye had greyed from cataracts, whereas the other was a violent purple, and they were always looking. Searching.

'Silas, I trust the birds have been released?' King Gathrax asked, his voice bouncing in tandem with the trot of his horse.

'Indeed, they have, sire,' Silas replied carefully. 'The last of them left the aviary last night.'

'And the chances of interception?'

Silas cleared his throat. 'Nightfall was our best option for discretion. It will limit the chances of the North seizing our message, but we cannot think they do not already know.'

'For your sake, Silas, I do hope you are confident in what you say,' King Gathrax replied, speaking down to him. 'Now remind me, how long until we are to receive a response?'

'I expect our sibling Kingdoms will need a day or two, just to mull over the news before responding. Let them take all the time they need,' Silas hissed.

'We do not have time,' King Gathrax said. 'Not if the North know about the mage.'

They spoke of me as if I wasn't there. Which I didn't mind entirely. Being invisible in their company was a relief.

'The moment the Kingdoms hear of your mage, they will be rushing to our borders, likely arriving before their birds bring back replies.' Whenever Silas spoke, his lisp made it sound as though he hissed. Which was fitting for someone who was more serpent than man.

'And what of my people, Silas? I trust you have worked on them thoroughly?' King Gathrax asked.

'Of course, sire,' Silas said, smiling quietly to himself. 'Once word spread of the passing of Maximus Oaken in the fire, followed by the announcement of your coming display, all thoughts shall no longer dwell on the incident. Our people are fickle. Give them something new to chew on, and they soon forget about their discarded scraps.'

Me. I was the scraps. I almost tripped as Silas's words settled over me. Dead. I was supposed to be dead. Not Julian, but me, Maximus Oaken. For a moment, I forgot where I was walking. Instead, my thoughts lingered on Beatrice. And I wondered, did she grieve for me?

'*Our* people?' King Gathrax's voice was sweet, divinely light, but there was something lurking beneath it. 'Did I hear you correctly, or are my ears deceiving me?'

The horse stopped. I heard the tightening of the reins, a squeak of leather against leather, followed by Silas's rasped exhale.

I risked a glance to find Silas looked at the ground as he replied. '*Your* people, my sire. Forgive my slip.'

'Forgiven,' King Gathrax said. 'But do not think for a moment I will not relieve you of your duties as councillor if I believe you may be forgetting who leads this Kingdom.'

'My apologies,' Silas said, drawing out the final sound in a hiss.

My feet were rooted to the spot.

'Are you waiting for something?' A poke slammed into my back as Silas knocked his cane into me.

'Julian,' King Gathrax called out. 'Is there a problem?'

I stiffened. 'No,' I forced out. 'Just trying to find my bearings.' I didn't dare admit I had no clue as to where to find the corpse.

'With haste then,' King Gathrax snapped. 'Time is precious, my son. Keep ahead.'

The Galloway Forest was endless. A sense of confusion baffled me as we surrounded ourselves deep within the towers of bark and leaves. I tried to keep my emotions neutral, unsure what punishment awaited me if King Gathrax caught wind that I was leading them astray. Or what punishment awaited my parents.

A fresh bed of leaves covered the floor, destroying all signs of struggle and footprints. Silas kept silent, but his unbalanced gaze settled on my back. That alone kept me moving.

'What *is* that smell?' King Gathrax scoffed what felt like hours later. The muscles in my legs burned, as did my need for a drink. Exhaustion, hunger and anxiety weakened me. I paused, taking three deep breaths through my nose. It was by the fourth that I smelled it.

Rot. It smacked the back of my throat and clung to it. I slapped a hand over my mouth, thankful for my empty stomach.

'It would seem we have found what we are looking for,' Silas said, reaching up to grasp the reins of the King's horse. A thud sounded as the King jumped from the saddle, followed by the crunch of boots as he walked towards me.

'Well done.' King Gathrax squeezed a hand on my shoulder. It was a gentle and caring touch. 'Silas, I trust this is kept between us.'

'Of course, sire,' Silas replied, trepidation in his voice as well as excitement.

King Gathrax released me and stepped ahead, nose upturned as he sniffed like a bloodhound. When he looked back to me, his bright eyes were alight with excitement. 'Shall we see just what mess you have left, mage?'

I swallowed hard, not wanting to see Julian's corpse again. Though it was always there, lurking in the dark of my mind. There was no escaping what I'd done.

We continued by foot. Silas tied King Gathrax's horse to a tree. The smell intensified as we prowled further on. It didn't take long until we found him. King Gathrax was silent as he peered upwards to the body of his child, hanging before us.

Daylight hid nothing. Its rays highlighted every inch of horror.

Julian's skin was grey. At least, what little we could see of it was. Large crows sat perched on his head and shoulders, beaks stained black with his blood. Every single one of them looked at us with beady, all-seeing eyes.

*He is ours.* They seemed to say.

Julian's bulging stare was a mix of yellow and red from where the creatures had feasted. The red jacket he wore did nothing to hide the branch that stabbed right through his stomach, the bark stained a russet brown. Julian's neck was at the most awkward of angles. A bone protruded and was being pecked at by one of the hungry birds. Some of Julian's innards had spilled from the open cavity the branch had created, swinging in the slight breeze.

I couldn't tear my eyes off him. And Julian, in turn, had his open, lifeless eyes pinned on me. But it was the mess of burned skin across his chest that captured my attention, spread out in the shape of a star. The material of his shirt and jacket hung tattered around it. Beneath the intense smell of rot, I could still catch the faint whiff of burned flesh.

'Cut him down.' King Gathrax waved a dismissive hand at the body. 'Remove him, then bury him here. Dig the hole thrice as deep and ensure it is covered completely. I do not want his body being dug up, by people or beasts. Give him to the earth, let it absorb him, bones and all.'

'Certainly,' Silas muttered, skin almost green. 'He will be so deep not even the Dryads will find him.'

King Gathrax turned to face me. I half expected tears, some glimmer of sadness. He smiled instead.

'Why don't you hate me?' My voice cracked. 'I killed your only son, and you offer me comfort.'

King Gathrax lifted the material to my face and cleared the tears away. I was shocked by his touch and dropped his gaze, unable to hold it any more. His delusion was all-consuming. As his words settled over me like ash, all I could focus on were my sodden feet.

'Hate is a powerful word,' King Gathrax said, standing back and marvelling at my dried face, 'but a magic is more powerful. A mage trumps such emotion. How could I hate you, when you are going to give me everything I have ever desired?'

I turned my back on him, his reply sinking into me like poison. It was easier to face the death I caused, then regard the look of pride on King Gathrax's face.

Silas unsheathed a sword from his belt, waving it around to disturb the flock of crows who claimed Julian. Once they had dispersed, Silas began hacking it down. Iron clashed against wood in a steady rhythm, dulling the blade in the effort. Once the branch had broken enough, Silas was able to pull Julian from his impalement. I gagged at the wet noise his open stomach made as it slid over the bark. When he was almost free, Silas stood back and allowed Julian's corpse to hit the ground with a dull thud, face down. Unmoving; a discarded puppet.

'Help him,' King Gathrax commanded, his voice swallowed by the thud of a shovel to earth. Another shovel waited, strapped to the side of the saddle. I took it without being told twice.

King Gathrax didn't command me to quiet. He allowed me to cry out my guilt. I cried until I had no more tears left, I cried until the hole was carved into the earth and Silas used his boot to roll the corpse into it.

And I cried until Julian's body was concealed by dirt, buried far, far beneath the ground.

\* \* \*

In the day and night that followed, I couldn't rid myself of the smell of rot, mud and death. It had lodged in the back of my throat, unmoving and persistent. Reminding me with each breath, or gulp of water, of Julian.

I was exhausted down to the bone. My skin itched as though it had been burned endlessly by the sun. My reflection, which wasn't mine at all, showed signs of disarray. Dark circles hung around my bloodshot eyes, my skin had paled, and my stomach cramped from lack of food. I had been provided with meals but could not face eating. Not when each passing hour away from my parents meant I was left to ponder their welfare.

I *had* to see them. It was not a desire, but a need. Which was why, when Silas retrieved me from the bedchamber that morning and informed me King Gathrax wished to have breakfast with me, I went.

'I admit I am not surprised by the sudden response from Queen Calzmir.' King Gathrax conversed with Silas. 'I did not expect anything less from her. Amilia surely enjoys being the first, no matter the situation.'

A folded parchment was held firm in his hands. I couldn't see the details from where I sat on the opposite end of the table, but I knew it had come from Queen Calzmir, her Kingdom nestled west of the Gathrax borders. The parchment was tied with a silken blue ribbon, the colour of their Kingdom.

'Gossiping wench,' Silas clucked, his tongue wetting his lips as he raised the fork to his mouth. The hulk of braised pork barely balanced on the prongs, and dripped juice down the napkin he had forced into his collar. 'Insufferable.'

'Which is exactly what we need. Allow her to spread the word of Julian, my mage. It will save you and your *mice* a job, Silas.'

It was one of his *mice* who'd scurried through the dining hall shadows. He was a young boy, hooded in a cloak, with the familiar red ribbon pinned to his chest.

'Then we shall welcome them with open arms... and cold tea,' Silas said, shooting me a look with his clouded eye.

'Which brings me to another concern,' King Gathrax said. 'Queen Calzmir hasn't seen Julian in four years—but she is a sharp woman. Do you truly believe we will convince her of our deception?'

Silas blinked, his grey orb drinking me in. 'You have done as well a job as you can to make *him* look the part.'

'It is his knowledge I worry about.'

I looked down to the plate of untouched food before me, hands resting beside the silverware as though I didn't know how to use them.

'Even if they do contest to him being my true heir,' King Gathrax said, 'the collateral will keep his actions in line. Julian, you will do as I please, won't you?'

'I will—'

'Romar is the farthest Kingdom away from our borders. It may take a few days for the news to reach them of the mage, then another two for them to arrive by carriage.' King Gathrax played with the food before him, deep in thought. 'When they arrive, Julian must display his power to an audience, it is the only way to show the truth of what he is. The more who hear news of the Gathrax Kingdom having a mage, the higher the risk a bird carries that same news to the North. They *will* lay claim to him.'

He growled as he spoke those last words, scratching his intent over my skin. Possession.

'My mice have been instructed to send an arrow through any unwanted bird who dares pass over our skies. We will keep the North in the dark.'

'For now.'

'And what if they already know?' The question broke out of me.

Silas mumbled something under his breath, but it was King Gathrax who replied. 'Then we prepare for a visit from the mountain worms.'

Mountain worms, a Southern term for dragons. A way to degrade them and take away their power and might.

'I say we let them find out.' Silas raised his glass in cheers. 'It has been many years since we were a threat to the North. It is about time they began to fear us.'

I looked at King Gathrax's face as it slowly slipped into a grin. 'You are awfully quiet, Julian. If you are ever going to convince anyone with sense that you are my heir, you better find your voice, and quick.'

I tried to keep my face straight as King Gathrax stood from the table and prowled towards me. He stopped directly behind my shoulder. Silas licked his lips in anticipation. His mismatched eyes glinted with something sinister.

'Do you have something to say?' King Gathrax leaned in and whispered. 'Something you may care to ask?'

'My parents.' It was the only thing I could say. 'I want to see them.'

'I am your father, did you forget?'

Panic sliced through me. 'I... no. I mean you are my... but...'

Silas released a slick, vile laugh that caused the hairs on my arms to stand. 'You play with him, sire.'

King Gathrax slapped a firm hand on my shoulder and squeezed. 'He is mine, I do as I please.'

Silas nodded with a knowing smile that sang with his agreement.

'Julian, Silas will retrieve you every morning over the coming days. You will listen to him, learn from him. Before our visitors arrive, you will need to know who they are, what they are and recognise unfamiliar faces by name. And I trust you do not need a reminder as to the consequences if I hear you are not progressing as I wish you to?'

'Allow me to see my parents,' I began, each word a struggle to force out. 'And I swear I will not defy you.'

'You are in no position to make requests,' King Gathrax leaned in close to my ear and whispered. The warmth of his breath made me cringe, but his hand kept me still and in place.

'It isn't a request,' I said, jaw taut.

Silas gasped, hiding his paled lips behind fingers.

My blood thrummed in my ears. The roar of it was so loud, it was as though a tidal wave of water cascaded overhead.

'How do I believe you will uphold your promise to care for

them, if you do not let me see them?' I asked, voice clear and confident.

There was silence. Then a laugh. King Gathrax slapped a hand on my shoulder and squeezed. 'You already sound much like him, keep it up and I will reward you for your good behaviour.' I tensed my shoulder, hoping he felt the tension.

My mind spun. I didn't imagine that would be his answer. Even Silas spluttered through a mouthful of roasted potato. '*But* when you can see them is down to Silas's discretion. Behave. Learn. Prepare for the arrival of our guests. Only when Silas is satisfied, will I be too.'

Satisfied, such a dirty word for a vile old man.

Short-lived relief flooded through me. King Gathrax read it in my demeanour.

'You see, I can be just, you simply have to cooperate.'

I stilled, looking to the snake of a man who watched me with unwavering eyes, crow's feet pinching at the corners, dreading his plans.

'I will prove to you,' I said, struggling to form the right words. 'Myself, I will prove myself to you.'

'Then we have an agreement, mage?'

I looked to his hand, at his manicured nails and fingers decorated with wealth. Then I took it and held firm. All I could see were my parents' faces in the darkness when I blinked.

'We do,' I answered.

'Good, I am glad to hear that. If you continue this, if you work hard, you will do more than simply see them as a reward. Play this game, do as I say, and you will have them returned. As I said before, we do not need to work against one another, we can find a way for our little situation to benefit us both.'

I straightened, grasping my glass filled with pressed apple juice and held it in salute. 'I'll drink to that.'

'As will I.' King Gathrax looked down the length of his nose, drinking me in with blue eyes brimming with pride. 'Obedience suits you, *Julian*.'

If it meant seeing my parents, I'd do anything. Even if that meant playing this game, even if it meant becoming the loyal hound this man wanted me to be. But the second the leash around my neck relaxed, I'd take my parents and run.

# CHAPTER 9

I was twelve years old when a man, no different to Silas Graham, broke into my family home whilst I slept. Mother was working late, likely tending a demanding Julian—this was a few years before the twins were born. Father was not home either, but I couldn't remember why. He should have been. No one was there when one of King Gathrax's drunken council members infiltrated my home, clambered on top of me and held me down until the skin of my wrists turned black and blue. He was a nameless man with a dark appetite. It seemed—in power—there were plenty of people willing to abuse their station.

Since that day, sleep didn't always come easy. Often when I closed my eyes, I would be dragged back to that time of panic and horror. I'd see those wide brown eyes and feel the splash of the man's dribble as it fell from his lip and landed upon my cheek. I'd recall the hot tang of his breath and the rough grasp of his ringed hands. My dreams always ended the same way the moment had. With my father barrelling into the room, dragging the man off me. What followed was the broken and bloody screams of the nameless assailant as Father beat him to a pulp in the corridor beyond the rooms.

He had killed for me that night.

I remember the chaos well. But I also remember being told never to speak of it. It wasn't until five years later I found out why, when the nameless man was no longer nameless. Raiyn Dalton. His body had been found in the gardens of the Gathrax manor. It was more a pile of bones by then, but the rings on his left hand had identified him.

It had turned out Raiyn had gone missing that fateful night. Father had killed him and buried his body, only for the remains to be dug up by starved wildlife during a long winter.

Was that why King Gathrax wished for Julian's body to be buried deep, deep into the ground?

I had expected there to be an inquisition. But there wasn't. Even knowing that Raiyn was dead, I struggled to sleep when I was alone. Which was why I stirred awake the moment a light thud sounded within Julian's room.

My eyes snapped open, and I was faced with a wall of black. Night had fallen over Aldian, and the hearth in the room had faded to cinders. The lack of light made it hard to discern what had caused the sound. Had Silas returned for another session of endless education about the Southern ruling estates? After that breakfast, Silas spent most of the day with me. Was that why I had dreamt of Raiyn? Why I woke with the crawling of hair across the back of my neck, and the damp smudging of sweat across my brow?

A cold brush of wind eased over me. It came from the direction of the window—which was odd because it had been closed earlier. I was certain of it.

Footsteps. I'd recognise the soft pad of feet even if the room was completely without light.

I sat up, gathering a lungful of air, ready to scream the

entire estate down if I had to. A figure stood, just as I knew they would be, half between the open window and the bed.

'Maximus, you're alive—'

The use of my name might as well have been hands gripping my throat and squeezing because I couldn't form a single sound.

Before me was a person. The outline was broad and strong, and coated in shadows. Two arms were outstretched towards me, lean muscles straining in desperation for me not to shout out.

I didn't need light to know who it was, their voice alone gave them away.

'Beatrice?' I whispered, not truly believing this to be real.

A thrum of hope lit through me as the figure stepped forward until I had full view of their face. I watched, numb and dumbfounded, as the figure lifted a hand to the strip of material covering the lower half of their face, and dragged it down.

'The one and only,' Beatrice said, eyes glistening.

'What are you—'

Beatrice pounced the final distance between us. In a blink, she'd slapped her cold hand over my mouth and held it firm.

'Quiet!' she hissed, eyes wide as her grip quickly softened. 'I don't have much time.'

Silence stretched out around us. Beatrice positioned her head towards the door and waited. It took a minute or two of stillness to confirm those stationed outside my door had not heard. Only when she was sure, did she remove her hand.

'Why… how did you get here?' I whispered, gripping hard onto her hand so she could not pull too far away. I feared this to be a dream. An illusion. But her touch was real. Warm and real. As was the smell of her. Even now, I could catch the whiff of hot coals and newly cooled steel seeping from her skin. I took a deep inhale, relinquishing myself to the familiarity.

'I have my ways.' There was something about the way she looked at me. The sadness that glistened in her eyes, which added to the strange tension between us. 'All this time, and it was you.'

My brows furrowed. 'Me?'

The days of frustration poured out of me. I had to bite down on my lip to stop myself from shouting at her. It wasn't her fault, but the feral desperation was almost too much to bear.

Before I could voice it, Beatrice reached forward and pulled me into her. The embrace melted all emotion within me.

'They said you died.' Her voice was tired. Broken. It quickly sharpened when she withdrew and smacked a fist into my shoulder. 'Dammit, Max. You actually had me thinking you had died.'

'I'm sorry?' The apology was strangely timed but felt as though it was the only thing to say.

'Don't be stupid,' Beatrice said, snatching the long braid of hair that had fallen over her shoulder, then discarding it back. 'Maximus Oaken, the lost mage, all along it was you.'

I allowed her to snatch my mage-marked hand and turn it palm up. The rough pad of her thumb brushed over the puckered lines of the scar, sending a shiver from my hand across my entire body.

'I didn't know.' I yanked my hand from her.

Even in the darkened room, I could see the furrowed wrinkle set between her thick brows. 'Then what the fuck, Max?'

'You're not making any sense,' I replied, unable to contemplate how she was even in this room, let alone what she was talking about.

'All of this has gone wrong, Maximus. You should have told me when you saw me before the festival. I could have helped you then. We would have been long gone by now.'

'I didn't because I was protecting you.'

She pressed a hand to her head. 'That is my job, Max. That was *my* task, but time blinded me and I gave up. And now I find out you were right in front of me all this time.'

'What task?' I pulled back.

'To find the lost mage and take them back home.'

'I don't understand. You're not making sense, Bea.'

'You don't understand? I'm the one who doesn't understand! Me, Max. The North has been waiting for you to show yourself for twenty-five years. I should have known. Should have guessed it was you. This god-awful place dulled my senses, just as my brother said it would.'

Confusion melted quickly into fear. As I stared at my friend, someone I had come to believe I knew, I saw someone completely different.

'You…' I found it hard to voice what my mind had already worked out. 'You are from *there*, aren't you?'

The North. A place were magic lingered and a Mad Queen ruled.

Beatrice nodded once. 'So long ago that I can hardly remember the place, but yes. I am, as are you.'

My hands gripped the sheets beside me, my knuckles turned white from the tension of my grasp. 'Have you come to kill me?'

Beatrice took a moment to reply, until her steel expression melted, easing slowly into the face I knew. 'No,' she whispered. 'Of course I haven't come to kill you. The Maximus I knew is dead. You died during the Dance of the Dryads, but servants whispered, speaking about you... about Julian. Dryads, Max. This is fucked. All of this.'

King Gathrax's concerns were right. The North did know about me. But he was so wrong because the North was already here.

'I need to get you out of here,' Beatrice snapped, fuelled suddenly as though she finally remembered what she was doing here. 'Now, Max, we need to go.'

Something my mother made me promise her chose that moment to fill my mind. *The moment you get the chance to leave, take it, no matter what.*

'Who are you?' I asked, distrust easy to grasp than any other emotion.

'Your friend.'

I shook my head. 'My friend is an orphan from Calzmir, someone I have known for years, certainly not someone from the North.'

'Max, the same can be said for you. A mage, I can't believe it. But we are going to need to put our secrets behind us for now. I need you to trust me. Get up,' Beatrice said. 'We are leaving.'

I didn't move. I wanted to, but I didn't. Couldn't.

'Max, come on, now is the time.' Perhaps Beatrice saw something in my gaze, but she quickly stopped herself. 'What is it?'

'My parents,' I said, voice cracking. 'I can't leave them.'

*No matter what.*

I blinked as I remembered the line of dead maids. I blinked again, recounting King Gathrax's warning loud and clear in my skull.

'He has them, he'll...' I couldn't form the words, for fear speaking them into existence would make them true. 'Hurt them.'

They would be more than hurt, I knew that.

'Simion is dealing with it,' she said, wide-eyed and firm.

'That name,' I muttered, as the man stepped free from the shadows of my mind and revealed himself. Warm amber eyes. Kind, attentive touch.

'My brother,' Beatrice confirmed, nodding.

'You don't have a family.' Questions roared through me. 'You've told me as much.'

Beatrice paused, toying with the accusation as though she was unsure how to answer it. Even in the dark, I heard her take in a heavy, weighted breath. 'It is complicated, but I can explain when we are far from here. Max, you aren't safe.'

'You know I can't leave,' I said. 'Not without *them*.'

Beatrice drank me in. As she opened her mouth to say something, there was a sudden noise from beyond the door. Clinking keys ruffled by the tired guard beyond, trying to find the right one for the room.

'Shit,' Beatrice muttered under her breath, staring daggers through my skull. 'Max, I will come back. Trust me, okay, you can trust me.'

'Julian?' A muffled voice called from beyond the door. 'Is everything all right?'

No matter what lingered between Beatrice and me, I worried greatly for her well-being. I pushed her, hissing through a whisper. 'Go, Bea. They'll kill you.'

'Fight them,' Beatrice sneered. 'Every step, everything they make you do. Fight them, Max. Don't let them win.'

She slipped through the shadows of the room, on soft feet, towards the open window. I found that I moved after her, bare feet slapping against the cold floor without care for keeping quiet.

'I can't,' I said quickly. 'They have already won.'

'I refuse to believe that.' Beatrice climbed onto the

windowsill effortlessly. Like a cat, prowling on all fours, she snapped her bright eyes to me in a final warning. 'Leave the window unlatched, Max. If it is closed, you open it. Understand? I *will* come back.'

The familiar snap of a key turning sounded at the door. I turned around to face it, blood thundering in my ears. By the time I turned back to Beatrice, she was gone.

I spluttered a gasp, feet slapping against the floor as I closed the space for the window. My hands gripped the stone sill, recognising Beatrice's warmth upon it as I leaned out.

There was nothing to see beyond it. Straining my neck, I glanced down to the ground, half expecting to see a body. But the dark ground was as it should be. Bodyless and empty.

Then I heard it. A low slither with a chorus of creaks. It took a moment for my eyes to adjust to the dark, but when they did, it was to see the ivy was moving. Like snakes, ropes of green-brown vine slithered across the wall just shy of my fingers. Living, brushing fingers of thorns and roots settled the same moment the door burst open.

'Julian,' a voice called the name from the now open door. I turned back to see a guard, eyes tired and cheeks flushed, sword held out in his arm. He scanned the room, searching for something.

I didn't respond straight away, not because I was choosing to ignore him but because my excuse had to be believable, my parents' safety relied on it. This would be reported to Silas come morning, and he couldn't know.

'I'm fine,' I said, swallowing the roaring emotion within. With all my effort, I hid the shaking of my hands as I reached for the window and closed it, still registering the brush of vine as it slithered and stilled on the outer stone wall. 'Just cold, that was all.'

The man stood there, watching. Waiting. His eyes flicked back to the window and then at me.

'Leave,' I commanded, voice spiked with forced authority. 'Before I tell Father you barged into my room, waking me.'

'But you—'

'Don't make me ask again.'

I didn't miss the sudden fear on the guard's face before he bowed and looked to the floor. 'My apologies, Julian.'

Only when the door was closed, and the familiar click of a lock fell back into place, did I open the window again. The cool breeze brushed over my skin, kissing the sheen of sweat across my forehead and bare neck. I looked out, noting the ivy had stilled and the night beyond was pierced only by the caw of an owl, laughing at me from its perch in the shadowed trees.

Simion. Hearing her speak his name lingered within me, knowing I was not alone when facing this. Until now I couldn't do anything but play this game. Now I knew I simply had to survive it, until Beatrice helped pull the board from beneath me.

Something unfamiliar sparked in my chest. It was hope.

# CHAPTER 10

'Wrong.' Silas's cane slapped against the wooden table, inches from my hand. I flinched, expecting the pain to follow. It didn't. Every time he brought his cane down, reddening my knuckles, I contemplated killing him. Dark thoughts didn't frighten me; they were what got me through. When Silas gifted me with pain, my mind replied with vivid images of him choking to death as slithering roots tightened around his wrinkled throat.

'From the beginning, again,' Silas droned. 'Unless you truly do not wish to see your dear mother. Or your father?'

This had been our routine over the past two days. From dawn until dusk, my days were full of grilling and questioning as Silas tested me on his lessons from the day. He had grown tired of my company too. Throughout our time together his demeanour cracked to reveal the true snake lurking beneath.

I ground my teeth together. 'I do.'

'Then do *better*. Again.'

We started our dance for the third time that day. His question followed by my answer.

'Who was the last mage to fall in the War of the Wood?'

'Mage Damian Gathrax the Red.'

'Why did the war begin?'

'Out of the Mad Queen's jealousy.'

Silas ran a tongue across his thin lip as he sauntered around the table. Hands folded behind his crooked back. When he didn't rely on his cane, he had a slight limp in his left leg, I fixated on it, filing away that knowledge until I needed it.

'And pray tell, of what was the wench jealous?'

I paused for a moment. Imagining the thoughts of a woman who had lived longer than any known in Aldian's history. The Mad Queen of the North. It was hard to understand her motivations. Had the South ever really been a threat to someone so powerful?

'The combined strength of the four Southern mages. Gathrax the Red, Calzmir the Blue, Romar the Grey and Zendina the White.'

With a short nod of Silas's head, we moved swiftly onto the next question.

'Before the War of the Wood, how would the family of the ruling mage pass down their heritage? Tell me, how did they pass on their gifts to their successors?'

I blinked my tired eyes and I saw the image of the Heart Oak lurking in the dark behind them. Tall and proud. 'From the Heart Oak, in the centre of the Galloway Forest. When a mage died, naturally or unnaturally, their heir would visit the Heart Oak and take wood from the tree—fashioning it into a wand. It was always the eldest, and usually custom for only sons to be deemed worthy. Except for Calzmir and Zendina, the only two families who allowed their women to behold power.' I added that last bit of knowledge in because I knew it would displease Silas.

As I'd expected, Silas mumbled something misogynistic beneath his breath. 'So, the Mad Queen desired to eradicate our power. For the twelfth time today, how did she go about it?'

'She burned it. Destroyed the Heart Oak with black fire.'

He *tsked*, passing behind me like a ghost. 'But a Heart Oak cannot simply burn by mundane flames can it, boy?'

The way he said boy made my skin shiver. It reminded me of another man, in the dark, long ago. I was beginning to think Raiyn and Silas were related in some way, it wouldn't surprise me.

They both beheld a predatory glare in their eyes.

'No,' I said, back stiffened. I couldn't see Silas behind me, but I sensed his presence. 'The fire was of Northern creation. It burned black. No water could put it out, no wind stifled it. It burned and burned until the Heart Oak, and leagues of forest around it, was destroyed.'

'Dark power, boy, a power that we have come to fear. To live day by day waiting for her to bring it to us again. To squash us where we sit powerlessly. But you. You will change that for us all, won't you?' Silas's hungry eyes met mine as he slipped back into view. 'With your help, you'll restore the power of this great family. And this time, that power will not be wasted.'

The door to the bedroom opened, and a familiar figure slipped in. Simion. A breath lodged in my throat, stifling me.

'Ah.' Silas clapped. 'Refreshments. Right over here.'

Simion didn't look at me once. Not as he crossed the room with a silver tray balanced in his strong arms. As with the first time I saw him, his presence seemed to be all that mattered in the room. Except now for an entirely different reason.

Simion was a Northern spy. He was Beatrice's brother, something I would've believed impossible until she told me.

Since her visit she'd not returned to answer any of my questions. But I still left the window open every night.

Silas was clueless of Simion's status as he snatched the bone teacup from the tray and lifted it to his nose. I fought to conceal any reaction on my expression, for fear he would notice something was amiss.

'Mint,' Silas called out, nostrils flaring. 'Camomile. And… honey. Well, I am impressed.'

Simion tipped his head, not once smiling. He looked at me. 'For you,' he said, his deep voice reverberating through the room.

As he gazed down at me, I, too, studied the planes of his face; how his cheekbones protruded with pride, and his jaw was sharp as steel and covered with a day or two's old stubble. His eyes were like Beatrice's, although his were sparked with flecks of gold, whereas hers danced with a multitude of browns among amber. Simion's skin was richer in tone, and his hair beheld a copper note that hid among the deep browns of his tight curls.

I hadn't realised I'd ignored the offer of a tea until Simion fixed his posture, took the cup by his own hand and passed it to me.

'Thank you—'

'Yes, yes.' Silas interrupted. 'That is more than enough. Go, and see that you leave the rest of the pot in my personal rooms. I will not be long left here.'

Simion tore his gaze from me, regarded Silas and replied. 'As you please.'

With that, he was gone. And I couldn't help but recognise the strange void that was left in his wake.

It had been two long nights since Beatrice had visited my rooms. I had hardly slept as I waited for news that Simion had located my parents and got them to safety.

The door closed shut, closing those questions away. Silas continued, unaware what thoughts speared through my mind.

'What do you know about a mage's power?'

I didn't register his question, not until the sting of his cane slapped against my hand. I almost dropped the teacup at the sudden pain. Although I managed to hold firm, it didn't stop the scolding tea from spilling over my knuckles.

'Their magic came from the dryads, which reflected the earthen abilities they would call upon. Conjure.' I wanted to reach for the journal before me. The golden, embossed name of Damian, the last Gathrax Mage, scrawled on its worn spine. It held the answers I needed. The very source of Silas's knowledge. Within its crinkled pages and bent edges, left from Silas's many readthroughs, it was our only source of reliable knowledge beside what stories had been passed down during the years.

To my left, sketches of the dryads, the spirits of the forest, were laid out across the table. The humanoid beings created from bark, leaves and mud. Glowing emerald eyes, wide as moons. Pointed teeth of twigs and stones. Moss-like hair and fingers of sticks and root. Magical beasts but also strangely... human. No one knew the origin of the dryads, besides what the childhood rhymes suggested.

*And from the deepest pits of the earth itself, when the ground was new and virgin; the Dryads danced. Where once the land was barren, life was breathed anew.*

'Continue...' Silas urged on, dragging me from my thoughts of the woodland sprites.

'They were able to *think* and *do*. Imagine a force of power and create it. Heal crops from the brink of ruin, control stone and make flora do as they so wished. Complete feats of pure wonder.'

Silas sighed, gaze drifting. 'Do *you* feel it?'

'Feel what?'

'The power.'

I flinched from his eyes tracing my skin. 'No.'

'I suppose you would not, since your wand is kept from you. Damian described it as an unfulfilled hunger when his first wand broke. He depicted the feeling as a burning ache in his stomach. And it lasted until he claimed another. Do you sense something similar whilst King Gathrax withholds yours from you?'

We had read that story of Damian yesterday. Silas referred to a time when the mage's wand snapped during a vengeful argument with his youngest brother. They were only boys, and Damian's brother was jealous that he was not chosen as the next mage. The fight also resulted in the youngest brother's death, the very wand that had broken in the tussle stabbed through his neck.

'I do,' I said, refusing to blink as I focused entirely on Silas and his sly, growing smile. 'I do feel it.'

It was an ache, eating at me over time. And it was fucking constant. Sometimes, a sharp pain stabbed across my stomach, and other times, the feeling was nothing more than a dull shiver. But regardless of the intensity, the discomfort never left me. I suppose I was simply growing used to it.

It was a hunger never satisfied.

'You must be practically murderous to get it back.'

*You have no idea.*

Something knowing passed behind Silas's eyes. 'Soon you and your wand will be reunited. It all rides on how you do tomorrow, for your next test.'

'Tomorrow?'

'King Gathrax has asked for our lesson to finish earlier than normal today. To allow you some extra rest before the *hunt*. A gift for your cooperation during our lessons and a final test before the other Kingdoms begin to arrive.'

The hunt. Of course. I had forgotten all about the annual event held by the Gathrax family.

'And it will not only be your wand you will be reunited with,' Silas said, drawing me out of my thoughts. 'If you do well, if you prove yourself, King Gathrax has agreed an audience between you and those you long to see.'

My blood ran cold, and my mouth dried.

'My parents—'

Silas leaned in so suddenly, his lips inches from the side of my face. It took everything in me not to flinch as he rested a hand on my shoulder and squeezed. 'Patience, Julian. Although I enjoy seeing you plead, it is best you do us all proud tomorrow. If not, when you see your parents, they may not be breathing.'

# CHAPTER 11

Becoming Julian Gathrax required more than knowledge. It was a physical change. The way I walked, the tone I spoke with, the promise of pain that the true Julian once held in his eyes. Blue eyes, like his father's, a colour I couldn't imitate. But I could fake the rest, making those around me fear me enough to not look long enough to discover the truth. I was being tested. I'd fail or pass—and the reward for doing as I was supposed to, convincing the Kingdom that I was the true, blood heir, was the only thing I cared about.

'Glorious weather, for a glorious day,' King Gathrax announced, as I took the final steps into the main foyer of the manor. I'd often wondered how this man could call himself a king yet live in a building such as this. Gathrax manor was no castle, not the type that the stories spoke of with towers and turrets, battlements and monstrous stone walls. I supposed it had little to do with money, for the Gathrax family had an abundance of it, and everything to do with the title being given to the Gathrax line after the destruction of the mages.

Before that time, there was no such thing as kings or queens, besides the mad one who dwelled far in the North.

Silas dwelled in the shadows, sulking close to the wall. 'Red suits him.'

I held myself straight, refusing to cringe at Silas's comment or the way his eyes scored over me.

'Have I kept you waiting?' I asked carefully, keeping up the false illusion I was to uphold. I must've done well for the King smiled, welcoming me with open arms.

'No matter,' the King said, 'what matters is that you are here. And Silas is right, red does suit you.'

He referred to the velveteen cloak that had been waiting for me that morning, wrapped in brown paper and tied neatly with a twine cord. A note card was attached with a single word scrawled over it. *Reward.* More proof that I was working hard and pleasing them with my act.

Although the crimson cloak was not the reward I cared for, it was the promise of seeing my parents after today's hunt that helped keep my emotions in check.

And for once, I was confident in myself. I would *not* fail.

I could hunt. Mother had ensured I was well-versed in fending for myself. I could skin a rabbit, gut a deer. My use of a bow required practice, but I knew the basics. It wasn't uncommon for us to slip from Gathrax manor with the purpose of finding meat when King Gathrax refused to provide us with rations himself. Although now, I had to wonder if she prepared me for other reasons.

I would have to play my skill down today because like stealing books from the library, King Gathrax wouldn't like knowing that when his servants suffered, we fended for ourselves. He enjoyed knowing we relied on him heavily.

'It would suit me,' I replied, mulling over each word. 'Since red is my family colour.'

The King's thin, pale brow raised above glinting sky-bright eyes. One corner of his lip peaked, flashing the slight yellow stains across his teeth. 'Indeed, it is.'

I forced a smile to match, feeling heat rise in my cheeks. 'When do we begin?'

Beyond the doors, out in the halo of daylight, a crowd had gathered. Noise filtered in, excited chatter and boisterous laughs that could only belong to those who knew wealth.

'I wished to have a word with you,' the King began, 'before we join our noble lords and their ladies. Silas has informed me of the sharp improvement in your attitude. As much as I enjoy hearing of your cooperation, I also am a man who lacks trust. So, you would understand my need to straighten a few...' he paused, scratching his chin with long, manicured nails. 'Details, before we begin.'

'There is no need,' I replied, gut twisting as it always did when he was close. It was hard not to drop my eyes from his and look to his wrist, knowing the wand lingered within the sleeve, strapped there with leather bindings. 'I understand what is on the line, *Father*.'

'Do you?' he asked, voice raised in pitch. 'Are you certain you understand?'

I closed the space between us, fists balled to stop my hands from trembling. 'Am I to repeat myself?'

It was a risk, speaking to him in such a way, but one that paid off as he threw his head back in a laugh. Silas joined in. There was heavy pat on my back, followed by the scent of lavender as the King leaned in close.

'I must say, you do him justice. But it will take more than insolence to convince those waiting outside of this door. Today, the hunt, is a test. You pass it, well you know what happens and who you get to visit. Fail—' His voice deep-ened, his fingers pinching through the thick material of the cloak, '—I cannot guarantee they will be breathing by sundown.'

'I understand,' I said, biting my lip.

'Very well,' King Gathrax said, releasing me. 'Silas will be keeping a keen eye on you. Do me proud, Julian, and I will return the favour. Oh, I do *love* the hunt.'

\* \* \*

The crowd clapped every time my arrow struck another woodland creature. Tied by a string, wild hare hung across the back of Master Gathrax's horse. I would've been the first to admit it: this praise felt good. It seemed having my parents' well-being on the line helped improve my aim. I hardly missed. When I looked to King Gathrax, who sat observing through the crowd, I expected to see disappointment.

There wasn't any to find. Only pride.

Each Gathrax lord and lady had a representative who partook in the hunt alongside me. It wasn't a competition as such, but dryads know I wanted to catch more. I quickly passed through my quiver of arrows, only to snatch more from the unsuspecting lord beside me.

King Gathrax laughed at my demanding display, deep belly chuckles bellowing across the crowd. Before it would have set a knot of unease in my chest. Now, I took it as praise and continued my show.

Hours into the hunt, my arms ached, and my aim was beginning to falter. To my luck, King Gathrax called an end to it.

Or so I thought.

'Now, now, before we call an end to the day's hunt, I would like to share some words with you all.' King Gathrax surveyed the crowd. One sweep of his gaze and he silenced the excited gaggle of Gathrax elite. Women and men, whose names I had been forced to memorise during my lessons with Silas. Names that mattered little to me as I kept returning my focus to the person selected for my demonstration.

'This year's *hunt* marks the special celebration that has occurred among my family. Events I am sure you have all been informed of and have spent days pondering.'

Every set of eyes fell upon me.

'As Silas's messages have informed you, my son Julian has discovered his mageship, and today we celebrate together that the once-great power of the Gathrax bloodline has returned. The dryads have deemed us worthy.'

I kept my chin raised. My shoulders rolled back. All I could contemplate was King Gathrax's promise.

I focused on the surrounding faces—each reddened with a mixture of excitement and disbelief, as King Gathrax forced out his speech.

Respect and awe gleamed in the eyes of those who dared to hold my gaze for long enough. I tried to hold each of their stares, forcing as much confidence in my eyes as I could muster. It was exhausting.

There was only one soul among the large crowd who oozed pure, boiling hate towards me. It radiated off her, high-lighted by her bloodshot, swollen eyes. Eyes that sang of grief.

Queen Remi Gathrax.

It was the first time I had seen her since the festival. And there was no denying it; she knew I was not Julian. She knew I had killed him. And she was not pleased to be playing a part in this game.

She stayed at the back of the convoy, handmaids fussing over the twins who also followed in suit. Neither child seemed bothered about me. I suppose the Gathrax family were all too familiar with death; it was their legacy, after all.

Remi's grey eyes sang with her want for it. Every time I looked behind me, she attempted to murder me with her gaze, eyes glistened with tears born from hate, not sadness.

I didn't blame her. Unlike her husband, she didn't find it easy to replace Julian. To her, a mage meant little compared to her own flesh and blood. I wasn't a twisted pawn for her gain. No, I was the murderer who broke her heart.

'My son, are you ready?' King Gathrax dismounted with Silas's help.

'For what, Father?' I asked, feigning boredom.

'Your final prey,' King Gathrax said with a smile, arms raised beside him. 'Surely, you did not think I would forget your favourite part of the hunt?'

The crowd buzzed with knowing energy.

'I enjoy it all,' I said. 'Father.'

'No, no.' He clapped a jewelled hand on my shoulder and squeezed. 'I have something better than hare and deer, my boy. Something to whet your appetite.'

He turned me around, faced me towards the belly of the forest, to the hooded figure who was stood, waiting, wrists bound by rope.

# CHAPTER 12

'Your final prey. I made sure it was a good one, just for you.'

My *prey* stood before us, hooded and whimpering. I couldn't take my eyes off them. Their clothes had been ripped and stained with filth. Even the fresh air of the day could not cover the stench that clung to them. I held my breath against the smell, but there was no escaping the truth of this moment.

Over the past days I had unearthed horrors I could never believe. Horrors I never knew people were capable of. Killing Julian Gathrax out of pure desperation. The murder of Gill and the maids.

But this was something else. My test was clear. Participate in the hunt, kill this person, and claim my reward. But how could I do it? How could I trade their life for the life of my parents? It crossed my mind many times, to draw the arrow, nock it and shoot—not at the hooded person but at King Gathrax.

Their head was bowed, whilst the crowd of nobility fussed and gossiped. I soon realised they began placing bets with

Silas, who slipped through the crowd with a pocket notebook in hand.

'He is speechless,' Silas called out, voice thick and breathless. The crowd mostly roared in response, some whispering behind hands.

'Did I not tell you today's hunt would be a special one? Just for you. All for you.' King Gathrax waved his hand towards the concealed figure ahead of us, then turned back to his adoring crowd. 'Julian is thankful, even words have escaped him.'

The crowd echoed his amusement as they forced out their laughter. Still, I couldn't speak, couldn't move.

'Say something,' King Gathrax hissed beneath the noise of the crowd. 'Quickly, boy.'

'I was promised a stag,' I snapped, my voice not sounding like my own. 'Where is it, *Father*?'

I forced the question out. Edging my words with whiny complaint, just as the old Julian would have done.

'Stag?' Silas jumped to King Gathrax's aid. 'Those creatures have not returned to these parts of the wood since *you* drove them all out last year. So, as you see, we have something much better. A challenge, just as you like.'

'Precisely.' King Gathrax pursed his lips. He wrapped his arm around my shoulders and squeezed his fingers into my upper arm. To anyone watching, his touch was a loving gesture between a father and his son. But the discomfort was invisible. His nails managed to stab into my skin through the thick cloak.

'I prefer my prey to run. The chase is what makes the hunt worthy,' I spoke again, this time keeping my face void of emotion. Bored, almost. Inside, all I could think about was the chance of this person being set free. Perhaps, if they could run, they could survive. The rope tied around their ankles would result in a very short hunt otherwise.

One heavy pat on my back, then King Gathrax released me. 'Do not worry, son. If you would prefer the prey to run, then that is what we shall let them do.'

'Good,' I said, choking on the word. There was nothing good about this.

I swallowed the lump in my throat, forcing down a wave of sickness. The bow creaked in my grip, fingers tightening until my knuckles were as white as fresh snow. King Gathrax leaned in close, mouth mere inches from the side of my face. A wash of his rotten-toothed breath cascaded over me.

'Do not miss your mark,' King Gathrax whispered, 'remember what awaits if you pass this test. Do me proud.'

The crowd shifted as Silas paced into the clearing, snatched a serrated blade from his belt and severed the rope that bound the hooded figure to a tree. He gripped the leash, looking back to us as though waiting for his command.

'Would you like me to count down for you, sire?' Silas asked, uncaring for the person who trembled violently at his side.

King Gathrax clapped, face alight with feral excitement. Hunger. 'Yes, you may do the honours, Silas. But first, remove their hood. If my son wants them to run, best they see where they are going, don't you think?'

Silas's thin mouth lifted into a razor-sharp smile, his eyes serpent-like. I held my breath as he raised a hand to the hood, gripped it and tore it free.

If King Gathrax wasn't still gripping my shoulder, I would've fallen to the ground.

'Dame?' Her name broke out of me.

I saw the silver-grey hair of the old woman first. The skin

around her eyes and head was a puzzle of purple and black. Angry bruises surrounded red, shallow welts. The pain she'd suffered was evident from the crusted blood across her hairline. Her eyes squinted as she finally saw daylight, then they rested on me.

'Dame.' Her name fell beyond my lips again. I couldn't fathom if it was a whisper, or a shout, as I regarded her with torrid horror.

'It took some time,' King Gathrax whispered, lips brushing my ear. To anyone watching it looked as though a father offered encouraging words to his son, 'but we finally found the traitor who allowed your mother access to see you. This is her punishment, one you will award her.'

A chill raced through my blood, seeping into my bones. As I looked upon her, my eyes blurred. Even after everything I had witnessed, this vision of her had the power to destroy me.

'Five,' Silas began his countdown, the crowd collectively echoing a moment after him. *Five.*

My heart thundered in my chest, filling my ears with a violent rush of blood.

'Four.' *Four.*

Guilt overwhelmed me. Guilt for knowing what I had to do, for my parents.

'Three.' *Three.*

Dame held my eyes, looked at me—*truly* looked at me as though she was the only one who saw who I really was.

'Two.' *Two.*

She closed her eyes and bowed her head. It was a subtle expression, but I read it for what it was. Understanding. She knew what I had to do, and she accepted it. That didn't make it easier.

'One.' *One.*

Silas's hand dropped the severed rope, his mouth moving in a final word that was not meant for me. *Run.* I read the word from his lips, hearing it in my head as booming as a crash of thunder.

And Dame ran, dashing into the forest, hands bound, stumbling over roots within seconds. The crowd erupted, cawing like crows over a corpse. The shock of the noise caused me to send the arrow skittering in the wrong direction.

Breathing failed me, there was only the beat of my heart. I lifted for another arrow, nocked it, held...

'I'm sorry,' I exhaled, as I released.

It missed again, steel tip burying into the forest bed, a few feet from where she ran. A ragged scream escaped her, reaching me even from our distance.

'Nervous, Julian?' King Gathrax called out, making me jump in my skin. 'You haven't missed all day, do not ruin your streak now.'

I didn't answer him. Refusing him gave me some sense of power, when, really, I had none.

I snatched another arrow from the quiver. I squinted my eyes, levelling the bow in the direction of Dame. Sweat raced down my neck, my palms were damp and fingers weak. It seemed my body longed to refuse me, whereas my mind continued its chant.

*He will punish your parents. They will suffer if you fail.*

Trees blurred the way of my target, giving her a shield of bark at her back. Every second that passed the further she was getting away. Thoughts seemed to fade, as did my conscience. Suddenly, I wasn't looking at the back of an old friend, but at the receding chance of protecting my parents from pain, or worse, death.

Dame tripped over something on the forest bed. I winced as her hunched body slammed into the ground.

It gave me a moment to act.

As I released the third arrow, all I could contemplate was how I had lost. My arrow slammed into her shoulder, jolting her back to the ground with a thud. The crowd erupted as Dame released a blood-curdling scream.

I turned my back, cringing at her screams of agony and looked directly at King Gathrax. I could steel my expression, but nothing stopped my eyes from filling with tears. 'Proud?'

*Please stay down, please stay down.*

One glance to King Gathrax was all I needed to know I had convinced them. His smile was proud, sliced from ear to ear. Silas clapped slowly, encouraging the rest of them to join in. Only Remi Gathrax refused to celebrate my success.

'Compliance is the key,' King Gathrax said with a clap, slow methodical slaps of his hands until the entire forest erupted in cheers.

I couldn't face them, couldn't look at their glee without wanting to shoot an arrow towards the crowd.

Facing Dame was easier. She was still, body splayed out across the forest bed, the arrow protruding from her back.

My emotions slipped from me, all the sorrow, sickness, sadness. All that was left was anger. A rage that paled the black fires that destroyed the Heart Oak all those years ago. Those flames couldn't compare to those I would spark.

Eyes dried, I wiped all remnant of weakness from my face. By the time I turned back to the King and his crowd, I was numb and empty.

The crowd stilled in fear. Monsters recognised monsters, and I had become one with far greater teeth, far sharper claws.

'Well done, my son,' King Gathrax called out, welcoming me into his arms. I melted into him, arms stiff at my sides.

'Does it suit me?' I replied, loud enough for them all to hear.

King Gathrax pulled me back, keeping me at arm's length. I caught my reflection in the wide set of his eyes.

'Does what suit you?' he said.

I narrowed my eyes, practically tasting the buzz of the crowd around me. 'Red,' I answered.

'Yes, yes, it does.' He turned to the crowd. 'My loyal supporters. Trusted and fair. The Gathrax bloodline has always been the strongest of the four estates. It had been when my grandfather, Mage Damian Gathrax the Red, dulled the powers of the other three ruling mages. Our blood was the purest. It is no wonder why it is my son, who has defied all odds, retrieved his wand and claimed that power once again.'

Everyone listened in utter silence. Even the twins were entranced by their father. His voice carried above the crowd, stilling all movement and sound. All the while, he didn't release my shoulder.

'May this be a blessing for us all. With the change of tides comes a shift in power. One that is going to cause great interest from our brother and sister estates. But there will be more eyes turning our way soon. The North will catch wind of my boy in due time, and when they do our skies will once again be filled with dragons come to claim him. We must be ready.'

A chorus of gasps passed over the crowd. People looked through the thick foliage of the woods to the sky, expecting to see the very beasts he threatened. For the first time, I fought the urge to smile.

I bore holes into the back of King Gathrax's balding head. *The North are already here, you fool.*

'Encouraging words.' Silas bowed to his king and stepped forward into the clearing. 'In the coming days, the remaining Southern rulers will be arriving to our borders. Birds have been sent carrying invitations of great importance and urgency. When their carriages carry them across the borders of our King's domain, we shall hold many councils, meetings that shall determine a new South. A united one. Opening borders, demolishing tensions. All for a single purpose.'

'Let the *red* rule!' someone called out.

The crowd buzzed at the shout, echoing it in return.

'Yes! The great *red*.'

I watched the corners of King Gathrax's lips quiver. 'Now, now.' He waved his hands to quieten the crowd, although the smile suggested he would prefer to let their frantic chaos continue. 'Let us not get ahead of ourselves. It is only natural, as the old mages ruled, so will the new. Julian, my heir, will unite us all under one name. A strong, *ancient* name.'

The crowd began to chant. '*Gathrax, Gathrax, Gathrax.*'

'When the South see a mage has returned, they will not refuse our request. If they do, well, they'll find their Kingdoms nothing more than ash. Then, when the North arrives, we will have the numbers to match. Tell me, my friends, how does that sound to you? More power. More land. More wealth. Is this more to your liking?'

Their cries bellowed, every shout lit up the forest, scattering birds from their nests above. Bows pumped skywards, as feet stomped on the ground. The entire clearing seemed to vibrate with pleasure.

'*Gathrax, Gathrax, Gathrax.*'

All I could focus on was Dame's limp body as the King's guards scooped her from the ground and carried her out of sight.

I added her name to the list of dead I left in my wake. I etched it into my soul, as grief prepared to pounce over me.

# CHAPTER 13

'You have proven yourself,' King Gathrax said, patting me on the back. 'Because of that, you are allowed to have five minutes.'

I couldn't speak. Not since we left the crowd of nobles, who would all be sharing some elaborate meal in the grand hall of the manor, likely boasting about the hunt. About me.

'Compliance is the key to success.' King Gathrax moved for the door to Julian's room—*my* room. He gripped the brass handle and turned it. 'Continue doing as I ask of you, and your visits with your parents will last for a far longer time. As much as you benefit me, I can equally benefit you.'

'Did you know?' I asked, body rigid and mind a storm. 'Did you know what she meant to me when you picked her?'

'Yes,' King Gathrax said plainly, voice raised in pitch. 'We must shed our past to make room for a new one. Perhaps if Dame did not betray me, it would have been another who was chosen. But, two birds with one stone as the saying says.' He paused, opening the door an inch. 'I told you it was a test. They are not meant to be easy, and I had to ensure you would do anything for me. You *would* do anything for me, wouldn't you, Julian?'

I nodded, losing sight of the world as I caught the view of someone through the slip of the door. 'Anything.'

'Five minutes,' King Gathrax repeated. 'Now go, do not waste it.'

My father sat on the edge of my bed as I entered the room. He didn't stand as he regarded me. It was as though I saw myself in his eyes, drinking in the vision of his son dressed in a red cloak.

The door clicked closed at my back, muffling the voices of the King and his councillor.

'What have they done to you?' Father asked, his deep voice itching across my well-dressed frame. He stood slowly; I could tell from his face that it pained him. He gripped the bed frame, using it as leverage, unable to put much weight on his foot.

There was no answering him, no words that I cared to share. In seconds, I closed the space between us and threw myself into his waiting arms. As always, I felt like a child in his hold. There was a reluctance as Father wrapped his arms around me, but it quickly faded.

He rested his chin on the top of my head, his breathing laboured.

'I killed Dame.' The admission burst out of me. 'I killed Dame because if I didn't, they would kill you.'

Father held me firmer, encasing me in the protection of his arms. All at once, I was twelve years old again when my father returned, broken knuckles and blood-splattered face, from killing the man he found in our home. Except, this time it was me who had done the killing.

'I am safe, your mother is safe,' he replied. 'Most importantly, you are safe.'

'Where is she?' The shock of seeing my father had blinded me to the fact he was alone.

'They only allowed one of us to see you,' Father said. 'Deborah refused, not because she didn't want to come, but because she thought it was best that I did.'

Of course, my reward was double-edged. I knew, without a doubt, King Gathrax only allowed one of my parents to come so he could continue holding the other against me.

'Where does he keep you?' I asked, the question rushing out of me.

'I am not permitted to say.'

I wanted to force the answer out of him, knowing if he told me I could inform Beatrice when she—*if* she returned for me.

'Do they hurt you?'

Father shook his head, although his eyes spoke another answer. 'We are well, you need not worry about us.'

'You are all I worry about.'

My father held my face in his large, calloused hands, eyes tracing over my troubled face, dyed hair. 'We are sorry, Maximus. This is our doing.'

I shook my head, eyes pinched closed as I refused to listen or see the pain in his eyes. My father was always a strong man, a strength I'd aspired to, and seeing him so weak was world-shattering. 'Don't say it, not now.'

'All right,' he said, exhaling as I melted back into his arms.

Me and my father had never spoken about that night when he killed a man to protect me. It was an unspoken secret, one of many it turned out to be. There would be a time we spoke about the mage-mark on my hand, and the reasons behind how it was possible, but in the limited time I had with him, I didn't want to waste it. King Gathrax was evil, but he was also true to his word. I would continue complying and passing his tests, knowing my parents would be returned to me.

'Do you remember that night?' I asked, not having to explain what I spoke of.

Father's body stiffened, his voice lowering in octaves as he replied. 'I do.'

I took several deep breaths, filling my lungs with the confidence to speak aloud the horrific thoughts that had buried themselves in my mind like thorns.

'You protected me from a monster.' I took a deep breath, steadying the canter of my heart. 'You always protected us.'

'I did what I had to do, for my family.'

I closed my eyes, losing myself to him. 'It is my turn to defeat the monsters. My turn to protect my family. You've shown me what it takes, and I swore to myself, promised myself that I would return the favour one day. Tell Mother,' I said, almost choking on my words. 'Tell her that I promise no harm will come to either of you.'

'Do not make promises when the price is steep, Maximus. Not if it is at the detriment to your own safety.'

King Gathrax needed me. He needed me for the power I gave him, which meant I was safe. 'I swear, I will do anything. You are all I have.'

Father cupped the back of my head, fingers brushing softly over it. 'I will tell her, my boy. But only if you promise me something in return.'

'Anything.' The word broke out of me, fuelled by the grief from Dame's death and the knowledge that this moment was limited. Worst of all, it was the same promise I had just made to King Gathrax.

'Don't forget who *you* are.'

# CHAPTER 14

*Compliance is the key.*

The words had etched themselves into my mind. And it seemed the ink King Gathrax wrote them with was the blood of those I loved.

I was haunted by Dame's death. No matter how I washed, the stain of it didn't seem to leave me completely. I couldn't sleep without seeing her, couldn't eat without my body wanting to expel every morsel. From the moment Father had been taken from my room after the hunt to the following morning, I knew little of rest.

I'd not only left the window unlatched, I had thrown it wide open. There was no preventing the evening freeze invading the room and ridding me of the little comfort left. Surely Beatrice would come—she had to.

But she never came. No one did.

Perhaps it was for the best.

By dawn, I was aware of commotion beyond my bedroom. There was the rushed pattering of feet and muffled conversations from unseen people. I couldn't make out the words, but the energy behind them was undeniable.

Whatever happened within the estate was important enough to keep Silas from visiting me for our lessons—not that I minded the reprieve, but I would've preferred my mind to be occupied than to have the space for dwelling on what had happened.

By the time I caught the familiar jingle of keys, and the smooth click of a lock being opened, I didn't have the energy to look up as Silas finally entered the room.

Soft footsteps, the door shutting, closing us in. I continued to stare at my open hands, pondering how they were not visibly covered in the blood of those who had died because of me. Dame. Gill. The servant girls. Julian.

'Good morning, Maximus.'

My blood ran cold. I snapped my attention from my hands to the man who stood at the other end of the room. A man who was not Silas at all.

Simion offered me a smile. It was short-lived and didn't reach his amber eyes that were, as they always seemed to be, fixed on me. In one hand, he held a plate covered in a bulbous silver lid. My nostrils flared as it recognised the warmed scents of spiced sausages and scrambled eggs. In his other hand, he carried a jug of water.

I stood abruptly from the bed. 'I won't come with you.'

He regarded me where I stood. His warm eyes trailed the entire length of me. From the mud-flecked trousers to my rumpled jacket. Clothes I had not changed since the hunt. Beneath his scrutiny, I found myself running my hands down the jacket, trying to iron out the wrinkles.

'That's not why I am here,' Simion replied.

Although we had hardly shared more than a word until this moment, there was something easy and familiar about him. It was likely a result of him looking so similar to his sister. Or was it the glint of misplaced kindness that still shone in those glittering, warm eyes?

'You shouldn't be here,' I said.

Simion scanned his eyes around the room. 'By here, do you mean this room or this building, this Kingdom? Which one is it?'

Was that sarcasm? 'The South,' I answered. 'Well, all of them.'

The upturn of one corner of his mouth caused a shiver to pass across my back.

'You best keep it between us then. I wouldn't want to find myself in trouble if anyone found out.' Simion strode forward, directly towards me. His hands were full, so he had to use a flick of his expressive gaze to give his next command. 'Sit.'

'For what?'

I couldn't help but focus on the curved lines of his arms. The shirt he wore, which up close proved to be a size too small, flexed at the seams at the power beneath it. How did he hide in such plain sight, when one close look would confirm he didn't belong here? His uniform didn't fit, his body was not shaped for the mundane chores of estate life. Yet it had been days since I had first seen him in the manor, and here he was.

'You need to eat something.' He discarded the plate on the bed beside me and then carefully placed the jug of water on the dresser.

'I'm not hungry,' I replied, unwilling to take my eyes off him.

'Okay,' he drawled, 'allow me to rephrase that. You *will* eat something.'

We stared at one another in contest. Me silently refusing the food, which he'd exposed by removing the silver covering. My stomach betrayed me with a mighty roar.

Simion, knowing I would not give in so easily, leaned his weight on one leg and placed a rather large hand on his hip. 'I'll make you a deal,' he said. 'If you finish the plate, and I mean the entire thing, I will take you for a walk.'

'A walk?' I echoed; it was almost comical.

His dark brows raised upwards with a quick flick. 'Yes, a walk.'

'But Silas…'

'Silas is busy and will be for the rest of the day. Silas has appointed me to accompany you. So, if you want to be let out of this cage, get chewing.'

I did as he asked. Not because I didn't want to refuse him, but because my stomach was lost to the enticing smell from the plate.

I finished it in moments.

'Better?' Simion asked from his seat in the armchair beneath the open window. I had moved it there last night, and spent most of the long evening in it, waiting for Beatrice to arrive. There was something in his knowing expression that told me he knew, which was why he didn't bother to close the window.

'If you haven't come to take me away from here, what do you want?' Was it my deep exhaustion that removed my patience, or perhaps the drawn-out discomfort that plagued me from being separated from my wand?

I couldn't hold my tongue.

'My *sister* is currently busy attempting to locate your parents, just as you had asked of her. And, for the record, if it was up to me, I would never have thought twice about looking for them. All three of us would be in the North by now.'

'Then I ask you again,' I said, shaking. 'What do *you* want?'

'Want?' Simion played with the word, chewing on it and making a face. 'I wanted to check on you.'

'Why?'

Simion shuffled forward until he perched right on the edge of the seat. He leaned his head in his hands, elbows propped up on his knees. 'Because your well-being is my priority.'

His reply caught me off guard, if only for a moment. As did the sudden intensity in his stare that narrowed as he looked at me.

'I don't even know you,' I said.

'I'm Beatrice's brother,' Simion recounted, not an ounce of a smile on his face.

'I've known Beatrice for years, and never did she tell me she had one.'

Simion screwed his mouth up as though I'd offended him. 'Just as I am sure she didn't tell you that she was actually from the North, she was a mage, and you are the sole reason my family was torn apart.'

I couldn't breathe beneath the weight of his words. They bore down on me, pressing in from every angle.

'I expected more,' Simion stood, 'from you.'

There was disdain in the way he looked at me. I finally recognised it. It lasted as long as his gaze did before he moved it towards the door and paced for it.

'Where are you going?' I found myself calling out.

He didn't stop. '*We* are going for a walk.'

*Compliance is the key.*

I called out after him, body refusing to stand. 'I cannot risk doing anything that they have not asked of me.'

When Simion turned back to face me, I expected to see his dislike for me. But his eyes had softened. I felt pathetic before him—hair bleached and dressed like a puppet in someone else's clothes. Was that why he looked at me the way he did? Because he saw Julian Gathrax? Or was it because he saw through the illusion, directly to the core of who I was. *What* I was.

'Silas has asked that you are paraded around the manor,' Simion confirmed. 'With the arrival of the Calzmir family comes more scrutinising and malicious whispers. It cannot be believed that Julian Gathrax is locked up in his room. Julian must be seen, walking freely around *his* home.'

Something felt wrong. In the days since the Dance of the Dryads, I had never been let out without Silas or King Gathrax in tow.

Simion reached for the door handle. 'Perhaps you should tidy yourself up. I'll wait for you outside. First impressions count, after all.'

I knew when someone was keeping something from me. Simion was a stranger, but I could recognise the flash of a lie in anyone's eyes.

\* \* \*

We walked for hours. Even when my legs ached, I didn't stop. Simion never strayed too far behind, but he was so quiet I could have forgotten he was even with me. It wasn't until we passed through the gardens for the second time that I realised what I was doing.

I was searching. Looking. Trying to find some proof that Maximus Oaken had existed.

Simion didn't question me when I finally took us to my home. Perhaps he didn't know what I was doing, since we had passed the servant quarters once already, but the first time I didn't feel brave enough to go. I was scared, in a way, of what I would find.

Which, when we moved towards my front door, to my home, where my family had lived for as long as I could remember, I discovered that those concerns were completely justified.

It was empty.

I stood in the barren front room. All there was to prove anything had even been there were outlines of dust where furniture had once been.

Behind me, the door clicked shut. It was the feeling of a door closing me in a place I no longer recognised. The room was as much a stranger as I was.

'This place, it means something to you.' Simion's deep voice echoed throughout the room. I didn't move, not as he stepped to my side and paused. Out of the corner of my eye, I knew he had looked at me. But I couldn't tear my eyes from the vision before me. It was as though he tore the very thoughts from my mind, which tingled with an unnatural cold presence.

'My home,' I said, voice cracking. 'At least, it was.'

Simion looked back to the room as his shoulder brushed mine. He was taller than me by inches. 'This was never supposed to be your home,' Simion said calmly. 'It shouldn't hurt you to say goodbye to it now.'

What was there to say goodbye to? All that was left were the memories that haunted the empty space. And no matter the emotionless, careless comment Simion had just made, there was no part of me that felt strong enough to bid it farewell.

'You say that as if I will go with you,' I said, as my eyes brimmed with tears and my body shook with anger.

'Because you will.'

'No,' I growled, speaking from some dark part lingering in me. 'Not until I make *them* feel this agony that haunts me.'

Simion didn't speak at first. He shifted his weight beside me until he pressed closer into me. The back of his knuckles brushed my forehead. 'Revenge is not always the relief you believe it will be.'

I scoffed as the first tear sliced down my face. 'Maybe. But I'm confident it will feel better than this.'

Simion regarded me, and I dared not look at him. I didn't want him to see how broken I was.

'We will get you away from here,' Simion confirmed finally. 'Then you will really understand what home is. Or at least, what it can be.'

'This is all I have ever known.' I raised my mage-marked hand as I shouted. Simion didn't flinch. 'I didn't ask for this burden! I don't know about the North. I don't know the secrets that you, Beatrice, everyone is keeping from me.'

'And that fury you feel, for being kept in the dark, should not be aimed at me. Your lack of knowledge is not my fault.'

'Then whose is it?' The tears fell freely. I became hot and uncomfortable in the red-velvet jacket. I longed to rip it off. 'Who is to blame?'

'Just as revenge will not suffice the fires of your anger, nor will the portioning of blame.'

'Answer me,' I demanded.

'*If* Beatrice can free your parents, then perhaps they will be the ones to answer you. Not me.'

I reached for him and grabbed his shirt. The material gathered in my fists, and I shook him. 'Then do it. Go and save them! What is stopping you? I thought the North were skilled warriors, what is taking you so long from saving two fucking people when you have had no problem fooling the Gathrax estate this entire time.'

Simion blinked, and the fire behind his stare scolded me. One look, that was all it took, and I released him.

'I'm sorry, I...'

'We've lost them,' Simion said so plainly I almost didn't understand him.

My heart jolted in my chest. 'You what?'

'We've lost your parents,' Simion confirmed, unblinking.

'How can you—'

'They left the Gathrax manor last night. Beatrice trailed them to the outskirts of Gathrax boundaries, but she couldn't follow any further.'

The room fell away from me. Everything slipped away as my mind digested.

'Max—' I didn't register that Simion was speaking to me. Not until he used my name, my true name, for a second time. 'Maximus, listen to me.' He laid his hands over my shoulders. Unlike the rough grasp I had just used on him, his hands were gentle. Soft. The sheer size of them should have weighed me down, but they were featherlight and... warm.

I stopped, enough to look at him directly in his eyes, to truly take him in. This close, there were so many other details I had missed before. Simion must have been near me in age, perhaps a few years older at most. Up close, hidden among the tight curls of copper-brown hair were strands of silver. Like stars in the night sky, they glistened when he tilted his head down to me. His skin was smooth, his lashes long and dark.

If he was no mage, he certainly held some power in his touch. It completely silenced me.

'Listen carefully,' Simion said. 'You need to hold yourself together. If only for a couple more days. We will see this through, and your parents will be okay. I swear it.'

'He... he lied,' I stuttered, mind falling back to King Gathrax. 'He told me to comply and I would be rewarded, but he is sending them away.'

'Jonathan Gathrax still has control over them.'

My eyes narrowed. If I had tears to spare, they would have been filled with them by now. 'Why are you helping me?'

Simion's fingers tightened, but only enough to send a familiar shiver across my back. 'Because I know what it is like to have lost someone you care deeply for. That feeling is enough to destroy you. Which is why, if it means you will come North with us without resistance, I will ensure that your parents come with us.'

We were interrupted by sounds outside the room. Simion let go of me, and I almost sagged in on myself. He turned, glanced to the door and spoke. 'I should see you back to your room before Silas comes looking.'

'I thought you said…'

'Walking the heir of the Gathrax estate around the manor, like a pheasant with its feathers on display, is one thing. Creeping through the servants' quarters is another.'

A blush crept over my face. The flick of Simion's eyes to my cheeks confirmed he had seen it.

'Silas is a bad man,' I said. 'I know the likes of him.'

'Oh, I know. I worry, not for my sake, but for his.' Simion said, tilting his head to the side. 'And now I have what has been kept from me for years, I will do anything, anything to make sure I never let her go.'

'Beatrice?'

'Yes, my sister.'

Pieces of a puzzle began to slot together in my mind. Before I could form the image, Simion took my hand in his, distracting me.

'Come,' Simion urged me towards the door. 'Dry your face before Silas sends his little mice to locate you.'

* * *

The Gathrax estate buzzed with energy. Servants raced through corridors, in and out of rooms and up the many grand staircases two steps at a time. Only when I passed them, did the chatter simmer to a faint whisper. I was all too familiar with the reaction. I'd done the same when I was Maximus and worked for the family; a family I was now a part of.

Heads bowed and eyes lowered. Not out of respect, but fear. The reaction made my skin crawl. If it had not been for Simion, lurking like a shadow beyond my shoulder, I would've turned around and fled back to the room. But, for the sake of my parents, if this is what had been asked of me, I would do it.

We didn't speak—couldn't speak—not with so many around us. It was in the quiet when all the questions came to me.

Was Simion a mage? Where had he been in all the years I had known Beatrice? Why did he regard me with such dislike in quick moments? And why had I torn his family apart?

He didn't wear gloves, so I tried to search his palm for a mage-mark. It didn't take long to confirm that neither beheld the telltale sign of magic. Then there was Beatrice. I had never seen one on her hand before. It wasn't exactly something she could hide when the use of her bare hands was pivotal to her work at the blacksmith's.

Questions followed questions. By the time we reached the main atrium of the manor, my head ached.

I paused at the top of the grand landing. It was curved in the shape of a half-moon, with a balcony giving way to a drop into the main foyer of the estate. I stood at the edge, gripping the banister, and peered down below.

The floor was covered in cases. Boxes had been piled high, leather-luggage containers almost bursting with their contents. All around them, a gaggle of servants fussed. They were all dressed in blue.

The Gathrax estate walls were either painted or papered in different shades of crimson. Even the woodwork throughout the manor had been stained a russet brown. Curtains were lined red, as were carpets and stair runners. Everything was red. Until now, with the arrival of the Calzmir estate.

It was… disorientating.

I gasped at the sudden touch of a hand on the small of my back. 'They've seen you now,' Simion whispered, close to my ear.

'Take me to my rooms,' I demanded, sounding more like Julian Gathrax than ever before.

Almost every one of the Calzmir servants looked up to where I stood. Hands covered whispering lips, and not one of them continued with their tasks as I stood above them. Seeing them was a reminder of my test. This was simply another one.

'Not yet,' Simion said, fingers drumming on the small of my back. 'Let them see you, Maximus.'

This time his use of my real name didn't affect me. All I could think about was being Julian—showing this crowd the illusion King Gathrax had constructed just to ensure my parents' safety.

It was becoming easier, slipping into the skin of the boy I had killed.

I only hoped it was worth it.

# CHAPTER 15

'I *am* impressed. Studying, even when I permit you a day's break from our lessons,' Silas said, as he entered my rooms later than afternoon.

I looked up from Damian Gathrax's journal, the words imprinted in the dark of my eyes every time I blinked. Reading was the only thing that took my mind off Simion and the revelation he had left me to simmer in. Since he had returned me to my room, the intensity of his gaze and words wouldn't leave me.

*We've lost your parents.*

'What do you want, Silas?' When what I really desired to ask was, what have you done to my family?

The ache in my legs echoed how long I had been sat on the bed, poring over the texts. Needles stabbed the tips of my toes and spread up my feet until I pressed them on the flagstone floor and added weight to them.

'I wouldn't ask such questions of me,' Silas drawled, flashing his cataract-ridden eye at me. 'You may not like the answer.'

Disgust danced through me, as did unbridled anger.

I slammed the leatherbound tome, shutting off the same story I had read over and over. The same retelling of the fall of Mage Gathrax the Red and his valance and bravery in the face of death. Each a ballad to his strength, written by those who followed him to his final breath. Biased accounts, I had determined by my third readthrough. There was not one perspective from anyone but a Gathrax. But it was something at least; it was knowledge. And knowledge was power, so I'd arm myself with it until I glittered like an armoury.

I held the journal firm, knuckles paling, as Silas slipped over the room towards me. One swing to his skull, and I could batter him away. In some sadistic way, I wanted him to act out on those dark thoughts he harboured. My body desired the excuse for some violence. Especially after everything Simion had said.

'I have come on request to prepare you for supper this evening,' Silas announced.

'I'm not hungry.'

Silas regarded me for a moment, taking in the sharp tone of my response. He smiled slyly, flashing every toothy gap in his mouth. 'You have a spark of him you know. Julian, that is. I sense him in you, a change perhaps. Finally, all my hard work is paying off.'

'Compliance is the key,' I said, repeating the sentiment that had filled my mind since King Gathrax first used it.

'That it is, mage, that it is,' Silas replied, eyeing me up and down. 'Shooting an arrow into the back of a woman you once cared about. How unkind, something Julian would've done. Allowing her death to be slow, painful. I admire your choice, I do.'

My skin itched where Silas's eyes tracked over it. Hearing

him speak in such a way about Dame almost ruined everything. I kept my lips screwed shut, knowing if I opened them, I'd unleash a storm over him, or I'd drown in my chest-cleaving guilt.

The tap of Silas's cane shuddered through my bones as he paced towards me. 'Your *father* has requested your presence for a supper, a final meal before tomorrow's celebrations. The Romar estate will be arriving by dawn, the Zendina estate later this evening. Oh, it is going to become busy for you. Gone are the times you can sit back in your room and enjoy the simplicity of a book. This, this is what it has all lead up to.'

There was no stopping Silas from plucking Damian's journal from my hands. Without something to hold, they fisted, nails biting into the softening flesh of my palms.

'Tell my *father* I decline his invitation.'

Silas smiled slowly, tongue lapping over his lower lip. I knew he won before the words even came out of his vile mouth. 'What were you just saying about compliance?'

He'd won, and he knew it.

'Let us not keep our King waiting,' Silas clapped. 'Shall we?'

* * *

I arrived at the dining hall before anyone else. Silas had spoken not a word to me the entire way there, only going so far to open the door for me to enter, then closing it behind me. He didn't follow me in.

The dining room was modest. A personal space for the ruling family of the estate to eat together. It wasn't a place for showing off wealth and hosting grand parties, there were plenty of other rooms for that. Narrow, barely fitting the dark pine-carved table in its centre, when the chairs were filled

with people servants would hardly have space to walk around
the table and serve.

Crimson curtains hung upon two of the four main walls.
They didn't conceal windows. During dinner, they would be
drawn to cover the many frames that were hung between
them—at least only when Queen Gathrax ate within the room.
She couldn't stand the sight of the preserved palms of mages
passed. I didn't blame her. It was a horrific thing to hang like
decoration. The skin had dried and curled at the edges, kept
only in place by the pins that secured them inside the frame. I
scanned them, eyes moving down the line of hands, each
showing the same markings that I had upon my own palm.

Mage-marks.

The scars on my palm seemed to warm as I regarded the
frames. I hoped, for my sake, Queen Gathrax would join the
feast tonight. I couldn't eat looking at the dried old skin
either.

A deep pomegranate-toned runner draped off either side
of the table, finished with impressive beading and tassels.
Besides the table and chairs, there was one other piece of
furniture. A chest of drawers at the end of the room, placed
beneath an arched, diamond glass window. Red candles
burned in black-iron holders beside freshly picked holly and
greenery.

I counted five chairs in total. Each with a full silverware set
placed on the table before them. For five guests. Myself, and
four others.

A breeze slipped inside as the door opened behind me. The
flames of the pillar candles danced in the gust.

'Julian, it pleases me to see you,' King Gathrax announced,
entering with his wife, hand in hand. Both were dressed in
finery; elegant postures and equally regal costumes. Queen
Gathrax was swaddled in a gown of ruby silk, making her

frame look narrower than usual. The gleam of the material matched the ostentatious gem that hung from her thin neck on its large, golden chain.

'I didn't have much of a choice,' I replied.

I stepped into the corner of the room, melting into the shadows. Their presence didn't frighten me, but the action was drummed into me from years of serving. The King's frown reminded me of my new station.

Without more than a subtle glance to where I stood, King Gathrax pulled a chair from beneath the table and urged his wife to sit. Whilst he fussed over the chair, Remi stared hateful daggers through me. This time, I returned them.

'Your display earlier today has truly injected some excitement into our guests,' King Gathrax said. 'Well done, Julian.'

I swallowed the urge to scream at the name, warring with the desire to fight him but knowing what would happen if I did. Raising the mask of Julian Gathrax was becoming as natural as walking and breathing. I reached down, past the guilt and shame, until I clasped that dark part of me and lifted it to the surface.

'Dare I ask what the occasion is?' I asked, hating the emotionless tone of my voice. 'What are we celebrating this time?'

'You, my son. As all our recent celebrations have been. It is all for you.' The King's excitement was a visceral thing. It smoothed the haunting lines across his face, making his eyes bright as cerulean stone. 'Silas had no problems with herding you here I see. Isn't life so much simpler if we all just get along?'

It wasn't the way I'd describe it. 'Yes, Father, it is.'

Remi scoffed into her napkin, concealing the flush of anger in her cheeks.

'Now, now, my love. None of that.' King Gathrax nodded

at his wife, ginger hair falling over his eyes. His jacket widened him, giving the illusion of a strong build when in truth he was nothing more than a needle beneath it. 'Take a seat here, please.'

He had walked to the opposite end of the table where his wife sat. For me, he did not pull out a chair, he simply waved a hand towards one.

'Now Julian, before our esteemed guests arrive. I trust you do not need reminding how important your behaviour is tonight?'

I swallowed hard, the sound audible. 'No reminder required.'

My eyes shot to the sleeve of his jacket. It shifted slightly, enough for me to catch the flash of leather hidden beneath it. I sensed the wand's presence. It took great restraint not to reach for my forearm and scratch the skin red raw. Over time, its call had reduced to a faint simmer, but it was there, none-theless.

'As I thought would be the case,' King Gathrax said with a smile.

There was noise beyond the door before it opened. Silas stood proud as two unrecognisable figures hovered in the shadows behind him.

Silas cleared his throat as the King stood, table jolting beneath his sudden change in stance. I remained standing, gripping the back of my chair, as I peered over his narrow shoulder to the display of blue which entered.

'May I introduce Queen Amilia Calzmir and her son and only heir, Camron Calzmir.' With a dramatic bow, Silas stepped aside, allowing the two new arrivals to enter.

Queen Amilia Calzmir was a tall, sharp woman. Every-thing about her was blade-like, from the narrow cut of her black eyes to the blunt line of her long, blonde hair. She had to bend her knees to enter. They clicked as she ducked beneath the door frame, moving with the grace and deadly precision of a swan. Giants' blood surely coursed through her veins.

Her nose was her most prominent feature, so long it overwhelmed the somewhat beautiful elements on her face. Her aged stare was crowned with wrinkles, even the corners of her painted lips were smudged with the painted liquid.

'Jonathan,' she exhaled, extending her hands out towards King Gathrax. She wore a silk dress of midnight navy blue. It was so dark the material was almost black, until it reflected the candlelight around the room. It was the colour of the deepest of oceans, where monsters lurked. Like water, it slipped over the hint of the curve at her hip, held by two straps at her narrow shoulders. Her skin, pale as bone, gave view to the multitude of veins beneath.

'Blue suits you well,' King Gathrax drawled, displeased at the use of his name, not his title. 'It really brings out the *depths* of your eyes.'

'As red suits you,' Amilia replied, her trill voice lacking welcome. 'It affords you a hint of colour in those hollow cheeks of yours.'

Remi loosed a bird-like chuckle, all to her husband's dismay. 'At last, some entertaining conversation.'

'Pleasure to see you too, Remi. I see you hold on to your youth as desperately as a—'

'And who is this lurking behind you?' King Gathrax interrupted before a civil war of insults broke out.

He gestured to the second figure who waited in the shadows beyond the room. 'No good just dallying out there, Camron, let me see just how you have grown.'

If Amilia Calzmir was a cold storm, her son Camron was

the opposite. He was the sun. Bright, fresh faced and devilishly handsome. Each step he took into the room was precise. Militant. Which added to the air of command that oozed from his posture. I placed his age in his late twenties, though from the look in his eyes it seemed Camron experienced more than anyone else his age.

I barely noticed Silas as he slipped into the room and pulled a chair opposite Remi Gathrax. He waved a hand and Amilia sat.

Which left Camron to occupy the empty seat beside me.

'Hello, Julian,' Camron said, tracing his obsidian eyes over me. Unlike his mother's, Camron's eyes were not cold. They were dark like coal, and I was certain there was a fire lurking beneath them.

The room was silent, as though our crowd waited on bated breath for my reply. I couldn't form one, not for fear of judgement.

'May I?' Camron said, brow peaking. They were pale, like his hair, which was the colour of sun-bleached sand. He had a faint dusting of freckles across the bridge of his nose, which he caught me looking at with a smile.

'May you what?' I asked, snapping out of the trance he put me in.

His midnight stare flickered to the chair I gripped with both hands. 'Your chair, may I assist?'

'Forgive my son,' King Gathrax said, quickly filling the awkward silence. 'He forgets himself.'

'It's no bother,' Camron said, as he reached for me.

I inhaled, taking in the fresh smell of salt and open air. It flooded my senses with pleasure. I inhaled a sharp gasp, expecting the brush of his hands. But it was a chair that he reached for, not me. He pulled it, gesturing for me to sit with a sweep of his large hand. My eyes fell to the sleeves of his azure jacket, which strained against the flex of muscle.

'Thank you,' I said, voice soft. Pathetic, certainly not the voice of the Gathrax heir.

Camron stepped back. 'It is my pleasure, Mage Gathrax.'

King Gathrax coughed from where he still stood, waiting, at the head of the table, urging me to move. I dipped my head, struggling to hold the heir of the Calzmir estates' gaze. His striking face was intimidating, as was his white-toothed smile and the single dimple on his left cheek.

I sat quickly in the chair with my back to Camron. I looked to the audience of four before me. Each who seemed to study us both with a mixture of expressions. Remi kept her face frozen in hate. King Gathrax smiled like a cat who found the cream. And Amilia Calzmir rolled her eyes, as though she saw this show for what it was.

Strong arms gripped the back of the chair and pushed gently.

I gripped the red cloth, heart picking up into a canter. Never had I been so grateful for King Gathrax to speak.

'How long has it been since we last hosted a feast?'

'Not long enough…' Amilia mumbled, forcing a sickly-sweet smile.

King Gathrax forced a laugh, but I could tell from the flinch in his blue eyes that he was barely holding himself together. 'At least, this time, we have something to celebrate. A feast to commemorate the coming *union*.'

I was aware Camron had pulled a chair beside me. His presence was a burning beacon, unable to ignore.

King Gathrax snapped his attention to the Calzmir heir and spoke. 'We have prepared three courses of food, each in honour of you, Camron. The freshest fish, mussels from the furthest reaches of the Unknown Isles. We wished to commemorate your recent adventures, since we have not had the chance to hear everything about them.'

'Oh, fantastic,' Camron said, refusing to spare King Gathrax a look. 'Because after months out in the ocean, eating fish is exactly what I miss.'

'Now, now,' Amilia cooed. 'Claws in, my darling.'

I don't know why, but my eyes dropped to Camron's hands. It wasn't claws I saw, but pink skin mottled by old burns. Camron must have sensed my shift in attention because he withdrew his hands and placed them beneath the table, out of view.

'My apologies, King Gathrax. I am sure the feast will be a... memorable one. No doubt,' Camron said, forcing a brilliant smile, 'the most memorable.'

'Perhaps Silas can pour us each a glass of wine, whilst we wait for the first course to be brought in,' King Gathrax added quickly, gesturing for Silas to do something.

'Yes,' Amilia clapped. 'Wine. Precisely what will make this evening... bearable.'

Wide-eyed, I looked to King Gathrax, who practically shivered in his skin. 'A sentiment we share,' he replied, as Silas hobbled into action, cane in one hand, bottle in another.

The sooner this was over, the better.

It didn't take long for the glasses to be filled and the food to be brought in. Food I had never even contemplated eating before. Mussels drowned in a lemon-infused soup, monkfish circled with a bed of boiled potatoes. Fresh bread, so crusted it flaked across the table like snow beneath the softest of touches. No matter what was brought in, the scent of food did little to distract me from the man beside me. Nor could I stop myself from looking at him. And I was certain he glanced at me, the shift of his body moving so slightly whenever my eyes flickered to him.

Conversation was lacking, replaced by the click of silver-ware against plates, and the torturous chew of food in teeth. My body moved for me, joining in those around me as I ate. I'd almost placed a forkful of fish in my mouth when the brush of a knee met mine beneath the table.

I jolted, kneeing the table so hard it shuddered, glasses clinking together.

'Julian,' King Gathrax said, thin brows raised, 'Is there a problem?'

I dabbed my mouth with the cloth, steeling my face to hide my panic.

'I am afraid, that was my fault,' Camron answered for me. He was the only one to continue eating, although he smiled slightly as he lifted his fork to his mouth. His lips were lined with freckles, I noticed. 'I have a habit of wandering in unknown territory.'

The hair on my neck prickled, settling only when our audience continued to feast. Camron chuckled beside me. Out of the corner of my eyes, I caught him reading my profile with deep intent.

'Are you enjoying your… fish?' I asked, not wishing to suffer in forced silence a second longer.

His knee brushed mine again, causing a jolt to burn up my spine. I was beginning to think it was not an accident, but a well-planned action. 'All tastes the same, don't you think?'

'Tastes like the sea,' I replied, unsure how to truly answer, because this was the first time I had ever eaten fish. It was an expensive meat to retrieve from the coastline. My parents could never have afforded it. Which, as I stared at the carcass and the small white bones riddled within it, I was glad for.

'And when did you taste the sea, Julian?' Camron replied.

A blush crept over my face. There was nothing I could do to stop it.

'I jest,' Camron muttered, winking. 'You're not wrong, in fact it does.'

Silas's lessons flooded back to me, giving my mind something to mull over. I knew all about Camron Calzmir and his expedition across the Thassalic—the endless oceans that stretched between Aldian and the Unknown Isles.

'Let us hope the pudding doesn't suffer from the same affliction,' I added, offering him a smile indicating my want for the conversation to end. I lifted my glass of wine to my mouth.

Camron Calzmir either didn't get the hint or didn't care to allow me the reprieve. 'You would not want to imagine what we suffered through when we desired something sweet whilst out on the seas.'

'Enlighten me,' I replied.

'Apples,' Camron said, urging this conversation along. 'An amazing and extremely versatile fruit. Imagine the different ways it can be devoured when desperate.'

Sarcasm, I recognised it well. Against my better judgement, it warmed me. It was familiar. 'Hmm.' I kept the glass to my lips, focusing in on King Gathrax's words as he sparked conversation with Camron's mother.

Camron took my diverted attention as a hint to cease the conversation.

'Amilia, we were truly sorry to hear of the passing of your dear husband,' King Gathrax said, lifting a fork full of fish to his mouth. 'And how equally apologetic we were for not attending the service of his burial. I hope our gifts sufficed our absence.'

Amilia hardly spared him a glance. Silas had told me of the passing of King Calzmir. It had been almost three years ago, and he'd died from a battle with a terrible sickness that ate away at his lungs, a sickness it was believed Camron brought home from his travels.

'The portrait was... interesting, however it did little to fill the void of my love's death.' Amilia's sharp, angular brow raised. 'Do not force sorrow, Jonathan. It does not suit you.'

King Gathrax's knife screeched across his plate, lips pursing white. On Amilia went, eating without acknowledging how her comment had sliced at him. It was hard not to smile; I had never known King Gathrax silenced by anyone before.

'I must say, years have been kind to your heir. Camron, what a man you have grown into.' King Gathrax turned his attention to the man beside me. 'A spitting image of his father.'

'Indeed.' Amilia replied, then her eyes were on me. 'However, I cannot say the same for your heir, Jonathan.'

I almost choked on the mouthful of food.

'He has developed in many ways since your last visit,' King Gathrax added, equally displeased.

'Handsome being one of them,' Amilia announced, shifting her stare to the man sat at my side. 'Do you agree, darling?'

'Very,' Camron said, almost too quickly.

The skin across my arms shivered, hairs standing on end.

Both King Gathrax and Amilia shared a look. A grin on both their faces. It was the first time either had regarded one another with a lick of kindness. It unnerved me.

'Then let us toast to that.' King Gathrax raised his glass, wine swirling like fresh blood within. 'To us. Gathrax and Calzmir. Great allies for years, soon to be united anew.'

'Here, here,' Amilia replied, joining King Gathrax by lifting her glass. Even Remi, her hand shaking slightly and her face lacking a smile, joined. But Camron didn't move. He sat still, back straight, gazing upon me as the room chimed with the clink of glass on glass.

The conversation that followed was of little interest to me. Both leaders of their respective estates discussed taxes, compared wealth and boosted about political matters that brushed over my head. I was just happy that Camron's attention had returned to the dessert before him.

I could hardly focus on mine, on anything really, beside the steady breathing of the man sat beside me.

'And there will be a display, I hope?' Amilia asked, chair screeching across the stone as she stood from the table. 'You promised me a show, something grand and magical. I may take your word for it, but the other Kingdoms are already talking, Jonathan. Not all can simply believe your son is suddenly a mage. We have questions, ones that require answering.'

'Answers, you shall get. But do not mistake me, Amilia, I care little of what Romar and Zendina discuss. Their opinions are meaningless. But yes, you shall all get the demonstration you crave.'

'When?'

My heart skipped a beat as King Gathrax reached for the wand hidden beneath the sleeve. I expected him to pull it out and show the room, but he didn't. I drowned in the burning jealousy of his proximity to it.

*Mine.*

'Tomorrow, after the ceremony.'

Amilia tipped her head, fingers pressed to the slight swell of her belly. 'I would like to discuss the details further before I retire for the night.'

Camron stood abruptly. 'Mother, I wish to speak with you first.'

Queen Calzmir's face was flushed white, ghostly. 'Not now, my darling.'

'Yes,' Camron said sharply. 'Yes, now.'

The sudden change in atmosphere sparked around me like lightning, fizzing in the air, only highlighting the smaller sounds of breathing, shuffling feet and Remi's slurping of more wine.

'You are welcome to join us, Camron.' King Gathrax studied the Calzmir heir with trepidation. 'In fact, your presence would be helpful for the finer details we must discuss.'

I didn't miss the look Silas gave Camron, and the one he returned to the vile man. There was a knowing between them, something that stretched further.

It was my time to break the tension, standing abruptly just as the demanding Julian would've done. 'I'm going to bed.'

Shocked and perhaps a tad disappointed, Camron looked at me. I held his stare, attempting not to lose myself in their darkness.

'I think that would be a good idea,' King Gathrax said. 'You will need your rest. We have a big day ahead of us tomorrow. Silas, see my son makes it back to his rooms whilst I direct our fine guests here, to the drawing room. Our home is far larger than theirs, it would not be hard to find oneself lost among so much comfort and wealth.'

Amilia's expression pinched into a disagreeable scowl, and she faced her host a final time. 'It's all the red that I find disorientating, Jonathan,' she retorted, as I allowed Silas to guide me to the door. 'I have always found the colour… displeasing. Although I suppose, I can get used to it.'

Camron kept quiet, but I saw him wince. I glanced up to him, neck straining, for the man towered over me by half a foot. He took my hand in his, lifted my knuckles to his lips and pressed a kiss to them. It was so sudden I didn't have a chance to react.

'It has been a pleasure,' Camron said, returning my hand to me. 'Sleep well.'

I didn't have the words to reply, not as Silas guided me away from Camron, out of the doors and into the quiet darkness of the manor. All the while, Camron's warmth didn't leave me, nor did the smell of salt and ocean breeze that lingered in his wake.

# CHAPTER 16

No matter if I desired it, there was no evading sleep.

By the time I returned to the room, I was knocked out before my head hit the pillow. I'd attempted to stay up—reading through more of Damian's journal—but found my eyes heavy and mind pleading for rest.

I was haunted by the stories on the page. The dreams were vivid, so real I could taste the burning black flames, and feel my skin boil from the intense heat.

Mage Gathrax the Red fought beside Mage Calzmir the Blue. He had conjured the very trees to dance as they reached for the Mad Queen atop her mount—her beast, her *dragon.* It spat pillars of burning ice across the world as it cut across Aldian's skies.

I was a bystander, unable to do anything as Mage Calzmir the Blue fell beneath the might of the creature. One blast of the dragon's breath and she had crystalised. And when she fell, body connecting with the muddied battlefield, she shattered. Broke apart into a million pieces of iced-coated flesh and blood, glass shards that flew across the battlefield until her remains were left to melt into the earth—forgotten.

Gathrax the Red was left. And he fought, just as his life depended on it. He raised his wand, pointed it directly into the gaping mouth of the dragon as the Mad Queen cackled upon its back and—

I woke, smashing through the membrane of the dream, gasping into reality. My mind went to the window first. It was open, but no one clambered through it. Still, something was wrong.

A change hung in the air.

Blinking away the sleep, I dragged my eyes through the haze of the room until it landed on the most noticeable difference. The door was open. In fact, it still squeaked on its hinges as though pushed by an unseen hand. Beyond it was nothing but shadow. I squinted into the dark, trying to make sense of what was happening.

Had Beatrice finally returned to take me away?

I jumped from the bed. The cold-stone floor shocked through my feet.

'Beatrice?' My whispered voice echoed through the darkness. I cringed at the sound as my heart thudded into my throat.

I braved a step from the bed.

'Simion?'

A figure slipped from the shadows, edging its way into the room. Before the features became clear, I stumbled until the back of my thighs crashed into the bedpost.

'I am sorry to disappoint you.'

I squinted as panic crawled up my spine.

The Calzmir heir swayed in the doorway, his face illuminated by the glow spilling in from the open window.

'Camron,' I said his name, toying with the way it sounded.

'The one, and only.'

'What are you doing here?' I glanced beyond his shoulder, trying to see if anyone else was outside the door. There should have been a guard, someone who sat vigil as they had every night since this hell began.

But the hallway was dark and deserted.

'Should I be concerned that you are calling out the names of other men?' Camron asked, looking behind him as he followed my attention. He almost tripped over himself, his body awkward and fumbling.

'I asked you a question,' I snapped, panicked.

'And I asked you one too.' Camron winced, his dark eyes flashing with genuine hurt. 'I know it is not custom, but I thought, what is the harm in breaking them and coming to see you. Not like custom truly matters. Not to them at least.'

Camron was clearly drunk, slurring heavily over his words. His steps were mistimed, he would have fallen if it wasn't for the bedpost he grabbed at the last moment.

'I think you need to leave,' I said, not needing to force the demanding tone of Julian Gathrax. The panic of having this man, this stranger, in my room was enough to draw up that feral part of me. 'Now.'

Camron narrowed his scrutinising eyes. In the shrouded room, they looked endless and black.

'I cannot tell if it is the lack of light that makes you look different or the long time between my last visit,' he said, pausing only to hiccup. 'And your eyes…'

Camron leaned in and I pulled back, offended by the alcohol on his breath. He noticed my reaction and looked shocked at himself. 'I am sorry if my coming here has made you uncomfortable. It was not my intention.'

Every muscle in my body tensed. 'Then what do you want?'

'I just… I had to see *you*.'

He made me feel very seen, that was for certain. He only took his eyes off me between long, heavy blinks.

'It is late, and you should be resting,' I croaked, voice shaking slightly. I despised how frightened I sounded, but there was nothing I could do. My eyes darted between the drunk man and the door. My chest felt tight with each inhale.

'Do I scare you?' Camron asked, a puzzled expression creasing his handsome face into a frown.

'You've broken into my room, in the dead of night, drunk. Yes, you frighten me.'

He ran a finger over the coarse hairs that shadowed his sculpted face. A light beard fit perfectly in the hollows of his cheeks, giving his jaw a defined, strong shape.

'Why do they lock you in?' Camron asked.

'Excuse me?'

He gestured back at the open door, swaying wildly. 'The door. It was locked and guarded. Usually, it is to keep people out, but I get the impression, this time, it is to keep you in.'

Words failed me. Excuses slipped through my fingers like sand. 'Perhaps it is to keep people like you out.'

'I hardly imagine that would be the reason. I am no threat, and if I was, then your guard would not have been so willing to give the key to me.'

'You keep telling me you are no threat, and I shouldn't be scared. But I am, and I would like you to leave.'

Camron leaned in closer. 'Your eyes... they are not as I remembered them.'

I fought the urge to lift a hand and cover them. Julian had eyes as bright as summer skies. Mine were green, and there was nothing King Gathrax could've done to change them.

Camron's eyes narrowed, racing across my face, seeing the truth that lurked beneath. I felt every graze of them everywhere they touched.

'And I am wondering if that is the reason Jonathan has you locked up in this cage. I tried to tell myself it was because he feared you—what you could do. But you seem... powerless, so that cannot be it.'

*Powerless.* The word stung.

'It is late.' I forced command in my tone. 'I should be in bed, as should you. Unlike your mother, who must have taught you that breaking into others' bedchambers at night is rewardable behaviour, mine warned me not to speak to strangers.'

Camron's entire face lit up. His eyes widened, and he thrust his finger towards me in a point.

'So, you admit we do not know each other.' He practically shouted, his voice dripping with glee. 'That we are strangers.'

I would've stepped back again, if there wasn't the bed in the way, as Camron took another wobbly step. This close, there was no hiding in the shadows. His features were on full display.

His white tunic was unbuttoned and untucked. The tie he had worn earlier in the evening had been removed, and the shirt drawn back at the collar revealed curled hairs across a well-formed chest. I first thought his trousers were black, but I was wrong. They were a dark blue, made from velvet, giving them a darker impression. Blue. Calzmir blue. He was without a jacket, and his summer-blonde hair was dishevelled in places, as though hands had run through them one to many times.

'The Julian I remember was never short for words... you seem too quiet.'

'I have got nothing to say to you,' I said, wishing to slam my hands into his chest and force him out.

Camron grinned, knowing he was backing me into a

corner. 'I prefer it. The quiet. But then, I don't think it suits you. Not really.'

'Camron,' I sneered, tension rising thick within me. 'Leave.'

'Answer me one question,' he said, some far-off sadness in his gaze that was lost for a moment. 'Why do they lock you away, *Julian*?'

I gathered he already knew the answer.

'For my safety,' I lied anyway.

'And yet your guards of choice are tired, untrained maids? They would do nothing to protect you once the North comes to claim you—or stop strangers like me from breaking in.'

'As you pointed out, we are not strangers.' I tensed my hand, mage-marked palm sparking at his comments. 'And I'm more than capable of looking out for myself. May you be reminded that I'm a mage—I do not need maids or guards as protection.'

Camron tilted his head like a dog, raised his hand to his chin and ran a large finger across its sharp edge. 'A mage, I believe that. But a mage without a wand. Helpless. Powerless. So, I ask you again, why the need for lock and key?'

'Get. Out.' My gut jolted, bile threatening the base of my throat. I was too slow to conjure another lie.

'Your *father* is adamant your new magic has caused some dramatic changes in you. Yet he keeps the wand from you, and I do not believe it is because of his desire for control. I think it is because he is frightened of what you may do with it.'

'King Gathrax has nothing to fear from me.'

'Formal, isn't it? Referring to your own father in such a way. I know he enjoys the flamboyant use of titles, but it is simply strange.'

Camron took another step, bringing with him the fresh scent of sea-salt once again.

'You're drunk,' I told him, now noticing the slight detachment in his stare.

'Nothing gets past you, does it?'

My cheeks warmed. 'It has been a pleasure—'

'I can see through the illusions of this place, *mage*.' Camron interrupted, brows furrowing over midnight eyes. 'I have experienced enough in my life to see through it.'

'Then you would know that prying in such matters will do you no favours,' I said, ignoring his closeness. In my mind, I saw flashes of everyone King Gathrax had killed because they knew the truth. Even though I didn't know this man, I didn't want his name being added onto the list of dead.

My conscience was frayed, it couldn't take another.

'If King... my father has already warned you of the changes my magic has caused, best you listen to him.'

'For whose sake, yours or mine?'

'Neither, perhaps even both. So please, go.'

Camron grinned, straight teeth flashing. I blushed. He was handsome. With his loose shirt and dark stare, he looked like a pirate from a story I had once read. And behaved like one, swaying where he stood. Even with the lack of light, I could see the mess of scars across his hands. His shirt had been rolled up to his elbows, and the marks went up even further.

He caught me looking and quickly rolled down his sleeve.

'Good night,' I said, stepping in close. I couldn't move away, but perhaps I could force him with my demeanour and make him leave.

'Maximus,' Camron said, finally backing away. 'That is what you were called before, wasn't it?'

Ice gripped a hold of me. I shook my head at him, unable to look into his sharp eyes.

'Do not worry, I won't tell anyone else,' Camron said, as he turned on his heel.

The question broke out of me. 'How do you know?'

The Calzmir heir stilled. I didn't need to see his face to know he was smiling. By the time he looked at me, his expression was stoic and straight. There was no moving as he lifted his finger and placed it, carefully, beneath my chin. Camron's touch was gentle, and warm—very warm. I didn't pull away, not as a shiver raced from the place of his touch, spreading across my entire body.

'I have my ways,' he answered.

'My name is Julian,' I lied, for the sake of my parents. This could be a test. He could've been sent here by King Gathrax to look for a missing piece to my new self.

'They can make you look like *him* on the outside, but I can see through this illusion.' Camron's eyes widened. 'I apologise if I have intruded too far, but I had to see you.'

A smirk lifted his lips finally. He leaned in close to my ear, closing the space between us. My breath rasped as his ocean-breezed scent washed over me.

'I am not like them,' Camron said. 'I want you to know that, before tomorrow.'

Could he hear the slam of my heart? He stood so close, it wouldn't have surprised me if he did.

'You are *all* the same,' I replied, voice trembling.

Camron drew back, dropping his hand back to his side before he stepped away. 'Injustice sickens me. This place… sickens me. What they have done to you, it…'

'King Gathrax will kill you if he thinks you know the truth.'

'No, that is not the power he holds over me,' Camron said, plain and simply. 'He needs me, as he needs you. I am sorry if my coming tonight has startled you. It truly was not how I wished for this to be. But here we both are, on this path. I suppose we make of it what we wish.'

I couldn't make sense what he meant. Not as Camron tipped his head, bowing with extravagance, then backed out of the room.

I stood there in silence and unravelled with a breath.

*He knows.*

With my back pressed to the door, I slumped to the ground.

*He knows the truth.*

There was relief knowing someone else recognised the horror I had been through. But there was also panic. Panic of what Camron would do with that information.

And who would suffer as a result.

I sat still for a while, lost to thought. Then I found enough energy to clamber from the floor into my bed, where I hid beneath the stiff feather-stuffed duvet.

It was only when I replayed over the entire meeting, trying to find out what I had done, or said, to ruin the lie, when I realised Camron had left the room unlocked. No maid returned.

Camron, unlike the others, had not locked me away.

# CHAPTER 17

Mist clung to the outer grounds of the Gathrax estate—
blanketing the world in an otherworldly sense. The fog was so
thick even the view of the Galloway Forest was disturbed. It
was as though a wall had been erected between me and the
world. What was most strange was the trail of servants—
dressed in Gathrax red and Calzmir blue—racing like ants
across the gravel below my window.

They carried boxes overspilling with an array of white
flowers. Large petaled daisies, ivory stained roses and lavish
draping of champagne hyacinths that dragged across the
ground at their feet.

Every now and then, they would look up to my window
and stare. And for once, it was not fear or hesitation they
regarded me with. Their bright smiles and whispered
murmurings spoke of something entirely different.

*Excitement.*

Camron had alluded to a day of celebrations, which
echoed something King Gathrax had discussed the night
prior. I hadn't the faintest clue what it was, but if it ensured

the attention was off me for a day—I welcomed whatever it was that kept everyone busy.

Silas didn't show for our morning lessons. Simion didn't turn up in his place, offering refreshments and a walk. And Camron, someone whose presence still lingered, must have been nursing a hangover in bed. I couldn't help but wonder if he would wake, embarrassed, at his behaviour the night prior. I only hoped he was so drunk that when he woke, it wasn't with the memories of what he had said.

Every passing second, I expected someone to rush in and tell me of my punishment for failing his test. That's what it had to be, wasn't it? A sickness stabbed within me, knowing Camron saw through this illusion, and what was at stake.

Another night of poor sleep had left me with a raging headache of my own. One that would only settle when I spoke with Camron. I had to ensure he would not reveal what he had figured out. For the sake of my parents, for his sake, Camron couldn't tell anyone. And I was prepared to become Julian Gathrax—threats and all—to ensure he kept his mouth *shut*.

The door to the room exploded open, tearing me from my view of early dawn. My shout of surprise caught the attention of those passing beneath the window, resulting in them scuttling away.

Beatrice stood in the doorway, breathless and wide-eyed. 'Maximus, we need to leave.'

My initial reaction surprised me. I was not thankful for her presence, or relieved to finally see her after so many days. Instead, I raced towards her, grabbed her arm and pulled her into the room.

After Camron had dismissed the guard beyond my door, they had not returned all evening or morning. Perhaps the manor was so focused on preparing the day's events that I had become an afterthought. Thank the dryads because it meant no one had seen Beatrice or stopped her. But from the panicked look on her face, I didn't think she cared if she was caught or not.

Hope swelled in my chest, making it hard to steady my breathing. 'My parents, did you find them?'

Her gaze did not falter from mine, but she kept her lips straight. 'No. But I can explain.'

Beatrice used the leverage of my hold on her, gripped my wrist and pulled me back towards the door.

'What do you mean *no*?'

Her golden eyes widened. 'I'll explain, but I am going to need you to trust me.'

I held my ground, pulling free of her grasp. 'Then I'm not going anywhere.'

'You have no choice, Max,' Beatrice growled, lurching forward to grasp me again, but I pulled out of reach just in time.

'Bea,' I warned, body trembling. 'Let go of me.'

'Maximus,' she scolded, speaking from a place of panic, using my name as a weapon. 'We don't have the time for this. Simion is waiting for us, we must leave.'

'I'm not going anywhere with you. Not until you tell me what is going on.'

'Something terrible,' Beatrice snapped.

'You disappeared for days and now return with demands?' Frustration riled within me. I couldn't dampen it. 'How do I trust you, when I don't even know who you are?'

Her cheeks blossomed with heat. My mouth dried as the face of my friend twisted into a scowl. 'The same goes for you.'

She moved, throwing the cloak from her side to reveal the leather that hugged her chest and stomach. It was a harness of sorts. One that held a staff of knotted wood upon her back. With a large sweep of her hand, she displayed it before me.

'Max, don't make me do this.' Her eyes—although overspilling with hesitation and sorrow—glowed from within. Magic, it had to be.

I raised my hands out before me, as if it had the power to hold back whatever Beatrice was prepared to do. No studying of old journals or stories about the mages of Aldian's past prepared me for this.

'Then don't,' I replied as calmly as I could, though terrified. 'The Beatrice I knew would never threaten me like this.'

The staff she held was wooden and—at first glance—was no different than a walking stick. Narrow and long, it had a knot of wood at the top, which was now pointed inches from my chest.

'I'm doing this for you. To keep you from harm. Please, just come with me. Walk out this door, and I swear you will never have to see this place again. There is a place of safety waiting, a place you will be looked after, cared for. This is bigger than you and your parents now. This affects Aldian, North, South, the fucking lot of it.'

The tears that blurred my eyes were not out of sadness. It was frustration. Power radiated from Beatrice in undulating waves that rippled across my bare skin. I knew, without a doubt, she could outdo me.

'I told you, I told Simion. King Gathrax will kill them, Beatrice. Do you understand that? They are all I have left, and he will take them from me. I cannot leave them.'

*Compliance is the key.*

Beatrice cocked her head and sighed. It was a defeated sigh. Not because my words had the power to win, but because she knew what was to be done. 'Your life means more than theirs.'

There was no power—no magic—with the ability to strip me down to the bone like Beatrice's words.

'How—' I said, jaw clenched. 'How could you even say that?'

'Because it is true,' she replied.

I shouted now, not caring who heard behind the still-unlocked door. 'You're just like them, you know. Telling me what to do, threatening me. You're all the same.'

The pent-up anger stormed inside of me. Like the beat of a second heart, it pulsed deep within. My palm spasmed in response to its call.

Beatrice's breathing deepened as she studied me. Although she kept still, the outline of her frame shivered with anticipation. Her stare glittered with unspent power.

I could smell it, the magic; it washed the air in thick clouds of oak and pine. It reminded me of autumn mornings when the northern winds cascaded over the wood with hints of damp soil and sweet maple.

It reminded me of Simion.

'Do it then,' I encouraged. 'Make me leave. Force me. Be just like *them*. And I swear I'll hate you forever, there wouldn't be a day I'll not resist you.'

Her staff dipped slightly. 'Fuck, Max.'

My shoulders rose at her remark, knowing she was backing down. The staff lowered another inch. Then I noticed the dark circles that shadowed her eyes; the way her skin was lacking in its usual warm tone. Even her posture, beneath the heavy moss-green cloak, had slumped.

'Simion is going to kill me for this,' Beatrice said, before settling her eyes on me again.

Relief flooded through me. 'This *is* the right decision, Bea.'

Beatrice shook her head, enough for strands of thick dark

hair to fall over her eyes and hide them. 'Your parents have been handed to new captors.'

The world fell away at my feet.

'I trailed them south-west from here. Max, we cannot leave you to go after them. You are what is important, we only can hope they are safe now.'

Camron. Had he known about my parents when he visited last night? The pity I saw in his eyes, the guilt that led him to drink himself into a stupor. But why?

My forehead creased as my mind fought to make sense of the situation. 'King Gathrax *he* needs them to make me comply.'

'Jonathan's signed a contract, shifting over responsibility to Queen Calzmir and her son.'

I looked up, numb to the world and everything within it. 'He can't hurt them any more?'

Beatrice shook her head. 'No—'

She stopped dead; her eyes shot to the door behind me. We both heard the pattering of far-off feet, getting closer.

'Something is happening today, and it involves you, contracts, deals. And it will happen. I don't know what they have planned, but I can guess.'

I wanted to question it more. But voices grew louder as they approached the room.

'... *where is his guard?*'

Silas. He was coming.

'Shit,' Beatrice whispered, looking around the room frantically.

'*Find his guard and see they are punished!*' King Gathrax screamed.

'Keep playing,' Beatrice warned. 'Dryads help you.'

'And you.'

In a gust of wind, Beatrice was gone. She flew from the

bedroom, skirting into the arched doorway that led towards the bathing chamber. The dark cloak barely escaped from view as the door was opened by another, unwelcome, visitor.

I looked upon King Gathrax and felt nothing but hate. It burned in my chest, gripped a hold of my throat and squeezed, keeping me breathless where I stood.

'What a day this will be, my son. A wonderful day, one to remember. One that will be written about,' King Gathrax called out, throwing his arms wide as though I would run into them. He didn't seem to care when I refused him.

Silas had entered behind, the tap of his cane grating me as he moved to the open window and closed it with a bang. The glass shuddered in its frame, mirroring the rattling of my blood.

'Beautiful skies. Perfect for such a day,' Silas said, filling the silence.

'Cat got your tongue?' King Gathrax asked.

I was frozen as he pulled me into a stiff embrace. My hands hung awkwardly beside me, fists clenched. Then he held me at arm's reach and leaned his face in close to mine.

The wand was in the holder at his wrist. It peeked from the sleeve of his red lapelled coat. Of course, I sensed it before I saw it. The familiar tug in my gut—which I had grown accustomed to—reminded me it always waited.

One swipe and it would be mine. I could take it and conjure the same power Beatrice had displayed. Except, I wouldn't hesitate to unleash it.

'You must look the part,' King Gathrax said. 'We have much to prepare. You need to be bathed, dressed and ready, to greet *our* guests. It would be highly improper if you were late.'

I tried to steady my voice, but there was no keeping the bite from it. 'Ready for what?'

He tapped my nose. 'It is a surprise.'

With one swift clap, more people flooded into the rooms. It was an army of maids and servants. I didn't even bother to look. All my focus was on the wiry man before me and the sickly grin he regarded me with.

'It is a wonder you have not caught your death,' Silas announced, as he re-entered the bedroom. I hadn't noticed he had visited the bathing chamber, so was surprised when he returned and Beatrice had not been found.

'All those windows left open,' Silas continued. 'No wonder your room is so unpleasant.'

Beatrice must have fled. I didn't know if that made me feel better or worse.

'Come, let us get you—'

'I want them,' I interrupted, voice shaking. I dared not call my parents by their title, not with the crowd around. But if what Beatrice said was right, they were far away from the King's hand, far from the punishment he no doubt longed to give them.

King Gathrax rolled his eyes, his grip on my shoulder tightened. 'You shall, if you comply. You know our deal.'

When he spoke, he could not look me in the eye.

I ran through the conversation with Camron, looking for a sign or a hint that he had this planned all along.

I had to speak to him, more desperately than before.

'Listen to me, Julian. Today will be historic. I have great plans for you. Strategies that will keep us on top of the South and its resources. With the help of a few, expendable parts along the way. I will need one thing from you today. And if you do it, I will take you straight to see your parents. I *promise* you.'

'Anything…' I said, marvelling at how King Gathrax refused to look me in the eyes whenever he spoke of my parents.

He lied to me.

'What do you need of me?' I asked, trying to calm the storm within.

His grin widened. 'Show them all your power. Show them the mage. Remove any doubt Calzmir, Romar and Zendina have. Prove to them why we—the mighty red—are worthy of power and *they* are not.'

Silas sniggered from somewhere unseen in the room.

'What do you say, my mage, will you do this for me? Display your power to our audience and show them why the Gathrax family will once again be restored to our rightful place?'

'I will,' I vowed.

Silas clapped, unable to control his excitement.

'Good,' King Gathrax said, patting my shoulder with bone-like fingers. 'Very good.'

I cleared my throat, feeling a swell of monstrous fury rise to the surface. I smiled, an honest true smile. A deadly smile. 'You'll all finally see the power of the mage.'

King Gathrax's eyes glowed and he grinned manically. 'Make me proud.'

I narrowed my eyes. 'Oh, I shall.'

\* \* \*

They stood me before the mirror and admired their work. I, too, admired it. Unlike the first time I was physical moulded into the illusion of Julian Gathrax, I was not displeased with what I saw staring back at me. My hair had been washed and oozed with the soft scents of honey and milk. My skin had been polished by dried sponges, scrubbed raw and drenched in fragrant oils.

I had been dressed in a suit, dark trousers and a jacket

decorated with ivory buttons, gold-rope trim and a shirt that over-spilled with frills across my chest. It had been made to fit my frame perfectly. The suit wasn't another set of clothes pulled from Julian's closet and forced upon me. This had been made to measure. As I moved my arms, the material dusted across my limbs like silk.

'Perfect,' Silas sang from behind me. 'Are you impressed with my choice?'

I regarded him in the reflection, noticing how he leaned on his cane and licked his lips until they glistened.

'It's fine.'

'Fine?' Silas laughed. 'It is more than fine. *You* are more than fine.'

My skin crawled at the thoughts Silas harboured as he studied my body closely. He could have had a suit made without taking my measurements. And he looked all too pleased with himself. His hungry smile was vile. I wished nothing more than to clear it from his face.

*Soon*, I promised myself.

A maid presented me with a cloak. The outside of the material was a deep black, matching the strange colour choice of the suit. But beneath, as I shifted and moved, a shiny red satin had been sewed into the design.

Gathrax red—it was a reminder. No matter how I looked, or how they dressed me, I belonged to King Gathrax.

From behind me, a maid gasped out loud. I looked back to see what the fuss was, to find Silas recoiling his fingers back from her direction.

'Keep your hands to yourself, Silas,' I warned, speaking to him through my reflection in the gilded mirror.

Disappointment crossed his face. It was as if I had slapped him on the back of the hand. Which I would never have done —because I would've preferred to cut it off entirely.

'It would seem someone has found their voice. And with perfect timing.'

I glowered at him, lips lifting above my teeth. 'You have been a good teacher to me over these days. Truly. You've given me all the knowledge I required. Teaching me what it means to be a mage. I believe it is time I *properly* thank you.'

'Is that so?' He pushed from the wall, folding his lanky arms over his chest, blush creeping over his pale face.

'Yes.' I nodded, biting down into my lip. 'I think it is time for me to teach you a lesson in return.' I waved off the young girl who fussed over the collar of my jacket.

He took a tentative step towards me. 'I am listening.'

'May I remind you, Silas, of your *place*. You are nothing more than a master of mice, whereas I'm the mage.'

The crowd of maids simmered to silence. The girl Silas had pinched was standing red-faced in the corner. I sensed their trepidation as if it thickened the air of the room.

'Do not forget who *you* speak to… boy,' he hissed, yellowed teeth bared. 'One word to King Gathrax and you know who will feel the punishment.'

Silas stepped, just as I knew he would, directly into my trap.

I strolled to him, leaving the mirror behind. The cloak swirled around me with flair. Shoulders rolled back, I didn't stop until the toes of my boots touched his. Although I wanted to cringe away from the rotten smell that seeped between his lips, I summoned everything in myself to hold my authority. 'But how can he harm my parents, when he no longer has them?' I whispered.

Silas paled. All the confirmation I needed to know that Beatrice had told the truth. 'Who told—'

I turned, cloak slapping into him. 'Thank you for that,

Silas. Truly. You have no idea what your knowledge has… unlocked in me.'

My parents *were* out of his grasp, which meant his leverage over me was gone. A spark of hope mingled with the pull of strange power that had been building. Deep, deep inside of me, it lingered and waited. It was starving, but would soon be fed.

*I promise.*

In that moment, I knew I would leave this place. With Beatrice's help, I would retrieve my parents and put miles between me and the Gathrax family. But not yet. No. They wished to see the mage—I would show them.

# CHAPTER 18

The floral scent of fresh-cut flowers surrounded me, intrusive and sickly. It stuck to my tongue and stung my eyes. Even Silas sneezed repeatedly. It was the only noise he dared to make around me since our confrontation.

Our destination turned out to be an old, stone building in the eastern gardens of the Gathrax estate. The flowers I had seen earlier now decorated the worn, wooden door nestled among large slabs of granite. White hyacinth framed stained-glass windows, which glowed with warm light from within. A sea of roses had been laid out on either side of the path we trod on, pearlescent as though snow had fallen across the path.

The years had been unkind to the building. Over time, the Galloway Forest had shifted its border and devoured the back half of the spired roof. Looking at it, it was as if the forest was halfway through a meal, devouring stone and mortar.

Through the dust-ridden windows, I caught shapes moving and shifting.

My ears peaked at the noise the thick stone walls did little to stiffen. A crowd waited inside, large enough that even whispers sounded momentous.

Silas swept ahead and opened the doors for me. It opened slowly, hinges screaming violently for the need of oil. As I stepped into the shadow of flowers and stone, every set of eyes trained on me. Everywhere I looked, I saw unfamiliar faces. And they all saw me.

'Stand for the mage,' King Gathrax called. He stood at the end of a narrow walkway through the crowd. My footfall softened as I moved from the stone slabs outside to the worn red-carpet runner that led me to him.

Whatever noise had been inside before I arrived had now lowered to a faint murmur. The rustling sound of bodies shifting and the scratch of wood against stone as pews were pushed across the ground.

My audience studied my every move, but I kept my eyes on King Gathrax where he stood at the head of the chamber, on a raised stone platform. Candles haloed him in gold light, reflecting the red that draped from his every limb.

He was dressed in a long, drowning robe of crimson. The strands of his auburn hair trailed over his shoulders like wisps of orange cobwebs. In the glow of the wall of candles at his back, the bald spots atop his head shimmered.

I drank in the room. It was a chamber of sorts. From the lined pews, low-beamed ceilings and walls of candle wax and flame, I knew what this was. I had read about it in Damian's journal.

A chamber of worship—one built by Damian by use of his magic—as a place for study and reverence. A room in which the memory of the mage would live on. And it was no wonder I'd not seen it before. Until now it had been closed off to the public.

Although the low ceilings were suffocating, the width of

the room was large. Beyond the pews stood pillars of stone. They were on either side of the chamber, levelling off into arched beams draped with red cloth and twisted in yet more white flowers. White and red petals dusted the floor beneath my feet as I walked to the head of the room, muffling the footfall of my boots.

Clusters of the four ruling Aldian estates stood together. Faces I couldn't work out, but names I had studied with Silas. Where the ruling colour I was used to was red, all around me were an array of different colours. Red, blue, grey and white. People dressed in uniforms that matched the colours of their Kingdoms and Queendoms.

To my left, I saw the bright whites of King Zendina and his solemn band of followers. Beside them was a sea of depressing grey suits, headed by a youthful woman in a plain dress of dove grey and storm-coloured silk. Queen Romar. Silas had told me she was the youngest leader of the four estates, but he didn't comment on her beauty, nor the steel in her eyes as she followed my movements.

To the right of the chamber, the Calzmir family stood solitary, separated from the rest of the crowd. Camron. His exposed, handsome features snatched at my breath, but so did the sorrow he regarded me with. It pulled down at his furrowed brows and kept his lips straight.

The woman beside him did not share the same emotion. How could one be miserable when adorned in such finery and wealth? Amilia Calzmir stood straight-backed and proud, with silver jewels pulling down at her ears and a choker of gold strapped around her neck. It stood out against the cerulean gown she wore; the glint of a ruby sat in the heart of her necklace.

Red in a sea of blue. Two colours that—if anything my lessons had taught me—had not gone together since Mage

Calzmir died, leaving Mage Gathrax open to the unkind jaws of the Mad Queen's dragon.

I took the steps up to the stage where King Gathrax greeted me. There was no resistance as he pulled me to his side and clamped an unwavering hand around my shoulders.

'He arrives at last, my son.' His voice boomed, echoing across the chamber. Even the flames of candles seemed to flicker as he spoke. He looked from me to the waiting crowd. 'Better late than never to such an important day. I must thank you all for waiting, so patiently, for his arrival.'

Queen Romar stepped forward, the crowd parting around her with ease. 'Then there will be no further delays?'

The fingers on my upper arm tensed, taking out the frustration her question created. 'If you step back in line, Stephine, then yes. We shall proceed.'

No one else made a noise.

'I wish to extend my thanks to all of you for journeying such a way to visit us. Lann Zendina, I understand you have been on the road for days, even missing your own celebrations and feasts, just to come and visit us.'

I caught the blush of King Zendina at the back of the crowd. He bowed his head, a sheet of black hair falling over his face. But he never looked away. The whites of his eyes were visible through the strands of his hair, it was unnerving.

'We would never turn down an invitation as welcoming as yours, Jonathan,' Lann replied. For such a small man, his voice was mighty. It shivered through the crowd around him.

I knew little of the Zendina estate, but I knew they were the furthest Kingdom south of Galloway Forest. Their lands were minuscule compared to Romar, Calzmir and the largest Kingdom of the Gathrax family. Nestled by the edge of the world, unlike the Gathrax Kingdom, Zendina had little money, wealth and almost no power. Yet their Kingdom was the most populated.

King Zendina had a long beard that ended at the narrow pinch of his waist. Even from a distance, I could tell I was far taller than him.

'You each bear witness to a spectacle. A miracle. Whatever you wish to name it, we can confirm one thing for a fact. I knew the moment word of his magic reached your borders that you would be keen to see it with your own eyes. I do not blame you for housing such intrigue for it *is* a sight to behold. It has been many years since we last saw such a display—'

'Get on with it.' Stephine Romar stepped forward once again. Her shaved head meant her face was entirely exposed and breathtaking. Her cheekbones were high as they were sharp. 'We've waited long enough.'

'Excited, I gather,' King Gathrax said, hate dripping from his cerulean eyes.

'We did not come to hear your waffle,' Stephine said, 'nor did we come to hear yet another history lesson of Aldian's past. The winds still carry the burning tang when the Heart Oak was destroyed, we all know what loss of power is like. Yet somehow fate has smiled upon your family kindly. How did Julian come to find a wand? Without the Heart Oak, it should be impossible. Care to explain those missing details, the ones your birds seemed to forget to add?'

King Gathrax released me, although I still felt the echo of his pinch across my upper arm.

'I can read the accusation beneath your question, Stephine.'

'As you should. I'm not trying to hide it from you. I haven't the time for falsities,' Queen Romar snapped. For someone so young she glowed with intensity.

I fought a smile as King Gathrax's expression hardened. He had, it seemed, met his match.

'Stephine is right,' King Zendina said, twisting the frayed end of his beard within his finger. 'Show us what we have travelled to see, if you would be so kind.'

So not everyone lacked the fear towards King Gathrax as Stephine did. It was clear from the tone and lack of eye contact that Lann Zendina acted carefully.

'I see the man you call a mage; I hear the rumours. But I do not see his wand, nor sense his power.' Stephine threw her silver eyes towards me, scrutinising. 'Show us, then we will consider listening to you.'

The crowd murmured in agreement.

'All good things come to those who wait.' King Gathrax's voice raised, stilling the conversations. He ran his tongue over his teeth as he extended a hand for Amilia Calzmir, who had stayed silent on her side of the chamber. '*We* first have a special celebration that must proceed. And then you will see his magic.'

'What is more important than proving your son is the mage you say he is?' Stephine's voice raised in pitch.

'A handfasting ceremony—'

I turned to face King Gathrax. The voices filtered out and taut silence flooded the room.

'—As you said, Stephine, you did not come here for a history lesson. I am hoping you remember exactly what a handfasting ceremony is?'

My lungs failed to take in a breath. Amilia Calzmir stepped forward, hand grasped in King Gathrax's hand, her gaze as sharp as blades.

Impossible. This was impossible. How could King Gathrax marry her, when Queen Gathrax—his wife—sat on a chair beside us. And not just marry her, but give himself to her through the ancient, magical bond of handfasting. It took one look around the room, and I knew the sentiment was shared.

Only Camron showed no signs of reaction. His expression was stoic and void as he continued staring at me. It seemed this was not news to him.

'It has been years since my family has witnessed, let alone taken part, in a handfasting. What better time than now? Both myself and Queen Calzmir have news we wish to share with you all.'

'Blasphemy!' Stephine shouted. 'Never have two estates united in this way. Not to mention, Jonathan, that you have a spouse.'

'Oh, Stephine, do stop squawking. It is not *I* who shall take part in the handfasting. I respect custom as much as the rest of you do. It will be my son, Julian, who will be partaking.'

'Father?' I asked, voice breaking, unsure what exactly to ask.

King Gathrax smiled at me. 'Your handfasting, my son. This celebration is for you.'

'No...' The word escaped my control and silenced the room before repeating the word louder. I laughed, shaking my head in disbelief. 'No.'

King Gathrax turned back to the room as shackles of dread tied around my soul and dragged me down. 'Nerves, that is all. It has been agreed that Julian will handfast with a Calzmir, creating a new, stronger alliance between two of the existing Kingdoms.'

My ears rang as if bells themselves hid within them. I looked to Amilia Calzmir, disgust twisting in my gut at the thought of being married to her. She was a widow, allowed to reclaim a partner, but not me.

No, I wouldn't.

It was Queen Calzmir's words that shattered me. 'My son has agreed to take Julian's hand. Forever joining the two Kingdoms whilst creating a new, harmonious one.'

Camron was suddenly before me. I hadn't even noticed he had moved. His broad frame blocking out the view of the room behind him. As I stared into his eyes, I saw no sadness. No sorrow. In fact, I saw nothing but empty and endless obsidian.

'No,' I repeated the word, finding it was the only one I could manage.

Camron simply nodded, closing his eyes as though the pain in mine was too much for him to regard.

The room was suddenly a chaos of moving bodies. Shouting filled the chamber, bouncing from wall to wall. I would have joined in, but my body didn't feel like my own. Because it wasn't. It hadn't belonged to me since the Dance of the Dryads. And soon, it wouldn't belong to King Gathrax either.

This was his play, a move on the board for more control.

The doors slammed shut amidst the shouting as armed Gathrax and Calzmir guards stood watch at every possible exit. The Zendina and Romar courts scattered, and it was then I noticed they were all unarmed. Not a single weapon hung from their belts. This was a place of worship, and they had each followed the rules of the chamber and left their weapons beyond its walls.

As with all other rules, King Gathrax was above them. He did not follow his own custom for it was his guards who raised blades, keeping anyone from leaving.

Camron placed a hand on each of my arms, leaning down into my line of sight. I expected him to be rough with his touch.

He wasn't.

'This is a lot to ask,' he whispered. 'But I am going to need you to trust me.'

'I won't...'

'Play along,' Camron said. 'I know this is not ideal. I know this is wrong. Listen to me and I can keep you safe. Just as I will your parents.'

His words reminded me why I was here. I didn't know if it was my own delusion, or panic, but I believed he spoke the truth. Not once did he drop his eyes from me as he spoke, nor did his face twitch in the telltale of a lie.

'Can you do that for me, Max?' Camron's thumb brushed the skin across the back of my hand. 'I know you've been asked a lot of already.'

His whisper warmed me; his tone held something beyond command. It was sympathy.

But still, I couldn't reply.

King Gathrax called out across the chamber room to calm the crowds. 'Now, now, respected friends and allies. Do not fight and fret. For this is a *happy* occasion, a new chance for the South to reclaim the power we once had. With the return of the mage and the joining of these Kingdoms, we will create a new more powerful force, undivided by borders, names and colours. How can we go against the North if we continue to be scattered—how can we each claim the same power my son has found, if we do not do it as one?'

'It sounds wonderful, doesn't it?' Queen Calzmir clapped as Camron left me and joined at her side.

'Silas,' King Gathrax called, and his councillor sprung forward, cane tapping quickly as he climbed the steps. 'The cords, if you will. There is no point for further delay, not when our guests all desire to see the power of my son, the power we will all soon obtain when we take the North.'

From the depths of his oversized pockets, he revealed two thin ropes. One was red, the other blue. Handfasting ties. My body moved against my frozen mind. I began taking steps away from them until King Gathrax noticed and whispered.

Silas grabbed me and pulled me up, although I sensed the reluctance in his grasp.

I stared at King Gathrax, hoping my hate could burn him where he stood. 'I will *not* do this.'

'You have no choice.' King Gathrax smiled, the face of someone who believed he had won.

Camron took my frozen hand. I looked down, grounded by his touch. My hand was small compared to his, nestled within his smooth palm, his fingers knotted to keep hold of me. He did not let go. Not even when King Gathrax stepped forward, blue and red cords in hand, and began weaving them around our wrists. He spun the cords like a spider weaving silk, binding Camron and me together.

My eyes fell on my wand hidden in its holder. It flashed beneath his sleeve, reminding me what I must do.

*Patience*, it sang.

Everything in this life came at a price. For me to get my wand, to access my magic, this was simply a cost to pay.

I looked for someone to fight for me, to stop this from happening. But only the presence of my wand whispered promises in my ear.

'Shall we begin?' King Gathrax's voice rained down across the room.

If no one would fight for me, I would do it myself.

'Yes,' Camron answered for me, distracting my attention. 'Bind us.'

# CHAPTER 19

Camron's stare was unwavering as King Gathrax instructed him to take over from Silas. His touch was gentle, fingers dusting across my skin like flecks of snow. The blue was tied first, signalling the Calzmir family. Next came the red cords, signalling the Gathrax family. The poisonous tang of bile crept up the back of my throat. It mixed with the copper of blood that seeped from my bottom lip. If I'd not dug teeth into it, I would have screamed.

'It will be over soon,' Camron replied, his voice a barely audible whisper. Only I heard it, as King Gathrax continued his speech about union, matrimony and harmony.

'Breathe,' Camron encouraged, 'Breathe with me.'

I envied his calm.

His lack of shock told me everything I needed to know. He had known this was to happen. Last night, full of alcohol and darkness, he knew. His touch brought me back to the moment at hand. As he twisted the ropes around our forearms, tying us together as one, he brushed the pad of his thumb over my skin. His fingers shifted subtly, offering me some peace. Even the tension of the rope against my flesh was soft.

Camron stopped when there was no rope left, when we were united by flesh and cord.

'Look at me,' Camron commanded. 'Do not look away. I *have* got you.'

I heard him, but it sounded as though he spoke through a body of water. His words were distorted and misplaced.

Although Camron's voice enticed me, I refused him. Instead, I dropped my gaze to his exposed forearms, marvelling over the scars littered across his skin. They left nothing untouched. Burn marks—old yet raw—mottled his ivory flesh. A map of tight skin, different shades of pink and brown.

There was a beauty to the scars; it was a landscape all onto its own.

I didn't flinch. Even if the cords didn't tie us together, I wouldn't have pulled away. The breathless gasp from Camron, as my fingers brushed over the rough field of skin, told me of his insecurity. And a deep part of me wished to help him conceal it from the crowd.

Handfasting had died out as a tradition alongside the mages—without their magic the bond created in a handfasting was mundane. That didn't stop me from pondering what finding the other half of one's soul would be like. In those quiet moments before sleep took hold, I had often dreamt of the love I would one day find. My dreams would conjure the person, forming the shape of a man who would one day keep me safe in our union.

I supposed, as I looked back up at Camron, he would have been a perfect fit. He was handsome, so much so it snatched my breath away. Even his eyes reflected the kindness echoed in his touch.

But he was a stranger, a person I hadn't known before last night.

Sickness crashed deep in my stomach, threatening me.

'As the ties of our lineage bond you together, may the cords of two souls join as one, united.'

The book King Gathrax read from was old and worn. The leather bindings almost fell apart in his very hands. As he turned the yellowed page, the spine cracked. On he spoke, reading ballads of harmony and love. Such wondrous words that didn't deserve to spill from such vile lips. By the third page, the chamber was silent. There was no more shouting or commotion. Entranced, they watched as witnesses. It wasn't entirely quiet, not with the thunderous beat of my heart, and the reply of Camron's, which I felt beneath my fingers where they laid across his scarred arm.

'... and, before the many witnesses, I pronounce you both fasted together through health and life, until the void claims you. *Only in death shall you part.*'

I called out as a burn spread over my palm, the pain both sharp and sudden. Camron shouted out too. I thought his pain was a result of my nails digging into his skin. I was wrong. The heat across my palm spread, spilling from the mage-mark and moving up my fingers, across the back of my hand and up my arm.

*Only in death shall you part.*

The cords—once mundane—glowed with power. It was as if they came alive from the burning touch of my skin. At once, they slithered on their own accord, pulling tighter on our arms so we couldn't separate. And beneath the cords, where they snaked over our skin, silver marks glowed to life. Phantom vines and roots shivered and twisted from nothingness and left opaque ink beneath where the cords squeezed its vice-like grip.

As suddenly as it began, the light faded and the burning ceased. No longer required, the cords unravelled themselves and fell to the floor between us.

'It is done.' There was a cold finality to King Gathrax's voice.

No one clapped. That was what was supposed to happen after a handfasting, was it not? Clapping and tears, smiles and shouts of pure joy.

Not here.

Camron marvelled at his hands, raising them before his eyes. He tilted his head, narrowing his dark stare at the silver vines. Not once did he smile. Not even when he looked back to me, nostrils flaring, brows furrowed over dark, glittering eyes.

'It's over,' he said, freckled lips trembling. 'Are you all right?'

As Camron had, I looked to my hand. My mage-mark was the same, but the silver inking of vine and root was a new addition around it. In a sense, I still felt them shiver beneath the top layers of my skin, spreading from my wrist, up my arm, stopping where the tingling skin spread to my shoulder.

'No,' I finally replied. 'I'm not.'

Camron sighed; a single crease pinched across his forehead. 'I know.'

We were both distracted from one another as a shout called out behind us, oozing with the same fury we both shared.

'If you believe such a display will mean we will follow you, think again!' Stephine Romar spluttered, as she ran a hand over the smooth curve of her bald head. 'This is wrong. It goes against everything our ancestors ensured would not occur. There are rules, rules even you are not above, Jonathan.'

'By all means,' King Gathrax replied, snapping the ancient

book shut with a forced smack. 'Those ancestors are welcome to strike me down.'

'They will not need to,' Stephine replied, eyes glittering with dark thoughts. 'I'll gladly do it for them.'

Her body seemed to quake with explosive anger, echoed across the members of her estate, who hovered behind her in a shadow of grey.

I longed for Queen Romar's support. A statue of unwavering strength, she had more power in her words than even King Gathrax. He flinched back a step at the threat in her eyes.

'Mage Romar the Grey was known for his passive nature and pathetic integrity,' King Gathrax chortled. 'Are you certain you are from his same line, Stephine?'

'*Fuck* you.'

Amilia Calzmir gasped, slapping a hand to her chest in utmost horror at such words. 'Unfathomable language.'

'It would be, to you.' Stephine snapped her attention to the woman in blue and sneered. 'The concept of women with a backbone is a foreign one to you, isn't it, Amilia?'

As if proving Stephine right, Amilia turned to Camron with wide eyes and shouted, 'Darling, will you let such a person speak to your mother like that?'

Camron didn't respond. He didn't so much as move an inch from my side.

'I expected as much from you, Stephine. When we storm the North and claim access to a power that belongs to us, I will remember your refusal,' King Gathrax added, drawing my attention from Camron. 'You can step back in line and follow, or we can make you.'

Stephine glowed with determination and took another step towards the bottom of the dais. 'Pray tell, how do you expect to force an entire Kingdom to follow you? My people are loyal to the Romar family and have been since the beginning of its reign. *Your* family name only fills their mouths with the taste of dirt and shit. They would sooner perish than pin ribbons of red above their hearts.'

King Gathrax refused Stephine another breath. He turned his focus on the sulking man and his small group of followers. 'Silence becomes you, King Zendina. Have you nothing to say?'

'I will not—'

'Wolves always prey on the weak.' Stephine placed her body in the middle of King Gathrax's line of sight, blocking Lann Zendina from view. Even though she was far younger than him, she stood her ground, steady and powerful as a mountain.

'Now, Stephine, act like a lady for once,' Amilia called out, red-faced and flushed.

Stephine bowed her knees and flexed her fists open at her sides. 'I can show you exactly how a lady acts in my lands, Amilia. Why not come down here and see for yourself?'

Amilia battered Stephine's comment away with a swift, jewelled hand. 'This is nonsense.'

'Coward,' Stephine spat, hands flexing at her sides to reveal the sharp nails that awaited. 'Your pursuit for power will lead you into the jaws of the North, and I will not stand by your side and watch. I have heard enough, we are leaving.'

'But we are not remotely finished here,' King Gathrax said, gesturing a hand to me. 'At least stay for the show, Stephine. Allow me to remind you why you should stand by our side, or perhaps remind you what happens to your lands if you do not support us.'

'Do not threaten me, Jonathan.'

He laughed, light and high. 'Stephine, you know me better than to threaten. I haven't the time for anything but promises.'

I wanted to scream at her, to tell her to comply. Stephine

turned on her heel and moved directly towards the guarded door.

Gathrax guards refused to move as Stephine stormed towards them, chin raised and shoulders back. She demanded with words but they held firm. She raised her hand only to be met with the pommel of a sword. The crack of it smacking against skull cut through me.

'Stop!' I shouted, finally finding my voice. *My* voice. I pushed past Camron. 'Don't lay another finger on her.'

A firm hand grasped my arm and stopped me from racing to her aid. I turned around, palm raised and ready to slap, but it was Camron. He pulled me to his chest; stone hard as I crashed into it.

To King Gathrax, it looked as though Camron was controlling me, just as he likely hoped he would. But only I heard what he whispered, lips tickling against my ear. 'Not. Yet.'

His whisper sang to my soul, fuelling the spark of fury that burned deep within. 'When?'

'Their time will come. Maximus, only a few more moments...'

My name—my true name—had become my greatest weakness. The use of it had the power to disarm me, distract me. It seemed Camron understood that, for he used it like a newly forged weapon, striking through my storm of emotions.

'King Gathrax came to me yesterday evening with the proposition, and I must say I was very pleased with his suggestions.' Amilia Calzmir paced the podium, peering down her nose to Stephine who could barely hold herself up, blood spewing down her forehead.

'Of course, when talking about taking control, I had the same question as you, Stephine. How will we make the other rulers of the South follow us? What will stop them from revolting? Yes, your soldiers may not be as trained and well-armed as ours but combine your population and a coup would be easy to orchestrate. But that is not what we want. We need your numbers as much as we need your support.'

Stephine refused the help of her Council members, practically growling as they tried to get her off the ground. The split flesh across her eyebrow spilled blood down the side of her face. When she flashed her teeth, her mouth filled with blood, spitting it down her chin when she replied. 'Get to your point, *crow*.'

'Our mage will raze your lands until there is nothing left…' Amilia continued, a winning smile plastered across her face. 'He will destroy everything, towns, villages, cities, even the pathetic manor you consider a home. Then we will take your people, your guards, soldiers, anyone of fighting age. And they will come willingly because what we can promise them is far greater than anything you can give them.'

Stephine's expression of strength faltered. She looked at me with a glint of fear. I shook my head, unable to stop myself, just to show her I wouldn't do what they accused. But it seemed she didn't see. To Stephine, I was a weapon, not Julian or Maximus.

'Money means little to my people,' Stephine said, blood-shot eyes wide.

'But what about magic?' King Gathrax asked, stepping in beside Amilia and laying a hand on her shoulder. 'We can give them something that has long been kept from them. We will give them power. I am under good authority that the North have access to their own Heart Oak, and we will not destroy it, but take it. We will take what is ours, what belonged to the South first. Do you truly think your followers will follow you when I can give them access to magic?'

Stephine laughed now, throwing her head back. 'The Mad

Queen will destroy you before you even step foot into Galloway Forest, if the spirits and creatures do not claim you first. We all know how this story ends, our ancestors experienced it. We had four mages, and still they failed. You have *one*.'

'One mage,' Amilia Calzmir said, glancing towards me. As her dark eyes fell upon her son, a prideful smile stretched from ear to ear. 'But we have power, power you could not begin to imagine.'

'King Gathrax, Queen Calzmir.' King Zendina stepped through the crowd 'Let m-me assure you my people will bend the knee. We trust in our alliance and would no-not throw it away for *pride*.'

'You are a smart man, King Zendina.' King Gathrax tipped his head in a bow.

'Pathetic man, as you all are,' Stephine spat with conviction. 'I do not bend to the Gathrax name. My ancestors didn't, I won't.'

'You will not be following beneath the Gathrax or Calzmir name,' King Gathrax said. 'For it will be a new Kingdom—a stronger one—which shall rise from the ashes and rule anew.'

Camron trailed his fingers down my forearm, lacing them around my waiting hand. He held it, squeezed and ran his thumb over the back in comforting circles.

'Oaken.' The freckles around Camron's lips flexed as he called out to the crowd. 'Named after my husband—Mage Maximus Oaken.'

King Gathrax turned, gaunt cheeks flushed red, eyes wide.

'Is there a problem?' Camron asked, voice light with a grin.

'That is not what has been agreed!' King Gathrax paced forward, vein bulging in his forehead. 'His name is—'

'Step back.' Camron's sharp tone clove the room in two. 'Jonathan.'

King Gathrax rocked back a step, lips mumbling over a response.

Camron seemed to rise in height, towering over King Gathrax with ease. 'You will watch the tone in which you speak to my husband. I care little how your tongue snaps to others, but to him I will see it torn out.'

'What is the meaning of this?' Amilia Calzmir snapped, stepping to her son's side. 'Camron, behave.'

'Quiet, *Mother*. Your voice is grating.'

I couldn't think straight, couldn't grasp what was happening as the tension in the room shifted in Camron's favour.

'Ah,' Stephine said. 'Now this is a show I would stay and watch.'

'Remind me, Jonathan, how is one supposed to address their king?' Camron tilted his head slightly to its side. His expression was one of calm, but even I recognised the danger lurking in his dark eyes. 'As you have just proclaimed to our esteemed audience, you have signed the papers for a new Kingdom. Am I not the King now?'

Reluctantly, King Gathrax turned to him, his face as red as his shirt. Even Queen Calzmir's expression was one of bewilderment.

'My husband's wand,' Camron commanded, hand outstretched. He stood tall, his confidence adding an entire foot to his posture. King Gathrax seemed to cower beneath Camron's glower. 'If you would be so kind.'

'It. Belongs. To. Me.'

'You promised them all a display of power,' Camron said, glowering down at the snivelling king. 'Do not go back on your word now.'

King Gathrax's eyes widened so furiously I believed the

whites would explode from his skull. Everyone waited, breathless, as both men held each other in contest.

'So be it.' Camron struck forward, grasping hold of King Gathrax's arm, exposing the wand holder beneath his sleeve. Jonathan cried out as Camron twisted his forearm.

King Gathrax tried to pull back, but his attempt was futile. Camron was stronger both in body and mind. With one hand, Camron pulled my wand from the holder, then thrust King Gathrax back until he was crumpled on the floor of the dais. Queen Remi stood, attempting to rush to his aid, but Camron lifted the wand and pointed it directly at her.

'*Sit.*'

My palm shivered at seeing the wand so close. In the back of my mind, I heard its call.

*Hello, again.*

Camron held still, calm fury to freeze Remi to the spot. He moved the wand across the entire room, as though he had the power to use it—though he didn't. Only I could call upon the power. 'All of you, please, sit.'

And they did, each and every one of them. Stephine Romar, Lann Zendina, their followers. Only the guards were left standing, unwavering in their positions.

Shivers coursed down the back of my neck, as I regarded the wand in Camron's grasp. As he touched my wand, the feeling mirrored across my sweat-slicked skin.

Jonathan's face boiled with bulging veins. 'I will have your head for—'

'Guards, please see that Jonathan is restrained. I do not condone threats to the Oaken name and its new Kings,' Camron commanded, his voice steady. Instantly, almost rehearsed, the two Gathrax guards in red marched forward and seized King Gathrax.

'Camron, give it to me.' I couldn't think of anything besides taking it. To my surprise, Camron didn't hesitate. He extended the wand out to me, laid out across his two large hands.

My breath faltered as I looked at it. An offering from the man I had been forced to unite with. My husband by more than simple law. My bonded.

I couldn't deny how my soul screamed for me to take the wand. I looked to Jonathan Gathrax, expecting him to give me a command or threaten me. Even now, as he was held down by his own guards, I feared his capabilities.

Until Camron spoke again, his voice digging into my burning desires, pulling them to the surface. 'Take it, Maximus Oaken. It belongs to no one else. No more shall anyone hold power over you like a blade, when you are the power. You are the blade.'

Again, the name echoed around the crowd. Over and over, it filled me with a sense of energy that I had not felt in days.

'Say it again,' I uttered, looking deep into Camron's eyes, losing myself to the midnight expanse of them. 'I want to hear you say it.'

Camron smiled. 'Maximus Oaken.'

Tension fell from my shoulders. My body seemed to move on its own, without need for control. I lifted my hand towards the offering, silver ink marks of the fasting lines sparking in the candlelight.

My name sang within me, called out by another. The wand.

*Maximus*, it said, *how I have missed you.*

# CHAPTER 20

Camron took my hand, folding my fingers around the hilt of the wand.

It was a gentle motion, one that made it impossible to look away from him, from the way his eyes seemed to soften with relief.

As my palm connected with the cool wood, a breath of power shattered throughout me. It was energy, pure and undiluted. It sang through my veins, shivered through bone and sinew, until I became one with it.

I looked around, not at the crowd, but to the shimmer of cords that connected me to the very world. They were faint, like the rays of sun lingering through a window, highlighting motes of dust in the air. I feared if I blinked, it would fade.

It didn't. This was power, this was my right.

And I would finally take it.

I looked from the wand, then back to Camron. I caught my reflection in the dark pools of his stare. My eyes glowed, reflecting his face in pools of green mist. The forest green now glowed with flames of jade. They swirled and danced, just as Beatrice's eyes had.

Camron took a steady breath, gazing down at me with unbridled awe. 'No one should ever be kept from who they truly are. And who you truly are... Maximus Oaken, is magnificence. Even a stranger such as me can see that. Now, it is time for you to tell them all your truth.'

Ominous thoughts passed my mind as I raised my attention to those who wished to control me.

'Release me,' King Gathrax called out, fighting pathetically against those who held him down. I blinked, I saw his death. A death I had longed for. It boiled in my blood and fuelled me to speak out.

'How does it feel?' I asked him, as the room seemed to fade away.

The King didn't answer me, instead hurled panicked threats. Not a single one hit their intended mark. 'You will all be punished for this—your families, those you love. Release me.'

'No,' I breathed, slowly lifting my eyes from Camron to the guards. 'Don't let him go.'

The guards nodded, wonder gleaming in their eyes.

'In fact, bring him to me,' I commanded. With a thrust, King Gathrax cried out as his knees cracked against the stone floor. The pain radiated in his shout. He attempted to fight against, but it was useless. 'You know the consequences of your actions, *Julian*.'

King Gathrax's threats no longer controlled me.

'My name is Maximus. Say it.'

Who spoke, me or the power? Did the wand use me as a conduit, making me its voice and my body its weapon?

'An explanation is required,' Stephine called out. 'Who is Maximus?'

'We have all been lied to,' Camron answered for me, voice clearing over the chaos of the room. 'And as the new rulers of the Oaken Kingdom, my first action will ensure you all see through those lies. Unlike Jonathan Gathrax and my dearest mother, I do not have hidden agendas. I have watched, as you have, the unfair treatment of our people for too long. War with the North would destroy us, just as Stephine has alluded to. I will not see our people sent to their slaughter, like lambs following the promise of power, power the North cannot provide us. The shadow of red and blue has crept over the South, threatening to smother anything else beneath its greed. Unlike them, I will not force your hand to follow us. Threats mean nothing in the face of loyalty.'

My entire focus transfixed back to my wand. I memorised the twisted design, the slight red stain on the wood and the narrowed point at its top, sharp enough to bury in flesh.

Above all, it fit perfectly in my hand, as though it was crafted for me, not found upon the bed of a forest—forgotten.

'And this Maximus?'

'Maximus was never the child of the Gathrax family, he was forced to become Julian Gathrax in pursuit of control.'

I looked up at the crowd, registering the confusion in. Above it all, how did Camron figure out the truth? All my hard work to keep up with this game, and still I had failed.

'Mage Maximus Oaken... forced to become the false son for the benefit of the ruling family, a family whose power shall be eradicated.'

Camron had said my name again. Each time it felt like a bolt of lightning to the chest. 'End this, free yourself, Maximus.'

'This has gone on enough!' King Gathrax screamed. 'Julian, you are mine. Your power is mine. Your—'

I saw red. It flooded across my vision and blinded me. Fitting, for it was the colour of the man knelt before me. It was all I could focus on as I lifted the wand and pointed it at him, inches from the screwed lines between his eyes.

'I warned you,' I said through gritted teeth. 'I told you my name, and you refused to say it.'

Jonathan Gathrax broke before me. His lips quivered as desperate tears sliced down his hollowed cheeks. 'I have children. Do not leave my daughters without a father. Not when you have already taken their brother from them.'

He was lying again. He didn't fear for the loss of his children. He feared for his own loss, the one staring him in the face.

'Did you worry about that when you took my parents? Did you think twice about what I have lost when you made innocent people bleed? Do you even know their names? Do you?'

'*Please...*'

I was vaguely aware that Camron had stepped in behind me. His presence was warm and comforting but did not overstep.

'His fate is in your hands,' Camron said. 'You decide how this shall end.'

I laughed. It was a strange, dark sensation to chuckle with so much power flowing through me. I laughed at how wrong he was. It was not my choice.

The wand desired this. King Gathrax had not only kept me from it but kept *it* from me. And the wand desired the same vengeance as I did.

*Allow me,* it said. *I will free us.*

'You've hurt so many,' I said, starring down to the pathetic excuse of a man before me. 'And it was all in vain. Their deaths mean nothing because you haven't won.'

Jonathan snarled and his eyes bulged. 'I should have done more.'

I smiled, shoulders shrugging his words off. 'Perhaps. But now it is too late.'

I—my wand—called upon the pool of magic that shimmered among the ocean of darkness inside of me. One simple thought, an acknowledgement to the power, and it was at my command. I gripped a hold of it in my mind and pulled, feeling the shimmer of cords in the air around me tug hard against the stone, the earth beneath the floor, the forest beyond the walls.

The room shook. Bricks and mortar broke apart, sending clouds of dust to settle across those who watched. Fissures spread beneath my feet, splitting the ground.

Power filled me until I became it entirely.

'Send my love to Julian,' I whispered above the noise of the chamber as it cracked in two. I heard the scratch of wood as another death mark joined the first at the base of the wand.

One for a father, another for his son.

Thick roots exploded from the ground around me. Tentacles of earth danced like starved serpents, each with a thirst for blood. Gathrax blood. Roots and vines overtook the room, filling through the cracks in the ground and walls. It was the Galloway Forest. It responded to my call. I was merely a conductor, gripping the wand as though my life depended on it, and the wild heeded my call.

Jonathan couldn't fight as my power found him. The guards who had held him had fumbled away, but that didn't mean Jonathan could escape. He belonged to me.

The earth swaddled his body in a casket of root and vine. I felt him within its grasp, shivering and screaming, but his fight was useless. His blue eyes bulged as the earth folded over him, the colour bleeding out and turning red. Jonathan

Gathrax screamed, giving an opening for my power to reach inside of him. A serpent of a root filled his mouth, slithering down his throat, breaking teeth and splitting the seams where his lips met his cheeks.

Blood was everywhere. And for the first time, the colour didn't offend me.

I reached down with the earth, farther and farther, until my power was everywhere. It was in the stone walls, the wooden pews. It was in the forest beyond and the ground far beneath our feet.

I was alive with it.

Then, in a breath, it was over.

I blinked as exhaustion rolled over me. My magic recoiled back, retreating into the cage it had forged in the pits of my stomach. When it was over, and my mind belonged to me once again, there was nothing but silence.

Jonathan Gathrax was dead. His body couldn't fall to the slabbed ground as the snake of roots and vines held him entrapped. Only his bulging, lifeless eyes were visible, staring endlessly at me, tears of blood and brain-matter leaking freely.

A firm hand rested upon my shoulder. Then a voice followed. Camron's gentle tone, an anchor to retrieve my focus. 'It is done, you are free.'

I blinked, unable to look away from the corpse, until Camron turned my body, guiding me to face the crowd. It was to see expressions of horror. But it wasn't the only reaction I found. There was awe and fear in every set of eyes.

'Long may he reign, Mage Maximus Oaken,' Camron called, raising my hand and the wand up to the sky.

It was Stephine Romar who bowed first, her voice full of authority as she called across the quaking chamber. 'Long may he reign. It is our honour to follow you.'

King Zendina, Amilia Calzmir and even Remi Gathrax all replied with the same sentiment. As did the crowd, who echoed it over and over until the words had carved themselves into my bones.

'May he reign. May he reign.'

# PART TWO

## THE TRAITOROUS CORDS

# CHAPTER 21

I flinched with every bone-thudding hack of metal against wood.

It took hours for them to free Jonathan Gathrax from his tomb of vine and root. When they finally stopped, I was thankful for the quiet. Even if it meant there was nothing distracting me from what I had done.

Camron had escorted me swiftly from the chaos, leaving me in a dark room through a door at the side of the chamber, with nothing but the promise of his return and my guilt for company. I contemplated running, but it seemed my body refused me. All I could do was sit and wait.

If it wasn't for the cracked walls, there would have been no light at all. Daylight spilled in between torn-apart stone where my power had gorged itself.

Shelves lined the walls, overspilling with books and cobwebs. Boxes of parchment and scrolls waited beside stacks of unused pillar candles, glass bottles and other unknown objects. Everything was shrouded in dust and age. It reminded me of the library, a comforting thought during such a time.

I was alone. I studied the binding mark that wrapped around my arm—left from the handfasting. Then my eyes passed to the wand, gripped in my hand. It was my only company. And at the base of the wood waited two death marks, reminding me of what I had done with this power.

Where I expected relief from King Gathrax's death, I felt nothing but emptiness. Exhaustion. Shock. I'd not only removed the strings of my puppet king, but sliced through them with great power and shattered him as though he was the one made from wood.

I should've felt something more than this—this hollowness. This wasn't freedom. The silver inking on my other hand confirmed as much.

'Maximus.' I looked up at the sound of my name. Camron stood in the doorway; his large hand gripped around the frame for support. The same silver markings were visible as his long shirt tugged back from his wrist. It danced across burn-scarred skin.

I stood abruptly, knocking the chair back onto the floor. The sound was sharp, disturbing the chamber of silence.

Camron's eyes lowered to my wand, then back to my face. His brows creased over narrowed eyes as he lifted both his hand and gestured to the wand.

'Should I be concerned with what you might do with that?' he asked, eyes flickering between my face and wand expectantly. 'Or can we talk?'

'That would depend on your intentions,' I replied.

Relief eased the lines that had settled across his forehead. Camron drew his fingers through his blonde hair, combing it back from his face. 'Perhaps we can both have a seat and discuss such matters?'

'No,' I said. 'You stay right there.'

Camron pursed his lips, his hands carefully clasping before him. 'If that makes you feel more at ease, I will.'

The words burst out of me. 'I've just been forced to marry a stranger and murdered a king all in the same day. I hardly feel at ease.'

His smile surprised me. 'Forgive me, but hearing you say it aloud truly puts into perspective just how real this all is. Unbelievable, actually.'

I raised my wand arm, pointing the tip at his chest. It was a threat. I knew one thought would call upon the power. The shimmering cords continued to thrum around me.

Camron's smile faded from his face as quickly as it had come.

'You knew,' I snapped, accusing. 'Last night, when you came to see me, you knew this would happen, didn't you?'

There was a part of me that expected Camron to deny my accusation. I'd grown so used to the lies, that it was a surprise when he didn't. 'Yes, I did. I do not want you to think I waste my evenings getting drunk for no good reason.'

'And what reason was that?'

Camron stepped into the room further, directly into a beam of daylight. Beneath the glare of light, I was certain his eyes brightened. No longer were they black, now they glistened with something richer. Flecks of navy shimmered as he blinked, regarding me with a straight face. 'I'd just found out my mother had signed away my future on my behalf. I was angry.'

'*You* were angry?' I barked. 'Believe me, Camron. You've no understanding of such a feeling.'

He nodded. 'That is a fair assumption, but, believe me, Maximus, I know anger. Very well, in fact.'

His use of my name was disarming. Did his smile return because he noticed the wand drop, or could he sense my fury dwindle, as though my name was the bucket of water cascaded over it.

My fingers tightened around the hilt of the wand as the next question fired out of me. 'What have you done with my parents?'

His face flushed. Camron refused to look away from me as he replied. 'Nothing—'

'If you harm a single hair.' Power flooded through me. From his flinch, I knew Camron sensed it. I couldn't smell or see it, but I felt it—deep inside of me—uncoiling like a serpent from its burrow.

'Your parents are safe.'

'I don't believe you.'

Camron slapped a hand—covered in the handfasting marks—over his heart. 'Your family arrived at my home early this morning. As soon as my people look over them, I promise they will get back on the road. I imagine they will be here by tomorrow afternoon.'

I shouldn't have believed him. But there was something about the unwavering way he looked at me, the way his eyes refused to drop mine. Camron spoke the truth, but that still didn't make this any better.

'I can help them,' I said. 'We don't need you.'

'There is no doubt that I have not yet earned your trust, but I will.' Camron nodded, agreeing with himself. 'Maximus, I assure you nothing will happen to them. I understand what you are capable of… Do you truly think I would put myself in your line of sight, knowing you could destroy me with a single thought?'

'I don't know what to think,' I said.

'How about you lower that wand of yours, then I can shed some light on this for you?'

The bones in my arm creaked as I lowered it. My fist didn't

ease around the base of my wand, but I no longer pointed it at Camron's chest. He walked further towards me, unbeknownst to the cords of power. As his body passed through them, they dissipated like dust only to reform behind him.

It was both breathtaking and horrifying.

Camron exhaled a shaking breath as he took his opportunity to close the space between us. I didn't move, my eyes tracking his every careful step. Camron lowered himself to the ground and picked up the chair I had knocked over. Once he righted it behind me, he gestured and said, 'Please, sit down and we can talk.'

'Why are you doing this?' I asked, thankful to rest my legs.

'Believe me or do not,' Camron said, 'but not everyone is driven by power and greed. Some of us just wish to do best with the situations we are given.'

'Even if that means marrying someone, just to have a grasp at their magic?'

'No, Max. That is not why I have done this—'

'I don't trust you,' I snapped, interrupting him.

'I am not asking you to. Trust is not something to be given, it is earned and, as you have said, we are strangers, you and I.'

'Stranger or not, everyone has wanted something from me.' I raised my mage-marked palm and held it inches before his face. Camron didn't flinch away. 'You're no different.'

I blinked, opening my eyes to find my hand held in Camron's soft grasp. I didn't pull away. He lowered my hand and rested it on the edge of his knee. His fingers—although iron strong—didn't pinch or grab. He was gentle and warm as he traced his fingertips over the puckered scars of my mage-mark.

'I admire your resolve,' Camron said, as a shiver shot up my arm, spreading like the unfurling of wings across my back. 'Unlike those who have used you, I have no intention to control you and you will see that in time. If I did, why would I have given you the wand? It doesn't bode well for the unbalanced power dynamic between us, does it?'

'What about this?' I raised my arm, flashing my silver-inked flesh.

'Ah.' Camron chewed his lip, eyes tickling the skin it looked over. 'Now, that is a problem.'

'One we are going to fix.'

'By fix, do you suggest breaking it?'

Even speaking it aloud sounded pathetic. From the gleam in Camron's eyes, he knew as well as I did that this bond was unbreakable. It would only shatter if one of us died.

Jonathan's words echoed in my mind. *Only in death shall you part.*

Camron paused before responding. I caught his eyes lower to his arm—where the silver ink twisted around his skin—then looked back to mine. 'Then who is dying, you or I? I have not risked everything only to kill you. So, would you kill me to break this?'

His words caught me, as did the softening of his eyes. Camron's face had the power to reflect an emotion so vividly. If it was an act, it was a believable one.

'Perhaps I should,' I said, hating how much I still sounded like Julian Gathrax. 'You want me to trust you, yet you have let this happen. You tricked me into this, you trapped me.'

'I did this to free you.'

'Free me?' I laughed. 'What difference are these marks to that of iron shackles? Jonathan has simply handed me from one king to another.'

I blinked and Camron's soft expression hardened. The flash of anger across his face both frightened and thrilled me —but not enough to raise my wand again or move away.

'I am *nothing* like him,' Camron said, chest rising and

falling dramatically. 'From the moment I found out about what he had done to you, I did what I could with what I was given, to fix their wrongs.'

I read between the lines to uncover what he suggested. 'How long have you known I was not the Gathrax heir?'

'A day or two after the body of the real Julian was removed from the tree and buried in the ground beneath it,' Camron said softly.

'How?'

The door behind Camron opened and a figure slipped in. I looked beyond his shoulder and my entire body stiffened. Fear thundered through me at the sight of the man, immobilising me. Camron didn't turn around to see who it was because he knew. The tap of Silas's cane bounced across every shattered wall.

'Both the Zendina and Romar estates have been returned to their quarters for the remainder of the day. They have agreed to leave come morning, and return to their homes carrying the Oaken banner,' Silas said, all without looking at me.

Camron faced him; the profile of his face still visible to me. Muscles flexed in his jaw, a deep frown set over his brow. 'Is that everything?'

I looked between them both. 'He told you, didn't he?'

Silas bowed his head at my accusation.

Camron exhaled a heavy breath. 'The Master of Mice. My eyes and ears. He has been feeding me information about you. Without his help, we would not be here, and your parents would not be breathing.'

'Liar,' I breathed. 'He is just as bad...'

I blinked and saw my power devour the frail man across the room. My knuckles ached from the phantom crack of his cane. I saw his reaching fingers and heard his taunting threats.

But when I opened my eyes, nothing had happened. There was no more death.

*Yet.*

Camron stood from his chair. 'Silas may be a sly man, but not stupid. Since the death of my father, my mother has been distracted from her focus on her estate. She gave me the responsibility to obtain information on our sibling rulers, with the intention of telling her what she needed to know. I just chose what to tell her and what to keep from her.'

'That is what you want from me… isn't it? To take over as ruler of your lands, but you overshot your goals and have ended up with the power to control the entirety of the South.'

It took everything in my power not to stand and unleash my power upon Silas. I expected him to look at me. If he had, I would have done it. I would have added another death notch on the end of my wand, just to never have him regard me again.

'Silas, come here.'

Silas evidently feared Camron from the reluctance to move. 'Yes, sire.'

Camron didn't watch as Silas paced the room. He winced with every step—clearly hurt from a fall during the commotion earlier.

'You have been an exceptional help,' Camron said, placing a firm hand on the vile man's shoulder.

Silas bowed beneath the sudden force. 'Thank you, sire.'

'Without the help of you and your mice, I would never have been made aware of Jonathan's lies.'

'Anything for you, sire.'

Camron turned his back to me and faced Silas. It meant I couldn't see the expression on his face, but I could see as he reached a hand into the band of his trousers and retrieved an object hidden beneath his shirt.

'But Silas, if I am honest, I have never cared for rodents much.'

'Pardon—'

Camron swiped his arm out before him. Light flashed across so suddenly it blinded me. I pinched my eyes closed for only a moment, and when I opened them again, it was to see Silas clutching at the skin of his neck.

'Stop!' I shouted, unsure where my desperation came from.

Blood blossomed beneath the press of Camron's blade. A bead formed from the small nick Camron had made in Silas's wrinkled skin. The Master of Mice opened his mouth, flashing discoloured teeth, but no sound came out beside a gasped plea.

Camron peered over his shoulder to me, frowning. 'Is this not what you want?'

'Not like this.'

'Thank you, thank you,' Silas sobbed, tears slicing down his face, his good eye flickering between Camron, the blade he held, then me. 'Spare me.'

'He is a dangerous man,' Camron said, 'one who does not understand the concept of loyalty. He proved this to me by turning against Jonathan. What is to say he will not do the same to me... to us?'

It would've been so simple to call for the power. Dryads know the wand thirsted for Silas's death, as did I. But enough blood had been spilled by my power. Julian might have seen Silas punished, but Maximus—the one who'd been buried—would've searched for another resolution. 'He is, which is exactly why his fate should be decided before punishment is served.'

Silas spluttered out a breath of relief as Camron relaxed the pressure of the blade. 'Speaking like a true ruler, just and kind. It would seem we balance each other out, Maximus.'

I ignored his comment, focusing on the snivelling man.

'I kept your parents from harm, I helped them… I helped them,' Silas sobbed.

'Do you want me to thank you?' I asked, fighting the urge to silence him forever. 'What about the rest you have seen harmed? What about those your hands grasp when you believe no one is looking?'

Silas fumbled over his words, snot and tears blending into one.

'His service has been invaluable, but I no longer require it,' Camron said, knuckles paling as he held onto Silas's narrow shoulder.

'Release him,' I commanded, 'Camron.'

Camron did as I asked, but not without pushing him forward in the process. Silas crashed to the floor, his cane falling from his hand and skipping across the ground until it came to a rest before my feet.

'What would you have me do?' Camron asked.

Without taking my eyes from Silas, I replied. 'There are many people who've worked beneath Silas, they are to be the one to hand out his judgement. Servants, maids, members of staff. If he is to die, it will be their choice.'

Camron didn't reply straight away. Instead, he paced the couple of steps to where Silas cowered. Camron knelt, the material of his trousers pulling against the strength of his thighs. 'What do you say to him?'

The question was not for me.

'Speak, Silas,' Camron said, 'for you seem to be good at it.'

'Thank you,' Silas spluttered. He was a broken man. I didn't long to admit it, but seeing him grasped in fear was an enlightening feeling.

'Don't thank me yet,' I said, scowling down upon him like

death incarnate, judging him for his actions whilst knowing how this would end.

Four guards came into the room, all without the need for command. Where they once had pins of red ribbon over their hearts, now the place was empty.

'Remove Silas,' Camron said calmly. 'Mage Oaken has requested that this man is tried for his crimes. Take him to your people, see they decide what justice looks like.'

Silas was dragged from the room, his feral screams the last thing to fade. Only when they became faint, far beyond the chamber, did either of us speak.

'You are a better man than me,' Camron said.

'Silas *will* die,' I said, thinking back to the crying girl earlier that morning. To the many who had felt the pinch of Silas's fingers, the scratch of his gaze. 'He will face his punishment, but it should be at the hands of those he has hurt.'

'He doesn't deserve your loyalty.'

'What do you know about loyalty?' I asked, drawing my eyes back to Camron. The word soured in the back of my mouth, loyalty not being something that deserved to be given to a man like Silas. 'Silas trusted you, and you would have slit his throat. What makes you any different to him?'

'The difference between Silas and me,' Camron repeated, toying with the question, 'is that his intentions were impure. Mine are not.'

'Words,' I said. 'Meaningless words.'

'But words nonetheless, you simply must decide if you believe them or not.'

Camron slipped the blade back into the band of his trousers, then crossed both arms over his chest and regarded me as the stranger I was.

'Do you fear what I am capable of?' I asked, not once losing the grip on my wand.

'Yes,' he replied, 'I do.'

'Good, then we finally see one another on equal grounding. I fear you, and you fear me.'

Camron stepped forward, the scent of salt and sea rushing over me. 'Then I ask, would you care to learn to trust one another, together?'

'Give me my parents, and then we can discuss.'

'I do not make promises I cannot keep,' Camron said. 'But I swear to you, I will have your mother and father returned to you by supper tomorrow.'

His promise hung between us.

'What now?' I asked.

'Well, it has been a long day, and I fear those that follow will only be harder. I understand it is not the custom for newlyweds to spend their first evening apart, but shall we make an exception for the rest of the day? Then tomorrow can be a fresh start.'

I didn't wish to tell him that the fresh start tomorrow wouldn't ever happen. Not because I cared to offend him, but because I had one goal in mind. I would leave with Beatrice, with my parents. Placing my trust in Camron was foolish. Now I knew where they were, I could tell Beatrice and Simion and leave to get them.

Finally, we would be free.

'Yes,' I lied. 'But if you come back to my room tonight, drunk or sober, then don't think your welcome will be as gentle as it was last time.'

A smirk lifted the corner of Camron's lips. It was dangerous, but beautiful, as all deadly things were. 'I am a man of my word, Maximus.'

'We'll see.'

# CHAPTER 22

I found Beatrice upon return to my room. She was waiting, head in her hands, sat on the edge of my bed. Only when I slipped through the partially opened door did she look up. And when she did, the sadness etched across her face was palpable, I could almost taste it in the air.

Beatrice stood abruptly, golden eyes trailing from the wand still gripped in my hand, up the silver inking of my fasting mark, then to my face. Expectantly, I thought she might say something—offer me some form of comfort that I so desperately needed. Instead, she raised her hands up to her sides as if to prove they were empty.

'If you are wondering where your wedding gift is, I haven't had the chance to get one yet,' Beatrice said, voice cold.

A laugh crept up my throat and burst beyond my lips. 'Fuck it,' I replied. 'I'm not exactly in need of a set of new glasses or plates.'

'Is this the moment I should offer my congratulations?'

I exhaled a long, heavy breath. 'I'd rather we didn't speak about it.'

Beatrice pouted and dropped her sorrowful eyes back to the inking marks across my wrist. 'This is bad, Max. I knew something was going to happen, but I never thought King Gathrax was capable of this—'

'I killed him.'

I expected shock to explode across her face. It didn't.

Beatrice's expression smoothed out the lines around her eyes and across her forehead. She took a step from the bed, leaning into the tall wooden staff that had been resting upon it. One look at the staff and my wand grew warm in my grasp.

'I know you did,' she finally responded.

'I killed King Gathrax,' I repeated, finally allowing myself to face the reality of what I had done. My knees buckled. I gripped the edge of the bed to keep myself standing.

'He forced me into an arranged marriage to better his position of power, and my new husband gave me a gift—not glasses or plates—but the chance to rid myself of the very man who has ruined my life. And I killed him with it.'

Beatrice released a long breath but didn't utter a word.

'Does that make me evil?' I asked.

'We've all done things, Max. What is one person's evil, is another person's good.'

'Murder is...' What was it? Was it bad when my father killed the monster who broke into our home and attacked me?

'Come and sit down,' Beatrice said, gesturing to the bed. 'Then we can compare our evils and see who trumps the other.'

I couldn't refuse her. Beatrice had gone from my closest friend to a stranger in a matter of days. Selfishly, I was willing to put all those secrets behind us just for a chance to feel what it was like before this... the wand, the Gathrax family, before Camron and these silver marks.

I thirsted for normalcy, and Beatrice could offer me that.

The bed shifted as we both took a seat. I didn't dare look into her eyes because I didn't want to see something I would not like. I stared at the wand in my fist and the two death notches scored into the base of the wood.

'The Calzmir gave you that,' Beatrice said, breaking the silence. 'King Gathrax would have never given you back your *amplifier*, but Camron has.'

'My wand?' I corrected.

'A wand is merely one style for a mage's amplifier. It's a very Southern design.'

I glanced at her, noticing how Beatrice glanced at the staff with a longing gaze.

'Then I gather that is yours?'

She nodded, reaching for it and wrapping her long, calloused fingers around its middle. Power spiked in the air around me. It was charged, like the sky before a summer storm before fading quickly.

'It is.'

My eyes drifted downwards. I didn't know what I searched for at first, until I couldn't find it. There were no notches in the base of the wooden staff—no death marks. Beatrice may have been a liar, but she was not a murderer.

I couldn't say the same about myself.

'You can ask it,' Beatrice said.

I tore my gaze from her staff back to her face, to find that she was studying me.

The question was pointless because, between the power that radiated from Beatrice and the staff she held in her hand, I *knew* she was a mage. But what I couldn't understand was how. How had she kept this from me? I had known her since we were children and never had I sensed such a thing.

'What happens next?' I asked.

Sadness etched deeper in the lines across Beatrice's face. 'We leave for the North, as planned.'

'Now?' I added, studying her eyes for the answer before she spoke it.

'No, not yet.' Relief rushed through me. 'I have sent Simion North, to provide a message to the Queen and her Council about these events. If they hear of your union, they will see it as a play of power against them. Simion can explain, he can delay the potential of retaliation, then he will come back, for us. In the meantime, I promised not to leave without your parents. I plan to see that through.'

I buried my face in my hands. 'Camron has said they'll return here by the end of tomorrow.'

'And you believe him?' Beatrice asked, body stiffening beside me.

I leaned into her, thankful for her physical presence. 'I haven't got the choice.'

'We all have a choice, Maximus,' Beatrice said softly, laying a hand on my knee. I looked to her, drinking in the familiar vision of my friend.

'All this time and you were a mage,' I said.

'I could say the same.' Beatrice nodded, thick curls of brown hair falling over her face. She swept them away, tucking them behind her ear. 'You might think I lied to you, but the truth is by the time I met you, I was so far into a new truth that my past meant nothing. I was... sent here many years ago. My goal was to search for something that was stolen from the North and return it. I didn't know—or would have ever believed—the person I looked for was you.'

'Who would send a child on a task like that?'

Beatrice looked towards the open window of the bedroom, her gaze travelling far beyond it.

'I've grown rather fond of this place,' Beatrice said, ignoring my question as she lost herself to deep thoughts. 'Regardless of the control, the poverty and struggle, there is a freedom in the South. Don't tell Simion I'm admitting this, but it pains me to leave.'

Another question sprung to mind. Where had Simion been all this time? I'd only ever known Beatrice as the young orphan taken under the wing of the blacksmith many years ago. She was supposed to have no family. Yet here she sat beside me—a mage, a sister and a Northern spy.

'You know, this changes everything,' Beatrice said. 'Everything. When the North finds out you have handfasted, they will no longer practise patience—of course, that is if they don't already know. I only hope Simion isn't too late.'

'Patience?'

'Your presence here—in the South—is a threat but nothing the North can't deal with ease. But this… this handfasting is something entirely different.'

'Because it is one less way they can control me,' I answered for her.

'No. It sends a message, even if you don't wish for it to, it does. It tells the North you are prepared to do anything in the shifting game of power. You've gone from a solitary mage to a mage with the potential of an army behind you.'

'You know I wanted none of this,' I said.

'Nor did I.' Her reply caught me off guard. 'It still doesn't change the perspective of those watching on. They'll see what they want to see.'

'I *am* coming with you, Bea,' I said. 'Either my parents come back as Camron promised, or we know where to find them. Then, we get far, *far* away from here. My search for a better life, Beatrice, that dream has never changed. Our dream.'

'I believe that,' she said. 'We just need to convince the North to hold off any... desperate measures they may take when they find out you are no longer simply the lost mage, but the new leader of the South.'

For the first time since Camron had given me back my wand, I desired to give it away. I lifted it from my lap and held it out to Beatrice.

'Then take it,' I said, rushed and desperately. 'Take the fucking wand, show it to the North and tell them I am no threat. Without this, I am nothing, right? So, have it and save me from this.'

Beatrice looked to my offering, then turned away from it.

My heart sank to the pits of my gut.

'Keep it, there might come a time when you'll need it,' she said, scratching her thumbnail across the wood of her staff.

Tension hummed between us. It thickened the air. 'What is it you want?'

'I want forgiveness,' Beatrice said finally, her voice cracking as she did.

'From whom?'

She held my gaze and I practically saw the cogs of her mind whirling within. Then her face hardened and she stood, the base of her staff smacking down onto the stone floor. The suddenness of it made me flinch back.

'*Them*. The North. Even if I wanted to force you out that door right now, I couldn't. Not without Simion, we need him to gain entry North. Without him, we wouldn't make it. So, until he returns, we wait and pray to whoever will listen that the North exercises patience.'

There it was again, the word patience.

Beatrice was red-eyed and breathless, gripping onto the staff for support.

I stood, levelling myself with her in height. 'And what happens if they don't?'

'Then expect to see the skies full of dragons and everything around you crumbled to dust.'

The threat in her words stunned me. Perhaps it was instinct, but my power uncoiled, tickling across my mage-marked palm, begging for me to release it.

Beatrice struck forward and took my hand in hers. She raised it between us, allowing the fading light of afternoon to dance across the silver inking that wrapped around my arm. 'We face the reality of this. The unbreakable vow. You are forever tied to the South, Max, whether you like it or not. But it doesn't matter what you like, not when this... this union may be the death of you.'

'It won't,' I replied sharply, 'be the death of me.'

She nodded as a shadow passed behind her eyes. 'If you asked me to break it, for you, I would do it.'

*Only in death shall you part.*

'No,' I snapped, unsure if it was me or the bond tying Camron and I together. 'At least not yet.'

She dropped my hand as though my skin burned her. 'There is no knowing what the North will do. Let's hope the years since I have last seen them have softened their hearts...'

The warmth of her fingers lingered on my hand. I longed for Beatrice to envelope me in her arms and hold me, but the distance between us was too great. Those days of comfort were long gone.

'I'm just one person,' I said. 'How can I be such a threat?'

'Because of what you are, Maximus.'

'Then tell me,' I said, reaching for her, but Beatrice pulled away. My hand dropped pathetically to my side. 'Help me understand what I'm facing.'

Beatrice looked from me to the door and then back to me.

'Danger,' she said. 'That is what we all face. Danger and control. We all belong to someone, Max. Whether it is— was… the Gathrax family, Camron Calzmir or those lingering far away North of the Galloway Forest. No one is free. Our choices are dictated, our lives are not even our own.'

'You're not exactly selling me on the idea of going with you,' I said, fear and power coiling within me.

'And nor do I need to. It is your only option. If you don't, no one is safe. Not you, me, your parents or the innocent people who live in these lands and simply want an easier life. Ruin and destruction do not discriminate, and that awaits if the North believe you are refusing them for nefarious reasons. I'll give you some advice, even if you don't wish to hear it.'

There was something driving Beatrice's desperate warnings and threats. This was not the person I knew—that much was clear. What also was obvious was the North had left a scar upon her soul, a deep one.

'Tell me,' I said, pleading.

'Don't use your wand. An open act of power will be seen as a threat. Hope that the North see reason and believe your story—that you stumbled upon your truth and you are no pawn or puppet for Southern power and control. Convincing them you are not a threat is the only option left.'

A breath lodged in my throat. 'And what if I fail?'

Beatrice shifted on her two feet, gathered herself, and took a step towards my side. 'Then we face the consequences together. Simion is my brother, but the time me and you have spent together has made us family. Max, I have got your back just as I know you would have mine.'

I gripped her forearm. 'Always.'

Her expression softened enough to reveal a glint of humour as she leaned in. 'Although don't expect me to forgive you.'

'For what?' I asked.

Her eyes fell to the silver markings across my arm. Every time I looked to them; it was as though I realised my new reality. 'I at least expected to witness the biggest day of your life.'

'Oh, fuck off,' I expelled a deranged laugh, relieved for a moment of lightness.

# CHAPTER 23

Silas Graham, the Master of Mice, was dead by morning.

Beyond my bedroom window, he hung from rope that strangled his thin, broken neck. A crowd had gathered around him, servants and maids, throwing stones and sticks at him, laughing and calling out with glee. Beneath the sway of his lifeless body, a small fire burned across the gravel. Before I realised what simmered within the flames, I smelled it. Charred flesh, boiled blood. Where Silas's hands used to be were now stubs of bloodied, torn skin, exposing bone, muscle and gore. His hands belonged to the fire now, never to touch anyone again.

I knew Silas would face punishment at the judgement of those he had affected over the years. His death felt as much my fault as Jonathan's and Julian's murder. Although my wand may not have been etched with a third death notch, the blood was on my hands.

I tiptoed to my door and opened it slowly. The corridor was empty, although I heard the light-hearted bustle of life far off in the manor. I'd checked outside the door multiple times during the sleepless hours of the night and had found the door was never locked, with no guard stationed outside.

Camron's presence was written all over my freedom.

By the time his first invitation to breakfast arrived, I had just changed into a fresh pair of clothes—form-fitting leather trousers and a matching long-sleeve tunic. It was all I could find in that wasn't red, but also fit me to some capacity. Still the tang of burned flesh lingered beyond the window, although the jeering crowd had long departed. Silas was left to the starving birds now perched on his shoulders.

'King Oaken has requested your company for breakfast,' a young maid said, smile beaming across her face. She had been one of those who'd thrown stones at Silas's body, but I also recognised her as the girl who had cried as Silas had me dressed for my handfasting.

It was strange to hear her use my family name when referring to Camron. When I finally reclaimed it, the name also belonged to someone else. 'No, thank you.'

'Camron asked me to get a valid reason if you were to decline his invitation,' she added, playing nervously with her braid of golden hair.

'Then tell him I'm not hungry.'

The maid toyed with my response but didn't question me further. I heard the quick patter of her feet running off to deliver my message, whilst I continued to prepare for my day. My *last* day in the South.

The next knock came as I donned a russet-brown jacket that belted at the waist and had many pockets. It was warm but also offered me a place to store the wand. I had no desire to use it—but also knew I needed to keep it close, just as Beatrice had warned.

My cheeks reddened when the maid entered my room for a second time.

'I'm sorry, Mage Oaken, but your husband insists that you have something to eat. He has asked if you would please come, or he may be offended.'

'Then you can tell him…' I didn't feel angry towards her, because she was simply the messenger, but my reply came out short. 'It is not the offer of food, but his company that offends me.'

She fumbled over her words. 'But sire, I don't think I can tell him that…'

'Then don't,' I said. 'In fact, let me give you a task and then you don't have to report back to him.'

This was a test. If Camron could command the staff, then so could I. I was the mage, after all. The new King, even if I didn't wish to accept it, nor care to.

'What is your name?' I asked.

'Isodel,' she replied.

'Then Isodel, would you mind preparing my room?'

She looked around me expectantly.

'Not this room,' I added. 'My old rooms, in the servant's quarters. You know my name, so I trust you know what I'm speaking of.'

'Are you certain you want that?' Isodel asked, reaching for her plait of blonde hair to give her hands something to do. 'This looks a fair deal more comfortable.'

'Trust me, soft pillows and lit hearths are not the comfort I am seeking. So, can you do that for me?'

She nodded, smiled and spoke. 'Of course, I can, my King.'

'Don't,' I snapped, feeling the swell in my chest. 'Don't call me that.'

If Isodel lowered her eyes to the floor any more, she would've fallen over herself. 'I'm sorry, sire.'

Guilt gripped me so quickly I didn't have the chance to apologise before she was off, running down the corridor.

* * *

I stood at the doorway to the rooms—Julian's rooms—for a final time. There was no love lost. Relief came like a breath of fresh air. If I never had to see these walls again, I'd be happy.

I contemplated taking Damian Gathrax's journal, but I had read it cover to cover. There was no knowledge it could provide me that the North couldn't when I arrived there.

I raised my hand, folded my fingers into a fist, all beside my middle one.

'Get fucked,' I said, quietly at first. Then I repeated it, as if a new energy of defiance flooded through me. 'Get. Fucked!'

It wasn't clear if I spoke to the room, the man who once owned it or everything that had occurred since I had first woken inside of it, but a sense of relief eased across my chest.

'What a mouth you have on you, Maximus.'

My blood cooled as I turned around, hand reaching for the wand in my pocket. Camron Calzmir stood before me in the corridor, bathed in shadows. The jacket he wore was a dark navy, with golden buttons and silver thread. Everything about his posture screamed of comfort, something I couldn't exactly relate to.

He smiled, flashing straight white teeth, and that alone sapped the shock away.

'Can I help you?' I asked, burying the ruder question I longed to ask.

Camron pouted, running a hand through his soft blonde hair. My eyes fell to his arm, and the muscles that flexed beneath the material of his cream shirt, stretching seams. I wondered if he got those arms from his months out at sea.

*No, focus.*

'I have come to see why Isodel never returned with you for breakfast,' he said softly. 'Now I see, it looks like you've made other plans.'

His dark eyes traced me from head to foot, drinking in my outfit of choice. I had the urge to step back so he couldn't devour me with his gaze.

Swallowing hard, I raised my chin and forced enough confidence into my form. 'Am I not in a position to refuse you, Camron?'

His pale brows raised in genuine shook. 'Of course, you can, but that doesn't negate my worry for you.'

'And why would you worry for me?'

He lifted his hand, flashing the hint of silver ink beneath his sleeve. 'Perhaps you slept so well you forgot we are... married. It is now my duty to worry, believe it or not.'

Married. Just hearing him say it aloud, so casually, made me want to scream.

'Oh, believe me, it is very much on my mind.'

His lips shifted into a smile. 'Am I on your mind?'

'Yes,' I snapped, narrowing my eyes at him. 'But not in the way you may think. Now, if you don't mind.'

'I do. Mind that is,' Camron said, stepping aside to allow me to pass him. As I did, I caught his sea-salt scent. 'Which is exactly why I have brought this.'

He raised a brown bag that sagged at the bottom. The paper stained with something soggy inside.

I eyed it, cautious. 'I'm more than capable of getting my own—'

'Pastry, fresh lathered with cinnamon and honey,' Camron interrupted. My cheeks soured with an onslaught of saliva. 'There are two, one for me and one for you.'

'Your persistence is an irritating trait,' I said, unable to conceal the grumble that erupted from my stomach.

'Well,' Camron said, eyes flickering down as he heard the sound. 'Persistence is not necessarily a bad thing.'

'Depends,' I said.

'On what?'

I inhaled, stomach rumbling again as the sweet scent of pastries filled my nose. 'The reasons behind it.'

'Perhaps we can discuss this on the way into town,' Camron replied knowingly.

Was I that easy to read? It was as though Camron could look into my intentions and grasp a hold of my desire. 'You aren't coming with me.'

Camron showed no signs of flinching. 'I sense you are going to be a challenge, which I admit I am glad of. There is nothing duller than complacency.'

I furrowed my brows, feeling the tension across my head swell. 'What does that even mean?'

'It means that Isodel warned me you planned to walk to town, and due to the obvious threats that lurk outside the safety of this manor, I cannot let you do that alone. So, before she prepares your new dwelling—which I think is truly a swell idea—she has prepared us a mount. We are riding into town… together.'

Isodel had warned Camron. *Dryads.*

'No,' I forced out, 'thank you.'

He shrugged, pouting deeper. 'Why not?'

'Because I…' I fumbled with an excuse. 'Because I don't need a chaperon or the company.'

'Okay,' Camron said, nodding. 'Then consider me a guard. You are the most valuable commodity South of the Galloway Forest—which means, you do not have the same forms of freedom you once did when you were simply Maximus

Oaken, and not Mage Oaken. So, we can continue this conversation, or get moving before these wonderful pastries cool and go to waste.'

'Is taking no for an answer another trait that is strange to a Calzmir?' I asked, frustrated.

'Yes, in fact, it is.' Camron said, turning his body, offering me the crook of his arm.

'You've got to be kidding me.' I rolled my eyes, unable to stop myself as his smile widened.

'No,' Camron said. 'Just as my stubbornness is a trait, as is my chivalry. So please, walk with me. As King of this new estate, I would very much like to update you on the matters that our little ceremony caused yesterday.'

Again, that title. King. It was a reminder that this man was solely in control of my parents' welfare, and I didn't want to piss him off. I conceded to his offer.

'Any news on my parents' arrival?'

Camron swept into pace beside me, his longer legs doing well to keep up with my quick-footed steps. 'That would be my first update for you, one you would have got if you didn't refuse my invite to breakfast this morning. As promised, and planned, they will arrive before supper tonight. Which means, we have some time to kill.'

'Interesting choice of words,' I replied, offering him a sharp glance. There was no ignoring the smile he regarded me with in return.

I looked away before it distracted me.

'There is something I wanted to show you, actually.'

I paused, unable to ignore the sudden seriousness of the atmosphere between us. 'If it is Silas, I have already seen.'

Camron's brow furrowed deeper. 'Not that, something better.'

'I guess if I ask you what it is, you won't tell me?'

'Ah,' Camron exhaled, leaning warmly into my side. 'It would seem you are already growing familiar with me. Don't you like surprises?'

'Hate them,' I said.

'Oh, Maximus, I am sure we can amend that.'

# CHAPTER 24

The horse bumped over the dirt path, forcing me to grasp hold of Camron to steady myself. His stomach was as hard as stone, the ridges and hollows of his muscles rippling beneath the press of my fingers. I was reluctant to hold on, until Camron took that away from me, guiding my hands around his middle as he said, 'After everything, I wouldn't want you falling off.'

I couldn't help but feel as though Camron had chosen a mare that didn't like me, just so I was forced to sit with my chest pressed into his back, and my arms gripped around him.

I was glad that his back was to me, so he didn't see how red my face had become.

Suddenly conscious of the heat of Camron's body pressed to mine, I wished I'd made a better effort to refuse him. But then again, I had questions.

Camron had promptly explained that my parents would return to the manor sometime in the early hours of the afternoon. What I didn't expect was the note he had given me, a single line of familiar handwriting scrawled across it.

*We are coming back for you.*

I would've recognised Mother's writing anywhere. The note hadn't made me trust Camron entirely, but it certainly helped his cause. It burned a hole in my pocket. If I wasn't holding onto Camron for dear life, I might have pulled it out and read it for the hundredth time.

The horse trotted down the long drive of the manor, passing the boundary wall in a blur. We slipped around the dirt track that gave view to the front entrance of the manor. It was full of carriages as the members of the Zendina and Romar families prepared for their journey home. I had enough to worry about, without thinking about what had become of Stephine Romar and Lann Zendina after the hand-fasting ceremony but, Camron explained, it seemed they left happier than they arrived.

With the promise of funding, supplies and the support of their new leaders. *Us.*

Even hearing him say it made me want to throw myself sideways off the horse. But then again, I was growing rather comfortable with his shared warmth, the steady rhythm of his breathing and the canter of the horse's hooves against the ground.

'Remi Gathrax and those two—rather vile—children of hers, will not cause us any further bother,' Camron added, his voice jolting with the trot of the horse. I was coming to understand that Camron rather enjoyed the sound of his own voice. Even if I didn't respond, he always had something else to say.

'My father called them devils.' The memory warmed me; Father's voice echoed in my head.

'That sounds like a rather tame description of the twins,' Camron replied. 'No bother, those *little* devils will never be a worry again.'

'Is that a polite way of saying they'll meet the same end as Jonathan, or Silas?'

The thought unsettled me.

Camron shifted in the saddle, forcing me closer into his back. 'Not at all. They will be given a home and servants and asked to live peacefully. Quietly. There has been enough bloodshed, and I hardly imagine you, or I, would like our consciences marred by more death.'

'Could we change the subject?' I asked, the mare agreeing with an expelled neigh.

'I think that would be a grand idea, husband.'

Discomfort uncoiled within me. 'Don't call me that.'

The rumble of Camron's laugh rippled beneath my palms pressed against his stomach. I released my hold on him suddenly, gripping the back of the saddle at an awkward angle, just so I didn't slip off.

'I jest, Maximus. The word certainly sounds as strange as it feels.'

'That is one way to put it,' I replied, unable to ignore how comfortable Camron seemed to be with the entire situation. It should have made me feel strange in his presence, but the flippant referral to our situation almost diluted the seriousness of it.

'I must admit, I admire you, Maximus,' Camron said, the honesty in his words plain. 'Not many people would have been able to survive what you have endured.'

Some of the tension eased from my shoulders as Camron spoke so openly about my experience. I wondered what Silas had told him but didn't dare ask.

'I had something to fight for,' I replied, staring ahead at the endless view.

'That you did.'

'Are you going to tell me where you are taking me?' I asked

for the fifth time, knowing his answer would not change. But I could be persistent as well.

'Are you going to be one of those overwhelming, needy partners?'

'And are you going to be one of those sly partners who keep secrets from the other?' I retorted.

'Well-played.' Camron's chuckle warmed me. 'I admit I did not expect you to have such a combative and dry sense of humour. Careful, because it may be my favourite trait already.'

'I'm not joking,' I said, brushing off his sarcasm.

'I do not doubt it.' Camron shrugged as a shiver passed over him. 'Consider my interest in your daily activity eradicated.'

As it had the four times before, my question went unanswered. Camron had the gift of diverting the conversation. Controlling it.

The morning had passed, the sun melting frost that coated the rolling fields around us. Thick, doughy clouds of grey hovered ominously over the landscape, promising snow in the coming days.

The horse jolted over a small ditch, forcing me to return my arms around Camron's stomach.

'Tell me something interesting about you, Maximus,' Camron asked, focusing on the road ahead. I could see the smudge of the main town in the distance, a dark stain of buildings that billowed smoke from chimney towers.

'There is nothing interesting for you to know.'

'Oh, come on,' he drawled. 'I understand this situation is not ideal. For you or me. However, I think we could both agree that we should get to know each other. It would be a pleasant use of our time if nothing else.'

The horse jolted over another ditch, sending me bumping into Camron's strong back. His hand pressed suddenly over mine, fingers encasing my fist and gripping on tight. 'I have got you.'

My cheeks stung a deeper red, my tongue stinging as I bit down on it before I could thank him.

'What's your favourite food?' I quickly asked, wanting to ignore Camron's gentle voice.

He paused at my question. 'So, you *are* interested in me.'

'We have to start somewhere.'

*Not that it matters, by nightfall I will be gone.* The thought was as sharp as lightning. *Far from here. Far from you.*

'Very true,' Camron said, withdrawing his hand from mine and returning it back to the reigns. 'If you were to put a honey-glazed gammon in front of me, then you have won your way to my heart.'

I found my lips curving upwards as the image of steaming meat covered in sticky honey came to mind.

'That is far too sweet for me,' I said.

'Sweet enough, are you?'

I rolled my eyes. 'Sweet enough to rot your teeth.'

'Dearest me,' Camron gasped. 'And what would you be doing in my mouth?'

*Fuck.*

'I am only playing with you.' Camron flashed a winning grin over his shoulder. 'Believe it or not, it was my father's weakness to sugar that caused mine. Before he died, he made sure those who worked for our family got to experience the same joys he did. Like the pastries I brought to you, he would've made sure every member of working staff in our manor would enjoy the same.'

'He sounds like a better man than many,' I said, unable to ignore the deepening of Camron's voice as he spoke of his father. It was as though the words became too heavy for him to bear.

Camron exhaled a breath, the tension in his stomach easing beneath my grasp. 'He was one of the best.'

Not able to dwell on the atmosphere for another moment, I changed the subject with another question. 'Cats or dogs?'

'Now that truly is one of life's hardest questions.'

'Answer it,' I said, squeezing his midriff. Camron stiffened in my hold, every muscle tensing again. 'Dogs. Now, depending on what you answer, will depend on whether I like you.'

'Dogs,' I replied, almost hoping not to displease him.

'Thank the dryads for that. If I even see a cat, my eyes swell to the size of apples. It's not a pretty sight.'

'Then I know what I need to do to keep you away from me,' I replied, fighting the urge to smile.

He turned over his shoulder to look at me, flashing a bright smile. 'Treason, to threaten your king?'

'Perhaps it is.'

'Hmm, how exciting.'

This time, I couldn't fight the swell of warmth that flooded my cheeks. From the way Camron's dark stare dropped, I knew he recognised the reaction. His slight amused glint confirmed it.

The sun finally burned through the clouds, enough to offer some warmth among the chill of the day. Ahead of us, the town looked different than I remembered it. It was alive with the bustle of noise and... laughter. Camron navigated the horse down the centre of the town's main road, passing Beatrice's smithery, which looked dark and empty.

Far ahead, the sentry line of trees surrounded the Green. It was strange seeing it again. Stranger doing so on the back of a horse as I held onto a man I'd been bonded too.

The deeper he navigated into the heart of the town, the more I noticed something on the people's faces.

'Everyone is... happy,' I spoke my inner thoughts aloud.

'Why would they not be? News has spread that Maximus Oaken has not only freed himself, but in doing so has freed his people. They are thankful. Thankful for what you have done.'

I followed their faces, waiting, expecting to see someone who hated me. My name was whispered on their lips. Not Julian Gathrax, but mine. Maximus Oaken. I found my lips played into a smile, mirroring the emotions that poured towards me in abundance.

'How do they all know?' I asked.

'Someone's little mice needed a new task,' Camron said. 'It didn't take long for all of Silas's previous charges to spread the tale of what happened yesterday.'

Camron slowed his mare, even lifted his hand to wave at a crowd who huddled on the side of the street.

'It seems those little mice didn't only spread news about Jonathan's death,' I said, noticing the many who looked at our embrace, the silver inking on our hands, then back to us.

'In the wake of dark times, sometimes the excuse to celebrate something is most welcome. I hope you do not mind, but I thought *your* people might like to know of our union. A wedding—no matter our thoughts on it—is as good an excuse as any to lift a drink and celebrate.'

'My people?' I asked, finding my arms tighten a tad more around him.

'Ours,' Camron corrected, 'if you would prefer.'

All at once, the burden of his words became too heavy. 'Perhaps coming here wasn't a good idea.'

'Maximus, I think we are about to have our first disagreement as a married couple—'

'Would you *stop* saying that!' I snapped, teeth flashing.

Camron's laugh vibrated through his back. '*I* think this was a wonderful idea. Let them see you for what you are. Silas had told me the Gathrax family rarely came to their town, so seeing you is meaningful. There can be no harm in letting them see you, their saviour.'

What Camron hadn't accounted for was the lack of red. Much like the estate we had left behind, there was no sign of the colour that once ruled everything beneath Gathrax control. No longer did the ruby banners hang over the street; empty wooden postings stood awkwardly in their place. I scanned the crowd, looking for red ribbons pinned to their chests, but I saw nothing.

'And will we be replacing the red with something else?' I asked. 'A new colour to establish our Kingdom?'

'Forgive me for reading between the lines, but that sounds like you are coming to terms with a possible... new future.' Camron looked over his shoulder, dark eyes squinting. In daylight, I saw the umber tones I hadn't noticed before. Flashes of light among the dark, like stars littering the night sky.

I rolled my eyes, using it as an excuse not to stare into his. 'You know that will not happen.'

'Maybe, maybe not. Only three weeks ago I was planning my next journey across the Thassalic. Now I am sat on a horse, walking through a new place, with a beautiful man clinging onto my back for dear life.'

His words settled over me, sending a shiver of pleasure across my skin. I was thankful, in that moment, for the thick jacket I wore, concealing my reaction beneath. Otherwise, he might have seen my skin prickle in gooseflesh.

'If parading me through town was your surprise, consider it a failure,' I blurted. 'I would very much like for you to take me home.'

Camron pulled on the reins, and his horse slowed to a stop. 'I made a promise to someone that I would take you to them. As it seems I still need to prove a lot to you, and I would very much like to start now.'

'Who're you talking about?' There wasn't anyone I could think of who I cared to see. Especially not this far into town.

Camron lifted a finger and pointed towards a building far down the street. 'There is someone who has been waiting to see you.'

'Who?'

His smile was the most honest, breathtaking thing I'd seen before. Then, when he spoke the name, it all came crashing down. 'Dame.'

# CHAPTER 25

The world stopped for a moment before a rush of fury shot through my core. How dare he mock me. If he knew her name, he knew what I had done to her.

'Dame is dead.' My entire body trembled. Tears filled my eyes, clinging to my lashes. Guilt and grief overwhelmed me, devouring the crowd around until it was only the two of us. 'How dare you.'

'No, Maximus, you are wrong,' Camron whispered, laying a hand over mine before I could pull away. I couldn't see his face, but the change in tone confirmed he believed he was speaking the truth. 'She is alive, very much so. I made sure of that.'

I couldn't think clearly enough to comprehend what Camron meant. *I made sure of that.*

'Go and find out for yourself. She is expecting you.'

\* \* \*

The care home was nestled within the shopping district of the town. One of the town's oldest buildings, with its weathered walls and mostly boarded-up windows, it stood out from the freshly painted shopfronts. As I stepped closer to the main door, my foot crunched over smashed glass from one of the broken windows above me. I couldn't fathom how anyone could live inside, especially not those who required the most care. It made my old quarters at the back of the Gathrax estate seem like a haven in comparison.

I was guided to a room on the third floor of the care home. It seemed Camron had sent word ahead of us because the nurse had been waiting for me. There wasn't much to say, not as I followed her to our destination. All the while I focused on holding back my tears which was all in vain as my eyes fell upon the impossible.

'Here he is, finally come to see little old Dame.'

Dame was waiting, tired face brightened with a smile. She held her arms out for me, beckoning me to her. Where I expected her to hate me, fear me, there was only love in her eyes.

'I'm—'

'Swallow that tongue of yours, Maximus Oaken, if you even think of apologising.'

I huffed out a laugh, tears falling, as relief crest over me.

I knelt before Dame, carefully resting my head in her lap as my tears stained her blanket. The material scratched my skin, but that didn't stop me from melting into her.

'*Shh*, Maximus,' Dame sang, voice soft as a whisper. 'Hush now, there is nothing for you to shed tears over.'

'You're alive,' I snapped, dumfounded. 'I killed you. I saw you...'

'I once told an old lover that it would take more than a blade to finish me off,' Dame rasped, coughing between every few words. 'The bastard didn't believe me. I only wish he was around long enough for me to prove him right.'

A deranged, misplaced laugh burst out of me. 'The rumours of you being an ox made of steel, they were right.'

'Ox,' Dame barked, brows furrowed over tired eyes. 'Is that what you whisper behind my back when I put you to work on something that displeases you?'

'Yes,' I choked out a sob and a laugh, all melded into one.

'Just you wait until I am out of here, young man. I will put you to work in the kitchens as punishment. Ox, dryads, I can't believe it.'

I gripped onto her hand, careful not to hurt her. Her bones were frail like glass, her skin delicate. 'I would like that.'

'As would I.' The lines around her eyes smoothed as a proud smile lifted her mouth. A faint glow of colour returned to her cheeks as her eyes fell to my hand, tracing over the silver inking.

'It has been many years since I last saw marks such as those.' I didn't stop Dame from lifting my hand, marvelling at the thorns and vines that twisted up my arm in beautiful, carefully placed swirls. 'What else have I missed?'

I longed to pull my hand from her, but she had seen it. 'A lot.'

'Well,' she urged, offering me the same scolding look she had given me so many times before. 'We have some time, so tell me.'

And I did tell her, not a single detail spared. I told her about the handfasting to Camron Calzmir, Jonathan Gathrax's murder, Silas's too. Dame was the first person I told of Beatrice and Simion, explaining the little information I knew. Dame was equally surprised to discover Beatrice was also a mage. Even if I longed to stop myself, I couldn't. The words spilled out, unstoppable as the tears that continued to course down my cheeks.

'I never asked questions when your mother arrived at my door, all those years ago. Perhaps I should have, but it was not my place to question a mother and child, longing for work, for sanctuary.'

'I never knew,' I said, fisting my mage-marked palm as though I had something to hide. 'I swear it.'

'Nor would I expect you to.' Her fingertips were ice cold, rough from years of use but beautifully familiar. 'Which is why I cannot understand why you would want to go North at all?'

Did she miss the part about my lack of choice? 'Because I can be free. They have promised me a life unlike one I can get here. Dame, you could come with us.'

'Darling boy,' Dame exhaled, shoulders sagging from the weight of her thoughts. 'My life is here. As is yours. This is your home, and by the sounds of it you have a real chance to make a change. Do better. Ask yourself, why did your mother risk the dark of Galloway Forest, simply to get you as far from the North as she could? It seems rather strange to be running straight back to them, when she gave everything to keep you away.'

Her words sank into me, slicing bone deep.

'Now, since we both are not planning on going anywhere for a while, can you do me the honours and push my chair closer to that window. It is torturous hearing the sounds of the world beyond it, and I have hours to spare, hours I could spend watching.'

'Anything for you,' I replied.

'Good, because you owe me a dance. Dryads, I regret not taking you out that library by the ear. If I had...'

*None of this would have happened.*

I leaned into her ear as I gripped the back of her wheeled chair. 'I promise, the second you are up and moving, we will be dancing so much you'll regret wanting your bones rattled.'

Her hand patted mine. 'Oh, dear boy. You truly know how to make an old woman feel special.'

The screech of the wheels was only another reminder of the dire state of the care home. Years of defunding from the Gathrax family had led to this. It had to change. Dame reached up, placed her shaking hand over mine and leaned her face into it. I didn't want to look at the leaking wound on her shoulder, but I couldn't help myself.

'Now that is better,' Dame said, closing her eyes as the warmth of sun cast across her face. Beams of light highlighted every wrinkle, every faded bruise. And when she smiled, my entire world brightened.

'Since you came all this way to visit me, pull up a chair and sit. I want to hear all about Camron Calzmir.'

A warmth spread across my face. 'He is a stranger.'

'A stranger, yes. But is he kind?'

'I don't know him well enough to answer.'

'Then you better find out some more about him. If not for your benefit, but for mine—'

A thunderous screech split the world in two. It was so loud that it shook the walls of the building, forcing me to clap my hands over my ears. It was a warning; in hindsight I should've known that. Because when the sound came again, the walls trembled and the ground beneath our feet shook so violently I lost my footing.

My body hit the floor. I pinched my eyes closed as dust rained down upon me. It took a moment to regain composure when a roar shattered my hearing, rupturing my skull.

'Dame!' I shouted, lungs invaded by dust and debris. The moment I opened my eyes, they stung from the cloud of it.

Beyond the ringing in my ears, I could hear my name. It was desperate and feral yet seemed so far away. I waved away the debris until I could see Dame's profile, and the horror that shone from her expression. Her lips trembled; her face coated in flecks of grey. As she lifted her hand, finger pointed towards the window, she said something. But I couldn't hear what. All I could focus on was the cloud of mist that expelled past her trembling lips.

I opened my mouth, only to find my breath fogged out as well.

'Dra—' The broken word came from Dame's mouth, followed by the hissing rush of ice. The crack of freeze spread across the walls, engulfing the window and frosting the scene beyond. It seemed to poison the air, making every inhale harsh. My lungs burned, my throat stinging with dust and ice. Before my eyes, winter devoured the building, spreading its frozen touch across everything around me.

I pushed myself up from the floor, trying to reach Dame. Without realising, my wand was in my hand. The moment the wood met my palm, the world glowed with iridescent cords— tying me to the element of earth around me.

Another sound exploded beyond the window, vibrating glass. A shadow followed, blocking out the natural light and bathing the room in shadow for a second.

There was no time to think. I was up, reaching towards the back of Dame's wheeled chair, ready to move her, when my ears pricked to the sound of wings. A pounding of large wings as if a flock of woodland kestrels flew outside. But no bird had talons as large as those that pierced the wall before Dame.

No bird had the force to rip the entire portion of brick apart.

No. This was *no* bird.

'Dragon,' I breathed, as the wall was torn away, exposing

the beast of horror beyond it. Red scales, gold eyes with a slit of black like a blade. Horns. Teeth as long as spears, sharp enough to pierce stone as though it was skin. The building groaned beneath the weight of the creature as its neck slithered through the gap, and it expelled a rumbling growl that stank of death.

I couldn't move.

The dragon's snout protruded through the hole, frigid air billowing from the slits in its nose. I blinked, taking in the vision of blood-red scales and an eye that flickered around the room—searching. The remaining wall of the room cracked loudly beneath the weight of its claws.

'Maximus, run!' Dame screamed.

Slowly its hulking jaws separated, exposing lines of pointed, serrated teeth the size of blades. A tongue, pink and forked, slithered out in search of its next meal. I saw it before it happened. The monstrous face tilted, its jaw opened wider, then it snapped Dame from her chair, dragging her out into the world beyond.

The dragon pushed from the building, rocking it down to the foundations from the force. Beats of horrid air cascaded over me, blinding me as the beast flew off into the distance. When I opened my eyes again, it was to see red. It was everywhere. Dame's blood smeared across the floor, the wall. Even the chair was gone…

Reality crashed over me thick and fast. I put up no resistance as two, horrifying facts melded as one in my mind.

The North had come for me, and *they* had murdered Dame.

# CHAPTER 26

The entire world trembled beneath the force of the creature's wings. I raced towards the shattered remains of the wall. My feet slipped over ice and blood, but I grasped the broken brick. I looked up into the sky, glimpsing the creature that still lingered above. Diving between clouds, I studied the shape of the red dragon. It almost didn't feel real.

A flash of light caught my attention. My eyes flew to the creatures back, drinking in the whipping ivory cloak and silver metal gleaming beneath the sun. Someone rode upon it.

*When the earth first moved, and the mountains cracked in two; out birthed Dragons in their hordes who claimed the skies as their new domain.*

From this distance, I could not see its features. But I heard it. Its cry sent burning anxiety across every inch of my body.

The streets beyond the care home were filled with screaming people. Their terror was powerful. I looked down to see them running, watching. I wanted to shout at them from my place up above and tell them to run and hide. To get as far away from here as possible.

Then a name flooded my mind.

*Camron.*

I searched for him among the bustle of the streets, but my effort was wasted. There was no finding him among the sea of bodies running, moving for shelter, whilst many stood, dumbfounded, staring up at me.

'Mage Oaken!' Someone beneath me shouted, pointing up to where I stood. The winds caught my hair, picking it up in dancing tufts, and quivered my jacket.

'Help us!'

My fingers tightened around the hilt of my wand.

'Please, mage, spare us from the North!'

Soon enough, they were all shouting, begging for me to save them.

Something warm ran across my hand, distracting me. I didn't need to look to know it was blood. Dame's blood.

*She is dead.*

Beatrice had warned the North would come. She *promised*. And now another life had been lost because I had refused to leave.

Another thought speared me with horror.

Had Simion done this? Beatrice said he went North, and now they were here. The timing seemed suspicious. Connected.

I watched the blood coil around my wrist, over my handfasting marks and carry on its descent to the floor where it puddled. Seeing it brought me back to reality.

My magic pooled in my stomach, twisting as anger took over. Like the raging waters of the ocean, its presence thrashed within me.

*Release me.* It sang in a symphony that sent shivers across my skin. *Release me.*

'They will destroy us all,' I said, unsure if I spoke to Dame's ghost or the presence of my power.

*No.* The thought was boiling.

'No,' I repeated aloud. 'I won't let them.'

With livid speed, I left the building and exploded onto the street, hand raised to block the sun out of my eyes. I searched for the dragon amongst the sky, but I couldn't find it. But it would come back.

I knew it—I sensed it.

It would come for me, just as Beatrice said. And if it wanted me, it could have me if it meant sparing the hundreds of innocent lives.

I pushed through the crowd, apologising to each person I barrelled through. The desire to help was powerful and unignorable. But so was the fear that had embedded into my gut. With each blink, I saw the blades of the dragon's teeth. Was that my end?

I ran across the street ahead of me towards the alleyway, blood thundering in my ears. I didn't look back to the care home and the destruction I had brought to its door, but I vowed I would fix it.

Legs and arms pumping, I kept up pace, unsure of where exactly I was headed. Then the shadow of the dragon passed overhead, and instinct took over. I ducked as more cries of terror lit the world. An intense cold nipped at my arms as I hit the ground and covered my head. Just in time, as frost—pure and white—spilled from the flying beast's jaw. It kissed buildings, smashed windows, and altered the very air where its breath touched. Buildings burst apart, exploding in clouds of wood and stone.

By the time I looked up, it was as if winter had finally arrived and claimed the world. Ice clung to the buildings, sleet fell around me from a cloudless sky. No matter where I turned, the pop and crackle of ice spreading across stone had replaced that of the screams of terrified people.

*Up*, I told myself. *Run.*

Leaning buildings towered above from either side, blocking the sky the further I ran down the alley. I risked a glance up but saw no dragon. But I could *hear* it.

Terrorising cries sounded ahead. Hearing them renewed my vigour. Adrenaline fuelled me, the wand held firm and poised in my hand.

The screams of the town would not cease, not until the North got what they wanted. Death. We had all heard the stories, we all knew what happened when dragons last filled Southern skies. Complete destruction.

The wand's smooth hilt was a steady force in my hand. I reached for the power, its familiar guidance poised for me. I knew little of the power's nature, but I trusted it would help when needed. Visualise, Damian's journal had explained. It would be no different than with Julian or Jonathan—once I opened myself up to the power, it would do as I wished.

I reached the opening of a street and stopped, skidding across the now-frozen path. Air cracked, each lungful burning as I inhaled. The world shadowed beneath the splay of sinuous wings, a gust of violent wind—and then the dragon was before me. The beast landed with such force I had to bend my knees to stop myself from falling. Glass windows from nearby buildings exploded, a torrent of broken shards fell like rain.

I raised an arm, covering my head. Every second stretched into an oblivion. My skin crawled as a feral clicking sound erupted from deep within the dragon's long throat, followed by a crawling hiss. I peered from behind my arm, getting a better view. My breathing was harsh and loud, no matter how I attempted to still it.

The dragon's back was to me, folded wings pressed tight

into its mountainous frame. Whatever it was focused on was standing on the opposite side, unseen behind its body, blocked by the muscled, barbed tail that thrashed left to right. It was unlike anything I could've ever imagined. Seeing it up close, without the broken remains of a wall to cover its body, I drank in every inch of it.

The ground beneath its talons had been gouged, deep scores etched into stone. Its body looked like a sculpture from blood, so red in places the scales almost looked black. Everything about it was both beautiful and horrifying. Its tail was as thick as a tree trunk and moved like a garden snake, crashing into buildings without care, tearing through walls as though they were made from paper.

But it was the figure sat upon the dragon's back that captured my attention, perched on a seat crafted of leather.

The Northern soldier was garbed, from helmet to boot, in polished silver armour. The breastplate reflected the white ice that clung to the buildings around them. The ivory cloak billowed, as though caught by an invisible hand.

I threw myself forward, screaming my grief, anger, desperation, hate—it all spilled out of me in a single breath. With it, my magic exploded. This time the power felt different. It was bright and crackling, not the same comforting warmth as when I called for vines to strangle Jonathan Gathrax to death.

Lightning crackled through the taut air, lifting the hairs on my body to standing. The sky broke; dark clouds gathering into view until the sun was blocked out and the town was cloaked in shadow.

A bolt of white, jagged light crawled across my skin, up through the wand and out its end. I turned my face away as the bolt of light exploded from my very soul and shot across the space towards my enemy.

My attack slammed into the side of the dragon's snout,

missing the Northern soldier by inches. It threw its long neck back, raised onto its hind legs and threw out its ruby-leather wings in a shield. In the chaos, I didn't see the Northern soldier fall from his perch, but I heard it. The crash of metal falling onto stone was faint beneath the dragon's pain-fuelled screams.

Frigid steam billowed out of its jaw, the temperature around me dropping so suddenly it snatched my breath. The dragon opened its jaw with a shattering roar, spraying a pillar of ice and wind skywards. I ducked down, not before the bite of freeze nipped at my face.

My magic had hurt him. But it had also alerted both the beast and its rider to my presence.

'The *traitor mage*,' the soldier shouted, voice raw and stern as he pushed himself from the ground, helmet askew and sword discarded in the street.

'No one else needs to get hurt,' I called back, unsure if the soldier could hear me over the dragon's monstrous caw.

I kept my wand pointed, stare unwavering.

'You're right. Only you need to die. So, you can resist, and others can perish, or you can kneel and save them all.'

What had Simion done? What had he said to the North to create such a reaction? Beatrice had promised me safety there, but here they were, ready to kill me.

'I've survived worse than the likes of you,' I said, magic boiling through every vein.

'Oh, have you?' The soldier straightened his helmet as his laugh reached me.

'Her name was Dame,' I replied, throat burning, anger lashing within me.

The soldier stalked for the sword and swept it from the ground. 'Their names do not matter, neither will yours. You will forever be remembered for being a waste of power and potential. The lost mage who was felled for betraying his own kind.'

The dragon had calmed itself enough to position itself behind the soldier. It levelled its gold-black eyes upon me, pinning me to the spot whilst it erupted in a pleasured purr. My wand felt suddenly heavy, brimming with a power that begged for release.

'What happened to the North wanting me alive?'

The soldier swung his sword around with dramatic flair. It only proved to me he didn't see me as a threat. 'They do, but I do not care what they want. We should have eradicated all Southern scum years ago.'

Power crackled in the air, filling my mouth with the taste of soil and dirt. It was as if I sensed what was to come, saw the soldier's action before he made his first move.

I acted with equal speed. A sudden crack of lightning split the darkening sky above as I raised my wand for it, calling for its assistance. The soldier raised his sword skywards too, collected the same power and thrust it towards me.

Lightning exploded between us. A shield of white, boiling light that crackled as our powers met. The line of magic hissed and fizzed, spitting flame onto the buildings and street.

Then it was gone. It gathered around the metal of the sword as though it drank it in. Then I noticed the sword was not entirely metal. The hilt was wooden, no different to a play sword. It gathered magic, leeching it in, absorbing it.

*Amplifier*, the soldier's sword was his amplifier. The soldier was a mage.

'So, the rumours are true,' he called out, ripping his helmet from his head and discarding it on the ground. 'You even received the *Oribon's* blessing before she stole you away. You faced the dragon's breath—is that why *she* is so desperate to find you?'

Sweat ran down my temples, sticking my clothes to my back. 'You can leave. Take your worm and go.'

My insult didn't meet its mark. The soldier titled his head, smiling at me as he levelled the sharp edge of his sword in my direction. 'Where is your *bitch* mother? Perhaps I will kill her, too, before I leave.'

I blinked and saw red. Gathrax red. Dame's blood. The world was coated in it, all but the faint misted glow of green that reflected off the sword's metal. My eyes. My mother's eyes.

'I warned you,' I said softly, as though it didn't matter if he heard me or not.

The sky cracked in two. I conjured a power from the haunting place of fury deep inside of me, so vicious and unforgiving. I might not have the skill to fight, but dryads knew I had the desperation.

Fissures of light fizzed through the dark clouds, breaking them apart so suddenly, even the dragon looked up. I gestured towards the skies, pointing my wand to the swirling mass of ire. Before the soldier could react, a bolt of stark blue light cast down upon him, charring the very air in its wake.

# CHAPTER 27

In that single moment of overwhelming emotion, I learned the most valuable lesson about the strange power inside of me. It had a knowing of its own, a diluted sense of what to do. It worked on instinct, not command.

It owned me.

Perhaps that was what it meant to be a mage. Being owned. Something I longed to be free of. But among this power, I had never felt freedom like it. If it was the price to pay, I would.

The Northern soldier reacted a moment too late. His gaze was pinned to the tip of my wand, expectant. But the stark bolt of light shot downwards from the sky, not from my wand.

The hairs on my arms stood on end. The soldier dove out of the way at the last moment. The clatter of his armour smashing against the street was buried by the explosion of scolding light and burning stone.

I refused to give him a moment to raise his amplifier. The wand moved my hand, slashing my arm upwards. The ground beneath the soldier rumbled and split. Out from its depths burst shards of rock that imprisoned him.

Glass and brick exploded; shrapnel smashing into me. The wall of rock I had conjured crumbled beneath a force from within. The soldier stood among the rubble, sword raised, as the rocks hovered around him, sharpened into the tipped points of spears.

In a blink, they shot towards me.

I turned my back, screaming, expecting my flesh to be torn apart. But the magic would never have allowed that to happen.

*I will protect you.*

When I turned back to face the soldier, pondering why I was not punctured by a multitude of earthen spears, it was to see a wall of stone fall back to the ground as though it was a wave of water.

The soldier didn't wait for my next attack. He raced across the street, bellowing his war cry. It ricocheted around the ruined buildings and glass-strewn street. Lightning hissed around the sharp edge of his blade and coiled around his fist in a glove of power.

I saw the desire for death flash in the soldier's eyes. His control over the power was well-trained, whereas mine was nothing more than a trust in something unknown.

We collided, limbs and flesh. He raised his sword in an arc above my head, then brought it down. I sidestepped, missing the blade's edge by inches. Before the soldier could steady his stance, I thrust my shoulder into his stomach, driving the wind out of his chest. We traded blow for blow. I cried out as the wooden pommel of his sword smacked into my back, one, two, three times. Perhaps he wished for me to release him, but all the pain did was turn my body to dead weight—which brought us both down onto the ground.

The crack of the soldier's head hitting stone was beautiful. His hold on me loosened for a moment, enough for me to straddle his waist. Before he could open his eyes, with the wand clasped in my fist, I drove my fist into his nose.

My knuckles came back pained and bloodied. The soldier wailed beneath me and raised his sword towards the side of my stomach. Before the tip so much as brushed the leather of my jacket, I lifted the wand and filled my mind with an image.

Roots slipped through the cracked ground and engulfed his hand. I saw it in my mind before it happened—envisioning the attack and making it real with a simple thought. With my spare hand, I rained down punch after punch, not caring where my knuckles hit. Skull, broken nose, split lips, shattered teeth.

The soldier didn't let go of the sword, but it didn't matter. My conjured roots ensured he could not lift it again. The air fizzed with the raging storm above as I shouted. 'I don't want to hurt you.'

That was a lie, I did. I wanted nothing more than to punish him for what he had said about my mother, for what he had done to Dame.

The man smiled up at me, eyes feral and teeth covered in blood flowing from his bent nose. 'But I want to kill you.'

He jolted his head upwards, screaming through the agony in his captured arm. His head crashed into mine with force. The crack was sickening, I blinked and saw stars.

The soldier broke free of my roots and shifted his weight from beneath me. Suddenly, I was the one on the floor. Pain radiated in my wrist as he slammed his boot down over and over, until my fingers spasmed and the wood fell from my grasp.

An armoured fist smashed into my stomach, then my chest, then crashed into either side of my face. The metal gauntlets cut into my skin as he attacked.

I raised my arms, bones bruised and battered, to cover my face. Until it all stopped.

'Look at me,' the soldier commanded. His voice was muffled in my ears, as though he spoke through water. When I didn't do as he asked, he kicked into my side again. That made me look. I gasped out, eyes wide, the breath driven out of me.

The Northern soldier towered above me. Unnatural lightning flashed in the sky behind his head, giving the sense that he wore a crown of pure power.

'I want to see the life leave your eyes as your death leaves its notch in my amplifier,' the soldier spat, teeth exposed as he grinned down at me.

'Fuck. You.' I spat in return; my mouth full of blood. Without taking my eyes off him, my fingers searched for the wand.

In that moment, I was back in the forest with Julian holding me down, desperately searching for something to save me.

As it had then, I prayed the wand would come to my aid.

The soldier raised his sword and pointed it down at my chest. His breathing was ragged, his face smeared with gore, both his and mine.

'You could have been great,' he said, teeth pink with blood.

My fingers continued to drum over the street, searching as the warm kiss of blood bloomed beneath the soldier's sword. I didn't struggle—didn't take my eyes off his.

'I'm not dead yet,' I said, as the tips of my fingers brushed something familiar, and a rush of power flooded through my arm.

'Allow me to rectify that. Then my dragon will feast on your flesh...'

The soldier's words faded as he glanced towards my hand;

it gripped my wand. His lips parted, but before he could gasp, it was over.

With one hand, I pointed towards the sky, calling down the lightning that buzzed through my veins. With the other hand, I grasped the end of the sword, not caring at the blade slicing through the soft flesh of my fingers and palm.

Lightning ripped from the sky. It tore down my arm, through my chest and filled me entirely. The hairs on my arms stood on end as bolts of white heat consumed me. I tasted the warmth across my tongue as it spread from my body to my mind. Like the beating of drums, the intense power built in pace.

I released it.

# CHAPTER 28

Pure, white-hot light spread from my hands and engulfed the blade. I pinched my eyes closed just as the power tore out of my other hand, shot up through the metal of the blade and met the soldier with a wrathful force.

In the peaceful dark, a death notch etched itself onto the base of my wand. I didn't need to open my eyes to know it was over.

The power vanished in a heartbeat—leaving me empty and weak. My insides were on fire. Every vein was alight with the stark fury of lightning as though it consumed me.

I blinked, opening my eyes to see that two storms filled the skies, two open jaws of a dragon lowering down over me.

'Maximus!' a familiar voice screamed.

The dragon's forked tongue slipped from between its serrated teeth. I had only enough energy to turn my head to the side as it dragged the rough textured flesh across my cheek. Rotten breath soured my senses.

Then the dragon retreated enough for me to open my eyes. Beatrice stood in the street, staff held high in defiance.

She glowed with power. Her amplifier was held out before her as winds snatched her dark hair and sent it into a fury—whipping around her face to obscure her scowl.

I tried to open my mouth to call but couldn't. My throat was raw and sparked with the remnants of lightning. I lost grip on my consciousness.

I blinked and the darkness claimed me.

Someone's hand lifted my head from the ground. I cracked my eyes open to find Beatrice cradling me to her chest. Her mouth was moving, but her words did not register. All I could sense was the droplets of her tears that fell over my face. It was soothing against the overwhelming burning that enraptured me.

Clouds dispersed beyond her head, the storm breaking apart. I expected the dragon to be above her, but it was nowhere to be seen. The world seemed still and silent.

I rolled my head, neck aching, to find the cause of the silence. A jagged spear of stone had pierced the ground, spearing through the dragon's neck. Its body hung awkwardly in place. Lifeless, gold eyes looked across the street, to the place its soldier's corpse lay, melted flesh, his armour melted, puddling beneath him.

Beatrice killed it. I knew it, even in my disarrayed state.

I blinked again, eyes heavy. I faced darkness for an eternity, unsure if I would ever break free of it. When I found the strength to open my eyes, it wasn't to see Beatrice cowering over me. A new face looked down, equally haunted with panic. A touch as warm as an open flame, skin that smelled as light as the open oceans.

'Cam… Camron,' I spluttered, voice broken.

The sky beyond him was moving quickly—no, we were moving.

'I have got you.' Camron's warm hand slipped behind my neck.

I groaned beneath his touch as he held me to his chest. Exhaustion kept me in place. All I could do was register the worry in his dark eyes, the way his jaw feathered and the lines across his forehead deepened.

Although I wished to lose myself in the darkness of his eyes, I drifted away. A crowd had formed, blurred faces looking at the destruction. Every eye was on me, fingers pressed over their hearts, boiling defiance reflected in every expression. I fought to keep my eyes open, not wanting to show such weakness to those who relied on me. People whose lives I had risked, simply for being here.

Then I found her again, Beatrice. She was on the ground, buried beneath three of Camron's guards. Her arms were snatched behind her back, and her cheek pressed into the stone of the street, her eyes set on me.

There was a knowing in her stare. Had she known what Simion was truly going to tell the North? Then I looked back to the dragon. Beatrice had killed it, to save me.

A sharp lash of pain erupted through my skull. I must've groaned because warm hands fell upon my cheek, turning my face back until all I could see was Camron.

'Look at me,' Camron urged. His voice was soft as silk. 'Maximus, you are safe now, you are with me...' Just his touch was enough to distract me from the pain.

My raw throat burned as I gathered in enough breath to force out a reply. 'They came, they said they would...'

'And the North will come again, but I shall face them by your side. I promise you.'

I couldn't hold onto a thought. Between my agony and the gentle lull of the horse, I was fading.

Camron lowered himself over me and pressed his lips to

my forehead. It was gentle and warm… so warm. The kiss lingered, dulling the pain that had latched onto every inch of me.

'Am I… am I going to die?' I asked, no longer able to keep my eyes open.

'No,' Camron growled through the darkness of my mind. 'I *need* you.'

# CHAPTER 29

My body was a map of bruises and cuts. In time, the blue-black marks would fade, and the skin would stitch itself back together—but the intense exhaustion would linger. Simply walking hurt me, but that discomfort was nothing compared to what I felt as Isodel revealed my biggest fear.

Camron had stationed the maid by my bedside. She had answered my rush of questions, explaining how I had lost an entire day since the attack. But it was her answer to one particular question that jolted me from my bed.

'You really need to rest,' Isodel fussed. 'If you don't allow your body to heal—' She continued speaking, but I didn't hear her.

I had pushed out of the manor's infirmary, unstopped by anyone who attempted to help Isodel calm me down. I hobbled from the bright, white-tiled room, moving swiftly through the manor with Isodel at my heel. I didn't care about anything but finding Camron. I hurried, barefoot, with nothing on but a loose linen tunic and trousers hanging off my hips.

My wand had been beside me when I had woken and was the first thing I grasped for. Now I held it firm, the world before me alight with the glowing cords of power. I moved through them like the strings of an instrument, feeling them pull and tug.

I was angry. At myself for losing so much time, at the world for constantly punishing me for a choice I never had. And it was that anger that had me thrusting the wand before me, its tip aimed at the closed doors. The wood bent to my will, caving inwards until I had full view of the throne room beyond.

'Is it true?' I shouted, watching as a sea of heads turned. Men and women, young and old, lined every inch of the throne room. Far beyond them, atop a dais, sat two thrones. One for King Gathrax and the other for his Queen. Except it was not the Gathrax family they belonged to any more.

Camron had sat beside an empty throne, two burning braziers glowing on either side of the dais, casting him in an ethereal glow. He stood abruptly, dark navy jacket straining against the pull of his frame, gold buttons catching the light. Even from the distance, even with the hundreds of people standing between us, I knew from looking at him that what Isodel had let slip was true.

'Please,' Camron said, speaking to the crowd without taking his obsidian eyes off me. 'Will you give me and my husband a moment?'

The thunderous shuffling of feet sounded in response as every person left the room. They parted around me like a river to rock. It was then I noticed the biggest difference to the throne room since I had last seen it.

Above my head, tethered across beams, pillars and stone walkways, the red dragon dangled within a web of iron chains. Its hulking body blocked out the natural light from the many stained-glass windows.

The vision should've horrified me, but it didn't.

When I spoke again, I hated how broken I sounded. 'Tell me it isn't true.'

As though I had the power to control Camron, he stepped down from the dais, not sparing a glance to the creature that hung in the air above him. 'Yes, it is true. I will not lie to you, Maximus.'

'The North…' I could hardly speak. Each word felt like a shard of glass in my throat. 'The North have taken my parents.'

He bowed his head. 'They have.'

Angry, hot tears dripped down my cheeks.

Camron reached out for me, treating me with caution as the wand continued to shake within my gripped fist. The doors lay scattered on either side of me, bent and broken from the force of my power.

He lifted a finger to clear the tears away, I swatted him away. 'Don't touch me, don't fucking touch me.'

It was one thing hearing Isodel tell me, but seeing it in Camron's eyes made it all too real. As did the dragon that hung above our heads. A multitude of horrifying images came to mind.

Breathless, I doubled over and wretched. This time I didn't stop Camron from drawing me to him. He was silent, rubbing circles across my back as I expelled nothing but water and bile from the pits of my stomach.

My head throbbed; my throat screamed with agony. 'If they are dead—'

'They are not dead, Maximus. I promise you that.'

I snapped, pushing him away with sudden strength. Camron stumbled a step, catching himself with wide eyes.

'How can you promise me!' I screamed, the room swaying beneath the rumble of my power. I would've shattered it, but the connection stabbed another jolt of pain through me. Even my magic, magic I never wanted, magic that caused all of this, refused me.

I fell to my knees, bones cracking against stone as the wand rolled out of my fingers. 'How can you dare say such a thing when you don't know!'

Camron raised his hands up, trying to subdue me as though I was a wild bull. 'This is just another play. A move the North had orchestrated that gets you a step closer to them. I believe, wholeheartedly, that your parents will not be harmed. They are merely bait.'

'Don't call them that!'

Camron lowered himself to the floor before me. 'This is my fault. I take responsibility, which is exactly why I am going to do anything you ask of me. Maximus, we will get them home.'

The more my head throbbed, the harder it was to breathe. I knelt on the ground, hugging my knees to my chest. There was a shuffle of footsteps and then the warmth of a body. Peering through lashes, I found Camron, his forehead inches from mine.

'Whatever you want to do, I promise to aid you. Ask anything of me, and I will do it.'

'Why?' I replied, noticing just how violently I shook as Camron grasped my upper arms. 'Why do you even care?'

He looked me dead in the eyes, orange-red flames reflecting within them. 'Because I know what it is like. When my father died... I would have done anything, sacrificed anything, just for another minute with him.'

'Then you know what I will do to save them,' I said. 'I—I will tear the North apart just to get them back.'

'I have no doubt,' Camron replied, his voice the calm surface of the ocean.

'Are you not going to stop me?'

Camron pulled a face. 'Never. My wish is not to make life difficult for you. I understand how important your parents are. And I have a responsibility in this. If I had not allowed Jonathan to sign away your parents after that dinner, they would never have been on the open road for the North to... take. They travelled from my home, which means the North knew. Someone must have told them our plans.'

'Simion.' The name oozed out of my mouth like poison from a fang. 'Beatrice's brother.'

From the look across Camron's face, I didn't need to tell him who Simion was. 'Beatrice Hawthorn insists he carried no such message.'

'Where is she?' I asked, mind going back to the last moment I saw her, on the floor, accosted by Camron's guards. *My* guards.

'A place she cannot be harmed. A place she cannot hurt anyone.'

Camron was wrong. Beatrice would never hurt me. I tore my eyes from him, gazing up at the dangling dragon, the fire glowing over its crimson scales, turning them a darker red, its eyes a brighter gold.

'I need to speak with her,' I said. 'I need to hear it from her mouth that Simion is not behind this.'

I couldn't imagine that Simion, the man with the soft touch, the stranger who offered me comfort during times I most required it, would've been the reason the North sent someone to kill me.

Camron's expression steeled as he nodded. 'If that is what you wish, I will take you myself.'

Silence thrummed between us as another thought assaulted me.

'If I ignore this, the North will come back, won't they?' I whispered.

'I do not doubt it for a moment.' Camron lifted my face to his. He was so warm. I wanted nothing more than to melt into his touch. 'But we will be prepared. Those men and women who stood in this room, they have willingly given themselves to our cause. They long to fight for their home, a home you have given back from the Gathrax rule. When news of the attack reaches Stephine Romar and Lann Zendina, I have no doubt they, too, will lend us their numbers. Max, you are not alone. Not any more.'

*Not any more.*

I shook my head, unwilling to recognise the spark that kindled within me. 'I cannot let another person suffer because of me.'

'That is not for you to decide,' Camron whispered, his breath fresh and welcoming. For a moment, I was lost to the shape of his mouth, the freckles which lined it. 'We stand by you, not because we have to, but because we want to.'

'I hate them,' I replied, eyes dried from tears.

Camron held my gaze, hand moving from my arm to my chin. I allowed him to touch me this time, to offer me the sense of peace from his warmth. It was as though he searched within me, found my passion and grasped it—pulling it to the surface.

'We will get your parents back,' Camron said, firm as his grasp. 'If it means building an army and marching across Galloway Forest, we will.'

'They have magic, they have dragons...' I faltered, one thought replacing the rest. 'I know what I need to do.'

'We, Maximus. Together. One thing is certain amongst it all,' Camron said, as the iron chains creaked above us. 'Without Beatrice Hawthorn, you would be dead. I may not believe what she has to say for her brother's innocence, but I do believe she has your best interests at heart.'

Beatrice had told me the North wanted me to return, that it was a personal task of hers. But the soldier had no plans to take me; he was going to kill me. I hadn't vocalised it, but that was one part I couldn't make sense out of. If the North wanted me dead, why would they take my parents?

'You trust her?' I asked, searching his light-drinking eyes for the answer.

'Not exactly, but I trust my instincts and they tell me she will prove of benefit, in time. But first, Maximus, you must allow your body to heal whilst I fill our lands with soldiers.'

My skin tingled where he released me. I leaned into the empty space he had been, watching as Camron picked up my wand with careful fingers. It was as though he touched me, my skin reacting as his fingers drew the length of the wand. I couldn't help but watch how the old burn scars across his hand flexed, shimmering in the glow of the braziers around us.

'This is yours,' Camron said, offering the wand back to me. 'Keep it close.'

I took it, almost disappointed to stop feeling his touch.

'I'll do anything to get them back,' I said, losing myself back in Camron's wide eyes.

He combed his fingers back through his blonde hair, disrupting the perfectly laid strands. He then stood, extended his hand out to me, scarred fingers steady. 'I know, as will I.'

'I hate them,' I said again. The need to voice the three words were almost unbearable.

'And they deserve that hate,' Camron said, stepping in close. He peered down the length of his straight nose, his mouth pursing into a perfectly bowed shape. 'Take that emotion, take that fire inside of you, and mould it. Use it. And when you are given the chance, burn them. Burn them all.'

# CHAPTER 30

No one stopped me as I stole into the Gathrax cellars.

It wasn't the first time I had found myself here, searching for liquid peace. On my eighteenth birthday I had wormed my way in, unsure on exactly what type of wine I was looking for, only that I wanted to be drunk. What started off as a dare from Beatrice ended up as a night I could hardly remember.

Mother had found me, covered in chunks of sick, the next morning. The look she gave me was as much a punishment as the hangover. I never got to ask her if Dame purposely put me on duty in the stables, mucking out dirtied hay, just to punish me for stealing. I knew, deep down, it wasn't that I had stolen, but rather the risk that my childish act had put upon my family. I hadn't been back since. Which was exactly why I was here now. I longed to rebel, just for the chance that my mother would miraculously return to the manor and scold me.

The cellar was a cold room, lightless and dry. Burgundy glass bottles filled shelves; large wooden caskets full of wine were stacked on top of each other. I contemplated taking two bottles of wine, but my goal was not to get drunk out of my mind, but just drunk enough that sleep would be easier.

By the time I reached my room—not Julian's room, but the modest dwelling that I'd grown up in—my body wished to collapse in on itself. I pushed the door open, not knowing what to expect. What I found sparked some sense of feeling in my numb chest.

My home was not empty as I last saw it. Furniture filled the space, albeit not the same our family once had. It was as though someone had gone through Remi Gathrax's bedchamber and deposited a large four-poster bed, a multitude of cabinets and draws. The freshly woven rug spread out beneath my feet smothered my hesitant steps as I entered.

If it wasn't for the ever-present strength of the glass bottle and the supportive frame of the doorway, I would've fallen over myself.

I closed the door behind me and shut the world and its worries away.

I lit the hearth as I had done many times before. It was such a mundane task I could've almost convinced myself that none of this had happened. Before the first stack of kindling dwindled in flame, I had uncorked the bottle and took my first hearty swig.

It was pale wine, tasting of sweet grapes, so sharp it clenched the insides of my cheeks. I drank and drank, taking comfort in the bite of fermented fruit as it burned down my throat and soothed me from the inside out.

The empty bottle was no more than an afterthought when Camron found me. I was vaguely aware of the shuffling of feet before three loud raps sounded on the door. When I didn't answer, Camron chose his moment to enter, pushing the door open enough to slip his head between the crack.

'This is where you have been hiding. I have been looking for you, Maximus.'

'Well, here I am. You found me,' I said, slurring over my words.

'You are drunk.'

I raised my hands up in the air and clapped. 'It seems it is my turn to drink myself into a state. Are you here to stop me, or join me?'

Camron's prolonged sigh echoed through my entire body. He looked exhausted. Over the day, aided by food and water, my body recovered somewhat from my overuse of power. In a way, I was glad for the bruises; the pain every time I moved, even slightly. It reminded me of what had happened, what I had lost.

'Take it from me,' Camron said, stepping into the room without need for invitation. 'Drowning one's sorrows will not help deal with them.'

'Are you speaking from experience?'

Camron's gaze narrowed, his jaw flexing.

The glow of fire accentuated the sharpness of his high cheekbones. It glowed in the pits of his dark eyes, turning them ruby, orange and gold. His blonde hair had been smoothed down over the side of his head, and he wore matching jacket and trousers with the shirt beneath unbuttoned down to the harsh lines of his chest.

I drank him in, pushing myself up onto my elbows. 'Have you come to provide me with a moral lesson, or is there something else you require from me, *husband*?'

Camron blinked at my use of his title. His lips pursed into a pout, eyes shifting from me to the bottle that rested at the edge of the bed. He bent down, picked it up, and held it before him. I almost felt the brush of his fingers against the glass echo across my skin.

'Well, for starters, you could have at least saved me a glass.'

I narrowed my eyes—it was the only thing stopping his outline from shifting. 'If you want a drink, I could tell you where to go and get one.'

He looked back to me; a single brow peaked. 'And leave you, alone? I do not think that is wise.'

'Because the idea of keeping me safe helps stroke your ego, or because you just can't keep away from me?'

I regretted saying it the second it was past my lips.

Camron tilted his head. 'Would it bother you if I said my answer was the perfect blend of both?'

I stood on the edge of a precipice. From both sides, the fall was great. I simply waited to find out if someone would push or pull me. To my disappointment, the alcohol did little to ease the storm of emotions. It only jumbled them together into a tangled mess.

'May I?' Camron gestured to the edge of the bed.

I found myself nodding without much of a thought.

The bed shifted beneath Camron's added weight. He kept his legs apart, elbows leaning on his knees as he supported himself, head in hands. Again, I was mesmerised by the scars across his arm. They began at his hand, slithering up into the sleeve of his jacket, until I could only imagine where they lingered.

'Can I ask you something?' I asked.

I studied the back of Camron's head. He was a stranger with the ability to make me feel comfortable and... cared for. My eyes fell from the perfectly laid strands of hair to the mess of scarred skin that reached just beyond the lip of his collar.

'Yes. I could do with the distraction,' Camron replied.

'What happened to your arm?' I asked, voicing the question I hadn't braved to speak aloud yet.

Camron glanced at me over his shoulder, just as I reached

a hand for him. My touch was feather soft, but forceful enough to conjure a shiver across Camron's scarred arm. His arm was almost hairless and rough to the touch. Was it his heartbeat that thundered beneath my fingertips or my own? It didn't deter me as I ran my fingers over the mounds of twisted flesh, delighting in just how warm his skin was compared to mine.

'Silas informed you during his lessons about what happened to my father, did he not?' Camron replied with a question of his own.

'He may have spoken about you,' I replied, 'a handful of times.'

'I know he did because I ensured he would.'

A tingling warmth spread over my chest.

'So you are aware that my father died to a sickness he had a short battle with?'

'I am,' I replied.

'Well, he was not the only one who was sick, Maximus. I suffered with the same plague, but I survived when he didn't. These scars are a reminder of that pain, a reminder to what I did to him.'

'It wasn't your fault,' I said, laying my hand upon his. Camron's fingers were splayed across his lap, fingers flinching as though they longed to reach out in return.

'I appreciate the light you see me in, but I am afraid I am going to have to spoil it. My father died because of me, because of the plague I brought home after my expedition. I didn't bring home new foods and mesmerising jewels from new lands. I brought home death.'

His words chilled me. I couldn't fathom such an illness that could scar one's skin like this. I would've found it easier to believe Camron had walked, face-first, into a fire and survived.

'The illness killed your father, not you,' I said, lifting my fingers from his hand and moving them to the back of his neck. His skin was hot and smooth. Camron didn't pull away.

'As so many people have said,' Camron continued, 'but every day I am reminded of what I did when I look in the mirror. It taunts me. I should never have come home—if I hadn't, my father would still be alive.'

I thanked the burn of alcohol for my lack of care. With the confidence it leased me, I knelt on the bed behind Camron and wrapped my arms around him, resting my chin on his shoulder.

'What have I done to deserve this?' His question came out in a rushed breath.

'Be quiet and accept it,' I said, 'Not everything has to be a joke.'

Camron kept very still. I almost read his body language as a sign of refusal, until his hands spread over my shoulders. 'I do not deserve it.'

'I'll be the judge of that,' I replied.

Camron turned his head enough for me to drink in his profile. His freckled lips lifted their corners as the firelight flickered in his deep, never-ending gaze. 'And how do I fare, in the short time you have known me?'

'I'm still deciding,' I said, suddenly conscious of the hammering of his heart.

'Let's hope we find the time for you to discover your answer then.'

It was becoming custom for me to say something and regret it the second it was out of my mouth. This time I wouldn't regret *anything*.

'We have tonight,' I said, voice light.

Camron's expression hardened, dark eyes narrowing as he regarded me. They seemed to drink me in, immobilising me.

'That we do, Maximus.' His voice stirred the handfast marks, making them slither just beneath my top layer of skin.

Heat flooded my cheeks, my gaze diverting. Had I crossed a line?

Camron reached for me and pulled me over him, not stopping until either one of my legs was draped across his lap.

The suddenness of it made me break out in a giggle. Then reality hit and I found myself straddling his waist, two guiding hands splayed across the lower part of my back.

'Hello,' Camron purred.

I stared deep into his eyes. Behind me the fireplace glowed, flames dancing, warmth kissing the bare skin revealed as Camron's fingers lifted my tunic up.

'Hello,' I replied.

This close there was no hiding from him. I grew conscious of the wine on my breath and the way I grew sticky with sweat beneath his touch. Camron noticed the shift of my eyes and moved his hand from my back to my chin. He held it, softly pinched, between his forefinger and thumb. 'Would it be poorly timed if I admitted the thought of you leaving displeases me?'

'No,' I said, 'it wouldn't.'

Camron smiled, exhaling deeply through his nose. 'Good.'

Time stretched between us, prolonged by the connection of our eyes and the way I laid my arms over his shoulders, entwining them behind his neck. The wine offered me one thing, but this—Camron, his warmth, his body, could offer me a distraction like no other.

'Kiss me,' I commanded. 'Please.'

I caught him off guard, delighting in how the surprise melted across his face.

'Are you certain that is what you want?' Camron's deep voice spurred through me, enticing me to rock my hips.

He wanted it, as did I, that much was evident from his hardening length pressed beneath me.

'Do *you* want me?' I added quickly, not caring if it was the wine talking or not. 'You've snatched me onto your lap, that is a rather suggestive thing to do.'

'Oh Maximus,' Camron said, dipping into the crook of my neck. His lips against my skin had my back arching, my chest pressing into his. Camron's arms hardened, his hands keeping me in place. 'You have no idea.'

When he pulled back, my moan was not born from pleasure but disappointment.

'*Want* makes it sound as though I have a choice in the matter. Maximus, I desire you. Like air to flame. But...'

'No, don't say that word.'

Camron's grin widened, his eyes glittering with unbridled mischief. 'But, you are drunk.'

'I am tipsy, at best.'

I chuckled at the way Camron tilted his head sideways, blonde strands flipping with dramatic flair. The skin around his nose crinkled as he screwed his face up in judgement. 'Your eyes are red as my mother's polished rubies—'

Slapping a hand over his mouth, I delighted in the brush of his lips against my mage-marked palm. 'I would rather you kept the comparisons to your mother non-existent when I am sat on your lap.'

Camron wriggled free, lips tugging against my skin as he did so. 'Do you plan on sitting upon it again?'

My entire body warmed as I leaned into him. 'Please, Camron. I can't think about them any more.'

His smile faltered, broken by the desperation in my plea. His thumb brushed over my chin, slowly lingering down my jawline, across my neck and into the collar of my shirt. He pulled back enough to expose the line of my neck. 'If it was a

distraction you longed for, Maximus, I could have provided it
for you.'

I rolled forward, shifting my hips so my ass brushed harder
atop his groin. That small movement undid Camron. The
hand on my lower back shifted down, his fingers nipping
through my trousers.

'Then be what I need you to be,' I said, unable to hide the
plea from my pitched tone. 'Take my thoughts, fill them with
something other than this torment. Don't make me beg you.'

Camron was silent, likely shuffling through a list of
excuses in his mind.

'I will only ask you once more,' he said finally. 'Are you
certain that is what you want from me?'

I nodded, feeling my heart swell in my chest. Did I want
him, or just what he had to offer?

'From my understanding,' I said, stomach jolting as though
I stood at the top of a hill, looking forward at a sheer drop,
'newlyweds usually consummate their union.'

'We are more than newlyweds, we are bonded.'

I swallowed hard as my next admission rolled out of me.
'Unless you die, or I die, this is unbreakable. If I were to act
against it, it would destroy me.'

Camron grimaced. 'There are many things I would wish to
do with you, Maximus. Destroy is not one, at least not in the
usual context.'

I placed my palms on his chest and pushed him. Camron
offered no resistance. He fell freely onto the bed, his back
pressed onto the sheets. I leaned over him.

'Careful with your choice of words,' I muttered, enjoying
every moment of this distraction. 'You might just regret it.'

'The only thing I regret is not finding you before you
downed an entire bottle of wine to yourself,' Camron said.

'Why is that?'

As Camron shifted his positioning, something hard pressed into my behind. 'Because when this happens between us, I want you to be of sound mind. Clear-headed. Not drunk.'

I sat back, lifting away from him. If it wasn't for his hold on my ass, I would've stood. 'And here I was thinking you found me attractive.'

'I find you more than attractive, Maximus. But I don't wish for you to wake up in the morning and look at me with regret.'

'Why do you have to be the better man?' I asked, shaking my head in reply to his accusation. 'Why can't you be like the rest of them, taking whatever you want, whenever you want?'

Camron sat up suddenly and raced his palms up my spine. My back arched beneath the press of his warmth, until I found my chest pressed into his and my mouth inches from his own.

His dark eyes flickered between my wide eyes and parted lips.

'You want a distraction?'

*Need, not want.*

I feared to move in case I ruined the moment of closeness. 'I do.'

'Then I will give you one, and come morning, when your mind is clear of the fog and you might desire another—you know where to come.'

Camron dipped his head towards me, tilting it to the left ever so slightly, and pressed his lips upon mine.

The kiss was shattering. For something so sudden and so soft, it had the power to flay me open and expose all my hopes and wishes. Camron cradled the back of my head in his hands and held me to him. As I melted into the warmth of his mouth, guided by the encouragement of his tongue, I had no clue what to do with my own hands. Not until they naturally fell upon his cheeks, where they stayed as we explored one another.

There was no room for thought. No room for care. All I contemplated was how he tasted like fire and his entire soul burned along with mine. I dissolved beneath him.

When Camron pulled away, I was breathless and red-faced. His lips were swollen and the tenderness of my own told me that mine must have looked the same. Camron was smiling, both with his eyes and entire face. As was I.

I leaned in for another kiss, only to find him pull away, tutting his tongue between his teeth.

'Tomorrow,' he promised.

Camron desired me. It showed in the tension of his muscles. I rocked back and forth, encouraging him with my body and eyes. I wanted more. But he pulled away.

'I won't beg for you,' I said, going back on my earlier promise.

His eyes lit up. 'Now that is a shame.'

'Is that what you want, someone kneeling before you, begging?'

He shook his head, blonde hair no longer settled and smooth, but wild and falling before his eyes.

'Tomorrow,' he repeated.

Camron's strength surprised me once again. He stood with me in his hold. I wrapped my legs around his hips as he turned around and lowered me onto the bed. When Camron pulled back, I dropped my legs, laying still as the world seemed to sway around me. In that moment, I knew Camron was right. I was drunk. And he *was* a better man than me.

'Good night, Maximus.'

'You're really going to leave me?' I leaned up, the bruises across my arms aching for reprieve.

He lifted a woollen blanket and draped it over my legs. Then he leaned over me and placed a final kiss upon my forehead.

'Yes,' he said, pulling back. 'I hope you dream well, or not at all, if that is what you would prefer.'

'Don't go—'

'Tomorrow,' Camron repeated a final time. There was a fire in his eyes, a desire. He struggled with it, his movements stiff and well-placed, as though he forced himself to stand away from me, forced himself to walk the room and open the door.

He spared me a final look, then he was gone, sweeping out of the room and closing the door firm behind him. All that was left was the warm press his body had left on me and the tingling across my mouth.

# CHAPTER 31

The chilled air of dawn did little to disrupt the maelstrom of embarrassment I was riddled with. Not even the ache across my skull, a gift from the wine, could distract from the mortifying replay of last night's events. I'd woken by the time the fire in the hearth was no more than crackling ember. No matter how hard I tried, I couldn't fall back asleep. I was acutely aware of how tender my lips felt and the faint whisper of Camron's warmth that still lingered all those hours later.

I couldn't face him. Just the thought of seeing him set me at a great unease. Not because I regretted it, but I feared that Camron did. My mind was already prisoner to thoughts of my parents and the North.

Which was exactly what led me to do everything in my power to prolong our next interaction; and there was someone else I needed to see. My guards didn't refuse me when I requested to be taken to her.

Beatrice didn't look up as I entered the old storage building just outside the reach of Galloway Forest. She sat on the floor, knees drawn up to her chest, chin hanging down as she surveyed an unimportant place on the floor.

A chain encased her ankle, thick bands of iron, which slithered across the floor where it was bolted to a stone wall.

'Did *he* do it?' The question shattered the silence.

Beatrice raised her chin and stared across the space towards me. It was a dark room, once a place meat and produce were stored to keep them cool. The sour tang of rot still clung to the heavy air. It was a windowless space; the only light came from gaps in the ceiling.

'I don't know,' Beatrice said, jaw fixed as her stare bore through me.

I stepped in, boots sloshing through melted piles of sleet and grime. The closer I drew, the more I saw her body tremble. Guilt tightened my throat, knowing I had slept in comfort when Beatrice had been kept in this place since the attack. I unclasped the cloak from my shoulder and brought it to her, draping it over her shoulders.

Beatrice held my stare, not daring to release it. 'I never lied to you, Max. Simion did go North to tell them Jonathan Gathrax was dead, to inform them of your handfasting to Camron and the intentions behind it—or lack thereof.'

'It would be easier not to believe you,' I said.

'But you do believe me?'

'You told me the North would welcome me; you told me the North was a place I could be safe.' I took a breath. 'The soldier, the one they sent, he had no plans to take me. He came to kill me, Beatrice.'

The iron links clinked together as Beatrice stood. Even imprisoned, Beatrice looked as though she had the power to tear the chains apart with her bare hands.

'I'm as confused as you are, Maximus. If the North wanted you dead, that would've been my task all along. Even if I failed, Simion would've finished the job weeks ago. Do you really think I would lie to you about that—'

'Would you do it?' I interrupted. 'If they asked you to kill me, would you?'

'No, I wouldn't.'

I believed her. But that didn't take away from the fact my parents were captives. Someone was to blame. 'Simion must've caused this.'

'Maybe,' Beatrice replied, gaze lingering elsewhere, 'but without him to answer for himself, we will never know.'

'Camron is gathering an army. He is prepared to go to war for me.'

'Do you truly believe an army is going to help you get them back? The North would decimate anyone and anything in the blink of an eye. You saw what one dragon did to the town, just imagine what a horde of them would do. I am not talking about a few, Maximus. I am talking hundreds.'

'Then what do you suggest?' I asked, heart in my throat.

'We go, as planned. We leave this all behind and get to the North before any more of them come looking for you. Then you can petition for your parents. Going willingly will save thousands. Camron's army will stand little chance against the power of the North. Bravery means little beneath the maw of a dragon.'

A chill raced down my spine. 'What is stopping them from killing me the moment I get there?'

'Me,' Beatrice said, reaching for my hand. 'I will stand by your side, Max. I told you this. Dryads, I killed a dragon for you. If anything, it will be my head on the chopping board for such a crime. Dragons are gods, like dryads. They are not creatures of myth and story—we live by them, with them.'

My thoughts drifted to the throne room, specifically to the crimson-scaled beast that hung from chains across the ceiling.

Its teeth were stained with Dame's blood. If Beatrice hadn't acted, it wouldn't have only been Dame's flesh stuck beneath the dragon's teeth.

'Simion *will* come for us,' Beatrice said quietly, voice dipping low enough that the guards beyond the door couldn't hear. My heart jolted violently. 'And when he does, you will need to decide to leave with us or not.'

I couldn't move. The thought of seeing Simion again tugged on my anger. 'Won't you force me, take me just like *your* people took my parents?'

Beatrice laid a careful hand on my shoulder, leaning in until she looked through her velvety lashes at me. 'I wouldn't force you to do anything.'

I longed to believe her, to lean into her words and allow them to take my torment away.

'Think about it,' Beatrice added, leaning her forehead to mine.

Closing my eyes, I allowed myself to dwell in her comforting touch.

'It is all I think about,' I replied finally, pulling back and breaking our connection.

Beatrice held my gaze. Then she said something that spoke to my soul. 'I hate them too, Max. I will not lie to you and tell you otherwise. The North is known for ripping families apart, they do it with ease and without thought.'

'And yet you still want me to come with you?'

Beatrice straightened her back. Her fists clenched at her sides, steady. Everything about her posture hardened, even her eyes seemed to shift. 'You are my family, and I will not allow them to take you away from me.'

I swallowed hard. 'And what about Simion?'

Beatrice softened only slightly. 'Simion is as much of a stranger to me as he is to you. I love him, naturally, but you,

you are more. A brother by choice is better than one who gains the title simply by sharing blood. I'm giving him the benefit of the doubt, Max. But I promise, if he caused this... if Simion lied, I would cut them all down and stand by your side, even if that means an army is at our back, facing magic and dragons. We do it together.'

I drank in the honesty behind Beatrice's gaze. For a single moment, I feared for Simion. But that worry lasted only for a moment.

'Guards,' I called out, voice echoing across the barren stone room. Feet pounded against the floor, followed by the screech of hinges.

'Yes, Mage Oaken.'

I didn't take my eyes off Beatrice as I gave them my command. 'Unchain Miss Hawthorn and see that she is returned with her staff.'

'But—'

'Do it,' I snapped, feeling myself slip back into Julian Gathrax's shoes.

'King Camron would...' The guard swallowed his words as I snapped my head towards him.

'Leave Camron to me,' I said, voice calm but forceful. 'Take Beatrice to Julian Gathrax's bedchamber. See that she is offered food, drink... Dryads, give her whatever she wants.'

I looked to Beatrice, smiling with mischievous pride. It was the very same look she had given me all those years ago, when I turned up at the back of her home, bottle of stolen wine in hand.

# CHAPTER 32

'King Oaken is currently visiting with Beatrice Hawthorn, as your message requested, Mage Oaken,' the guard said, standing vigil outside Camron's chamber as though the empty room still required protecting. There was a slight tinge of annoyance to his voice, one I couldn't ignore. 'I have been asked to inform you that he will return shortly, and you are welcome to wait inside.'

Two thoughts sprang to mind. Firstly, Camron had received my request for him to provide Beatrice's amplifier back to her. Secondly, he had expected me to visit him. I couldn't decide if his knowledge of my visit was born from last night, or something else. Even as I stood before his door, the guard waiting for my answer, I could almost hear Camron say one single word, a word he had repeated to me with hopeful promise.

*Tomorrow.*

'I'll wait inside,' I replied, flushing, eyes looking everywhere but the guard. 'Thank you.'

Camron had taken residence in the guest wing of the

Gathrax manor. I entered into a large foyer, a seating area and table perfectly positioned near a lit hearth, which spoiled the air with heat. There were two adjacent rooms, both separated through arched doorless frames, covered only by a curtain of sheer material that danced languidly in the draught.

Like all the other rooms in the manor, I knew this one well. But in the short time Camron had been here, he had claimed the chambers and made them almost unrecognisable. Boxes and cases had been piled up across most of the walls, overspilling with blue garments. Books stacked high atop the table. Some were left open, spines snapped, waiting for someone to finish reading them. It was a silly reaction, but I longed to relieve the books of their forced discomfort. Folding a page was one thing, but breaking the spine was practically criminal.

'What a monster,' I said to myself, smiling at the thought.

I found myself moving through his personal space, drinking in the details of what it said about him. At first glance, the room looked untidy. But even amongst the mess it seemed everything had a place.

The rest of the foyer was normal, nothing amiss or out of place. Until I stepped through the sheer curtain, into his bedchamber, and found what waited beside the unmade bed.

Armour, unlike anything I had seen before. It hung from a mannequin of sorts, crafted from red scales, each one far larger than my splayed hand would be. They overlapped one another, leaving no room for skin to show. The armour was separated into different sections—a breast plate lighter in colour at its narrowed peak, fading to a deep ruby where it overlapped with scales; gauntlets rested over a deep maroon vambrace; and beneath the mannequin were scale-covered greaves.

The skin of my finger bit into the sharpened edge of the

breastplate, almost cutting it from the smallest of brushes. It was ice cold. Tough in form yet flexible in design. I pushed the armour with a tentative hand, watching it move freely.

'If you would like one to match, I could see it done. There is plenty of the dragon to spare.'

I stiffened, withdrawing my hand as though I had been caught doing something I shouldn't have. Turning, I found Camron, a grin cut across his face. He leaned against the stone doorframe, arms folded over his broad chest.

'I didn't hear you come in,' I said, steeling my expression. Simply seeing him brought a rush of emotions back.

'No need to apologise, I have nothing to hide from you. If I did, I would've asked my guard to keep you out.' Camron pushed off the wall, striding towards me in a few long steps. With his sudden proximity, a wave of his scent brushed over me, sea-salt and bleached wood. It seemed to ease the tension from my body, removing it entirely within seconds.

'Everyone has something to hide,' I replied, feeling small beneath his dark gaze. 'It's *why* they hide which is the concern.'

'Wise words. But isn't it part of the fun to figure those secrets out?'

I looked back to the armour, unsure if I could hold Camron's stare. Something amused him, his light-drinking eyes glittered within unspent enjoyment. It was all so distracting.

'What do you think the North's reaction would be when they find you dressed in the corpse of a dragon?' I asked.

'Well, I'm sure they would not appreciate it,' Camron said, stepping directly behind me.

'We both know that is an understatement.'

He exhaled through his nose, the air tickling my neck. 'I've done a lot of research on dragons, and it was believed their scales can withstand violent drops in temperature. It may not be becoming to dress myself in its corpse, as you've so clearly pointed out—'

'But…' I drew out, knowing the word was coming.

'*But*, I do so knowing there is a chance I will not be ruined beneath the ice and wind the creatures can conjure.'

I wondered which book had suggested such knowledge. No doubt one of the books laid out on the table in the foyer.

'You seem to have a way of knowing information others don't.'

'Knowledge is more than power. Perhaps I can offer you something to drink, and I can share some of this power with you?'

'After last night, I would prefer a clear head.'

'Ah,' Camron breathed, eyes dropping to my reddening cheeks. 'Last night. I hope you are not embarrassed.'

'Embarrassed?' I choked out a laugh. 'What's there to be embarrassed about?'

Camron leaned in, lips a hair's breadth away from mine. 'I could list a few things, although I wouldn't necessarily agree that they should make you feel such a way. Come and sit. There is much to discuss.'

There was no resisting as his arm swept in mine. With a reassuring force, he turned me away from the armour and swiftly moved us back into the main foyer.

'Beatrice Hawthorn is a passionate woman,' Camron said, gesturing for me to sit on the plump, green velvet sofa. He had to clear a few books away, quickly depositing them on the table, adding it to the mess.

'I gather your conversation went well then.'

He nodded. 'I have had the pleasure of being around many in my life, but I must say Beatrice makes the others dull in comparison.'

Something sparked in my chest, a discomforting feeling which I couldn't place.

'So, you are not displeased that I had her freed without consulting you first?'

'No, as long as you are not displeased that I had her imprisoned in the first place.'

I couldn't answer because I wasn't entirely sure.

'Do you trust her?' Camron asked, standing with his back to the burning hearth. The glow of the flames haloed his powerful frame in an array of orange and reds.

It was distracting, watching him. Again, the thread pulled between us. 'Yes, I do.'

Camron's gaze drifted from me. 'I have no doubt that Beatrice cares about you. That much is clear. I think it would be sensible keeping her close, in the coming days. As she pointed out, I could do with as much help against the North as possible. Two mages are better than one.'

Camron tugged down at the cuffs of his shirt, straining the material as he did so. I had noticed this was something he did in moments of disquiet and wondered if it was because he longed to hide his scars.

'And if they do come, the North that is?' I asked.

'I do not want you to worry about it, you have enough on your mind.'

There was something intoxicating about being in Camron's presence. When I was with him, it made thinking about anything else difficult. Beneath his glittering dark stare, I was a leaf caught in a storm. All I could ponder was what thoughts went through his mind.

'I can't just sit around and wait for news about their well-being,' I said. 'At least with Jonathan, I knew if I behaved, they would be safe. But now, I have no idea what has become of them. Are they hurt? Are they…'

I couldn't finish, couldn't dare say the word aloud.

In a blink, Camron knelt before me. My skin shivered beneath his unfathomable heat as his thumb traced calming circles across the back of my hand. 'If the North wished to kill them, they would not have gone to the lengths they did to take them away. The carriage was almost untouched, the guards escorting them... they all survived.'

My body stiffened, hardening to stone. 'Can I speak with them, the guards? I want to understand what happened.'

Something flashed across Camron's face, so quick I couldn't place it. 'Of course, if that is what would help.'

A moment of silence followed. Although neither of us spoke words, our locked gaze conveyed our unspoken thoughts. I felt seen, not just with his eyes but with his very soul. I was bare beneath him. Camron had unravelled me, twisting and twisting with some unknown power, leaving me as starving for his touch as I had been last night.

'So, Maximus Oaken, tell me why you came to see me,' Camron asked, a single pale brow raised, his lower lip caught between perfectly straight teeth. 'Please, stroke my ego as you so pointedly put it during our last encounter.'

A warm brush of heat exploded across my neck, likely staining my skin a deeper shade of red.

'You tell me,' I replied, voice feather soft, 'since your guard seemed to know I was going to come, even before I did.'

Camron dropped his eyes to the silver inking marks across our joined hands. 'I had hoped you would come. That is different to knowing.'

'Why?' There was a part of me who hated hearing how breathless and meek I sounded. Another part enjoyed giving the power to him, if it meant I was awarded a break from it.

'Well, you could say I enjoy your company.'

'Here I am,' I said, gaze dropping from the intensity of his.

'Yes.' Camron squeezed my hand. 'There you are.'

There was so much I wished to say, but I couldn't seem to grasp a single coherent thought.

My eyes fell to Camron's lips. I longed to count every freckle, to keep a tally of the details of his face. Entirely entranced, I hadn't realised I lifted a hand to his jaw until my fingers scratched with the rough brush of his beard.

Camron exhaled a moan that soon became a hungered growl. Before I could react, he crawled over me. Stunned, my back pressed into the sofa as I edged down, allowing his body to hover over me. We moved, all without my need to take my hand from his cheek.

'I see what you want from me. I can feel your desire,' Camron said, face inches from mine. If it was possible, his eyes darkened, voice deepened. 'So, act on it.'

The muscles across my stomach hardened as a thrill spread through me. 'I don't know what I want.'

It was a lie. The sly tip of his lips told me he knew it too.

'Then allow me to be the one to show you.'

Camron dove upon me, lips pressing into mine. The connection undid me, ruined me. There was nothing but him, his strong mouth caressing mine, his salt-tainted scent, the taste of his tongue as it joined with mine.

I moved my hand from his cheek, threading my fingers through his blonde, perfectly laid head of hair. Camron groaned into my mouth as I tightened my hold, pulling on the strands until pleasure and pain melded.

Teeth nipped at my lip, punishing me. I laughed, unable to stop myself as his mouth continued its expedition, moving from my lips to my jaw, tugging my jacket from my shoulders until he had access to the soft of my neck.

I arched into him, pushing my pleasure into the hard swell of his.

Books fell to the ground with a thud, knocked by Camron's rushed, clumsy limbs. All I needed to do was give into his guidance as he moved me into a position that pleased him.

He explored me with his warm mouth. His tongue lapped at the small parts of skin he nipped with teeth. I was laid across the sofa lengthways, Camron upon me. His knee separated my legs, slotting himself between them. One arm was outstretched, keeping him from falling completely atop me, the other slipped beneath my neck and held me in place.

I was breathless, even though I had hardly moved.

Perhaps it was our union, bound together by an ancient magic, that intensified our connection.

'Off,' I snapped.

Camron pulled back suddenly, worry creased across his blushed face.

'Take *this* off.' My fingers fumbled with the gold buttons of his jacket, pathetically trying to pry them apart. I caught his pleased smile before his lips pressed back to mine.

We giggled into one another's mouth, the laughter erupting from a place of childish glee. He leaned away long enough to pull his shirt, half-unbuttoned, over his head.

Dryads, his body was beautiful. Half his torso was a twisted maze of scars, spreading over his shoulders like folded wings. I wanted to touch every inch, to show him what I thought of it. Whereas one side of him was covered in scars, telling the story of his survival, the other was entwined with the handfasting mark. Silver thorns twisting over his forearm, his biceps, his shoulders… Dryads, he was divine.

'Maximus,' Camron said, delighting in a moment of pause.

My name had never sounded so beautiful.

'Maximus,' Camron said it again, drawing the single word out into an everlasting hiss. My skin puckered, every inch his mouth and hands had touched felt scorched. He looked at me as though I could give him the world. As though I held the key to something wondrous—something great.

'I want you,' he moaned.

'Then have me,' I replied urgently.

Urgent because I wanted the talking to stop.

Urgent because if he didn't kiss me, I'd be forced to beg him.

Camron's expression hardened suddenly, his mouth parted and breathing ragged. When he spoke, it was from a place I couldn't comprehend. 'I would burn them all, for you. I want you to know that.'

I believed his every word. It frightened and thrilled me. In that moment, Camron beheld more power than my wand. He was my shield, my sword.

'Dryads,' I swore, 'help whoever stands in your way.'

Camron dipped back into my neck. His reply was muffled as he continued devouring me, mouth and tongue. 'You have no idea.'

# CHAPTER 33

The door to Camron's room burst open, shattering the moment like glass over stone.

I supposed, all good things come to an end. Some sooner than others.

Camron dropped his forehead to mine, eyes closed, his body tense beneath my touch.

'This better be worth it,' he growled.

Heat flooded my cheeks. I dared look beyond Camron's shoulder. Because there, at the door, not bothering to divert his eyes, stood the same guard who let me in.

'Spit it out,' Camron shouted so suddenly the blood drained from my face.

'There has been sighting of another dragon, my King.'

It was as though the guard had thrown a pail of water over me. Freezing cold and entirely debilitating. Whereas I couldn't move, Camron shot to action. He pushed from me and stood, half-dressed. My clothes were still on, the jacket pulled partially down one arm, the buttons of my trousers unlopped all but one.

'Where?' I asked, dread coiling through me.

I sat up, panicking as I grasped at my pocket, locating the shape of the wand. Before I could pull it free, I heard a sound that would conjure fear in the dead: an explosive roar sounded beyond the manor, glass vibrating in the windows, walls quaking.

The beast flew above us.

Camron looked at me, fury carved across his handsome face. He grasped my upper arms, his fingers bruising skin. I couldn't contemplate the discomfort as I lost myself to the sudden, boiling desperation that twisted his dark eyes.

'It sounds like we have a visitor.'

We both knew what this meant. 'They came back for *me*.'

'Listen to me, Maximus,' Camron said, tightening his vice-like grip. 'Go to Beatrice, do not stop running until you find her.'

I couldn't believe the words out of his mouth. My attempt to pull away was useless.

'I'm not leaving you—'

The room shook, battered beneath the winds of gargantuan wings. A shadow passed beyond the window, bathing us in darkness, followed by the frozen bite of winter as ice crackled over stone and glass.

'Go!' Camron pushed me from him. The force was so sudden I stumbled to the door. The way Camron looked at me, with intensity that boiled the air between us, kept me rooted to the spot. Until he shouted again, spittle flying out of his mouth. 'Now!'

I stumbled back another step, wanting to tell him I could protect him. All it took was one look in his eyes and I knew it would be wasted.

'You said you would be by my side,' I said.

Camron started to say something, but then shot forward

with viper precision, snatching me into his arms and planting a final kiss upon my mouth. It would've been easier to close my eyes and lose myself to it, but I couldn't deny the unsettled feeling in my chest.

'I'll never leave you, Maximus.' His voice dipped to softer, familiar tones, 'I will *always* be right behind you.'

Then I ran, legs and arms pumping, until Camron and his words were far behind me. With every step panic seized me. All I could think about was the dragon and the destruction it could cause.

Screams exploded behind every closed door. As I passed windows, I tried to get a look, but the dragon moved with such speed it was no more than a smudge across the grey sky.

With every step, I saw the red-scaled monster as it tore Dame apart. One fucking moment, that was all it took. Her blood, her ribbons of torn flesh, the bent spinning wheel of her chair.

Magic drummed through me, hastening me to Beatrice. It quivered in the bricks beside me, the wood of the floor. Even the air sang with it, a different type of magic, hotter, sharper.

By the time I reached Julian's room, I was made more from magic than blood, sinew or bone.

Beatrice was waiting, staff in hand, russet-brown cloak clasped over her shoulders. A satchel hung at her side, bulging with unseen items.

'It's Simion,' Beatrice said the second I entered. It was as though those two words made this all okay.

It didn't.

I almost didn't register her words above the pounding of my heart, distracted by how oddly calm she looked.

My fingers tightened my wand, unable to stop myself from reaching for the cord closest to me. The wall beside me cracked, a slithering line breaking wallpaper and plaster and brick.

'Breathe,' Beatrice said, 'no point in tearing the building down.'

'Simion…' I couldn't get my words past the lump in my throat. Before I could try again, a wave of ice spread across my skull. I pinched my eyes closed, pressing fingers into my temple.

*I had nothing to do with what has happened to your parents.*

The voice was a caress, a soft brush in my mind as though someone stood within it and whispered.

'Listen to him, Maximus.' Beatrice moved to me, a sense of trepidation in the way she regarded me.

Him. *Simion.*

He was in my mind, infecting it with his presence. It was as though he was a thorn, embedded. There was no knowing how Simion did it, how he infiltrated my mind with power I never believed possible.

Simion's voice uncoiled within my mind. *There is so much for you to learn.*

I looked to the window behind Beatrice, the one I had kept open for her to return, just as she had asked for me. Then I blinked, and the dragon made its first attack.

Talons pierced the wall, breaking through it with ease. Black wings beat violently outside, shattering glass, trembling the world as though it was made from parchment. The window disappeared, torn away beneath the force of the dragon.

Cold wind gusted into the room, encasing us both. Beatrice's thick brown curls danced around her head, blocking the view. By the time it stilled, I was able to watch as the sleek, elegant creature dropped the chunk of wall from its talons, wings pounding to keep it aloft.

Unlike the red-scaled dragon, the one before me was pure beauty, but as deadly as the first I had seen—the one Beatrice had killed, and Camron had turned into armour.

A marvel of polished obsidian scales covered its entirety. They glistened as the dragon thrashed its swan-like neck. Two curled horns protruded from its skull, spiralling back like a crown of ivory. It had the face of a wolf, scaled with glowing lavender eyes and frills tracing the length of its powerful body. I was mesmerised as the dragon separated its jaws and loosed a wind-curling growl, flashing rows of sharp, serrated teeth.

Beatrice grasped me, urging me towards the torn-out wall. 'The North didn't send that soldier to kill you. Nor did Simion betray us; he isn't to blame for your parents' capture.'

*I promise, I had nothing to do with this.* Simion's voice echoed his sister's words.

I'd yet to see him, but with some strange certainty I knew he sat upon the dragon's back. Thick leather bindings were wrapped around its sleek torso, tied together with iron clasps, likely holding a saddle of sorts in place.

A wall of raw, frozen honesty slammed into my mind, blacking the world out for a moment.

*I* will *take you to the North and I* will *see your parents returned to you.*

Whatever power he had over me, it moulded my mind until I was convinced. I didn't so much as hear his honesty but felt it, as vicious as the dragon's ice, as pounding as the earthen magic that surrounded me.

'If we do not leave now, the North will see the South levelled. Simion is the last chance. Maximus, we need to leave.' Beatrice gestured to the door at my back, to the people screaming throughout the manor. 'For their sake.'

As it had been since I first discovered the wand in my

hand, I was pulled in all directions. It was impossible to discern what decision was mine, or what was placed upon me by others.

*Quickly*, Simion encouraged.

Beatrice grasped my shoulders, levelling her eyes with mine. 'Forget everything. Forget Simion, the North. Do you trust *me*?'

Her question soured in my mind, churning my stomach into knots. One look at Beatrice and I knew she was prepared to leave, with or without me. The satchel full of supplies, the cloak. I couldn't answer her, not until I filled my mind with a silent question. *If you've lied to me, I will kill you.*

An eery silence followed, stretched out in my mind as I tried to grasp onto the caress of Simion's presence. Just when I believed he hadn't heard, a response came.

*I do not doubt it for a moment.*

Shouts sounded from beyond the room, raised voices, the thunderous stampede of booted feet. Guards. Above it all, I heard Camron as he screamed for blood.

Death waited everywhere. If we didn't leave, blood would spill. Beatrice and Simion, or perhaps Camron. I couldn't face it. I couldn't see anyone else die because of me.

'We get my parents,' I said, looking at Beatrice, knowing the same sentiment thundered through my mind. 'Then I leave with them. I get away from all of this.'

Beatrice looked at me, deep in my eyes. Then she nodded, two firm dips of her head. 'My promise hasn't changed. I stand by you, no matter what we find when we reach the North.'

I believed her, with complete confidence. Beatrice didn't need strange magic to convince me.

The black dragon landed upon the wall of the manor, gripping into the stone for leverage. All at once the cold presence left my mind, signalling Simion's retreat. He had won, he knew he had. But I also knew this was the choice, the right one. If the North had my parents, I would go to them as they wanted.

I faced the door, looking into the corridor beyond and the noise of Camron and his guards getting closer. My fingers drummed across the base of my hand, the cords of power brightening to new peaks as they filled my vision. Filling my mind with my intention, I thrust the wand out before me and watched the corridor crumble. It caved in on itself, stone and mortar piling high, creating a barrier between the room and those who wished to enter it.

As the dust settled, brushing over us in a cloud of grit, Beatrice placed a guiding hand on my shoulder. 'Camron knows you're safe with me.'

Tears prickled in my eyes, blurring my vision for a moment.

'Take me to them,' I said, feeling a weight lift from my shoulders. I spoke of the North; I spoke of my parents. No more would I rely on others for their safety. Jonathan, Camron, Simion. They failed me, each in their own way.

There was only one person I could rely on. Myself.

Beatrice winced, if only for a moment. 'This is the right decision.'

I couldn't tell if she was speaking to me, or herself.

Magic tainted the air, infecting my lungs. Beatrice's eyes glowed with a golden-hued mist. She turned her back on me and lifted her staff before her. Vines came to life, slithering from their place on the crumbled wall. They entwined together, serpents of earth, twisting and solidifying into a bridge, stretching from the broken wall directly to the dragon.

'Together,' Beatrice said from my side.

I afforded myself one look back. The handfasting marks

seemed to shiver on my arm as my thoughts went to Camron. *I will always be right behind you.*

I held onto his promise. I knew, somehow, I would fix this. When I retrieved my parents, dealt with the North and relinquished my wand, my power. I would return.

To *him*.

# PART THREE

## THE LOST MAGE

# CHAPTER 34

I screamed into the blue abyss. It wasn't from fear but freedom and elation. My stomach jolted violently as I peered over the dragon's hulking frame. The ground was so far away. Galloway Forest blurred beneath us, a patchwork of emerald, russet and gold.

There was no room for talking this far from the ground as the winds screeched terribly in my ears. I knew—as everyone did—the sheer size of Galloway Forest, but seeing it from such an angle gave a new impression of how endless it was.

The dragon—Glamora as Beatrice had named her—kept us airborne until the colour-changing sky muted my mind. There was a sense of reunion between the beast and my friend, as though they recognised one another.

Beatrice sat at the front of the leather saddle ahead of me, Simion statuesque at my back.

Hours into our flight and my body ached. The stiffness of the saddle and the numb tingling in my legs only joined in with the rest of my discomforts. Stinging cheeks, ears pinched cold, mouth parched.

There was little warning, besides the shift of Simion at my back, before the dragon changed course.

Bile coated the back of my throat, an acrid sting. I couldn't stop myself from shouting as Glamora contracted her wings into her body, folding them away, allowing us to dive towards the patchwork of the forest's canopy.

Beatrice howled in delight, throwing her arms out on either side of her. I longed to grab them and pull them in. Her hair billowed around her head, thick curls whipping like snakes in the torrents of winds.

The wall of thick green foliage came up so fast I expected to crash right into the trees. Everything was a blur. I gripped tight around Beatrice's waist, feeling the tug of leather straps around my thighs which kept me in place. Somewhere in my panic, I recognised arms around my waist and the press of a face into my back.

As the wall of trees shot towards us, I heard the beast's wings snap out. The sudden jolt snapped my body back, as Glamora caught the wind; the sudden resistance of air slowing our descent.

Steady arms squeezed my waist as the chilling presence of Simion's power brushed across my skull. Even if I wanted to refuse him entry with his strange power, I couldn't. Damian's journal never depicted such an ability, nor did the general knowledge of mages speak of it. As though sensing my thoughts, Simion's voice unfurled in my mind.

*There is much you don't know about us.*

Us. He used the word as though I was a part of it.

*The same could be said for you.*

In a strange way, I felt his humour to my response as though the feeling leeched from him. *I'm sure.*

I glanced back at Galloway Forest. We were so close I could almost reach and touch it. My mind was so quiet, I thought Simion had left it. When he filled my skull with his voice, I didn't bother smothering my disappointment.

*Do you know how the forest got its name?*

Glamora glided over Galloway Forest. Her dragging claws tickled across the reaching branches as we skimmed over the forest like a pebble across a lake. Beatrice looked over her shoulder at me, a smile cut across her face and her brown cheeks glowing with excitement. She showed no signs she heard Simion's voice, which made me wonder if my mind was making it up.

*No, no. I am very much here. Answer the question.*

It was not words that filled my mind, but a visceral feeling of unknowing. Simion must've understood because he continued. When he spoke again, images exploded throughout my mind.

*To understand the home you were taken from, you must know the story behind how it began. This may feel familiar, but once I am finished, you will understand a different perspective of a story the South has spoiled with propaganda and lies.*

*There was once a human and a dryad who fell in love. When the moon took its place in the sky and the sun bid farewell for another day, the man would run into the forest to greet his beloved. Night after night he would return, sharing tales of his day and listening to the songs the dryad had to share. Trust blossomed like spring flowers between them. As a gift, the dryad gave him something to represent her love. She couldn't give her heart, for without it she would perish, so, instead, the dryad gave him a piece of her that he could always carry with him. A reminder, during the long days they were separated. In his hand, it looked no more than a mundane piece of wood. But in truth, it was far more. It was imbued with the magic of the dryad, and the man came to know of it as the first amplifier.*

I saw flashes of colour in my mind. Simion blinded my

senses and replaced it with his own. As he continued, his voice lulled me, the world seemed to slip away.

*Miracles occurred in the South. Harvests flourished, crops grew healthy and full. People from all over came to see the man and his spectacle. Yet not all showed him such respect and awe. Some grew jealous of his power. They starved for it. A group, small but mighty, held resentment in their hearts. Burning, hot, evil jealousy. One night, when the moon hid beneath the clouds, unable to watch the coming horror, the jealous four followed the man into the wood to witness the origin of his power. When they found the man with his lover, they ambushed them.*

*Blood was spilled.*

I tore myself away from the vivid images Simion's tale painted in my mind. It was familiar, but different. Thirsting for more, I urged him to continue with a single thought.

He obliged without hesitation.

*As death came to claim the man, the dryad contested. Using her power, before the eyes of the jealous four, she gave up her life and encased them both—a sacrifice of her love. You have come to know their tomb as the Heart Oak. In truth, it is one of the terms the North and South share. From that point on, the jealous four cut their palms and bled upon the tree. In a twist of cruel fate, they claimed it for their own. From that night, the jealous four took offerings from the Heart Oak and claimed the power they longed for so desperately.*

'Gathrax, Calzmir, Zendina, Romar.' I listed the family names aloud, each one snatched by the tearing torrents of wind.

*His name, the Dryad's love, was Galloway. The forest was named after their story, a story that has been forgotten purposefully.*

A shiver raced across my neck as Simion leaned in, his power fading from my mind in a single, draining rush. 'They stole a power that never belonged to them.'

Relief flooded through me when Simion leaned away. It

was short-lived as Glamora expelled a roar, a flock of birds fleeing in fear. The dragon's wings flapped like the sails of a ship, catching the wind as she slowly lowered. It circled a clearing beneath us, expelling a few more sky-shattering calls that sang with warning.

By the time Glamora landed in the clearing, the powerful beat of her limbs had caused the trees on all sides to bow and bend. All I could hear was snapping branches, until her claws sunk into the clearing and the world finally stopped moving.

'That wasn't so bad, was it?' Simion's deep voice rumbled behind me.

'It was *incredible*,' Beatrice replied, shoulders heaving with each breath.

'Get—me—off.' My words came out, broken and breathless.

'Oh, come on. You get used to—'

'Now,' I demanded, feeling my entire body tremble violently.

Simion grunted as he lifted both legs to one side of Glamora's back and slid down the length of her extended wing. As he stood on the ground, he made sure to pat the dragon's hide in thanks as he surveyed the clearing around us.

It was modest in size. All around us, walls of thick oak and towering pine devoured the views beyond. Between the trunks all I could see was shadow. Even though the sky above still harboured the light of early dusk, inside the forest it was as night had already claimed Aldian.

'This will do for the night,' Simion said. 'Me and Glamora have spent days flying North, then back to you with little time for rest. Glamora needs to feed before we even think about continuing.'

'We shouldn't have stopped until sundown,' Beatrice said

from her perch on Glamora's neck. 'Camron *will* come after us.'

'No,' Simion corrected as his amber eyes darkened. 'He will come for *him*, and he would be a fool to do so. I told you, Glamora needs to feed. If Camron is foolish to follow, Glamora will eat well.'

I swallowed the urge to speak on Camron's behalf, to offer Simion a warning in response to his.

'Underestimating him would not be wise, brother.' Beatrice shot him a look which could've flayed skin.

Simion stiffened. It was clear whose side Beatrice was on.

'It is done,' Simion replied, gazing to his sister with a look of sadness. 'One night, Bea, then you are home.'

It didn't take much for me to notice something unsaid between them.

'The longer we waste, the longer I'm kept from my parents,' I said. 'I want to go.'

'There are many things I want, and a belly full of food and a well-rested body are two of them,' Simion replied, brows furrowed as he regarded me.

My body trembled, exhausted and emotional. 'Fuck that. You either take me to the North or...'

'Or what?' Simion snapped through a laugh. He leaned on his hip, large hand resting for leverage. 'If the North wanted them dead, they would be. Trust they are being kept alive for a reason.'

Heat rose in my face, blood thundering with a captive storm.

'Simion,' Beatrice scolded, 'be considerate.'

He paused, shifting his stare between us both. Simion then stepped forward and extended a hand. I studied his offering as though it was a viper. There was no way I was accepting his help to get off the dragon.

Simion pouted, stepped back and gestured dramatically. 'Go ahead, I'd love to see this.'

I didn't dismount with the same grace as Simion, but I also didn't fall like some fool. Taking my time, I slid down Glamora's side, using the twisted bones and horns that protruded from her scales as leverage. It was only when my feet met the soft texture of her wings that I lost my grip and fell the rest of the way.

'Certain I cannot help?' Simion stood above me; his hand outstretched once again. My cheeks blossomed with heat as I regarded him from my place on the ground. Pine needles dug into my palms as my fingers curled into claws.

I battered him away. 'Fuck off.'

Simion smiled to himself. 'So be it.'

I stood, dusting the debris from my trousers. My back and neck were stiff, my legs awkward as I took a few steps around the clearing.

'Sky legs,' Beatrice called out. She had dismounted and stood by her brother's side. 'How your bones feel like jelly, we call it sky legs. You get used to it, over time.'

Glamora lifted her onyx-scaled neck from the bed of the forest floor and turned it around to face me. She was just beyond Beatrice and Simion's shoulders, and I couldn't help but feel as though she was smiling at my discomfort.

'Shall we get this fire going?' Beatrice clapped, side-eyeing both me and her brother. I admired her attempt to ease the tension between us. 'It would be good to get some light before night truly settles—it will be the only thing deterring unwanted visitors from... visiting.'

# CHAPTER 35

We navigated the dark forest in silence. Over half a day away from Camron and the estate, it was abundant. Untouched. Unspoiled.

As I moved around monstrous tree trunks, whose roots devoured the very ground, I could not help but feel we had been the only people to ever walk here. In the shadows of the trees, the forest felt ancient. The air was thicker, and the sounds muffled.

'I do *not* trust you, Simion. I want that to be clear.'

He hadn't objected when I offered to help him gather kindling for the fire. It wasn't that I longed to spend time with him, but he held answers even Beatrice couldn't give me.

'And I am sorry if you think I care,' Simion replied, sharp as a blade.

I bit into my lower lip, fighting the urge to pull my wand free. 'You went North and suddenly my parents were taken. Seems strange, the timing.'

'Then you also believe I am to blame for your attempted murder?' His question caught me off guard, stifling me. 'Since you are so confident your mind has been made up, care to explain to me why I would assist in such a way, knowing you are the only thing keeping my sister from me. From her home. If you die, my sister fails. Her task isn't over yet. She needs you, so I need you. Alive, preferably.'

Until Simion had put it so plainly into words, I hadn't thought about it like that.

'Because her *task* is to return me to the North.'

'Exactly. Perhaps it is my turn to ask you a question,' Simion said, snatching branches and twigs from the ground.

'Depends on what you want to know,' I replied, putting myself to work. Only moments after leaving Beatrice, I was beginning to regret joining Simion. It was clear my presence displeased him, which was a feeling mutually shared.

A feeling which hadn't always been the case.

There had been a time when his presence offered me comfort. No matter what I thought of Simion, I couldn't forget that.

'Beatrice, what is she like?' he asked, diverting the conversation.

I paused. 'She's your sister. If anyone knows her, it would be you.'

Simion didn't look at me. He busied his hands, collecting wood. 'I don't know her. Not in the way you might believe. Since she was exiled from our home so many years ago, it is hard to believe it was even during this life. The girl I knew was... different. The woman I see now—she's a stranger.'

'Is this lesson supposed to remind me just how unkind the North is? Because if so, don't waste your breath.'

Simion shot me a sharp look. There was something comforting about seeing his dislike for me. In the moments when it was gone, I grew too comfortable with his presence.

'You *are* to blame,' he said. 'Your presence tore my family apart. If anyone understands hate, it is me. My one and only sister sent from her home for something that had little to do with her.'

'Is that resentment I see in your eyes, Simion?' I snapped, as my fists balled at my sides.

Simion stood deadly still as he regarded me. When he spoke, it wasn't with a plain response, although I felt like it was answer enough. 'You were her duty. To find the lost mage and return him. It was a task given to Beatrice, and if, and only if, she completed it, could she reclaim her place in the North.'

'Then it is done. I'm here, aren't I?'

Simion expelled a shaking breath. 'Not until we pass into Northern lands. But we are close.'

I turned my back on him, unable to look at the gleam in his eyes. Gone was the man who had offered me comfort, gone was the man who promised to help me. All this time, it was never me he wished to aid. He simply wanted to get me North, so Beatrice could finally return.

There was a brush of ice in my mind, followed by the caress of Simion's presence. *I'm sorry. This isn't your fault. I spoke out of line.*

'No,' I replied. 'You said what was on your mind.'

Part of me wished to remind Simion that I wouldn't be his problem for long. Soon he could have his family, and I could have mine.

'It has been a long few days,' Simion added, softer this time. *It is no excuse for me to talk to you in such a way.*

'Where is your mage-mark?' I asked, diverting the conversation. 'You must have one to be able to infect my mind the way you do? What power is it, what else do I need to know before we reach the North?' I peered at him over my shoulder.

'Our mage-marks are given at birth,' Simion said, tugging

down the collar of his shirt to reveal his chest. In the faded light, I could make out the leather cord tied around his neck, a wooden carved dragon dangling between the curves of his stone-hard chest. Then I saw the mage-mark. The three inter-linking circles of raised flesh rested over his heart.

I wanted to step closer and inspect it, but Simion released his collar and the mage-mark disappeared.

'In the North, our mage-marks aren't displayed on our palms. That is a Southern custom—as is the choice of an amplifier being used in the design of a wand. When we are born, we are gifted our marks above our hearts. You've never seen Beatrice's mark because she's never found it necessary to show you.'

Simion was right. I'd never seen Beatrice in anything but her blacksmith leathers or high-necked tunics. 'And what of her staff?'

'Her *amplifier*,' Simion corrected, 'was kept from her. I had it. When you first revealed yourself, I was the first to come South, with Glamora. I brought it with me.'

'You're telling me there was a dragon in the South this entire time?' I asked.

'Galloway Forest hides many secrets. Believe it or not, dragons are not the blood-thirsty creatures your history paints them to be.'

Dame's death filled my mind once again.

'Fifteen winters,' Simion said through gritted teeth, breaking the silence. Suddenly inches from me, he stared down at me with his large, brass-gold eyes. The pile of kindling was no more than an afterthought, dropped at his feet. 'Fifteen years I was kept from her.'

'You can blame me,' I said, 'but I had no knowledge of what I was. Or what I caused.'

Simion's breathing was laboured. His chest rose and fell so rapidly I almost reached out and placed a hand upon it.

'Your eyes,' he said. 'They're green as the forest, just like your mother's. The eyes of a traitor.'

I shook my head, unable to hold his stare. 'Then why punish Beatrice if my mother is to blame for taking me away?'

Simion exhaled slowly. 'My mother assisted in your *abduction*. If my mother was kept around long enough to serve punishment, she would've been. But the North thought it better to send a child—my little sister.'

His words settled across me like ash. 'Your mother died?'

'Exiled, but unlike Beatrice it wasn't to the South. It was from Aldian.' Simion said, mind haunted by painful memories. I saw his struggle in the widening of his eyes, the paling of his skin. 'I don't even know if she's still alive. In a way, after years of never hearing from her, I hope she is dead. It would be a good enough excuse as to why she never fought her way home.'

Everything clicked into place.

'Now I understand why you hate me.'

Simion recoiled from my words, lips parting slightly. 'I don't hate you, Maximus.'

'Your eyes say otherwise.'

'You were nothing but a child when you were taken,' Simion replied. 'It was many years before the inquisition discovered my mother's involvement and dealt her fate.'

'Why?' The single word hung between us.

'Be more specific,' Simion growled.

'Why was I taken away?'

Simion took a moment to reply. 'I cannot answer that.'

'Cannot or will not?'

'Both. I don't know the reasoning behind your mother's actions. Which proposes something else I cannot understand.'

There was something about his expression which tightened my chest. 'What?'

'Why would the North take your mother when she is not welcome back?'

'To use them, to get to me,' I said, overwhelmed by all this talk of murder and punishment. It cemented just how cruel the North were.

Simion held my stare, although I knew he didn't have the answers I required. 'Seems strange.'

'If they're harmed…' I growled, my magic purring deep in the bowels of my stomach. 'The North will never get what they want from me.'

Simion's face softened, the lines around his pursed lips and narrowed eyes smoothing out. 'Which is why I am confident they will be safe.'

'You said the Queen didn't give the orders to have me killed,' I said, 'but that didn't stop the soldier from trying. What's to say there aren't others willing to ignore orders? Maybe same people have my parents?'

I hadn't thought about it until now. The prospect poisoned my mind, sinking talons into it with vigour.

There was something Simion wasn't saying; I recognised it when he looked away as he replied. 'Until we reach the North, we will not know.'

'Teach me about them,' I said, reaching for the wand in my pocket. The brush of solid wood against my sweat-slick palm was calming. Knowledge was power, I knew that. But magic was magic, and I needed it.

The North were dangerous. Monsters who punished children. Monsters who tore families apart.

'What would you like your third lesson to be?'

A smile creased across my face. I withdrew my wand and

pointed it directly at Simion. He flinched, slowly raising hands up at his sides, regarding me with wide, pleading eyes.

'Don't do anything you might regret.'

Peering down the length of my wand, I studied Simion as my magic flooded through me. The forest came alive with breath, life and, most importantly, power.

'Magic,' I snapped the word in demand. 'Teach me. Not from the perspective of Southern journals. Teach me to enter minds, teach me the power you have. I want it all.'

# CHAPTER 36

Simion stiffened beneath the point of my wand. Whilst his gold eyes twisted with defiance, I caught slight signs of hesitation. He couldn't hide it from me. The frantic flickering of his gaze and the way his fingers didn't stop shaking. I may not have known control, but it seemed my erratic ability had its purpose.

'If it's a duel you seek, you are wasting your time with me.'

I flicked my wand in warning. 'Do I scare you?'

'Understanding one's own strength, and matching it to an enemy, is not a display of fear. There would be no point fighting you because you *would* win.'

Pride twisted my gut. 'You're a mage, are you not?'

Simion lowered his arms to his side, refusing to look away from me. 'Yes. But you harm, and I heal.'

I swallowed the discomfort of his words. *You harm.* 'And yet you can walk through my mind. What ability would that fall under—control?'

'Lower your amplifier, Maximus.'

I didn't, at least not straight away. I flicked it at him,

delighting in the step Simion took back. I slipped it back into my pocket, the shimmering cords fading from sight.

'How do you do it?' I asked, feeling somewhat bare beneath Simion's amber stare. 'The mind-speak.'

'Mind-speak,' Simion repeated. 'I haven't heard it called that before. I like it.'

'Answer me.' It was so simple to slip back into the tone of Julian Gathrax. It had almost become too familiar.

Simion lifted a single brow. 'I'm what is known as a gleamer in the North. It is a term given to the Children of the Forest who are gifted with passive abilities. Healing, telepathy and empathy-based magic. Abilities better-suited behind the lines of war.'

Damian's journal hadn't depicted such a power before. 'Where is your… amplifier?'

Simion's full lips lifted into a sly smile. 'So, you are learning.'

He reached for his collar, but this time he didn't pull it down. Instead, he threaded his finger beneath the leather cord and fished out the necklace from beneath his shirt. Once it was free, he pinched the wooden symbol of the dragon and held it up.

'I carved it when I was old enough to hold a knife.' Simion twisted the symbol around so I could see the rushed markings and messy design. 'It is customary for a mage to claim their own amplifier and craft it. It's said to solidify the bond between the magic and its wielder.'

'But the Heart Oak was destroyed.'

'Then how is it you are holding an amplifier, Maximus? Because you are right, your Heart Oak was burned to nothing but a husk. In the North, we have our own. Did your mother give it to you?'

A chill raced across my shoulders. 'I found it.'

'Found it?' Simion said through a forced laugh. 'Impossible. I get you want to protect your family, but pretending it wasn't given to you is a ridiculous attempt at dishonesty.'

The skin across my palm shivered. Even if Simion didn't believe me, I *did* find this wand. Or it found me, when I needed its protection and power the most. 'Then it doesn't matter if you believe me or not.'

Simion screwed his mouth, running strong fingers across the length of his perfectly carved jaw. 'Regardless of who gave it to you, without your amplifier you cannot access your potential.'

'Then if you're a gleamer, what am I?' I asked, not wanting to continue the conversation about my wand.

'You and Beatrice are what is referred to as a battlemage. Your abilities are physical in their manifestation, one of the three titles the North gives to its mages. You could tear the ground in two—some can pull lightning from a cloudless sky, a gift to children blessed by *Oribon*.'

'That name...' Oribon, it filled my mind, each echo reminding me of how familiar it was. I blinked and was back in Gathrax town, standing down the soldier who came to kill me. '*He* said it, the soldier who attacked me. He said I was blessed.'

'It is a crime your mother kept you in the dark for so long,' Simion said plainly. 'Oribon is the oldest known dragon. God of the sky. As the dryads represent the element of earth, the dragons represent its sister, air. It isn't known why Oribon chooses to bless certain children over others, but those who experience his breath can call upon the storms, can bond with a dragon, uniting human and beast, as one.'

Every inch of my skin buzzed with energy. At some point I had stopped listening to Simion, focused solely on one detail.

'I can bond with a dragon?' The thought was both thrilling and horrifying in equal measure.

'There is a potential, Council willing.'

'You said there were three...' I urged, wanting more, thirsting for the knowledge Simion could offer me.

'Yes, there are three types of mages. Elder is the third title given to a mage who has the abilities of both a gleamer and battlemage, although their kind is as rare as the dryads themselves.'

The darkening forest faded around me. 'There is so much...'

'You didn't know?' Simion finished for me. 'In Wycombe there is a school, a place where those with access to magic are sent to learn and train their abilities. You would do well to complete a term at Saylam Academy, it may even quench your thirst for a duel.'

My mind couldn't comprehend a school for mages, let alone a city with a name. Beyond Galloway Forest, I'd only ever known the land above it as the North. It was a nameless, dangerous place and yet it had a name.

'Yet they murder, punish and steal. The North is no different to the South.'

'You've mistaken me, Max. I never alluded to them being any kinder of a place,' Simion said, tilting his head.

'What's your point?'

Simion took a step towards me, and I took one forward as well. 'You tell me.'

My back stiffened. 'You seem to know so much about what I have been through. Then you should also know what happened to those who wished to control me.'

'Yes,' Simion said plainly. 'You kill them. To me, that sounds like you are no different. I'd go so far as to say you'd fit in well.'

The wand was back in my hand, all without a thought. This time Simion didn't flinch away. He stepped into it, the tip of my wand digging into his hard chest.

Simion's power slithered at the back of my mind, reminding me he was there. Ready and waiting. *I would be careful, Maximus. There are people North of Galloway Forest who will smite you down the second they catch wind of the hateful intent that occupies this mind of yours.*

'Get *out* of my head,' I hissed, feeling the ground swell beneath my feet as I called upon the instinctual power.

'You're untrained. Sloppy.'

'Fuck you,' I spat at his feet. 'Fuck you and fuck the North. Fuck your schools and battlemages and dragons.'

There was no hiding the slight smirk across Simion's face. He was enjoying this.

'My mother and father,' I sneered, 'they did it for a reason.'

Simion's smile faltered. 'The man you call Father had nothing to do with it.'

'What did you just say?' The words came out as a breathless gasp. It was as though Simion had slammed his fist into my gut.

'Nothing.' Regret crept across Simion's face, hidden only when he turned away.

I raced forward, grasping hold of Simion's upper arm. I spun him around to face me.

'Don't you dare walk away,' I sneered, ire burning hot throughout me. 'What do you mean *the man I call my father?*'

For the first time since our altercation, Simion didn't smile at me. He didn't frown or glower. His face was smooth and his eyes heavy with sorrow. 'I'm sorry, I—'

I slammed my palms into his chest, feeling the force vibrate through my bones. 'Stop apologising for your words. Say them, with your chest. Stop being weak.'

Simion shook his head. 'It isn't for me to say.'

'Pathetic,' I shouted, desperation fuelling me as it pieced details together in my mind.

The Northern soldier had blamed my mother. *Your bitch mother.* His words thundered through my mind. Every time Simion had referred to my abduction from the North, it was always my mother he mentioned.

Never my father. Why?

'He is not from the North,' Simion said, brows furrowing.

'But... but that doesn't make sense.'

Simion's eyes glimmered in the dusk of the forest. Everything was deathly quiet; I could hear his heartbeat as well as mine.

'He is not your father, Maximus.'

'No,' I laughed, feeling a strange swell across my chest. 'You're lying, of course he is.'

Just as Simion had done back at the manor, he didn't simply slip into my mind, he pushed his emotions in. There was no hiding from the truth as my body boiled with his honesty.

'Max,' Simion said, 'I think you should get some rest whilst you can.'

'I'm not going anywhere until you explain—'

'Maximus,' Simion interrupted, so close to me he had to look down his nose to regard me. 'He can tell you himself when we get to the North and find them. I'm sorry, I don't think before I speak, and I shouldn't have...' He sagged forward, as though guilt weighed heavy on his shoulders.

I pushed away from him, head thundering. It was as though Simion had taken a knife to my stomach and gutted me. Except it was not a blade which buried, soul deep, inside of me. It was his words. Words which haunted me as I left

him, words which repeated over in my mind, growing louder
and louder the more distance I put between us.

*He is not your father.*

# CHAPTER 37

Tears burned in the corners of my eyes, cutting silently down my cheeks as I faced the dark. I tried everything I could not to sob audibly, not wishing to draw unwanted attention.

It had been two long hours since Simion had spoken five words that tore my world apart, and I'd barely held myself together. I found it easier to keep quiet, as Beatrice skinned the rabbit she'd caught, then roasted it over a bundle of burning twigs and served it up. I knew she sensed the tension, but not once did she question it.

Had she known? All this time, whilst she concealed part of her life, did she keep this from me?

Simion didn't bother to converse, which I was thankful for. Once he'd finished the bland chewy bits of meat, he'd rolled over on his draped cloak and hadn't moved since. I didn't have much of an appetite, but in the spirit of not wanting to draw attention to myself, I finished what I could, followed Simion's lead and found a spot beside the fire to sleep. I used the cloak and laid it out across the pine needles. As my tears finally flowed free, I rolled over and faked sleep.

The warmth from the fire barely reached me. It only teased me in moments of comfort before dissipating in a cold breeze. I brought my knees to my chest and held on for dear life—hoping the little heat left in my body would not leave, unsuccessfully.

Simion didn't seem to share in my struggle. My resentment for him peaked as I heard gentle snores emanating from his direction. How could he rest after being the sole reason my world felt as though it was crumbling around me?

Galloway Forest was a place of deafening silence. The fire at my back cast my shadow across the wall of trees before me, whereas the rest of the world was engulfed in darkness.

I focused on the flickering light, willing it to take my mind off my father. Perhaps it was the glow of flames that brought Camron to mind, but suddenly I was transported to my bedroom in my family's quarters, to my drunken night when I practically begged Camron for a distraction.

I could've done with a firm drink and even firmer hands, to distract me.

Being lost to the memory didn't last long as Simion's snore peaked into a breathless choke and the warmth of the memory dissipated.

*Simion lied to me. He blamed me for his sister's and mother's respective exile and wished to cause me pain because of it.*

I rolled over carefully, not wishing to ruin the quiet across our camp. I hadn't heard a sound from Beatrice in a while.

As soon as I rested on my ache-free shoulder, I found that she wasn't sleeping at all. Beatrice sat beyond the flames, staring at something pinched between her fingers. I first thought it was a bone, left from the rabbit's carcass. I blinked, unsure how a bone could reflect the flames. The orange-gold light glowed across her tawny skin, casting harsh shadows across her lower face whilst catching in her eyes—eyes that suddenly raised to me.

'You're awake,' Beatrice said, almost surprised. Whatever she held before the fire was quickly placed into the folds of her russet cloak—a feather. I recognised it just before it was taken from view.

'Can't sleep either?' I asked, cheeks warming as Beatrice recognised the tears upon them.

She gripped her staff and the darkness shifted behind Beatrice, as though she controlled it. The sudden change unnerved me, until I realised it was not some unknown power she possessed, but a dragon. Glamora was almost invisible, her obsidian armoured body curled in a ball, scales drinking in the light of the campfire. For such a big creature, she had the ability to blend in and become almost forgettable. A word I never imagined would be tied to such a creature.

'Galloway Forest can be an unforgiving place. There are dangers lurking in the shadows,' Beatrice replied. 'I thought I'd stay up, keep a watch, so you can sleep.'

I leaned up my elbows, feeling the ache of muscles screech across my back. 'Want some company?'

Beatrice nodded; a crease of worry etched over her brow. 'You're crying.'

I drew my sleeve up and cleared my damp cheeks. Beatrice produced a waterskin from her belt and held it towards me in offering. 'There's no need to hide those emotions from me. I know you, Max.'

I eyed the waterskin suspiciously.

'It's strong,' Beatrice confirmed, shaking it.

'I should've known,' I replied, fighting the urge to smile. Beatrice liked a drink as much as I did.

I pushed myself up, snatched the cloak Beatrice had given me and drew it back around my shoulders to fend off the chill.

As I joined her, she shuffled over, patting the ground in welcome. I couldn't ignore the gleam of hope in her eyes, it caught the glow of light and sparked with it.

'You can do the honours,' she said, passing the waterskin into my numb fingers, 'just make sure you save me some.'

I thanked her with a pathetic grin, took her offering and lifted the neck of the waterskin to my lips. Tipping it, head cocked back, I downed the contents in a hearty mouthful. Alcohol burned down my throat, spreading a new type of warmth throughout my innards. I hissed out through my teeth, feeling as though I was moments from breathing fire. Glamora reacted to the noise, shifting at our backs, the ridges of horns down her spine rippling like the surface of a lake.

'What's in this?' I said, as the burning soothed to a numbing caress. 'Wytchfire?'

'Scorches your insides, just like a good spirit should,' Beatrice agreed with my sentiment, snatching the waterskin and taking a swig for herself. She hardly reacted, only blinking rapidly a couple of times. 'Burns like a bitch, but dryads, it's refreshing.'

It was so easy to slip back into our old ways together. Before the lies came out in the light. In moments like this, it was as though there was no mistruths between us, which was all well and good until they came flooding back tenfold.

Beatrice shuffled beside me until her arm pressed into mine.

'Just because you love your parents does not mean you have to like them,' Beatrice said softly.

I didn't take my eyes off the flickering flames as I replied. 'So Simion told you?'

'He didn't have to. Simion means well, I want you to know that. Even in the years that I have not been with him, his bashful sincerity has never changed. I don't remember much before I was exiled, but one thing I couldn't forget is Simion's tendency to speak before contemplating the consequences.'

Beatrice handed me the waterskin again. I took it gladly.

'*They* lied to me. All my life my mother kept the truth locked up and my…' I choked on the word. Only another swig of the spirit had the power to clear my throat enough for me to say it. 'My father isn't my father at all.'

I longed for Beatrice to tell me I was wrong.

She didn't.

'I've come to learn that it's best not to dwell on the actions of others, even if it affects the course of your own life. Trust me, Max. I've been angry for a long time. I resented my mother and wished she never even had that title. It would be lying to say I didn't spend my first years waiting for her to find her way back to me. To save me and make this all right again. But, alas…'

'Maybe something stopped her?'

Beatrice shrugged. 'Sometimes, those closest to us act in ways we could never comprehend, but it is important we give them the chance to explain.'

It was Beatrice's turn to find the comfort of a drink. Her fingers were cold as I took them in my hand and wrapped them around the neck of the waterskin. 'Do you think the pain you've experienced would mean something if you had the chance to speak to your mother?'

'I'll never know.' Beatrice stiffened, gaze lost to the fire. 'She is gone, Max.'

'Nothing is ever simply gone…'

Beatrice knocked her shoulder into mine. 'If I understood why my mother did what she did, would it have made my experience any different? Maybe it would've eased my life if I understood her reasonings. But, unfortunately, those are childish hopes and dreams. I cannot ever speak with my mother again, that opportunity was taken from me. But you, you can speak to your father, allow him to explain. Maybe then you will see through your hurt and understand.'

No matter how calmly Beatrice spoke, I sensed an anger beneath her words.

'How can you not hate me?' The question burst out of me. 'You were punished for something you had no part in. How can you bear to look at me, knowing what my life has caused you?'

Beatrice's eyes widened in horror. 'I hate what you represent, but not you. Never you.'

I swallowed the lump embedded in my throat. 'If it helps to hear it, I'm sorry.'

Beatrice leaned into me and rested her head on my shoulder. It was a position we were familiar with—comforting and close.

'I wish it wasn't you, you know. You were one of the few people I dared to allow myself to get close to. Perhaps I knew deep down that there was something different about you. Or familiar, I should say.'

'Well,' I said, taking a deep breath until my lungs were filled with charred wood and ash. 'I wouldn't change a thing.'

'You know what,' Beatrice whispered. 'Neither would I. In a way, I wish we were still back in Gathrax, with nothing but blissful ignorance between us. I can't tell you what I would give for that to be real.'

'I thought you'd be happy to finally be going home?'

'Home.' Beatrice spat the word out. 'I'm not sure I would call Wycombe home. I've always dreamt of returning, but now it's my reality, I'm not so sure. Home isn't a place, it's a people. And the home I carved for myself in the South was full of far more comforts than I remembered from before.'

Simion stirred and we stopped speaking. We watched, still

as rabbits beneath the glare of a hunter, as Simion rolled onto his side and faced us. The glow of the campfire licked across his handsome face.

'He is my home,' Beatrice whispered. 'Out of everything I have been through, all the days, weeks, months and years that passed since the North sent me away, *he* is family, but—you are my family too, Max.' She paused. 'I admit, for a moment, I allowed myself to imagine us carving a better life in the North. It was the only concept that made returning bearable. Now, after what they've done, I'm not so sure.'

I gripped her hand and squeezed. I longed to tell her it was possible, but how could I stay in a place whose rulers used my parents as bait? How could I tell Beatrice that the silver marks on my arm, the ones that bound me to Camron, gave me a sense of a future I never imagined possible?

'What is it *you* want, Max?'

I opened my mouth to answer, only to realise it was a question I had not been asked before. It had always been assumed—even by me.

'Answers,' I admitted. 'Answers… from my parents. I want to hear the truth, all of it. I want to hear it from their mouths, no one else.'

I released Beatrice's hand, reached into my jacket pocket, and pulled the wand from the holder. The flames illuminated the dark twisted wood and the three death marks at its base. 'They kept me from this. I must believe they did it for a reason, Bea.'

Beatrice reached out and ran her fingers over the hand-fasting marks across the back of my hand.

'And this?' she asked. 'If given the choice to break the bond, would you take it?'

'Are you offering to kill Camron again?' The thought churned my stomach.

'No, because I believe Camron wants what is best for you.'

'You sound certain,' I replied, side-eyeing her.

Her fingers brushed over the folds of her cloak, an uncon-scious action. 'We have spent enough time around terrible people to know when one of the good ones come along. Camron is willing to go to war for you, not because of what you can give him, but what he can give you.'

*I would burn them all.* My chest warmed as Camron's words coiled through me.

'I want to be able to choose my future, not have it decided for me.'

'*Only in death shall you part,*' Beatrice recited the same words Jonathan spoke during the handfasting ceremony. 'Until one of you dies, your union is unbreakable. Going against such ancient magic will destroy you.'

How could I tell her that isn't what I meant? Just the thought of Camron dying tore me apart. It was a terrifying weakness.

'I've come North because I don't want Camron to send an army,' I said, feeling the swell of disdain towards magic rise within me. 'I don't want anyone else to die in my name.'

'My noble friend, I knew I liked you.'

'How did you do it?' I asked.

'Do what?'

'Survive,' I said. 'We both know how unforgiving the South can be, yet you conquered it alone, and so young.'

A sadness drew down Beatrice's face. 'We're similar, Max. We both survived. I remember when it happened. Not in a matter of words and actions, but in a feeling of being exiled from a place I felt safe in. Do you know my mother was kept in Wycombe until she knew I was being exiled because of her? She was thrown out of Aldian knowing her actions had affected me—a child who'd barely seen ten winters. I was taken by the Council and discarded in the heart of Galloway Forest. A place no different to this. After days of travel and sleeping in clearings, much like this, it was the Calzmir Estate I found myself in. From then, it was all a blur. Someone found me and dropped me in an orphanage until I was old enough to leave by myself. I looked for the lost mage for a couple of years—searching for signs or news of someone with magic. I knew the person would have been around my age, but the South is a big place. I settled in the Gathrax Estate when I gave up. Took up a job with the local smithy and quickly settled into a new life. I was tired, very tired of having to search for you. I survived because I chose between finding a way back home or carving a new one. You know what decision I made.'

Beatrice spilled her heart out before me, tears pooling in her wide eyes before falling down her beautiful, grief-stricken face.

'I'm sorry,' I said. 'For what you have been through because of me. Because of my family.'

'I don't blame you,' Beatrice said, before taking a gargantuan gulp from the waterskin. 'We're both products of our parents' actions. If anyone deserves the blame, it is them.'

Clearing her tears with the back of her hand, she added, 'I regret to say we are out of alcohol.'

I shot her a look that caused her to splutter with a laugh. 'Dryads, how dare you!'

She knocked her shoulders into mine and I returned with a tap of my own.

There was one final question I longed to ask her, something which plagued my mind since she had asked me the very same thing. 'What is it you want, Bea?'

Beatrice smiled, but it didn't reach her eyes. There was something she couldn't conceal from me, a power I had only seen in glimpses. Amongst her grief, there was anger. Unspent vehemence.

'You should get some rest,' Beatrice said, ignoring my question, although her eyes seemed to answer it for me. 'We leave at first light.'

Her refusal was answer enough. Suddenly, I had another reason for wanting to find my parents. It wasn't only to see that they were safe from harm, and to get the answers I deserved.

I needed them to apologise for ripping Beatrice's life apart.

# CHAPTER 38

Flying on dragon-back was *not* the cure for a hangover. Every dip in height and sudden jolt as Glamora navigated the torrents of wind, I thought I'd vomit. Beatrice suffered too. Although she rode up front, her fingers were practically forged into her temple. Even her multitude of groans and moans could be heard above the roaring sky.

Simion was sat, ridged, at my back. He'd not spoken a word to me. Even with Beatrice, Simion seemed to bite his tongue. He had no right to ignore me; it wasn't a luxury I had, as his arms wrapped around my waist whilst we glided through the sky.

The threat of bad weather held off, but there were more clouds than yesterday. It made viewing the expansive wood below us almost impossible. Glamora kept above the cloud line, her wings steady and stretched out beside her. The sun beat down on us, casting Glamora's impressive shadow across the sea of clouds, her mace-like tail disturbing them as she dipped and weaved.

I was becoming accustomed to the chill this high up; how

it stung at my cheeks and had my eyes streaming. I'd not felt this awake in weeks.

It was hours into our travel when the frozen brush of power tickled the back of my skull. I knew what it meant before the voice followed.

*Maximus.*

I stiffened as my name sang through my skull. There was no knowing how I could keep Simion out, and he knew it. But that didn't stop me from ignoring him, pretending he had not infected my mind.

*Maximus.* It came again, louder. Sharper.

Winds ripped at my hair as I peered over my shoulder. Simion was already looking at me, an expectant glint in his eye.

I gathered my response, choosing each word and forcing them out towards the cold presence of Simion's power. My inner voice was broken and awkward, but the emotion behind it was clear. *I preferred it when we ignored each other.*

*I'm sure you did, but there is something I want you to see.*

It was a strange feeling, to have someone else invade your mind. Panic clawed at the thought of what Simion would find—

*Don't worry, I'm not prying. Simply speaking.*

Before I could answer, Glamora changed course. She angled the front of her wings down and dove her long neck through the ocean of cloud. I held my breath as the wall of silver raced up to greet us. As we passed through, the clouds left a sheen of moisture across my face. Only once the dense rush of air passed did I dare open my eyes again.

Simion's presence in my mind retreated. He didn't need to tell me what he wanted me to see.

I smelled it. One inhale and my nose filled with the acrid scent of burning.

The centre of the Galloway Forest was a large clearing; charred and black. Void of life. A graveyard of wood and ash, as if a star had fallen from the sky and landed, leaving nothing in its wake. I knew I looked upon the Heart Oak, I'd seen enough paintings of it, heard enough stories.

Surrounded by blackened ground was the skeletal corpse of a tree that spanned far larger and taller than any I'd seen before. For miles around it, there was nothing but destruction.

Unlike before, I had a new perspective of the place. This was where the dryad and her lover had forever entombed themselves from their enemies. It was a graveyard. The very place the first mages from the four ruling estates came to reclaim their wands and the very reason the North returned and destroyed them.

The devastation was unforgivable. It was as if the fire was new, fresh. But it had been close to a hundred years since the North burned the Heart Oak.

But like any scar, the presence of pain lingered.

# CHAPTER 39

Glamora returned us to the ground, just shy of the Heart Oak's destruction. We had flown for a long whilst after we passed it, but still the air was poisoned with the smell of death. Spread across the forest bed, ash rested like newly laid snow. The moment my feet touched the ground, the question burst out of me.

'Why did the North destroy the Heart Oak?'

It was Beatrice who answered as she fussed with Glamora's reigns. 'They didn't.'

'You have been brought up to believe many lies,' Simion added. 'I shouldn't blame you for your idiocy, no matter how laughable it is.'

Heat rose in my cheeks. 'You really are a nasty prick.'

'I've been called worse, believe it or not.'

'Trust me,' I said, stepping ahead and making him be the one to chase after. 'It's not hard to believe at all.'

'Stop. I'm going to get wood for the fire,' Beatrice announced. 'Both of you sort out your differences. Please, for my sake.'

There was a part of me who wanted to ask Beatrice to stay, but I couldn't form the words. Not as tingles spread at the back of my head, signalling Simion's entry.

'Don't,' I snapped, 'you dare.'

It retreated as quickly as it came. 'At some point, you are going to need to keep me out yourself.'

'Then you can add that to our list of lessons,' I replied sharply. 'But first, I want to understand the Heart Oak's destruction. If the North didn't burn it, then who did?'

His brow peaked, arms folding over his chest. 'The South.'

'Bollocks.' I laughed, eyes rolling. 'Why would they destroy it when it was the only thing providing them power? Seems rather counterproductive, doesn't it?'

'To understand it from a different perspective, you must first know the importance of the Heart Oak to the North. It is clear you know why the South coveted it so greatly, but it was also a sacred place to us, one our Queen grieves to this day.'

I waved my hand before me. 'Continue.'

'Galloway and his dryad mate had a child,' Simion said, so plainly, as though this new information didn't have the power to silence me. 'And that child you know as the Mad Queen.'

'Is that even possible?'

'You are asking if two beings can create a product of their love, when you can access magic? When there is a dragon prowling behind you? Ask yourself, why would the daughter of the first Heart Oak destroy it? Would you go and kick down your parents' gravestone?'

'No,' I answered.

'Our Queen didn't fly south and destroy your mages because their power threatened her. That is a pathetic notion your people spread—how could those four mages best a broken-hearted woman, on dragon-back, with an army of battlemages riding the skies beside her? She waited years, grew into her power and built an army. She destroyed your mages to avenge her parents, she did it because it was the South who bathed the Heart Oak in fire. She would've left them alone, if they kept to themselves. But they didn't want to do that.'

I stared at Simion, gobsmacked. 'That can't be true.'

'It is fact.'

'I think we've made it clear that destroying the Heart Oak wouldn't benefit your *Mad* Queen or the South.'

'Careful,' Simion said, so quietly it sent a shiver down my back. 'Otherwise, you may just find out why your people gave her such a title.'

I mocked a bow as though Simion was the Queen and I was apologising directly to her. He bit down on the insides of his cheeks, nostrils flaring. 'When you put your amplifier into the fire the night of the festival… did it burn?'

He was mocking me; he knew the answer. 'No.'

Simion reached into the collar of his shirt. He withdrew the wooden amulet that hung from the leather cord around his neck. His amplifier. My eyes traced the carving of the dragon as Simion's finger stroked down its curved spine. 'Exactly. No mundane flame can burn Heart Oak. It was the product of an ancient power, Maximus. Dryad made—God made. Only wytchfire—the dark destructive obsidian flame, has the power to kill a god.'

'Wytchfire,' I echoed. 'Finally, something both the South and North agree on.'

'When the Queen and her army invaded the South, it was to find the source of the wytchfire—destroying your mages was simply a bonus. It was believed the Southern mages had stores of it and were preparing to use the flame to destroy Galloway Forest in its entirety.'

I blinked and saw the destruction we had flown over hours before. 'Did she find it?'

Simion shook his head. 'No. The South is not the enemy and never was, no matter if your people enjoy preaching otherwise. It is why we've not invaded since. Well, until we came for you.'

'She didn't return because the mages had been killed.'

'Magic is not the enemy in this story, Max,' Simion said, returning his amplifier beneath his shirt. 'It is merely the victim of another threat. The South were tricked. Or you could say manipulated by another for their twisted gain.'

My mouth dried at his words. 'Who has the power to do that?'

'Wytchfire can only be created by a phoenix. They are natural enemies to the dryad for as long as the gods have existed.'

'You keep referring to the creatures as gods.'

Simion smiled—*actually* smiled. It was bright and brilliant. 'That is because they are. Four creatures for the four elements. The South turned those four mages into gods, whilst forgetting they would've been nothing without the dryad who created the Heart Oak.'

I took a breath. 'This is all so much to take in.'

'It's barely scratching the surface. Max, we're stopping here for a short rest,' Simion said, interrupting my racing mind. 'If I was you, I'd start forging walls of steel in your mind. When we reach Wycombe, there will be others who will root through your mind whether you like or not. If you wish to keep your secrets, start protecting them.'

I blinked, watching black flames devour forests and birds made of fire and ruin. Among the distraction of Simion's words, I hadn't noticed he had wormed his way back into my head. But there, beneath it all, was the slithering chill of his presence, probing the outskirts.

'Care to add *protecting my mind* to your list of lessons?'

Simion shrugged my comment off, eyeing me with the same suspicious glare I gave him. 'You should've taken a leaf out of Camron's book when it comes to guarding your mind—his is impenetrable.'

'Perhaps I would've, if you didn't come back on Glamora ready to destroy everything if I didn't leave.'

Simion paused, his hard expression slipping. 'I wouldn't have done that, Max.'

'No?' I asked. 'Because I got the impression you enjoy causing pain.' *Since you shattered my world with five words.*

He knew exactly what I referred too. Simion stepped in close, the sudden proximity catching my breath in my throat. I saw my reflection in his wide eyes, how he regarded me as though I was one of his biggest regrets. 'I *never* meant to hurt you.'

His honesty was so vivid, it took my breath away. All at once we were back at Gathrax manor. Simion was the man who offered me comfort, the gentle touch and kind-eyed man who looked at me when everyone else pretended I was someone I was not.

'You do not need to accept it, but I'm sorry.'

'I do,' I said, quickly looking up to him through my lashes. 'Accept it, that is.'

Relief pulled down at his shoulders. In a single exhale, the tension ebbed from his face. 'Beatrice was right about you.'

'In what way?'

Simion paused. 'Ask me that question when we get your parents back and I will tell you.'

# CHAPTER 40

'What's wrong with you?' Beatrice shouted, hands raised before her as she attempted to steady the black-scaled dragon. Glamora thrashed, thrusting her long neck from side to side, her tail breaking the charred trees near her.

Our camp had gone from quiet to chaos in the blink of a moment.

'Something has unsettled her,' Simion said, his face ashen as he focused on the dark of the wood.

Glamora pushed off the ground, rose onto her hind legs and kicked out like a horse, wings flaring wide. Beatrice tumbled backwards just in time, barely missing a large claw from piercing her chest. The dragon's roar shook the clearing; an unnatural cold wind ravaged across us. Simion fell back from the serrated teeth that flashed before him.

There wasn't room for thought, only action.

I took a step forward to help Simion, but the ground trembled as Glamora pounded her limbs upon it. Over and over, it was as though the very skin of the world was ready to crack.

'Get down!' I shouted at Beatrice as the dragon's mace-like

tail raced towards her. Just in time, Beatrice ducked as the spiked tip smashed into a tree, narrowly missing her. Upon impact, the tree exploded into shards of splintered wood. My breath was knocked out of me as Simion tackled me. We slammed into the ground, as another crash sounded from beside me. I turned my head to see the taloned limb of the dragon scoring marks into the dirt ground at my side.

'I've got you,' Simion said, leaning over me, eyes wide. He was so close I could feel his heart thundering within his chest. With a great heave, Simion rolled us across the ground before we were crushed beneath the weight of Glamora's pounding limbs.

The world turned upside down. Glamora beat her wings furiously, battering wind over Simion and me, keeping us pinned to the forest bed.

We couldn't do anything but watch as the dragon launched herself into the air, roaring and screeching.

Beatrice screamed, her voice rasped and sore. 'Wait!'

Simion's harsh breathing washed over me. He covered me, his body acting as a shield from the world.

'Are you all right?' he asked, flushed and breathless.

'Fine,' I replied, although my back ached from the fall. If Simion had not tackled me, the large body of the broken tree would've crushed me. One look to my side and I saw it, laid out across the ground where I had stood.

'Are you?' I asked.

Simion's amber stare flickered across my face, drinking me in. Up close, there was no hiding from one another. Suddenly, I was all too aware of his details. The way his forehead was never smooth, always marred by lines of worry. The scar across his eyebrow, which almost looked deliberate. How the scent that clung to him was fresh pine, like that of the forest itself.

'Alive,' Simion replied, finally withdrawing his weight from me. He stood, his back blocking out the view of Glamora flying away from us. Our chance of reaching the North, gone.

Simion offered me a hand and I took it.

A heavy thud broke my line of thought. I looked to Simion, wondering if he heard it. His grip on my hand faltered slightly, his eyes widening. When he opened his mouth, a string of incoherent mumbles came out, as the side of his face began to droop.

'Simion?' I spluttered his name, grasping his shoulders to keep him steady. But he was dead weight, a muscled body falling upon me. There was nothing I could do to stop his descent.

'Bea,' I shouted, not removing my eyes from Simion's open-eyed gaze. He didn't blink, only the leaves before his lips shivered. He was breathing. I pressed my palm to his chest, welcoming the steady but faint beat of his heart.

Beatrice was by us in seconds. Her knees cracked against the ground as she grasped her brother and shook him. 'Fucking dragon…'

But it wasn't Glamora who did this.

Simion didn't move, didn't speak. His lips were frozen in place, his eyes bulged.

'Take out your wand,' Beatrice said calmly, pulling her staff from the leather-strapped holder on her back.

She didn't need to tell me twice. I grasped the smooth hilt, welcoming the rush of power as the forest burst with cords of shimmering power.

'We are under attack.'

A cold sheen of sweat spread across my forehead and neck. Beatrice crouched above her brother, eyes squinting into the shadowed line of trees.

'Who?'

Camron? Had he finally reached me. Deep down, where my magic bloomed in my gut, I felt a wave of what could only be relief. It lasted all but a moment.

'Not who. What.' Beatrice peered over her shoulder at me, eyes narrowed and full of silent warning. 'If we don't get Simion to Wycombe, he will die.'

Panic rose in me, a tidal wave of unignorable power.

'But Glamora...' I raised my eyes to the sky in search for the dragon. She couldn't be seen anywhere.

The air hissed as a sharp projectile shot from the dark of the surrounding trees. It moved with blurred speed, cutting the air as it narrowly missed Beatrice's shoulder. Instead, it embedded itself into the ground beside us.

My magic roared within and around me, warning of another arrow.

Beatrice brought her staff down upon the ground with both hands. The force echoed through me, followed by the gushing explosion as the ground before us raised like a cresting wave. Shadowed beneath its height, I looked to my friend. Her head was bowed, eyes closed, as she forced her magic through her amplifier and into the earth.

'We're going to need to fight,' Beatrice said, straining through her concentration. 'Or we die.'

Something embedded into the wall of earth that shielded us. Then another and another. Thud. Thud. Thud.

Beatrice pushed out her staff. As she did, the shield of earth became a wave of mud and soil, racing away from us, towards our assailants.

Without the protection of her conjured wall, I could see them. Bright yellow eyes shone in the hidden depth of the wood, so many of them the forest looked as though it was on fire.

They were not arrows which shot for us, nor had Camron found me.

'Remember I told you there are dangerous things lurking within the shadows of Galloway Forest? Well, these are the worst of them.'

# CHAPTER 41

'Worcupines,' Beatrice said, her body tense as the monsters prowled from the shadows. They looked no different from a wolf. With matted coats of stone-grey fur, sharp talons and maws overspilling with jagged teeth. Their limbs thick with muscle and scars.

I was rooted to the spot, caught beneath their gaze. I sensed their hunger just as they likely smelled our fear in the air. I would not die. I would not perish beneath these creatures when my destination was so close.

The worcupine who led the pack was the largest of them all. It was as tall as Beatrice, its four legs larger in width than mine. Dark strings of saliva oozed from its jaw, smudging down its thick hide. It held its head high—inspecting. The others followed its lead, their bellies scraping across the ground as they followed.

A mane of sharp spikes framed their thick necks. Black and brown needles flexed and quivered with each step they took. The needle-like spikes were the same that had shot past Beatrice's shoulder only moments before. As the worcupines moved, the needles clicked together in an unnatural symphony.

My heart hammered in my chest, my throat. All I could focus on was the power around me and the knowledge that I would tear this forest apart if it meant surviving.

Beatrice stiffened beside. 'Keep still, Max. Any movement and we're done for.'

My palm grew damp as I tightened my grip on my wand. The mage-mark rubbed against wood, reminding me of its presence and power.

'If we are lucky, they will leave us alone,' Beatrice added.

'Luck has nothing to do with surviving this,' I hissed, as the five worcupines fanned out in a line before us.

'They've not come for us,' Beatrice replied.

'Then who?'

'Glamora.'

Unlike the rest of the pack, the smaller of the worcupines buzzed with frantic energy. It must've been a pup, snapping its jaw back and forth, tongue lapping across its stained teeth. There was something unpredictable about its movements.

'Still,' Beatrice warned. 'Keep still, Max.'

'But—'

The younger worcupine howled. The noise was rough, three sharp yaps and then it pounced, breaking away from the pack and racing directly for us.

'Beatrice!' I cried out. Before she could react, I called on my magic, reaching deep within. It didn't take much thought for it to listen; with the wand in my hand, there was no barrier stopping me from commanding it.

The ground beneath the charging worcupine exploded in a cloud of dirt.

I used my movements to guide my intention, flicking the

wand skywards as roots of all sizes burst from beneath the creature. In a blink, it was engulfed entirely.

The roots punctured through its hide. One had exploded through the soft flesh of its neck, silencing it from crying out.

'Now we are well and truly fucked,' Beatrice said, as the remaining four creatures erupted in howls of warning.

Blood thundered in my ears as my power tied me to the earth itself. It was almost hard to hear Beatrice above the storm in my skull.

I held the image of my attack in my mind, shifting it to something new. With a jolt, I brought my wand down, feeling the slight resistance of flesh and root. The worcupine slammed downwards, the force shattering bone. But I wasn't finished. The earthen bed of the forest liquefied, like sand, and devoured the creature whole.

Breathless, euphoria rushing through me, I looked to Beatrice and spoke. 'One down, four to go.'

'Two each?'

Beatrice pounced from the ground, twisted within the air and missed the snapping jaw of the largest worcupine. She flipped over the beast's back and brought the base of her staff crashing into the side of its jaw. The beast lost its footing and skidded into a heap on the ground. It cried out, shaking the trees with its croaking voice. More black gore spilled, but the beast did not stay down for long.

Movement in my peripheral vision caught my attention. Three of the creatures circled me, growls rumbling deep in their throats. The mane of needles flexed, shivered and stood on end. In the light of day, I saw glistening liquid oozing from their tips.

'The needles cause...' Beatrice shouted, as she twisted the staff in her hand, fending off yet another attempt from the largest worcupine. 'Paralysis!'

With a whip of my wrist, the trees above the pack shuddered. I screamed, forced my arm down and willed the branches to follow.

*Cords, visualise, intention.*

A resounding crack exploded around the clearing. The trees above the worcupines shed their limbs, one by one. Branches, large and small, snapped apart and fell. The ground trembled as they landed. Two of the creatures managed to dodge the falling weights, but the one who raced towards me was far too focused to notice.

The branch caught the worcupine across its lower back, with a crunch of bone and the wet smash of flesh. Like a cherry between teeth, the creature popped, splattering the ground around it in a sunburst of dark blood.

'What happened to two each?' I shouted, drunk from the wave of power that crest over me.

'Protect my brother,' Beatrice called back, scorning my misplaced humour. 'Focus, Max!'

The final two creatures moved. I threw myself to the ground just as they pounced from either side of me. I covered Simion with my body, my ribs aching as I rolled over him, skidding across the pine-covered floor.

Hot breath invaded my nose as a worcupine stalked forward. I scrambled backwards on my hands, fear burning within me as I heard the other creature behind me. I was trapped between them both.

Intense emotion overwhelmed me as the eyes of the creature peered to Simion. A tongue, long and white, lapped out for him.

Fury returned with force. 'Don't *fucking* touch him!'

It snapped its jaws twice, lowered onto its front legs—and pounced.

I couldn't focus enough to grasp the cords and fill them

with my command. All I could do was throw my hand forward, stabbing the tip of the wand towards the incoming creature's belly.

The air crackled with light and heat. One thought and my veins boiled with liquid fire, my flesh prickled as the air around me charged with power. As I thrust the wand up, burying it into the soft underbelly of the beast, I released the build-up of energy as though it was merely a held breath.

A streak of white, hot lightning shot out of the worcupine and sliced into the sky. Blood misted the air, charred flesh filled my nose.

The dead weight of the creature fell suddenly onto me. I tried to duck and managed to get most of my body out of the way. But the force of the creature's fall snatched my wand from my hand, leaving it buried deep in its gut.

There was no time to retrieve the wand, not as the final worcupine charged.

It charged. I threw my body to the side. The ground shuddered with the force of its fall. It missed, skidded on its paw, then turned to face me with its feral, furious maw.

*No.* I looked to my wand, no more than a thorn in the belly of the dead worcupine before me.

The reserves of magic sloshed within me, but it was as useless as a flame without air. Without my wand, I had no chance.

There was a whiz of air as two needles embedded into the ground in front me. The worcupine shook its neck and released another rain of needles. I ran. Legs burning and lungs ablaze, poison-tipped needles landing in the ground behind me.

I called for Beatrice, powerless to stop the beast that moved for me. She couldn't help even if she wanted to.

Locked in battle, she barely coped against the monstrous worcupine whose roar sounded like laughter.

A cold tingling spread across the back of my skull, distracting me from the world. A voice, faint as a whisper on the winds, shuddered throughout my mind.

*Glamora.*

I knew without a question it was Simion. My mind was full of the thunderous beat of my heart, but beneath it was Simion's weak voice. *Glamora.* He said the dragon's name with more strength this time, as though the word strained him. *Up.*

A rush of cold wind crackled over me, followed by a hulking shadow. The shape in the sky blocked out the sun for a moment, casting the clearing in darkness. Behind me, the worcupine stopped running. It released a starved howl that rippled across my skin.

'Max,' Beatrice cried out. She moved like water, twisting and turning, her staff an extension of her very being. 'Wand!'

Beatrice had been right; it was the dragon they wanted. Glamora distracted the worcupines, enough for me to take my chance. She cut across the sky, casting icy bouts of wind over the clearing. Frost crackled over tree, froze glass to dagger like blades.

I took my chance and ran.

Simion was there, laying helplessly on the floor. I searched for him in my mind but found nothing. That didn't stop me from pushing out a sentiment to him.

*You won't die today.*

Wasting no time, I grasped the blood-slicked handle, placed my foot on the concaved chest of the corpse, and pulled it free. The moment my skin encountered the wand, the barrier within me fell.

The magic was mine once again.

Power oozed from every pore in my body. I pushed every

ounce of my presence into the earth around me and
commanded it to do my bidding.

Dried needles of pine that littered the ground shifted,
lifting into the air. Thousands of small earthen spears hovered
in the space between me and the creature, so many they
blocked it from view.

Glamora baited its attention, circling the clearing. The
worcupine had no idea that death lingered behind it.

Satisfied, I flung the wand forward and willed the pine
needles to follow.

The worcupine could only release a wheeze as it was
stabbed over and over, the pine needles embedding themselves into every inch of flesh they could find. Countless cuts
and puncture wounds caused the creature to bleed out
furiously.

It fell, its body spasming, into a puddle of its black blood. It
may not have been dead yet, but its doom was pending.

My head spun as my energy gave up on me. I stumbled
forward, unable to stay upright, reserves exhausted.

I watched as Beatrice fought the larger creature. Sweat
gleamed across her brow, strands of hair stuck to her neck in
tacky chunks. I could see her losing energy just as I had. Her
movements were slowing, becoming frantic and aimless.

Even tired, Beatrice was formidable. A force of nature.

Poison-tipped needles shot from the worcupine's mane,
missing her by inches, littering the ground around her feet.
On she fought, eyes glowing with power and ground rippling
wherever her staff touched.

Glamora dove for the ground, wings folded into her
hulking body spearing towards the worcupine. Beatrice risked
a glance up, and I was certain relief washed over her face.

It was the distraction Beatrice needed. With both hands on
her staff, she slammed it into the ground. Her power rippled

beneath me—violent and raw. Just as the tension built and I believed the ground would cave in, a pillar of stone shot up beneath the worcupine and sent it airborne.

The dragon threw her wings out at the last moment, ceasing her fall. She snatched the flailing worcupine within her jaws in one fell swoop, serrated teeth sinking into the creature's underbelly as though it was butter.

Beatrice stood firm as blood rained down, coating her entirely.

Glamora beat her wings, taking her higher into the sky.

With the little energy I had left, I was up and stumbling towards Beatrice.

'We need to get Simion to a healer,' Beatrice commanded, wrapping her arm over my shoulder. We leaned equally on one another and hobbled over to Simion.

A loud bang sounded behind us just as we reached him. I gasped, gripping onto Beatrice, unsure if we could fight another worcupine.

But the creature that made the noise was not alive. The alpha worcupine was no longer in the jaws of Glamora, but in a heap on the ground. I studied the mess of muscle and broken bone, bile stinging my throat.

Glamora cried out above us with glee, spitting a river of ice across the blue expanse.

It was a war cry; it was a warning.

'More will come,' Beatrice muttered, hands carefully running over her brother's body. When she rolled him onto his side, my eyes veered to the thin spike that protruded between his shoulder blades. The material around it was stained dark with blood and yellow-green pus. The smell which followed smacked the back of my throat.

'It's bad, isn't it?' I said, choking on the sour air.

'Very,' Beatrice answered, eyes red.

Glamora landed among the clearing once again. Her teeth were stained black with the creature's blood, her dark scales glistened with it. We both carried Simion over to the dragon. Glamora bowed low to the ground to help us get him on.

'The worcupine is the sworn enemy of the dragon, and protectors of the dryads. Unlike the latter, the worcupine have been left within the wood only to grow feral. Time has ruined the once docile creature. Max, we shouldn't still be alive.'

The needle from the worcupine now clear in daylight, I reached for it, wanting to pull it from Simion's back. The back of my hand stung as Beatrice slapped it away.

'If you take it out, the poison spreads quicker. Leaving the needle in is keeping Simion paralysed, not dead.'

'What do I do?' Desperation laced my voice. 'Tell me what to do!'

All I could think about was how Simion had been the one to offer me comfort during my time of need. Now, with him beneath me, I felt helpless. Powerless.

'Hold him,' Beatrice said, forcing me up onto Glamora's back with a push, 'and don't you dare let him go.'

# CHAPTER 42

Glamora climbed higher and higher into the sky, wind screeching past my ears. She flew faster than she had before. Without Simion behind to steady me where I sat, I was vulnerable. One harsh jolt and I feared I would end up like the worcupine Glamora had dropped on the ground. Or worse.

I refused to take my hands off Simion's chest. I focused on the subtle beat of his heart pattering beneath my palms, the gentle rise of his chest. His mouth was parted, his eyes wide and trained on me. Beneath his unwavering gaze, I had no ability to hide from him.

*Si-Simion.* I forced my voice out into the void of my frantic mind. His name rang throughout my skull, skipping across bone like a stone over a lake. Nothing. There was no tickle at the back of my mind.

Beatrice's back was towards me, her hair wild and free around her. She leaned into Glamora's neck, holding on for dear life. As she ran hands over the magnificent scales, urging the dragon on, I could almost *hear* her plea with each encouraging stroke.

The ache within me was terrible. As the magic faded, and the adrenaline followed soon after, every muscle burned, every bone ached. My stomach spasmed with the need for sustenance, something to replace what had been taken from me.

When I fought the Northern soldier and his dragon, I had raced towards the limits of my energy and thrown myself over the edge. I had come close with the worcupines—if any more had attacked, I would've been no different to Simion.

Black blood dried across my face, my skin tacky to the touch. If I looked anything like Beatrice, it must've been a horrific sight.

But we were alive.

*Simion, you better not die on me.* I filled my mind with the command.

Unable to hold his wide, amber gaze, I leaned forward and placed my forehead on his chest. He was cool, the opposite to Camron's warmth.

It was faint at first, the familiar cool tickle of his presence. I dared to move from my position over Simion for fear it would break the connection. Then a voice oozed from the shadows, tired and meek, but undoubtably there.

*Are you worried for me, Maximus?*

The answer was simple. I needed more than wanted for him to survive. For his sake, and that of the woman riding before me.

I filled my mind with my response. *I don't want your death weighing on my conscience.*

It wasn't exactly a tone I heard in his voice, but more a feeling—as though our connection allowed me an insight into his pain. It echoed between my shoulder blades, just where the worcupines needle was embedded in his.

*Careful, I might start thinking you care about me.* Simion's reply faded into a whisper, ebbing away like dawn's mist.

My knuckles gripped his damp tunic, paling beneath the force of my hold on him.

*No.* I thrust the word out. *Beatrice has lost enough because of me; I don't think she would forgive me if she lost you too.*

*Strange.* I heard the humour in his voice, it was slight, above his resounding pain. *Because that isn't what I feel in you.*

A spire—towering and as white as fresh chalk—protruded through the thick clouds before us. Against the night it seemed to glow as though a star had been captured within the stone, pulsating an incandescent light from its surface. It was the first thing I saw. I didn't know what woke me until Glamora released another roar. It lit the obsidian sky in a stream of ice-cold winds, burning like blue fire.

We had arrived. We'd made it to the North.

My hands ached as I continued to hold onto Simion. I hadn't let go, not once, even when I slept.

*We are nearly there, Simion. Hold on.*

The tower must've been thousands of feet in height to rise above the clouds. Perhaps more. Its white walls were smooth. The waning moon cast its silvered light across the tower's surface, making it glisten as though it was made from ice, not stone. Gargantuan roots slithered up the tower's body, as though holding it up. The roots themselves were thrice the width of Glamora's frame, the thorns far more deadly than her ridges of horns and protruding bone.

Glamora flew through the night, directly towards the tower's crown.

Whereas the tower's body was smooth and straight, its head lifted in three equally pointed spires, like the three forks of a trident. It was only when we reached its walls that I could see that a podium stretched out across the tower's top, a disc-like shape that reflected the moon's iridescent glow from within. The three spires of the tower's crown were not in line, but two in front and one placed back. In the furthest spire was a door, large and arched. Sweeping out of the door were five figures, illuminated beneath by the glowing stone.

Beatrice glanced over her shoulder towards me. Her thick length of hair cast across her face, but there was no hiding her storm of emotion. I was no gleamer, but I sensed the desperation and dread flooding from her.

The powerful, frantic beats of Glamora's wings calmed. She glided around the tower's top, slowing her speed until it was safe enough to land.

My eyes focused on the five cloaked figures who greeted us. They stood in a triangle form, patiently waiting for our arrival. I couldn't help but imagine what we must've looked like as we came into view. Covered in blood, exhausted and wide-eyed, this was likely not how they pictured us.

Glamora landed, raised up onto her hind legs and beat her powerful wings. Not a single member of the crowd flinched as her cold winds billowed over them. Glamora soon settled herself, bowing her long neck and lowering her wings on either side of the glowing platform.

'You have to help Simion,' Beatrice shouted, throwing herself down Glamora's wing until she stood before the crowd. I couldn't seem to move, as though the unseen eyes hidden beneath cloaks kept me immobile.

'What happened?' a sharp voice asked.

I veered my gaze to the figure standing before the others. I held firm on Simion as the figure lifted hands to hood and lowered it. Her skin was a rich brown that glowed with vitality. A striking face was framed with a shock of white hair, two eyes of pure gold which scanned us all in turn.

'Worcupines,' Beatrice answered. I couldn't see her face, but I sensed she spoke through gritted teeth. My friend's demeanour had stiffened, her fists balled at either side as she regarded the woman.

The woman raised a hand and gestured to the crowd around her. 'Take my nephew and see he is healed.'

I looked between the woman, to Beatrice and then to Simion. I suddenly saw it: the similarities were striking. Beside her thick white hair, they each had amber eyes and skin warm with colour.

'Certainly, Elder Leia.'

I jolted back as Simion shifted beneath my hands. Beneath an unseen force, his body lifted from Glamora's back, rigid and stiff, and levitated towards the two cloaked figures. I fought the urge to reach out and pull him back.

I looked to the cloaked figures; they both held their arms outstretched before them, as though guiding the air. There was not an amplifier in sight, but I simply didn't look in the right place. They didn't hold a wand, staff or wooden-handled sword. Flashing from the sleeve of their cloaks was a thick band of wood around their wrists.

Simion followed behind the two cloaked figures who walked calmly towards the door at the far end of the podium. I didn't take my eyes off him until he disappeared into the shadows of the tower.

When I focused back on the group, it was to find the woman—Elder Leia—looking directly at me. There was nothing kind about it.

Glamora shifted beneath me as though sensing the emotion radiating from the woman's eyes. I moved my hand into my pocket and reached for the calming presence of my wand.

'I wouldn't do that, Maximus Oaken.' Then a strong voice filled my mind, like nails scratching over stone. *If you wish to see the light of day come morning, you will come peacefully.*

Unlike when Simion used his power, there was no warning before Elder Leia's voice boomed throughout my skull.

'Stand aside, Beatrice,' Elder Leia said, 'or do you wish to join the traitor mage?'

Glamora exploded beneath me in a vicious growl as the final two cloaked figures moved towards her. She thrust her long neck around, barring a mouthful of serrated teeth.

'Maximus, you are under arrest by command of the Queen.'

'What?' I said, but no one heard me above the shouting and roaring. Beatrice reached for her staff, ready to fight for me. Elder Leia threw back her grey cloak, exposing a shorter staff of wood strapped at her hip.

Magic radiated in the air around me, crackling alongside the ice hissing within Glamora's parting jaw.

'I'll come!' I screamed this time, my throat burning with desperation.

Everything seemed to calm. Even Glamora bowed her head into submission, her roar fading into a rumbling whimper.

'Willingly,' I added.

Beatrice stood before Elder Leia, her face coated in dried blood, her eyes blinking back furious tears. 'No, Max. This isn't right, this isn't what was promised.'

'At least the traitor mage sees sense.' Elder Leia stepped around her niece.

Beatrice gritted her teeth, her jaw flexed. 'He hasn't—'

'It's okay,' I whispered to Beatrice, as I climbed down from Glamora's back. As soon as my feet touched the glowing white platform, the hands of two mages were on me.

There was no fight left in me, not as they reached into my pocket and took my wand, nor when they drew my arms behind my back. There was a cold kiss of metal on my skin, followed by a *clink*.

'Did you believe you could simply walk freely into our borders with the promise of war at your back?'

'No,' I replied. I understood, with one look at Elder Leia, she was very aware of Camron's promise to me. 'I came to prevent it.'

'Do not play coy with me, child.'

There was no denying Elder Leia still lingered—unwanted —in my mind.

'See for yourself,' I said, tapping my temple.

She tilted her head, eyes narrowing as a grin picked up the corner of her lips. 'I shall.'

Claws ripped through my mind, tearing it, searching. I held her stare, refusing to let myself scream.

In a moment, it was done. Elder Leia no longer smiled when she regarded me. Although her expression had softened, she had not completely released the distrust evident in every flicker of her eyes.

The images she had rifled through were burning in the dark of my mind. Julian hanging from a tree, a puppet of death. Jonathan drowned in a knot of root and vine. The Northern soldier's melted flesh and charred bone.

She saw it all.

*You may not wish for war, but an army still builds in your name.*

*Then give me what I came for.* I forced the words out in response, each sharp as steel.

'Bring me his amplifier,' Elder Leia said aloud, hand outstretched, ignoring me. If hands were not holding me, I would've fallen to the ground. When Simion retreated from my mind, it was the brush of cool breath dusting across the back of my neck. Elder Leia was not so careful, not so kind. Her nails clawed, leaving scars in their wake.

My core ached as my wand was taken from me. It was in her hands in a matter of seconds. As her fingers moved across the wood, it echoed across my skin.

'And what of these three deaths?' Elder Leia asked, drawing her nail over the notches across the wand's base. 'Crimes must be answered for.'

'Destroying a common enemy is not a crime,' Beatrice hissed at her aunt's side.

Like a viper, Elder Leia snapped her attention from my wand to Beatrice. 'The years have softened you, Beatrice. Quiet, before you join the same fate. Don't think for a moment I believe you have succeeded. It is merely by the grace of your brother you have returned with the traitor mage —without his aid, you would have failed.'

Beatrice's expression sharpened. She lowered her chin to her chest, looking at Elder Leia through a line of thick lashes. With her face covered in a mask of dried blood, her eyes wide and wild, Beatrice was formidable.

Before she could act on something she would regret, I called out to her. 'Beatrice, I'll be fine. Make sure Simion is okay, find my parents…'

*Compliance is the key.* The voice I had not heard in days returned to my mind, loud and clear.

'My parents,' I said, as the uncaring hands dragged me towards the tower's door. 'What have you done to them?'

There was no denying the look of confusion that cut through Elder Leia's disdain. It lasted only a moment before I was drawn into the shadows of the building, leaving my answers just out of reach.

# CHAPTER 43

They took everything from me. My wand, my clothes, My dignity.

I was all stripped down to dirtied flesh in a plain smooth-walled cell. The cloaked figures who brought me left without a word. Perhaps they didn't care to watch me wash myself with the bucket of water provided, the water so cold it surprised me it wasn't completely frozen. Using the damp cloth, I cleared the blood, grime and days of travel from my skin until the water was left murky.

I stood in the centre of the stone room, hands clutching at my naked body, shivering. My skin had barely dried by the time a new guard arrived—this one was masked and garbed in silver armour with a familiar curved dragon etched into their breastplates. Just like the Northern soldier I had killed.

They provided clothes—placed them in a pile before me and said *dress yourself*, as though my presence bored them.

Over the day that followed, I had long given up on the hope that this misery would end. When morning arrived, a masked guard brought in a wooden bowl of food. Grey sludge, thick with soggy oats. At first, I left it untouched, but my pride soon waned—broken down to nothing but the hours of solitude.

Much like the tower, the cell glowed with incandescent strands of ivory, with white veins amongst the stone which emitted light. During the day, it was not as noticeable. At night, the veins lit up as though stars lingered within—always keeping some form of glow within the empty room.

There was a handless door buried seamlessly into the wall. It didn't open by hinges but pushed forward until a thick slab of stone hovered, allowing guards to enter. Magic. There was a narrow slit of a glassless window on the wall opposite the cell's entrance. Six iron bars prevented anything from coming in or leaving, except cold air. If I stood on my toes, I could glimpse the world beyond. For as far as I could see there was sky. I had to be high up in this impossible tower, from both the view and the freezing temperatures alone. The cold seeped into everything. The stone floor, the thin mattress laid out across it. Even the walls couldn't hold in heat. If it wasn't for the fitted black trousers and long-sleeved shirt I was provided, I was certain I'd freeze to death.

How much time passed, I wasn't sure. I slept, and woke, slept and woke. No matter what state I was in, two thoughts filled my mind. First, my parents and their well-being. Then there was Camron, his warmth, his kindness. It seemed, even miles away, he was my comfort. If I closed my eyes, I could almost feel his warmth over my tacky skin.

I woke to the heavy thud of footsteps beyond the closed door. I rolled over, body stiff and pained, glancing out the window. The sky was painted in orange tones, bleeding dawn out across the land.

'Wait for me outside.' The deep voice was muffled by stone, but I knew who it was without question. My thoughts were confirmed as the cool trickle of power slipped into the back of my skull.

'Simion...' I breathed, pushing my aching limbs until I stood.

The stone slab lifted. Simion strolled in before the guard controlling the stone had the chance to put it down. If I took my eyes off Simion, it was only to look at the now-open door, pondering how far I would get if I ran.

Simion paused only when he was close to me, his amber eyes trailing me from head to foot.

'You look better than I last saw you,' I said. Simion wore a cream tunic, long-sleeved, beneath silver armour across his chest and upper arms. His trousers were like mine, a black fitted material, and his boots polished into an inch of their life. Pinned by silver clasps at each shoulder, a long white cloak fell behind him, swishing with every move he made.

'Have you been harmed?' he asked sharply. My eyes caught the tense fists. I knew he fought the restraint to reach for me. In a strange way I wish he did.

*Answer me, Max, did they hurt you?*

Ice-cold fingers traced my mind, and then Simion was in it. The presence of his voice brushed through my skull, snapping me out of my shocked trance.

'No,' I choked on the word.

Simion studied me, searching for something. When he couldn't find it, he shifted his gaze to mine and held it. 'I'm sorry it has taken so long to come for you. It was never my intention to leave you here.'

'Then what is your intention?' I asked.

'You are coming with me.'

Even if I wanted to move, I couldn't. This didn't feel real.

Images of Simion flooded my mind, his paralysed body laid out before me, his unblinking eyes. I still felt the ache in my knuckles from where I had held onto him.

'Even in this predicament, I still sense your concern for me,' Simion whispered.

'I don't worry about you,' I replied, although we both knew it was a lie. Since I'd been taken to this cell, I had thought about Simion a never-ending number of times. And Beatrice.

'They are going to kill me, aren't they?' I looked to the ground, unable to hold his stare.

Simion didn't respond. Instead, he closed the space between us and wrapped his arm around my shoulders. 'No one is going to lay a finger on you, have I not made that clear?'

'Elder Leia... she said I would be tried for the three deaths—'

'My aunt says many things, most should be heeded, but on the odd occasion it is best to ignore her. Which, in this case, I urge you to do.'

I swallowed hard, wishing I could put on a brave act, as if none of this concerned me. But it did. Once again, I found my fate in the hands of others instead of myself. 'Has my punishment been decided?'

'There will be no punishment, Max,' Simion replied.

I looked back to him, relief lasting all but a moment. 'Then what did you come for?'

'To take you with me.' Simion's voice was soft. 'As I said, I would've come a lot sooner, but I had some rather nasty poison to expel from my body before I could speak with the Council. Will you forgive me for my tardiness?'

I appreciated Simion's ability to lighten the situation at hand, but something wasn't sitting right with me. His tone was light, but almost misplaced.

'You are free, Max, but until you speak with the Queen, I

have been entrusted to keep you under my watchful eye. Unless you would prefer to stay here… That is your choice.'

'You know what I want, Simion. I want my parents.' I trembled as pure, overwhelming emotion burned tears in my eyes. How did this man have such an ability to make me feel so… exposed?

Simion drew me into his arms. My entire body froze— shocked by his touch. He placed a hand to the back of my head and held me close.

*Nothing will happen to them. I—we promise that.*

Simion held me to him, refusing to let go.

'Take me to them,' I whispered, voice muffled by his chest. 'Please.'

'Come on, let us talk about this when we get out of here.'

There was something about being this close to Simion that caused me to shudder and lose all confidence. 'Simion, what are you not telling me?' I reached out and grabbed him as he began to turn away from me. His skin was cold but firm, my fingers hardly circled his wrist.

Simion stopped resisting, immobilised by my touch as though I harboured the same poison as the worcupines. He looked over his shoulder at me, sympathy evident in his dark eyes. This time I did not shy away from his stare.

'Tell me,' I said. 'Is it Beatrice? Have they done something to her?'

'Beatrice is fine and waiting for you,' Simion replied, still not looking at me for more than a second at a time. 'Please, we can go to her and talk about it.'

'Then what… no.' He caught my gaze, finally, refusing to look away. My knees buckled as I caught my wide-eyed reflection in the pools of his gaze. 'No.'

*My parents.*

The caress of Simion's power flooded my open mind and filled it with four, destructive words. *I am so sorry.*

# CHAPTER 44

My knees slammed into the hard floor of the cell, pain reverberating up my spine. 'No,' I said, broken and weak. 'No, no, no.'

Each time the word came out it was more furious. It boiled in my throat, scorching my insides until the cell echoed with my scream. Simion reached for me, hands holding my cheeks.

'I'll destroy them,' I shouted, voice echoing over the room, body trembling violently. 'I'll kill them all, Simion. All of them.'

Simion inhaled deeply. I longed for him to speak, but he didn't.'

'Speak, say something! What have the North done?'

If I had my amplifier, the room would have been torn apart. A storm raged within me, all-consuming. It shivered beneath my skin, coiled in the very pits of my soul. All I could do was hold onto Simion's eyes, unable to control my breathing.

'Nothing,' Simion said softly. 'The North have not harmed your parents, I promise.'

A spark of relief kindled in my chest, but quickly flickered out when I continued to feel the horror that occupied Simion's mind. 'Then I want to see them, please Simion. I need to know they are okay.'

He shook his head and my entire world burned to cinders. 'I can't do that for you, Max.'

A burst of strength flooded my body. I brought my arms between us and thrust them hard into his chest. Simion didn't waver, not even a step. He continued holding my face in his hands, staring deep into my soul.

'Bastard,' I screamed, swapping fists for open palms, continuing to rain down my blows on him.

Simion didn't pull back. 'I can't take you to them because your parents are not in Wycombe.'

I almost didn't hear him beneath the thunder of blood in my ears. 'Then take me wherever they are, do it now—'

'They never came to the North, Max.'

I paused, unable to do anything as his words settled over my mind like ash.

'You're lying,' I spluttered, almost laughing at the notion. 'Don't lie to me, Simion. I know they are here. They have to be.'

His power flooded through me, filling me with a window into his emotion. There, beneath my storm of fury and panic, a spark of clarity burned hot. Simion. It was him, his core. And as I had before, I sensed something that had the power to completely undo me.

It was not words he pushed into my mind, but the feeling of weightless honesty. It flooded my body, undeniable in its power.

'I have no reason to lie, Max, not to you.' *Your parents are not here. They were never taken. The North do not have them.*

Elder Leia's confusion suddenly made sense.

I shivered, teeth chattering. Squeezing my eyes closed, I couldn't focus on anything but the furious storm scorching through me.

'Camron,' Simion spat the name as though the word disgusted him. It was enough to cut through my body and scare my soul.

I pulled away from him, scrambling until my back pressed against the cold wall. 'What about him?'

'He lied. To you. To us. Your parents were never intercepted by the North, never taken. Max, the North has informants across the South—and it has been confirmed your parents still reside in Calzmir borders.'

'But…'

Simion dropped his head, gaze lost to a place on the floor by his feet. 'I've failed you.'

'No. This was your plan all along, wasn't it? To turn me against the South, that is what you are trying to do—'

'They're still alive,' Simion interrupted.

'Camron,' I whispered to myself more than Simion. Where the handfast marks inked my skin, it burned as though torched by flame. I looked down at the marks, my mind thundering with questions. When I said his name, it was a deep, visceral growl. '*Camron.*'

'We will figure it out,' Simion said. 'Together, you, me and Beatrice, we will make sense of what is happening.'

I burst from the ground, forcing myself to stand as though lightning shot through me. 'Then I need to leave, I have to go and get them.'

Simion held my gaze. 'You know it isn't as simple as that.'

'Are you going to stop me?' Fury boiled my blood.

'Yes,' Simion replied. 'If you wish to return to your parents, it will be with our support. The North will help you, Maximus. Then and only then can we go. Together.'

I fisted my hands, nails scoring marks into my palm, teeth cutting into my lower lip. I wanted to feel something that wasn't this useless panic. Simion's threat about death and punishment mattered little compared to the worry of my parents and their safety.

'Why...' I breathed, stomach twisting. 'Why would Camron lie?'

All at once, the memory of Camron's warmth faded. Before I would've grasped onto it, but now I let it leave me.

'I don't know.' Simion exhaled a long, tense breath from his nose.

Once again, the skin beneath my handfast mark stung. I longed to draw my nails over it and scratch it free from my flesh. Shame ruled my mind.

*This isn't your fault, Max.*

'Yes,' I said aloud, unable to fill my mind with anything but self-blame, hate and embarrassment. I allowed Camron to fool me. He preached about trust and blinded me with his warmth. If what Simion revealed was true, Camron had lied for a reason—manipulated me into this very position. All I could think about was *why*. Why did he do this? Why did he lie to me?

'Which is why I must be the one to fix it,' I added. 'No matter what.'

Simion *saw* my dark thoughts, he knew what I longed to do.

'And the first step of that is getting you out of here,' Simion said, extending a hand for me. I looked at it, untrusting, as though he held out a viper for me to grasp.

Scorned by others, I wouldn't allow my trust to be so freely given. Not to Simion, to the North, to anyone—I could only trust myself.

# CHAPTER 45

I moved through the world in a blur. I was a phantom, lost to the horrors of my reality. If Simion hadn't guided me with his hand in mine, I would never have moved from my cell.

I thought the formation of guards was for my benefit. I quickly realised they were here for Simion. When they regarded me, it was with eyes full of distrust—full of hate. But when they looked at Simion, it was with a glint of respect.

The guards reminded me of the mage who attacked Gathrax town—the one who tried to kill me but ended up as melted flesh and steel. Although these didn't wear pointed helms with fronts crafted into the shape of a dryad's face, they did have silver armour, a stone-grey cloak flowing behind them and the curled emblem of a curled-up dragon etched onto their breastplates.

Battlemages, all of them.

Simion kept me to his side as we navigated the maze of dark stone corridors. Every now and then I forced myself to drink in the details around me. We walked for an age until the corridor opened to an expansive room. There was the sound of rushing winds, echoing over stone. It wasn't until the battlemages at the front of our formation moved aside that I saw the cause.

In the centre of the grand room there was no floor. A dark pit of shadow fell away to nothingness. I looked across the walkway that hugged the wall around the circular space. There were no other doors and, most notably, no stairs. There was only the drop before us and nothing but the corridor at our backs.

One of the battlemages produced a mace from beneath their cloak. It was no surprise to discover the weapon was crafted from dark wood. Her hair was so black it had a slight blue sheen beneath the glowing veins of the stone walls. It was cut in line with her angular jaw but shaved on one side. Her fringe fell shy of her eyes, making the bright-blue hue stand out.

And out of them all, her eyes alone had the power to flay my skin. She had the type of stare that warned others away, a silent power that was not a result of magic.

The air spoiled with the promise of magic as she lifted the mace before her. At first, I couldn't understand what her attempt was for. Then I heard it. A soft whoosh of something large disturbed the whistling air, coming from far beneath us in the shadows of the pit before us.

A circular platform hovered into view and lined up perfectly with the pathway we stood on. It was a large disc made from the purest of white stone.

'Thank you, Mage Leska.' Simion placed his hand gently behind my elbow and urged me forward. He didn't seem to flinch as she stepped from the solid ground of the pathway onto the hovering slab of stone. The guard, Leska, held it afloat with nothing but her power.

'You're welcome, Mage Hawthorn,' Leska said, deep voice

resonating around the space. She bowed her head slightly. It was clear Simion held rank over these battlemages from the way they rallied around him.

As I stepped in past her, Leska raised her azure eyes and levelled them with mine. Disgust rolled off her in undulant waves. I refused to look away as I followed Simion onto the platform of stone. I only stopped when the battlemages joined us, blocking her from view.

My stomach jolted as the stone podium dropped violently. Simion held firm onto my hand, keeping me in place. Through the urge to vomit, I cast my eyes out into the blurring walls and tried to make sense of what I saw.

The tower was endless. As the podium fell through the dark pit, I saw that it was created from different levels. Over and over, we passed circular balconies lit with the same glowing stones the tower was built from. There was no requirement for firelight or daylight, not when the stone provided something better.

No matter how hard I focused on my surroundings, it was hard to make out anything given the speed we moved with. All the while, Simion didn't let go of my hand. Heights never bothered me and, after flying on Glamora, I had almost become comfortable with it. But I sensed Simion's concern in the hardening grip of his fingers around mine.

Our descent slowed. It was then I noticed that some of the other shapes we passed were not part of the tower, but other stone podiums that rose and fell around us. People stood upon them, looking at us. No, they looked at me.

*What is this place?* I stretched out my question, flickering my awareness up the ever-constant trickle of Simion's presence. Since we left the cell, he hadn't withdrawn completely from my mind. It was oddly comforting.

*Saylam Academy.*

I looked around again. Simion had spoken about the academy before, but I hardly imagined anything like this.

*Those are students of the academy,* Simion said within my mind, *some are academics and teachers.*

*They hate me.* I saw it in every face. Even the battlemages who surrounded us, the emotion oozed from them.

*They don't know you.*

The stone platform collided with the ground, sending me off kilter. Simion steadied me.

'You'll get used to it,' he said aloud, offering me a warning smile that flattened as he looked down at my hands. *You're shaking.*

I didn't realise how violently my hands trembled until they were captured within his. His brown skin stood out against the cream tunic beneath his silver armour, his touch feather soft. *I can help you, but only if you allow me.*

I tore my gaze from my shaking fingers to his eyes. They were gentle, his brows furrowed, and full lips pursed.

*Since when have you asked for permission to mess with my thoughts?*

Simion pouted, a single eyebrow lurching. *I would never alter your thoughts. Even if I wanted to, which I don't, it is not a power I possess. But your emotions, I can. Do you give me permission?*

I didn't have it in me to question his offer. My energy was vacant, and my mind was far too preoccupied with the hateful stares around me and the knowledge that Camron had lied to me.

*Yes.* My reply reverberated between us.

Before the word could fade from my mind, an overwhelming wave of calm washed over me. I blinked and was transported to another time. No longer did I stand upon a stone platform, stood before countless eyes full of judgement and disdain. I was in a bath, surrounded by the faces of Gathrax servants. And there was Simion, his gentle hand brushing over the curve of my back.

He had done this before—calmed my emotions when I needed it most. A warmth spread beneath my skin at the thought, and I knew Simion recognised it. Although he didn't say it, I *felt* it.

The feeling lasted a beat, then disappeared when Simion dropped my hands. When I opened my eyes, my mind was clear. I could still recognise my worries, but they weren't as overwhelming as they had been.

'The carriage awaits you at the bottom of the steps,' Leska interrupted, as she hooked her mace back into her belt. 'Best we leave before we gather more of a crowd.'

'After you.' Simion agreed as the crowd of battlemages parted, allowing us both to walk through them.

I looked up and saw an endless void of darkness. We stood in the middle of a grand chamber, flooded with people carrying piles of books, scrolls caught between arms and satchels strapped over shoulders. There were lines of bodies waiting to step onto podiums, to move between the different levels.

Tall glass windows took up every wall I could see, spilling a cool light across the chamber, illuminating even the smallest of details. The air was alive with the chatter of people and the gentle rush of air. Stone podiums continued to lift into the bellows of shadow above us.

The world moved on around me, all without knowing how mine was now in ruin.

There wasn't much time to drink it all in as Simion urged me forward, the swarm of battlemages not dropping formation for a moment. Leska led the way; we cut through the stone chamber and hordes of bodies were forced to move out of the way. No one seemed to mind, not as their eyes fell from me to Simion.

'Stay close, Maximus,' Simion warned, as we moved into the sunlight that poured in from a towering archway. All I saw beyond it was blinding light. I raised a hand and blocked my eyes as we left the academy and stepped out into the world beyond.

Wycombe took my breath way. I would've stopped walking if it wasn't for the battlemages at my back. The city was vast. There was no knowing where it ended; as far as my eyes could see, there were rows of buildings, giving way to streets, giving way to more buildings. Everything was made from stone. There was not a single building with a thatched roof. This place—this city—was more than I could've ever imagined.

I followed at Simion's side, taking the many steps down from the academy entrance. Rivers of vine and root wove around the stone beneath my feet. I followed them, turning back to see the roots growing larger as they reached the academy's outer white walls. As I had seen when I'd arrived, the roots climbed the exterior of the tower, wrapping greedily around it.

A firm hand pressed into my lower back, and I turned to see Simion looking at me. 'Watch your step, Max. Now is not the time to fall before a crowd. Eyes up, back straight.'

At the bottom of the steps stood a carriage. It was cut from a dark red wood and decorated in silver trim and gold painted swirls. Four horses fussed at its front, held together by reins connected to another silver-plated battlemage in the rider's seat.

The door to the carriage was opened before Simion could reach for it. As the battlemages fanned out at our back, it was Leska who stood beside the open door. She shared a quiet word with Simion before he clambered inside. Then her blue eyes fell on me, her face twisting into a scowl. Her hand gripped my upper arm and squeezed, nails pinching skin.

'The man you killed meant the world to me,' Leska hissed, fingers tightening. 'I will *never* forget that.'

I couldn't take my eyes off her. Her hate was so palpable it tainted the air. I knew Leska spoke of the soldier who had ridden south on his red-dragon and ravaged Gathrax town. Who'd murdered Dame.

'Blood for blood,' I replied, holding her gaze, refusing to release it. 'He murdered innocent people; I simply returned the favour.'

The lines in her face deepened. Leska looked me up and down, disgust removing any ounce of beauty. Then she spat on the ground at my feet.

'Traitor Mage.'

I slipped inside the carriage before Leska could say another word. The door at my back slammed, a hand slapped the outside of the red-wood frame and the carriage shot forward. I caught a flash of blue eyes pass beyond the window and understood the promise that lingered in them.

I knew, if I ever saw Leska again, she would make me suffer for what I took from her. In a strange way, I welcomed it.

* * *

*Traitor Mage.*

Leska wasn't the only person to call me that. The Northern soldier I had killed had spat it at me, as had Elder Leia upon my arrival to Wycombe. It seemed I had a new title—one to add to the handful I'd collected over the past weeks.

Julian Gathrax, the False Son. Maximus Oaken, the Lost Mage. And now this: Traitor Mage.

What title would I have next?

The scent of salt and sea crashed into me. I pushed thoughts of Camron from my mind as a fresh wind lifted my greasy curls from my forehead and coated my damp skin. My eyes fell past Simion and took in the endless view of ocean and sky.

The world was blue—different shades of it, from the open, cloud-speckled sky to the crashing expanse of ocean.

The carriage ride had passed mostly in silence. Simion had leaned back and closed his eyes. He looked as exhausted as I should've felt. But whatever magic he had used on me had drawn away any negative emotion. I knew I should've worried over my parents, but I couldn't grasp the emotion no matter how hard I tried.

Simion had severed it, pulling it just out of reach.

Should I have said something to him? I wanted to; Dryads, the silence was insufferable. But his closed eyes and crossed arms kept me quiet. Instead, I stared out the window, drinking in the view.

Our destination was a cottage nestled upon the edge of a cliff. Its white painted walls had worn from years of sea spray and wind. Smoke billowed from a single chimney stack, signalling that someone was inside waiting. Beatrice, no doubt. I almost sensed the familiarity of her proximity.

Once out of the carriage, Simion talked to the guards in hushed tones. I took a few steps forward, and my stomach jolted, my knees buckling. Beneath me was a sheer drop of white chalk that ended where the cliff met the sea. Jarred teeth of rocks cut through the water as the waves fought against one another.

A roar filled the sky, causing me to stumble back a step. I

looked up into the dome of heavy grey clouds, as another roar responded to the first.

Dragons. Two of them flew overheard, twisting scaled bodies danced and played among the sky. The largest of the two had a body armoured in pale cerulean scales. The other dragon was a dark moss-green with brown colouring at the tips of his wings and under its hide. Into the sea they dove, wings folded close to their spear-like bodies, only to explode once again from the rough surface of the ocean. It was magnificent.

'On a clearer day, you can see the Nest from here.'

Simion stood shy of my shoulder. I hadn't heard him close in on me, but when I turned to look at him, I saw the carriage moving off into the distance, a cloud of dust at its back.

'Over there,' Simion said, leaning in as he pointed off into the distance—his sudden closeness made my skin tingle. 'You see, those collection of islands are where the battlemages keep their mounts—the Nests are far enough from Wycombe that we do not need to live directly beside the dragons, but close enough to call upon them when they are required.'

I could see the faint outline of protruding shapes in the distance. It looked more like shadow—smudges of earthen fingers reaching out of the ocean. Dragons flew through the skies above the islands. There were so many of them, I couldn't begin to comprehend what I saw.

Besides Glamora and the nameless red dragon Camron had turned to armour, the creatures had only ever dwelled in stories. Until now.

'I never imagined the North would be like this,' I whispered.

'You'll get used to it,' Simion said, lowering his arm and stepping back again.

I swept my gaze over the world, drinking it all in. Far in

the distance my eyes caught the faint shadow of Galloway Forest. It was so far away it was blurry, but I would recognise the dark blanket of woodland no matter where I stood.

I thought it was a trick of the light which made it seem as though the line of sentinel trees shifted and moved.

My eyes narrowed, desperate to make sense of it. Simion must've sensed I didn't follow him because he stopped, turned back and followed my line of sight.

'The trees,' I breathed, a hand raised over my eyes to block out the sun's glare. 'They're moving.'

When Simion replied, I could almost hear the smile in his tone. 'Those are dryads, Maximus.'

I didn't dare believe him. Thick bark-coated coats, limbs like the branches of ancient trees, crowns protruding from heads thick with foliage.

'*Dryads*,' I breathed, 'So this is where they went.'

'Wycombe has much to protect itself against. Besides our power and dragons, our kin, the dryads, keep unwanted visitors out, and those they want in.' Simion leaned in, his breath tickling the sensitive skin of my ear. 'Except they let you go, no questions asked. One must wonder why?'

I couldn't fathom it, but, then again, I had ridden on the back of a dragon and could command the very earth to do my bidding. What was next, a phoenix or nymphs? Reluctantly, I tore my gaze from the dryads, back to the cottage behind us.

'Is this your home?' I asked.

'No. I cannot say mine is as peaceful as this. I thought you would appreciate something less... crowded,' Simion said, winds lifting his cloak, making it dance at his back. 'And this is far enough away from the city for you to rest, but close enough for the Council to remain content. They don't wish to lose you again.'

A spike of emotion rose in me. Simion's power had smothered the flame in me, not extinguished it.

'They may not have a choice,' I replied, as my anxieties
returned like a racing tide.

We both turned towards the cottage as the door opened
and Beatrice stepped out. Tears filled my eyes, blurring the
view of my friend as she carefully leaned her staff against the
outer wall.

'Camron...' I called out to her, voice breaking under the
weight of the truth. 'He lied.'

'I know,' she said softly, jaw set with tension. 'I know, Max.'

I stumbled through the rotten wooden gate and up the
stone-slabbed pathway. Beatrice moved towards me, catching
me in her arms as I threw myself into them.

'Everything is so wrong,' I cried, tears soaking into the
shoulder of her loose shirt. The intense smell of rose from the
large bushes buried the sea-salt air that poisoned my mind
with images of Camron.

'We are going to work this out, Max. Together, okay?'
Beatrice said, powerful calloused hands rubbing across my
back.

'I'm an idiot, a stupid fool who trusted someone so easily
when I never truly knew him.'

Simion kept his distance, but the cool trickle of his presence lingered in the back of my skull. It was moments like this
I longed to block him out. Did Simion see the flashes of
Camron and me in that room, with the warmth of fire and
alcohol to keep us company? The memory, which had not
long given me comfort, now punished me.

'We don't yet know his motives, Max, but I promise we
will help you figure this out,' Beatrice said, pulling me from
her and keeping me at arm's length. There was a determination in her eyes that calmed me.

'You still trust him?' I asked, the sadness twisting into wrath.

'I trust he cares about you,' Beatrice said. 'That much was clear. We can only hope he has lied for good reason.'

'And what would that be? What could he possibly want from me that is worth this deception?'

Beatrice dropped her head, looking away with a heavy sigh. 'I don't know.'

She was lying.

# CHAPTER 46

Night had fallen across the world, bathing the sky in a navy-black blanket littered with clouds. I sat on the damp ground, ignoring the moisture seeping into my trousers. The grass around me was crusted with dried salt from the ocean spray that thickened in the air. I drew the heavy grey cloak Beatrice had given me, tugging it around my shoulders against the cold.

A solitary dragon—its colouring impossible to make out in the dark—flew among the clouds, crying its song across the ocean. It was both beautiful and rough. I thought of Glamora and wondered if she was resting with the hordes of dragons who made their home within the collection of islands off the coast—the Nest, as Simion had called it.

The ground rumbled beneath me when the carriage finally arrived.

I didn't look to confirm it was Simion who had returned—his presence traced a featherlight finger at the back of my mind. Then he was there, standing on the sodden ground beside me, offering nothing but silent comfort with his presence.

'Is it true?' I asked, before he could utter a word.

'It is,' Simion said, voice void of any emotion. 'News has reached us that Camron plans to march for Wycombe.'

Simion had kept away all day. When I asked Beatrice why, she had explained that he was petitioning with the Council to help retrieve my parents. It took little more digging to uncover his urgency.

The North believed an army were on their way. They didn't know the army they were threatened by was made up of innocents, no more skilled with a pitchfork and torch than a weapon. This army was only patriotic civilians, willing to lay their life down for mine.

After seeing the dragons, the academy of mages, Leska— the South stood no chance. The North would crush them in a heartbeat.

'I'm not your responsibility,' I said beneath a rush of wind. These words had built within me all day; I couldn't hold them back any longer. 'I'm not your sister. I'm not someone you need to waste time helping just to keep yourself occupied.'

Simion didn't say a word as he sat beside me. A small part of me felt the need to ask him to go away, when the other part of me—the bigger, louder part—knew I had been outside because I had waited for him. The more my emotions returned to me throughout the day, the more I needed Simion. I craved him—craved what his power could offer. But my pride kept me from asking.

'You have an uncanny way of seeing me for who I am,' Simion said. 'Bones and all.'

I glanced at him, catching the profile of his face and the faint silver curls at his temples, lingering in his dark hair much like the stars in the sky above us.

'What has been decided?' I asked.

'The Queen and her Council have agreed that they will be sending a number of battlemages to the South.'

My heart dropped like a stone in my stomach. 'To destroy him?'

'To talk with Camron. They will not fight, not unless they must.'

'When?' I had to go.

Simion stiffened. 'They are readying their dragons and will take flight immediately.'

'And my parents, what about them?' My lungs constricted, panic returning in full force.

'*I* have it in hand.'

'And *I* shouldn't need to rely on anyone else to protect them.'

Simion moved enough that his arm brushed mine. 'Beatrice adores you. I owe you my life for what you have given my sister in the years that have passed.'

'No, you don't owe me anything.'

He turned to look at me. Where his eyes grazed my skin, it left it feeling as raw as my insides. 'That, Maximus, is for me to decide. You brought my family back to me. I will do the same for you. Consider it payment, a thanks. Then we are even.'

'Even?' I scoffed. 'This is all some game to you?'

'Believe me, I don't see this as a game. I see this as a chance to prove to you, and to myself— Dryads, it is to prove to Beatrice the North can be different to what you believe. It isn't all bad, it can be home. It can be a future.'

Simion silenced himself, his eyes scanning out across the oceans, searching for something he longed to find.

There was only one person left he didn't have. I didn't

need him to voice it to know thoughts of his mother filled his mind.

I swallowed hard, unable to stop myself from speaking. 'Can I ask her name?'

'Celia. Celia Hawthorn,' Simion said, knowing exactly who I asked after. I saw the grief in his eyes as he looked out across the landscape.

'It's a beautiful name.'

'Was,' Simion corrected.

I leaned into his arm, longing to take my cloak and encase him in it. 'Just because she is gone, doesn't mean her presence cannot linger. The name *is* beautiful, Simion. Not was, it is.'

'That doesn't make hearing it any less painful,' Simion replied. 'She left, me and Beatrice. Now, my sister is all I have left.'

We fell back into silence. All I could focus on was his laboured breathing and the way he was taller than me, even as we sat side by side. The faint silver light illuminated the bow of his mouth, the high prominent cheekbones and the square line of his jaw, flexing as he gritted his teeth.

'The Queen wishes to speak with you tomorrow,' Simion said quietly, diverting the conversation.

There was a crack in my chest as fear snapped open my ribs.

'Okay,' I replied, because it was the only thing I could think to say.

'No, it's not,' Simion said. 'Nothing about this is okay.'

My eyes fell to his hands. They were balled into fists upon his lap.

I reached out and laid my fingers carefully on them. Like a rosebud to sunlight, his hand unfurled beneath my touch. I didn't have Simion's power, but I could still offer him comfort in my own way.

Simion glanced to my hand, contemplated it, then exhaled a breath, tension ebbing from him like waves over a shore.

'I'm ready for my next lesson, Simion. Teach me how to protect my mind,' I said, longing to distract Simion from his turmoil. It was strange, but I felt as though it was my responsibility.

'Now?' Simion asked. He kept his hand beneath mine, deadly still.

'Show me how to protect my thoughts from those who will want to infiltrate them. It doesn't take much to know the Queen and her Council will deploy any tool necessary to reach a verdict of my loyalty. And in truth, I'm still unsure who it lays with.'

Simion flinched. 'It isn't as simple as—'

'Teach me,' I interrupted, refusing to release his gaze.

Simion's amber stare traced across every inch of my face, searching. Then he moved, shifting his weight around until he was sat, cross-legged, facing me. I did the same, the muddied ground squelching beneath me, as I turned to face him.

'Intention and execution,' Simion said, reaching up and pressing a cool finger to my temple. I closed my eyes as a shiver raced over my entire body. 'You must first intend to protect your mind— a wall around it, the strength of which is determined by your mind's ability to imagine. Blocking your thoughts from a gleamer is no different than calling upon your own magic. When you use your magic, you see what it is you wish to do and, with intention, you do it. This is no different.'

His cold power echoed in the back of my mind, letting me know he was there.

'What about my amplifier?' I asked, 'Don't I need it?'

'This is one power you don't need your amplifier for.

Camron is not a mage, and yet his mind was closed. It is will; it is practice.'

I stared deep into him, noticing the flecks of sea-salt across his russet skin. '*Show* me.'

'Create a wall,' Simion guided softly, his voice mixing with the rushing winds and crashing waves far below. 'See it in your mind, build it brick by brick and don't stop until you turn your skull into a fortress.'

It was hard to do anything when all I could focus on was his finger pressed to my temple. Each time I attempted to erect a protection, it fell like ash in a breeze and his presence in my mind only built.

'It's as if you don't want me to keep you out,' I said, opening my eyes to find him closer than before.

His palm followed his finger as he flattened his hand against the side of my head. Gently, he held my cheek as though it was the most delicate thing in the world.

Perhaps it was his touch, or hopeful gaze. Maybe it was his ability to calm the storm within me and make me feel as though I had nothing to worry about beyond the moment we experienced. Or maybe it was my selfish desire for a distraction—from the world, the lies, the truths of it all. Whatever the reason was, I leaned towards Simion, closed the gap between us and pressed my lips to his.

Simion kept still, eyes wide and watching. Then they closed, the tension in his face smoothed and he melted into me. I did the same. Hands grasped the side of my face, fingers trailing into my scalp. His tempered exhale brushed over my face as our kiss deepened.

My lips parted, my tongue slipping free. His joined in— brushing, caressing.

There was nothing rushed about it. It was as though we had all the time in the world.

Deep in my core, something unfurled. It peeled apart, one by one, the petals of vulnerability flaking away until the sensitive bud at the centre was open to the world—

Pain overcame me. It was unlike anything I had known before. It boiled through the skin on my arm, twisting my muscle, boiling my blood.

I jolted from Simion, blinded by agony, gasping out.

'What is it?' Simion spluttered, panic creased across his face.

I couldn't answer. If I opened my mouth, a scream would've burst free.

My arm—my fast-marked skin—felt as though it had been torn apart. It lasted only a moment, a second when my lips had met Simion's, then faded. Only discomfort lingered, reminding me of my crime.

Infidelity.

*Only in death shall you part.*

I stood abruptly, wincing as the invisible fire trickled across my arm. 'I shouldn't have done that. I'm not thinking straight. I'm sorry...'

Simion stood too. 'It's my fault, I gave you the impression...'

I turned my back on him, cloak sweeping out around me, before he could finish. The windows glowed with orange-red firelight and the door was nothing but a shadowed hole. It was as if the cottage was a witness, watching as I went against the handfasting and kissed another man.

'Maximus.' My name carried on the wind. I knew it was Simion because he followed up with speaking it out into the void of my mind. *Maximus, wait.*

I threw a wall up around my thoughts, not of stone or brick, but newly forged steel. It shot up with a single thought, born from desperation to keep Simion out.

One thought and Simion's presence faded. He didn't chase after me as I approached the cabin.

Beatrice turned as the door slammed open, a questioning look on her face. I didn't linger in the front room long enough for her to speak. With my heart beating viciously in my chest, I focused on my bedroom and didn't stop until I was shut behind its door.

I sat on the bed, silver-inked arm held to my chest. I didn't release it until the pain subsided. When it did, I inspected my arm to find new marks, torn flesh. But it was unmarked, besides the silver ink. But the pain had been real. And I knew what it meant.

I was trapped.

*Only in death shall you part.*

# CHAPTER 47

Sleep evaded me. Night passed slowly into dawn, torturing me with the passing of time. Whenever I closed my eyes, I saw him, Camron, haunting me with his lies and secrets. Even during my waking hours, my skin itched with the discomfort gifted from going against the bond.

It was not as debilitating as it'd been when I'd placed my lips upon Simion's—but it was enough of a reminder. A warning.

I tried to think back to the moment, but it was shrouded in the fog of agony. Had Simion thought I'd pulled away from the horror of the moment? I pressed the heels of my palms into my eyes until I saw stars flash in the dark.

'Dryads, help me,' I begged, face buried in my hands.

Being with Camron felt as though I was being pulled down a ravine, thrashed from side to side with no control. With Simion, it was different. A languid flow down a lazy river, slow and tempered, so I could take in the world around me.

I changed, knowing I couldn't hide in my room forever.

The cottage was oddly quiet, so much that when the pounding of heavy footsteps suddenly began, I couldn't stifle my panic.

Wood crashed into stone as my bedroom door was thrown open. The force shook the wall as Simion strode into the room. Seeing him pained me, reminding me of the feeling of broken bones and blade-scored skin.

'We're under attack.' He was wide-eyed and breathless.

I moved instinctively for my wand, but I didn't have it.

Simion paused, swallowed hard and I practically felt the terror radiating off him in waves. 'Wycombe is burning.'

Confusion sunk its talons into my mind.

'I can't find Beatrice,' Simion repeated, 'I can't find my sister.' He was frozen to the spot, gripping the stone wall for support. His chest rose and fell rapidly. I reached him in four long strides, placing a hand over his heart. Through rib and flesh, his heart slammed rapidly. He was dressed for battle—as though I saw him for the first time, I drank in his powerful body garbed in armour. Simion fumbled with the belt around his waist, tightening it and making the sword in its sheath clang against his greaves.

He tore his eyes from the space they'd been pinned to beyond me and looked me dead in the eye. 'I don't know what is happening, Max. But it isn't good. I need to find her.'

Simion took my hand and guided me from the bedroom. He didn't stop until we were outside in the cold dawn wind.

The smell hit me before I'd even taken my first step outside. Smoke. The air was thick with it.

I moved without thought, stepping down the cottage's pathway and towards the cliff edge beyond. There, in the distance, a shadow slithered lazily up into the sky, where it spread like a dark stain across the world.

I lifted my hand, upturned, before me and caught grey

flakes. One landed on the tip of my finger. I crushed it between my thumb, smudging the ash between them.

The sky rumbled with thunder as a dark shape separated from the plume of smoke and flew towards us.

'Simion,' I shouted, pointing as the dark mass broke from the plume of obsidian smoke, flying towards us with great speed. 'Is that… Glamora!'

I raised a hand to my brow but, even from a distance, I recognised the shadow of wings and claws that cut through the discoloured sky. At first, I had thought the dragon was black in colour because it was covered in ash, but as it grew closer and the light licked off scale obsidian scales, I knew who it was.

The moment Glamora touched down on the ground, Beatrice threw herself off and ran towards us. Her face was smudged in ash, her dark cloak almost white from being covered in it. She was coughing, violently, as Simion held her up.

'What's happening?' The question fell out of me. Beatrice didn't seem fazed because she answered so quickly it was almost rehearsed.

'I went to smooth some of my grievances with Elder Leia. Thank the Dryads because the attacks started. She… she told me to come and get you. Both of you. We must go directly to the Heart Oak—the Council await us.'

'Who is attacking?' Simion asked. 'Beatrice, is it the South?'

Is it Camron?

She looked her brother dead in the eye and shook her head. 'The fire is black, Simion.'

*Wytchfire.*

'There are fires all over the city,' Beatrice continued. 'Every mage has been called to protect the Queen and her Heart Oak. We must go, now.'

There was the familiar tickle of Simion, but the steel fortress I had erected was still there. He withdrew before I could even lower it and allow him entry. Something was off. I sensed it deep within me.

'Then we go,' Simion said, gazing back to the burning city.

Beatrice's amplifier was strapped around her back, held in place with leather bindings over her clothes. Like me, she wore a similar fitted black outfit, with thick leather boots. The only difference was she had her amplifier, and I didn't.

'I'll stay,' I said, as both siblings moved towards Glamora. 'I can't help without my wand.'

Simion broke away from Beatrice, concern creased across his strong bow. Ash had fallen into his tight, brown curls. 'You're right. Until we know the threat has been dealt with—'

'No,' Beatrice snapped, a flash of panic passing behind her eyes. 'Max needs to come. He... Leia said he must. Simion, we cannot leave Max alone. What if *they* come for him next? He wouldn't stand a chance.'

Simion looked from me to his sister and back again.

'Fine,' he said, gritting his teeth. Firm hands grasped my arms, holding me in place. The look Simion gave me was riddled with panic. 'But don't leave my side. I'll protect you.'

\* \* \*

Glamora pounded across the cliff face, wings spread as she readied to catch the winds beneath them. With the powerful force of her legs, she pounced into the skies, just as the ground gave way to the sudden cliff. We rose into the roaring winds, below us was nothing but ocean and cliff. We joined the clouds, climbing higher and higher. Once we were above them, the chill of sky nipping at my cheeks and nose, I could see the spire of the Saylam Academy ahead.

Suddenly, we were surrounded by dragons. Hordes of them passed us as we flew towards the city. I stifled a cry as dragons burst from the belly of clouds beneath us, slicing through the plumes of white, so close to us that Glamora jolted from side to side to keep out of the way. I glanced behind me, to see a mass of the creatures flying away from the Nest, leaving the peace of their islands behind, towards the destruction laid upon the Northern city.

With a giant cry of warning, Glamora changed course. Bile burned at the back of my throat as Glamora took a sudden dip, diving beneath the clouds. The towering spire of Saylam Academy was before us. The shard of white was dusted with ash as the billowing clouds of smoke now raged around us.

The city was a blur. The streets were full of people who watched the skies as the dragons sped above them. I could see the beasts as they flew above smouldering buildings—pouring their icy breath across the flames to quell them.

Glamora's dark shadow passed over black-tiled roofs, towering white buildings, and smaller homes that reminded me of the cottage we had only just left behind.

Dots of angry red flames ate their way throughout Wycombe city, spreading from one building to another. Every now and then I saw a flash of boiling black fire, flickering across streets as though it moved on by an unseen force.

I watched as another dragon, with scales as green as Galloway Forest's canopy, shot towards the fire. It spread its spiked jaws wide, unleashing a river of dragon ice across it. The freeze cracked against the side of my face. The dragon reared around before crashing into a building, turned its course back and released a second bout of frozen wind over the black fire.

This didn't put it out, but it certainly helped calm its spread. *For now.*

Wytchfire—it was everywhere I looked. Riling black flames, nestled among red and orange, hungering for the city and everything within it.

In the centre of Wycombe, the city seemed to open. The buildings lessened and the streets widened, until it gave way to another building—even more breathtaking and other-worldly than Saylam Academy. Wide and tall, made from moss-covered bricks. Through the broken roof, the largest tree I had ever seen stretched skywards. Full and green, large birds flew in and out of the shaded belly of the foliage, fleeing the oncoming destruction of the fire that spread towards it.

My eyes shifted down the monstrous tree, to the roots that spread out beneath it. Large and demanding, they devoured entire walls, weaved in and out of the broken steps that led up to the entry of the castle. Looking back, it was clear to see it was the roots of this tree which stretched miles into Wycombe city, all the way to Saylam Academy, where it spread up the spire as though connecting it to the heart of the city.

'Heart Oak,' Simion shouted into my ear.

Heart Oak. The very same tree that was burned by wytch-fire in Galloway Forest now stretched out into the smoke-stained sky around us. It was a twin—a sibling to the one that had been destroyed.

Jonathan Gathrax had lied about many things, but this was one thing he spoke the truth of. There was power here. A place the South could use, claim amplifiers for themselves, and even the balance of Aldian's power.

Wonder stole my mind, capturing it and refusing to let it go. It was beyond anything I could've ever imagined seeing. Stolen from the many paintings in the Gathrax family library, it was as though this tree was copied down to the fine detail.

Then my mind went to the burned corpse of the Heart Oak—the one burned by wytchfire all those years ago. As hot and sharp as the flames beneath us, I had the urge to protect the tree before me.

It was visceral, unignorable.

An explosion of heat burst from beside us. Glamora careened away from the blast as stone and rubble filled the sky around us. Beatrice's stomach tensed, muscles hardening beneath my grip.

Simion held firm too, shouting when we almost fell from the dragon's back as she dipped and wove amongst the chaos.

The sudden flare of heat nipped at my skin, followed by a flash of boiling red flame. A building opposite the castle had burst apart, sending rubble raining down across the street before it. Chunks of stone careened into the buildings at its sides, smashing glass and destroying walls—leaving a cloud of dust and ruin in its wake.

Buried deep within the roaring flames, there was not a soul in Wycombe who couldn't hear the shrill squawk of a bird. Glamora reacted, unleashing a roar so visceral, the air before her jaw crackled with ice.

My eyes trained on the shattered building, to the flames which twisted into a cyclone before darkening to the black-tainted flame of wytchfire.

# CHAPTER 48

A formation of armoured battlemages stood shoulder to shoulder around the entirety of the castle. They looked formidable as the flickering fire reflected off the dryad faces of the helms, amplifiers of all shape and design held at the ready.

There was magic in the air, twisting and powerful as the first inhale of spring.

Glamora cut across the skies above them, blanketing the army of battlemages in shadow. The lower we got, the more I could taste the magic in the air. By the time we landed, my skin itched with it.

One of the battlemages broke away from the line before the grand steps leading up to the castle's stone-pillared entrance. It was looking more as though the castle was a shrine than a place of residence. It was certainly not the type of place I would've expected a queen to live.

Leska tore her helm off, her black hair ruffled over stern eyes. 'We are about to raise a wall of defence. Any later and your entry would have been refused.'

'Just in time then, where's Elder Leia?' Simion asked, command thick in his deep voice. He was breathless, hand never straying far from the pommel of his sword.

Leska's sharp blue eyes fell on me, her face twisting in familiar disgust. I didn't react, refusing to show how her presence bothered me. In her eyes I could read the title she had last spat at me.

*Traitor Mage.*

'Your aunt and the rest of the Council have retreated into the catacombs,' Leska confirmed. 'Until the assailant is found and dealt with, they are to stay out of harm's way.'

Simion placed a hand on the steel pauldron across Leska's broad shoulders. 'If it is what we believe, then a wall isn't going to keep them out.'

'We are out of options,' Leska said, radiating with her own aura of command. 'Nothing else matters but protecting the Heart Oak.'

'How did *it* get in?' Simion asked.

'Not through Galloway Forest. The dryads confirmed no sign of our borders being infiltrated, nor have the scouts discovered anyone lingering within the forest either. It would seem *it* has been let in, from the inside.'

Relief uncoiled in my chest knowing it wasn't the South who attacked the city.

Beatrice stepped forward and, to my surprise, Leska shot her a look of distaste. 'Have the candles, lanterns and hearths been extinguished within the castle?' Beatrice asked.

'Every last one,' Leska confirmed. 'Doused in water. No one is setting a fire inside.'

Beatrice stayed silent, picking at the skin around her nails.

'Good,' Simion answered for his sister. 'Then let us hope your wall keeps them out long enough.'

Leska's jaw clenched. 'Hope won't save us.'

Glamora beat her leathery wings, casting wind at our backs as she took to the skies. It didn't take long for the dragon to assist with casting her river of ice across the nearest flames.

'Follow me, and I will get you through the line,' Leska said. 'Once you pass it, you're on your own.'

The stone street beneath Beatrice thundered as she tapped her staff upon it. Leska may not have noticed, but I saw the slab crack as Beatrice radiated power. 'After you, Leska.'

We ran, following Leska towards the line of battlemages who split enough to allow us through. Simion kept pace at the front of our group, Beatrice at my side. Before we reached the castle's entrance, I stumbled at the sudden surge of magic at my back.

The air grew heavy, making breathing close to impossible. Deep in the pits of my gut, my magic coiled and thrashed, begging to join the explosive release from the battlemages at our back. But without my amplifier, it was useless.

I turned and watched as the cobbled street rippled like liquid. Vines of brown and emerald burst from the bellows of the earth, reaching skywards. Towering slabs of stone raised in their wake, lifting high from the ground until we were shrouded in shadow.

My eyes traced the length of the line for as far as I could see. Before every mage, the vines slithered and danced, twisting among one another until a trellis of knotted earth blocked the view of the city. Between the stone and the earth, two layers protected whatever attacked the city from reaching the Heart Oak.

'Come on,' Beatrice said, helping me before Simion reached us. My magic stirred, desperate to aid the battlemages around me. 'We need to get inside.'

Gripping her forearm, I hoisted myself up.

'*Shit.*' Beatrice hissed; pain evident on her face.

'You're hurt,' I said, releasing her quickly, glancing to the arm she cradled.

'I'm fine. It's nothing,' Beatrice replied, pulling her arm into her side as though I had burned her. This wasn't the first time she lied to me. I tried to catch her eyes, but Beatrice did everything to look away. I couldn't press further because Simion was there wrapping his powerful arm around my waist, guiding me away from the magnetic pull of power behind me.

* * *

My eyes longed to make out the details of the castle's interior, but everything was shrouded in darkness. The flames that had once burned proudly in the many iron-wrought braziers had been extinguished. Water dripped from the cool iron, puddling on the ground and splattering over the walls. All that was left were the ribbons of grey smoke slithering from their charred wicks.

Simion was at my side, Beatrice up ahead.

'It is a phoenix, isn't it?' I asked through heavy breaths. 'They're the ones behind the attack.'

His gold-flecked eyes fell upon me, brow furrowed. 'All signs point that way.'

'But why would they attack?'

'Perhaps for the same reason they helped destroy the Heart Oak all those years ago,' Simion said.

I stopped running, my thighs burning and my lungs on fire. Gripping my side, a knot formed between my ribs. Each breath pained me, jarring through my body.

'Which is?'

'Some believe the phoenixes are jealous of the power we

hold. Others believe they fear us. Unless we can commune with one, I don't think we'll ever know.'

'Simion, Max,' Beatrice called out ahead of us. She stood before an open door, beside her a hunched figure waited. It was the garish light which haloed them both, glowing at their backs, which caught my attention.

I felt it what waited beyond the door—it was power. Pure, undiluted, ancient power.

I glanced at Simion, wondering if he sensed it too. He showed no sign as he used his hand on my lower back to urge me forward.

The figure revealed themselves to be a gleamer. She spoke through the shadows of her heavy cloak, her voice thick with age, comparable to the creaking of floorboards, each word rough and slow. The only visible part beneath her cloak were her bright green eyes that crept over my skin like a spider.

'Simion Hawthorn, we have *not* been expecting you.'

Simion bowed his head slightly, a sign of respect to the older woman. 'Elder Leia requested our presence.'

'Are you suggesting I am lying? I am the Keeper of the Chamber and I know all who are to come. You, Simion Hawthorn, were not expected.'

Simion shot Beatrice a look, but she ignored it. Instead, Beatrice pushed past the woman into the ominous green glow beyond.

'Wycombe is under siege,' Beatrice snapped. 'If you haven't noticed, *crone*. Perhaps you can gleam your way into my aunt's mind and inform her that we are here. Believe me, she will wish to see us.'

'And who shall I say is joining you?' the old woman asked, unbothered by Beatrice's insults.

Beatrice levelled her eyes with mine. 'Leia will know.'

'On your head be it, Beatrice Hawthorn.'

Beatrice grimaced, eyes narrow and voice raw. 'I've experienced worse than the wrath of my aunt.'

'Yes, yes,' the old woman sang, her tone sickly sweet. 'That you have. Now, follow me, all of you.'

The ominous light and sense of power came from the very centre of the room we entered. The Heart Oak towered before us, rippling roots cast around the chamber, devouring walls. The ground was littered with leaves, most of which covered the faded runner carpet we walked upon.

At the front, the gleamer led us with Simion at her side. Beatrice kept near me, although always a step behind.

The closer we grew to the gargantuan trunk of the Heart Oak, the clearer I could make out a strange detail in its base. A throne—stone devoured by wood and root—sat empty and waiting.

'It feeds off her,' Beatrice whispered, following my line of sight. 'Without the Queen, the Heart Oak would rot. It needs her, just as she needs it to provide amplifiers for the mages.'

I gazed back to the plain stone design of the throne. There was nothing wealthy and plush about this place. It was void of the comforts, warmth and details you would expect royalty to surround themselves with.

Besides the budding, thumping glow of life that emitted from the Heart Oak, it was not a giving feeling but a taking one. It pulled at me, much like my power had reacted to the battlemages when they called upon their magic—the Heart Oak drew me in with a siren call only I could hear.

I counted ten strange-shaped trees on either side of the room—each completely different to each other. They were soldiers of wood, standing guard before the Heart Oak. It was not only the tree itself that blossomed with radiant power, but these smaller figures. Knots of roots and branches formed

these trees into the twisted shape of humans. And their faces
—eyes closed and coated in bark.

'Dryads,' the old woman croaked. As I turned, she was
inches before me with eyes glowing of raw jade. 'We leave
them to slumber.'

My mouth dried to bone as I looked back to the dryads,
waiting for someone to tell me the woman was wrong. But I
knew, deep in my core, that these trees were not mundane.

They were gods.

'Go on without me,' Beatrice said, as we got halfway
through the room. We all turned and looked at her, standing
with her staff in one hand as though it was a sword of great
legend. 'I should help the battlemages keep the Heart Oak safe.'

'No,' Simion spat. 'Bea, we stick together.'

Beatrice didn't move. Simion inhaled, ready to say something else, but Beatrice silenced him with a single look.

'This is my home, Simion. Let me protect it.' Beatrice
glanced at me, cocking her chin in the direction of her
brother. 'He'll keep you safe.'

I reached out and grasped her hand before she turned.
Lightning fast, I pushed up the sleeve of her top and revealed
the blistered mess of brown skin beneath. It lasted a moment
before she pulled back, putting space between us.

'Why are you burned?' I muttered.

She tore her arm from me, pushing down the sleeve.

'The city is on fire, friend.' Beatrice didn't smile as she
replied. She continued stepping back. 'What did you expect to
happen?'

There was something she was holding back.

'You can tell me,' I whispered, not wanting Simion to hear.
If Beatrice was hiding something, it was for a reason. 'Whatever is going on, let me help you.'

She paused, her chest heaving. I saw her contemplate my offer, warring internally with herself. 'You can, soon enough.' Then she raised her eyes over my shoulder and looked at Simion. Her entire faced softened. 'Look after him, Max.'

Simion broke the strange atmosphere which blossomed around us. 'Beatrice is right, her power is best suited outside with the rest of the battlemages.'

I steeled my expression as I turned to face him, burying my concern for Beatrice. She was my friend and I trusted her. I had to trust her because out of everyone left, she was the only sliver remaining of my life before—and I longed to hold onto it.

# CHAPTER 49

Without firelight to guide us, Simion offered me his hand. I refused him at first, but he persisted. I had expected the sharp stab of agony to thrum up my arm. It didn't. There was only the soft brush of his palm and an anchoring hold as fingers knotted with mine.

Soon enough the impenetrable dark gave way to a soft violet hue of light. Even then, Simion didn't let go of me. His calm, steady presence was a welcoming thing.

I looked up to the terrifying roots that devoured the stone ceiling above us. Across it, mould emanated the purple light— it dripped in puddles, spreading its reach of light across the chamber. Down here, it smelled heavily of earth. The air was thick with moisture, each lungful of breath filling me with the sticky, almost sweet, aroma the glowing mould emitted. I was far too focused on the impossibilities of my surroundings to notice Elder Leia rushing towards us.

'Simion Hawthorn, how *dare* you bring him here of all places!' Elder Leia shouted. Simion barely had a chance to stand in front of me as she threw herself forward, eyes wide and alight with fury.

I wanted to stand before Simion, to shield him with my body. 'You requested my presence.'

'In what world do you think that would ever be a possibility!' Elder Leia ripped me away from him, her fingers biting into the skin of my upper arm. With a great heave, she pulled me tight to her side.

Leia attempted to gleam my mind. I kept her out, solidifying the steel wall with burning intention. Like nails scratching against glass, Leia prowled the perimeters of my thoughts—searching, waiting for a way through my fortress.

'Take your hands off him,' Simion growled, face twisted into a mask of contempt.

'Remember your place.' She swatted his request away with the back of her hand. 'Simion, I expected more from you.'

I saw a realisation settle over him. 'The same can be said for you,' Simion hissed, fingers drumming on the handle of his blade. It didn't go unnoticed by Elder Leia. She tightened her grip, her scowl sharp enough to break skin.

'You didn't give Beatrice this order, did you?' The question broke out of me.

I already knew the answer before she replied.

'My order!' Leia barked. 'I haven't spoken to that insolent girl since you arrived. Why, Simion, would I ask for you both to come at a time like this?'

'But—' Simion began, but I quickly interrupted.

'Beatrice lied,' I said, finding the word difficult. Simion snapped his entire attention towards me.

'Where *is* your sister?' Leia spat. 'I want to know what game she thinks she is playing.'

Beatrice had never been to see Elder Leia. If that is not where she'd been last night, then what had she been doing? I knew, without a doubt, the burn on her arm held the answers.

'She went to help the battlemages...' Before Simion could finish, Elder Leia shot a glance to the silent gleamer who had guided us here.

'Go, retrieve my niece,' Leia said, flicking her head as though she commanded a child. 'Bring her to me so she can explain what she wished to gain from this.'

'Yes, yes,' the old gleamer sang. Then she turned on her little legs and shuffled back to where we had come from.

'Since you are here, *Traitor Mage*, you'll face your judgement before the Queen.'

'The city is under attack,' Simion shouted, rushing in front of his aunt to block her from moving. 'Now is not the time.'

The violet glow of light cast over Elder Leia's bone-white hair, turning the thick strands lavender. A possessiveness washed over me as Elder Leia jolted me into step beside her. As though my eyes were drawn to it, I looked towards her ivory-cream shawl and felt what lingered beneath.

My wand pulsed through the folds of material, a beacon of light in the dark. It was so close I could've reached out and grasped it— Dryads know I longed to. My ocean of magic sloshed as violent as a storm, demanding release.

'Do you forget yourself, Simion?' his aunt asked calmly. There was a lurking danger in the woman's stillness that sparked more fear in me than when she shouted.

'I'll go, Simion.' I couldn't take my eyes off him as I replied.

He shook his head, defying me. 'Not alone.'

'Yes,' I snapped, giving into the desperate fury my proximity to the wand created. 'Alone. Don't make this any harder than it needs to be.'

Simion stiffened, flinching slightly from the bite of my words.

The scratching at the back of my skull intensified. A flash of pain thundered behind my eyes as Leia continued her attempt to gain entry.

'Have you something to hide, Traitor Mage?' she asked.

I looked her dead in the eyes, refusing to show any weakness. 'Yes.'

Leia recoiled physically, her eyes narrowing. I offered her a smile, a brilliant toothy grin that only painted more disgust over her face.

'Take me to your Queen,' I said, as my fingers twitched with the urge to strike out and take my wand from her.

Leia leaned in close, lips purling back into a snarl as her wide eyes traced over every inch of my face. 'You would do well to remember she is your Queen too.'

'Find Beatrice,' I called out to Simion, who lingered behind us. There was a part of me that longed to withdraw the walls around my mind and allow him access, just so I could tell him what I had seen on her arm, so I could share my concerns. But I couldn't do it, not with Leia lurking. 'Make sure she is okay.'

Simion didn't reply. His silence hurt more than Leia's grip.

Without a word, he left me.

* * *

The Queen stood proud in the centre of a crescent moon of steel-plated battlemages, breastplates emblazoned with the curled dragon. Among them were other grey-cloaked gleamers, and a handful of mages dressed in the same ivory-cream shawl Leia wore. Elders.

Regardless of the power stationed around her, the Queen radiated as though she was a star resting among the night sky. Like the Heart Oak, she glowed faintly. I blinked, the vision of her was imprinted in the dark of my mind.

The Queen settled her gentle, silver eyes over me as we stepped into the modest chamber.

'Maximus.' Her voice was clear and powerful. 'You have returned to *me*.'

Elder Leia thrust me forward. 'It would seem the Traitor Mage desires—'

I watched, dumbfounded and voiceless, as the Queen raised a hand and silenced Leia with a single gesture. 'Thank you, Elder Leia, but your explanation is not required. What matters is he is here.' The Queen lifted her eyes. 'With me.'

Leia bowed quickly, but not before I could see a flush of crimson flood over her cheeks.

Like the rest of the catacombs, evidence of the Heart Oak's roots protruded through the walls, ceiling and floor, giving off the violet glow from the mould that coated it.

I couldn't take my eyes from her. The woman was the very epicentre of stories I had grown up with. I'd seen her depicted in paintings, sat upon a ruby-scaled dragon, her face frozen in a demonic scream as she brought destruction to the South. But standing before her now, it couldn't be any further from the truth.

She was nothing like the reputation that surrounded her.

The Queen was tall and thin, standing inches above those around her. Her face was wrinkled like the melted wax of a candle. She wore armour, but it was not made from steel or iron—her frail body was encased in the bark of a tree. From her pauldron, breastplate and vambraces, a rough encasement of bark had been crafted into a formidable outfit. It was not a dragon emblazoned across her breastplate, but the face of a dryad.

'Maximus, step closer so I can see you better. I regret to admit that my eyesight is not as it once was.'

I did as she asked. There was something drawing about the

ancient woman's presence. She must've seen over a hundred years. The Mad Queen, the child of Galloway and his dryad lover, the woman responsible for the destruction of the Southern mages.

She tilted her head as I stepped in close, inspecting with striking green eyes. Her long, dark hair was speckled with strands of silver, held in place with a wiry crown of vine and leaf that settled across her brow. When she straightened, I could've sworn her bones creaked.

'Do you have nothing to say, Child of the Forest?'

My throat dried as I parted my lips. 'What would you have me say?'

The Queen twisted her thin lips, the furrowed skin around them deepening. 'I see the spirit within you, Maximus. I am happy to see the South has not smothered it in the years you have been kept from me.'

Elder Leia stepped up to my side. 'Maximus Oaken is responsible for the death of one of your battlemages. Not only has he murdered a peer, he has conspired against you by handfasting to King Calzmir, in an attempt to unify the South in contest of your rule. Not to mention the army that looms in his shadow. My Queen, he must answer for his crimes, as many have before him.'

The Queen regarded Leia; as she did a new presence flooded my mind. It was as malleable as a breath of air, but as powerful as a spear of stone. It passed through my defences as though they were never there.

*It would seem you have been busy. Tell me, do you admit to these accusations?*

The room, the castle, the entire world, seemed to fade away as the Queen filled my mind. Her power was unlike anything I had felt before. It was demanding and overwhelming, but there was also something tender about it. Her presence didn't pain me or cause me discomfort. It was almost... reassuring.

*To part of it.* My reply echoed across my skull, bouncing from bone to bone.

*Then there is much to discuss, in regrettably not enough time.*

'Leave us, all of you.' The Queen spoke aloud this time, all without taking her eyes from me.

Leia bowed her head again, frantically scrambling for an excuse. 'That would not be wise, my Queen.'

'I did not ask for your opinion,' the Queen replied, voice a gentle lull. 'All of you wait outside. I must speak with Maximus. Alone.'

Leia buzzed with energy. One look and I could see her lips forged together, as she held back what else she wished to say. Still, no one moved.

*Now.*

The command thundered in my mind, almost brought me to my knees. It seemed I wasn't the only one to hear it; not a single soul was left standing still. Every battlemage, gleamer and elder, flooded in unison towards the arched doorway we had entered. Even Leia left, skipping out of the room on quick feet, cursing under her breath as she did.

The Queen didn't speak until the door closed, leaving us alone.

'Please,' she said, gesturing forward. 'This would be your moment to explain yourself. That is if you wish to combat the allegations put against you.'

'Is there a need?' I asked, as I drank in the vision of the woman before me. 'You've been inside my mind; you know the answers you seek.'

The Queen smiled, a true beautiful smile that lit up her aged face. 'There is that spirit again. Yes, Maximus Oaken, I know the answers. But hearing them from you would be a pleasure.'

'I killed the soldier because he was going to kill me. At your command.'

Her smile faded instantly, replaced by a scowl that darkened the emerald of her eyes until they were the colour of Galloway Forest's underbelly. 'No, that was not my order. I need you, Maximus. Alive, not dead.'

*Then who wants me dead?*

'The very same people who conspire against me, within my own home. Not all of my people believe I act with their best interest in mind. Many would wish to see me fail.'

'The attack on the city,' I began, 'do you think those responsible for seeking to kill me are behind it? Because I have arrived?'

'Perhaps, perhaps not. Time will tell, our assailants cannot hide forever. What matters is you are here, you are safe.' The Queen reached out her spindly fingers to me. 'May I see your fasting mark?'

I couldn't refuse her even if I wished to. Lifting my hand, I lowered it onto her palm. A bolt of power sparked beneath her touch, flooding the length of my arm and across my back.

'I didn't ask for this,' I said.

'I know,' she replied softly, my skin itching as her bright eyes surveyed the thorned inked vines around my wrist and up my arm. 'We do not practise such a union in the North. Love should not be a shackle, but freedom. And you wish to break free of this, I sense that, but you also know what must be done for that to happen.'

I swallowed hard. The Queen released me, but her touch lingered. 'Regardless of what you may think of me, killing Camron is not something I think I can do.'

'Good,' she replied. 'Death is not always the answer.'

A question rushed out of me. 'Except you flew over Southern skies and murdered four mages.'

'I said it is not always the answer, but sometimes—depending on the circumstance—it comes in rather handy. Mad Queen, that is what they call me in the South. I admit, I rather enjoy the title and the picture it paints of me. Indulge me, Maximus, what do you see?'

As though encouraged by her question, I scanned my eyes over her again.

'Do you see madness when you look at me?'

'No,' I replied. 'I see someone who acted out of the need to avenge her parents.'

'Ah, so we have something in common,' she said. 'An attribute we share, one of many I must say. Do you know why I exiled Celia Hawthorn?'

'Because she helped my mother take me away from the North,' I replied, the words echoing around the chamber.

'Not entirely right, Maximus. Yes, Celia helped aid your mother in taking you away, but it wasn't from the North. It was from me. Everyone has a purpose in life, some more important than others.'

*It was from me.* I was trapped beneath her gaze, unable to move beneath the weight of her words.

'You are very important to me, Maximus,' the Queen continued. 'More than you could even imagine. Your purpose outweighs any of those around you—to me, you are the most sacred thing in all Aldian.'

'Why?'

The Queen raised a hand and traced it down the length of my face. Her touch was smooth yet firm, motherly, almost. I blinked, surprised to find tears glistening in her eyes.

'In the years you have been... lost, I have contemplated Deborah's actions. I do not blame her. It was a hard realisation to swallow, but I admit that I understand. She carried you, Maximus, knowing how important you were to Aldian, to me. But like the unconditional love of a mother to her child, she could not stand to give you up.'

'Give me up to what?' I repeated, my chest swelling with heavy breaths.

'The Heart Oak needs us to survive, in turn the dryads need the Heart Oak to bond with us. It is part of the circle of our purpose and, believe it or not, I will not be around forever to fuel it. Time is unkind and mine is limited. I am tired, Maximus, but I cannot go until another can replace me. You… are that other.'

I fumbled back, knocked down by her words. 'Other? This doesn't make any sense.'

'You are mine.'

'No,' I said, eyes filling with tears of fury and desperation. 'You're lying.'

The Queen stepped forward into the incandescent glow of the Heart Oak's roots. The light exposed her exhaustion. Tiredness deepened her wrinkles, made her posture bow as though it was a physical weight.

'You are a product of my seed, Maximus. Deborah was chosen out of many to carry you; she is as much your mother as I am. It is a secret I have kept from my Council, from Wycombe and those who live here.'

'I don't believe you,' I spat, clutching my chest as my heart thundered within. My throat burned with bile; my stomach twisting into knots. 'I *won't* believe you.'

'Do you feel it?' the Queen asked, as she reached a shaking hand towards the root above her head. 'Do you sense the Heart Oak, Maximus? How it pulls, saps and draws from you? We are different from the rest—whereas the mages rely on the Heart Oak to provide them with amplifiers, you can create your own. As can I. This tree is a product of my essence, just as it is yours.'

I didn't dare look up because there was no need. I did feel it, deeply—the Heart Oak called for me. There was a gravity that drew me here.

'Me and you, we are Children of the Forest, Maximus. A product of humans and dryads. Except you are… vital to our continuing efforts. Without you, we will not be ready for when—'

The Queen's eyes flew open, stretching wider than they had before. Her face broke apart in a silent scream, but only a rasped broken sound came out as she clutched at her throat. I couldn't move forward an inch as she fell to the ground, the whites of her eyes bulging and red.

I stood, rooted to the spot, shocked. She pushed herself up onto a shaking arm and reached for me, her emerald eyes— my eyes—pleading as the skin around them blistered and bubbled as though a fire burned through her veins.

'Maximus,' she gasped, fingers crawled towards me, yet still I couldn't move. Smoke slipped from her skin, which broke apart in fragments of ash. The smell of burned flesh bit at the back of my throat, filling my lungs with each hulking breath.

I finally moved—my knees cracked against stone as I threw myself towards her. The Queen fell into my arms, her eyes fluttering into the back of her head. I brushed my fingers over her face. Her skin boiled with heat.

'I am sorry,' she spluttered, as the wrinkled skin around her lips charred.

'Tell me what to do!' I pleaded. She burned to the touch, but I refused to take my hands off her. There were so many questions and even more answers lurking within this woman, but I knew she was dying in my arms.

'Help!' I shouted, the word scorching my throat. 'Help the Queen!'

The door behind me burst open, followed by the pounding of feet rushing in.

'What have *you* done!' Elder Leia shouted. She attempted to pry me away, but it was useless. I couldn't let go.

My fingertips hissed as I brushed away the Queen's hair from her brow. Where I touched, the skin shattered like ash, revealing the hissing black flame that danced beneath.

Hands grasped on my shoulders, drawing me away. I only released the Queen because of the cool, gentle voice that seeped into my unprotected mind.

*It is me, Max,* the voice said, *I'm here.*

*Simion?*

*I've got you.*

I turned and buried my face into Simion's chest. He encased me in his arms as the crackling of flesh in fire sang at my back. The thunderous beat of his heart slammed into my cheek as I pinched my eyes closed, willing for this hell to end.

'It wasn't me!' I said, voice muffled by the press of his hard chest. 'I didn't do it.'

'I know,' Simion replied, his hand brushing over the curve of my head. 'It isn't you, Maximus. It's… the Heart Oak is burning.'

# CHAPTER 50

Chaos reigned around the Queen as gleamers and elders attempted to heal the damage that continued to ravage her body. Helpless, I stared down at the smouldering body, at the way her skin fought to knit itself back together, only to be torn apart by more black flame.

Simion held me to him. His arms wrapped firm around my middle, keeping my spine pressed to his torso. His breathing was heavy, his heartbeat frantic. It matched my own.

'Keep it up,' Elder Leia barked, commanding those around her. 'Do not stop healing her.'

Where their hands brushed over blistered flesh, it became fresh and pink, only to bubble and break again. Their attempts were futile, I knew that.

'We have to do something,' I said, tears streaking down my face. 'Simion, you have to help them.'

His jaw tensed as he regarded the burning Queen. 'Until the source of the wytchfire is destroyed, the flames will continue to devour her.'

'Then we find it,' I snapped, shouting over the chaos of the room. 'I can't just stand and watch.'

Elder Leia lifted her red-rimmed eyes at us, her hands covered in gore and flesh. She lifted a finger and levelled it at me, glaring down the length of her nail in threat and promise. 'You've done this,' she said. 'You brought this to our door.'

The accusation flooded through me. I longed to tell her she was wrong, but I wasn't certain.

Simion released me, his hand falling back to the hilt of the sword at his hip. His knuckles paled with tension; the veins bulged on the back of his hand as he held on for dear life. 'That won't help save her,' he said calmly, but a threat lingered in his warm eyes. 'Aunt, we haven't got the time to play this blame game. We must find the phoenix and destroy it before the Heart Oak is ruined and she... the Queen dies alongside it.'

Leia recoiled, shocked by Simion's words. 'Where is Beatrice?'

Simion's gaze hardened. 'We didn't find her.'

Adrenaline sparked within my chest. Viper sharp, I turned to Leia and extended my hand. 'Give me my wand.'

Her eyes bulged in her skull as my command settled over her. She held the Queen cradled in her lap, like a mother would a child. I didn't want to look away from Leia and show defeat, but I couldn't help but gaze down at the Queen. Her eyes were barely open, her chest rising and falling so faintly I could've missed it. She was lost to the never-ending circle of healing and suffering.

'No,' Leia glowered, not bothering to tell me she didn't have it. We both knew she did. It called to me, sang to me, demanded me to claim it.

'*She* could be in danger,' I said, unable to steady my breathing enough to control the frantic rush of my plea. 'I cannot help you with the Queen, but I can help find the source of the wytchfire and destroy it.'

'You're not trained,' Leia replied, stammering over her excuses. 'Nor can you be trusted.'

The possessive coil within me tightened as I stepped in close again. At the back of the crowd, the battlemages stiffened, a clink of armour followed by the brush of feet over stone.

'It is *mine*,' I said, the demand more a growl. 'Give me my wand.'

Leia's face contorted into a mask of fury. She parted her lips, inhaling a deep breath as she prepared to refuse me, or command the battlemages to take me down, but before she could say anything, another voice raised.

'Maximus is… right,' the Queen croaked, lifting a bloodied, flesh-melted arm towards Leia's face. Where the tips of her fingers touched, she smeared gore in four, straight lines across Leia's jaw. 'Return his amplifier, Leia Hawthorn, you shall need him.'

It was as if I no longer mattered to Leia. Her entire attention fell to the Queen as a visceral sob broke out of her mouth. Tears ran the length of her striking face, dripping down her nose and falling upon the Queen's cheek. As the tear touched the Queen's skin, it hissed and fizzled into a puff of steam.

'Do it for Wycombe,' the Queen rasped, blood splattering out over her teeth. 'For Aldian. For me.'

The room seemed to still for a moment. Even the gleamers hesitated for a second as the Queen forced out those final weak words before closing her eyes and losing herself to the devouring pain.

Leia didn't look back at me as she reached into the folds of her cloak and produced the length of wood from within. Her hand shook as she lifted it towards me. My eyes locked onto the tip of my amplifier. 'Take it. Prove me wrong, *Traitor Mage.*'

I took my wand carefully from her fingers, prying it with ease until the base was lodged perfectly in my palm. Upon impact, a rush of power shot from the bowels of my being into every blood vessel, vein and bone. I pinched my eyes closed and gave into the rush of it. Like a breath of fresh air, the connection to my power blew the cobwebs from my mind and rejuvenated me.

*Hello again,* it seemed to say.

'Hello,' I replied.

A strong hand fell upon my shoulder, drawing me out of the connection and back into the catacomb.

'We need to go,' Simion said, his voice a cool breeze across the back of my neck.

I locked eyes with him. His brows lifted as he regarded me. I sensed his desire to say something else, but his lips held firm and he nodded instead. Then we were running from the chamber, leaving Leia and her mages to continue the endless cycle of torture, attempting to keep the Queen alive.

\* \* \*

I focused only on the path ahead, and not the one I'd been forced to leave. The Queen's words, her revelation, lingered in the far reaches of my mind but, if I dared acknowledge it, I feared I wouldn't see this through.

The phoenix had to be destroyed, it was the only option. Simion had unsheathed his sword as we ran from the catacombs, up the winding ancient stairs slick with moss and wet stone. The iron blade caught flashes of the glowing hue of light from the mould—leading our way as though it was a beacon.

When Simion suddenly stopped, I almost ran into the back of him. 'What is it?' I asked, thighs burning and breathless.

There was little space between us as Simion turned to face me. Bathed in the ominous hue of light, his amber eyes looked otherworldly. With his spare hand, he lifted it to my brow and brushed the hair from where it had grown tacky against my skin.

'I have to get something off my chest,' Simion said, his voice echoing in the narrow stairwell around us. 'I don't want to regret not telling you.'

I hesitated, drawing back a step to put distance between us. 'Now isn't the time, Simion.'

He refused the distance and stepped in close again. 'There is never a good time to announce something so raw, but Maximus I must do it. I've spent years not speaking what was on my mind, and I refuse to allow such weakness any more.'

There was a softness to Simion, a tenderness that was rare to find. It was buried beneath his soured expression and short temper, but it was there.

I gripped the wand in my hand, just as Simion held firm to his sword. It felt fitting to hold a weapon when under his gaze, because he made me feel as though I needed to protect myself —not from him, but from the way his gaze threatened to tear down all my shields and expose me.

'Last night…' Simion said, filling the silence.

The memory of pain lingered across my marked arm. 'No, not now.'

'Yes, now. What happened last night, I take full responsibility. It wasn't your fault, the kiss, your reaction. I want you to know I do not think bad of you for it. Please, don't allow it to drive a wedge between us. I promise I will not put you into such a vulnerable position again—on my life I swear it.'

I exhaled a shaking breath, wishing nothing more than to push past him and hide from the truth.

'Do you think that's what I want to hear you say?' I asked.

Simion paused, his eyes searching mine for the answer to my own question.

'I thought… I thought you were embarrassed. Your reaction was…' He took a deep breath, steadying himself. 'Yes, I do.'

Before Simion could step away, I reached for his stomach and laid my hand above it. He gazed down, almost surprised, at the connection.

'I kissed you, Simion, it was my fault if anything, and my reaction was not because I was embarrassed, nor was it regret.'

'Then what was it?' His deep voice thrummed around the dark around us.

'It hurt me, Simion. I did it because it's what felt right in the moment. But… it hurt me.'

His warm, gold-flecked eyes fell to my arm, more importantly to the silver fast-mark inked across my skin. Realisation hardened his stare. 'I didn't even contemplate the chance,' Simion said. 'The bond between you and Camron, of course, it would punish you for acting against it.'

My hand fell away from his hard stomach as Simion stepped back. The distance was minimal, but for a moment it felt gargantuan. I allowed my hand to fall to my side, fingers twitching as though they longed for something to do.

'I never want to be the cause of pain,' Simion said, his eyes pinned to his hand.

A hot flush spread up my neck and over my cheeks.

'It isn't your fault,' I replied, willing him to look at me. He didn't. Simion kept his eyes on his fist, which encased the leather-hilt of his sword.

'My lack of judgement and selfish desire blinded me. Maximus, I'm sorry.'

Before I could persist his innocence, Simion turned his back on me and moved back up the steps. I stood still, captured by the hollow swell that filled my chest. I couldn't bury my thoughts, nor smother my anger. It fuelled me forward, chasing after Simion as he raced, sword held before him, towards the Heart Oak in the chamber above us.

He didn't turn back to look at me, not as the stairwell filled with a heavy cloud of smoke. Snakes of dark grey lingered on the ceiling above, staining the air with an acrid scent. Simion fought through it, the crook of his elbow held above his nose and mouth. I followed, wading my way through the ever-growing cloud before us.

A flash of black flame flickered in my peripheral. I almost tripped up the final steps as I regarded the wytchfire. It danced across large roots at my side, charring the bark, blistering the wood and boiling the amber sap that bled from it.

It didn't take long to follow the roots to its source, to find the Heart Oak alive with writhing black fire. It hissed and spat as it ate up the hide of bark, licking far up into the canopy of leaves above.

'Dryads,' Simion cursed, the blade held at an angle before him. Except it wasn't a curse at all. I followed his gaze to see the line of trees that guarded each side of the chamber room. They writhed, completely engulfed in wytchfire. I thought the sound that emanated off them was created by the fire itself, but I was wrong. Completely wrong.

The dryads screamed, twisting and flailing their wooden limbs as the fire consumed them.

Realisation had me running towards them, fuelled by the shrieking pleas. Dryads, they were dryads, and they burned in godly fire.

Magic flowed down my arm, begging to be released—but before I could act the wind was knocked out of my lungs as strong arms wrapped around my waist and hauled me back.

'We cannot help them,' Simion shouted above the roaring flames. Heat bit at my exposed skin. The room was unbearably warm, my flesh boiling beneath my clothes.

'I have to do something,' I pleaded.

'And we will,' Simion said, firm. 'We will, but first we must find the phoenix. Only when it is destroyed will the fire stop.'

All around me the flicker of obsidian fire spread, charring the stone walls and devouring the Heart Oak at our backs.

Even if I wanted to help find the phoenix, I hadn't the faintest idea where to look. They were creatures of flame, spirits of fire—but in a room completely engulfed in it, there was no knowing where it hid.

'We need to keep moving,' Simion said, before a barrage of coughs hacked at his chest. He was unable to speak again as the smoke invaded his lungs, so he filled my mind with his cool presence, cutting through the heat lathered across my skin.

*Focus, Maximus. To help them, we must find the source—*

A deafening crack sounded at our backs; the sound so violent it made us recoil from one another. I was the first to turn, ready to see the bark split apart and the Heart Oak shatter.

But it was not the Heart Oak that split. It was the throne. I would've searched for the cause, if the figure standing before it didn't distract me.

Midnight eyes widened above a freckled smile.

'If you would be so kind, remove your hands from my husband.'

# CHAPTER 51

Camron Calzmir pushed himself to standing, strong hands gripping the stone throne for leverage, a grin sliced across his handsome face. The black of his light-drinking eyes gleamed with the orange-red firelight around him. Over his shoulders, the air rippled, unseen strands of heat reaching from his broad back. I watched, unable to move, as he took several steps away from the throne, whilst his gaze cut through me as I languished in Simion's embrace.

'Camron.' His name ebbed out of my numb lips. My mind whirled, trying to make sense as to what stood before me. Camron's strong, tall body was garbed in the armour of red scales. Flames reflected off the rough surface that spread across his breastplate, highlighting the black strips of metal holding it all together. Every fold of metal and placement of dragon scale enhanced the power of his body.

'Hello Maximus,' Camron exhaled, the obsidian flames across the Heart Oak behind him, flickering in tandem with his voice. 'Did I not promise you I would burn it all?'

Simion hesitated when I stepped from him. There was a

slight force of resistance, but it didn't last long.

'He did this,' Simion hissed, confirming what my mind had already concluded. 'Camron is—'

'Growing irritated at your proximity to my husband,' Camron answered for him, eyes widening at Simion. I watched as they stared each other down. Simion lifted his blade, catching the dancing glow of fire across it. Camron stood terribly still, not concerned about the weapon levelled towards him.

'Look at me,' I called out, voice raised above the roaring fire. My skin grew irritated by each passing second, slick with sweat and red raw from the proximity to the unnatural heat.

Camron did as I asked. As he shifted his attention to me, all tension faded from his face. The lines across his brow smoothed and the sharpness of his stare melted into a recognisable gentleness.

'What have you done?' I asked, my question barely audible over the wailing dryads and the wild, crackling black flames that devoured them.

'Everything I promised you.'

Disgust coursed through me, smothering the familiar tug of the thread that tied us together.

'You look at me as though I am a monster,' Camron said, an edge of sadness to his voice.

'I don't know *what* I'm looking at,' I replied, as I attempted to regain connection with my power. Seeing Camron—the shock and impossibility of his presence—had smothered it. Camron stood among furious black flames, as though it was nothing.

'Yes, you do,' Camron said, gesturing with his hand as though he longed for me to stand beside him. 'You have the knowledge. You know who I am.'

'Deranged.' I spat the word out as anger boiled deep within

me. My entire body trembled with it.

Camron tilted his head inquisitively, pouted and then seemed to nod in agreement. 'That and other things. My expedition across the Thassalic was rather… bountiful.'

Breathless, I stepped towards Camron as he spoke. Simion's cool presence thrashed against the newly restored shield around my mind, but I wouldn't allow him in. I needed to focus.

'You lied to me,' I said, unable to tear my eyes off him as I spoke. He tricked me, betrayed me, fooled me. Perhaps I should've cared for what he was saying, or his reason for being there, but all I could contemplate was this man had my parents, kept them from me and manipulated me up to this very moment.

Sorrow pinched at the corners of Camron's burning eyes. 'And I am sorry, Maximus, I truly am. But I promise no harm has come to them, I have kept them safe and cared for.'

'Why would I trust a word that comes out of your mouth?' I asked, noticing how the flames around me seemed to shrink the closer I got to him. I didn't need to question it to know Camron was in control. I didn't know how, but whatever happened to him during his travels had changed him—had given him access to powers I couldn't comprehend.

My head pained as Simion continued slamming his mental fists against my shield, trying to gain access. I sensed him, pacing like a shadow at my back, refusing to create distance between us. Blade drawn, and prepared to fight, Simion's presence alone gave me the confidence to continue moving forward.

'I required a way into Wycombe. The city is guarded, protected by the deceitful dryads to keep us out, and you in. Believe me, Maximus, it pained me to lie to you. I never wished for that to happen, but when I was given the option, my only option, know that I did it with the best intentions for us both.'

'Liar,' I spat, body trembling with power.

Camron flinched; brows creased as he stumbled over his next excuse. 'Sometimes, lies are born from a place of caring. I care for you, and I see your passion, it burns hot within you even now. You, Maximus Oaken, care for me.'

I smiled, unable to hold it back. It was disturbed and misplaced, but perhaps the most honest reaction to his admission. 'It would have been easier to believe you were different. You promised to give me a better life.'

'And I can—'

I drew my arm upwards, dragging the tip of my wand from the floor until it pointed directly at Camron. Where my power flowed and my intention touched, a fissure split the slabbed stone beneath my feet and raced ahead with vigour and furious speed. In its wake my destruction coughed up clouds of dust and debris. All my fury, all my confusion and desperation, flooded out of me. And as I screamed, the sound blended with the wailing cries of the dryads.

It was over in a moment.

Without dropping his smile, Camron sidestepped my attack, missing it by inches. The throne behind him was not so fortunate. As the fissure met it, the throne exploded apart, throwing slabs of stone and bolts of shrapnel in all directions. Simion shouted something as he dove out the way, iron and stone clattering. The crash of his body against the floor reverberated in my bones.

I turned, humming with power, only to watch a chunk of the throne landed exactly where Simion had stood. It took a moment for the room to settle from the chaos, enough for me to hear the slow, methodical clapping of Camron as he paced before the gaping hole in the Heart Oak's base.

Panicked, I tore down the walls around my mind and reached out.

*Are you hurt?*

*No.* His relief coiled within my very being, potent and freezing. *But we have to stop him.*

My chest rose and fell with each hulking breath. All my focus was on Camron.

Something had sliced a small cut across his cheekbone, red gore spilled freely down the side of his face. It either didn't bother him, or Camron just hadn't realised he had been wounded. Seeing the blood made me swell with pride for a moment.

Even monsters bleed.

'It is believed a successful marriage is built on the foundations of trust and forgiveness. It is not easy to forgive an attempt on my life.' Camron slowly lifted his hand to his cheek. His tips smudged the blood across his face, staining the tips of his fingers a furious crimson. 'Everybody has their limits, darling, please do not test mine again.'

'Stop this,' I said, ignoring the threat that darkened the glow of his eyes. 'Whatever you are doing, whatever you wish to achieve, stop.'

As Camron widened his smile, the black wytchfire around the Heart Oak roared with renewed vigour. 'I cannot, Maximus. It is not in my nature to give up. In fact, I often think my tenacity and determination is what allowed me to survive the burning plague. Unlike my father, a man I had often looked up to as kind and gentle. He didn't survive the possession because he was not worthy. But you, Maximus, you are strong and violent and driven. You would be the perfect choice to host a phoenix within you. You cannot even begin to believe the deception, the secrets, Aldian is built on. But I will tell you it all. Allow me to finish this and put an end to the dryads' unworthy creations. Balance must be restored and, once it is, we can go home, together.'

*Possession.* As Camron spoke his eyes had shifted, glowing with the spark of fire within.

*Destroy the source of wytchfire.* Simion's voice sang to me. *He is the source.*

'And my parents?' I asked, trying to close the space between us.

'Waiting for you,' Camron replied. 'They cannot wait to see you, darling. Once I am done here, and the Heart Oak is nothing more than smouldering ash, I will take you to them.' Camron smiled to himself. 'It is all you have ever wanted. The powers you are given by the dryads cannot help you. But my power, what I can offer, will ensure no one can control you again.'

I kept my face void of emotion, blinking doe-wide eyes and forcing a smile to spread across my face. 'No one but you, husband? Is that what you mean?'

Camron's smile faltered, his dark eyes twisting with the reflection of fire. 'Your words suggest one thing, but the passion inside of you—it tells of another desire.'

*Maximus, don't listen to him.*

Camron raised a finger and placed it directly over my heart. As he did, something within me jolted as though he, too, commanded not only the fire around us, but the one coiling within me.

'I know I have lied to you, but unlike the others, it is not out of the need of control,' Camron said, relaxing his finger until his palm rested over my chest. His focus was solely on my eyes and not on the tightening of my fist upon my wand. 'I have missed you, regardless of your... transgressions. I do not hold them against you.'

Camron knew what I had done. It was confirmed in the

sharp flicker of a gaze towards Simion. The handfasting mark across my arm tingled, burning like the wytchfire that licked up the towering Heart Oak at Camron's back.

'Did it hurt you too?' I asked, voice soft.

Camron's jaw tensed, his reaction relaxing the knot of unease in my stomach. 'Terribly.'

'Good,' I said, smiling once again. I stepped back from him, slowly moving until there was enough space between us. 'Then I'm going to need to ask your forgiveness for something else, if you have it in your heart to offer more to me.'

'Have I not made it clear, I would burn the world for you?' Camron's smile faded as quickly as it came. 'What would you need from me, darling?'

My lip curled upwards, flashing teeth as my magic sparked within me. Lightning fizzed through my veins, hot and sharp. The flash of brilliant light illuminated across Camron's armour as it collected across the body of my wand. One blink, one breath, and the power was free.

The force of my attack pushed the hair from my ash-coated face, forcing me to squint until I saw nothing but black. Before I closed them entirely, it was to see the shock pass over Camron's face.

I smiled into the dark, exhaling as relief flooded my limbs.

'Did I not warn you?' Camron hissed, violence in the feral tone of his deep voice.

I threw my eyes open to find him standing, unharmed.

Beatrice stood before him, breathless. Her staff was held out before her as though it was a long sword. Lightning crackled across the tip of the knotted wood before she battered it away, grunting with the forceful swing of her amplifier. I watched as the ball of lightning crashed into the stone wall, splintering it. Where it hit, the wall was charred black.

'I can't let you do that, Max,' Beatrice said, her voice barely an audible whisper. 'Please, don't.'

'Bea,' Simion shouted at his sister. 'Step away from *it*.'

'No,' Beatrice replied, dragging her attention between me and her brother. 'This must be done.'

Camron stepped forward and lowered a careful hand on Beatrice's shoulder. She winced, enough for me to notice, but she didn't pull away.

*I can't reach her.* Simion's voice flooded my mind. *She's keeping me out.*

'Beatrice and I had a rather insightful conversation during her time in my capture.' Camron glowered over her shoulder. 'I admit, if you had not asked me to see her, perhaps we would not all be here now. As I see your passion, Maximus, I saw hers. I was able to divulge her intentions and we both came to a mutual understanding. The North deserves punishment. Although for differing reasons, our shared goal was vital.'

I barely heard what Camron said next. All I could do was study Beatrice's face, searching for a reason to convince myself she didn't have a hand in this. I dropped my focus to her arm and the burned skin beneath.

'They tore my family,' Beatrice said plainly. 'I'm only repaying them with the same loss they gave me.'

'And we will,' Camron said, whispering into her ear without taking his eyes off me. 'We will make them all pay. As I told you, Beatrice, my husband would never think different of you for your actions. He understands the need for vengeance more than anyone.' Camron lifted his burning eyes, resting them upon me. 'Don't you, darling?'

Tears brimmed in Beatrice's eyes, brightening them. Regardless of the tears, there was no washing away the determination set within them. I held her stare, wishing I had Simion's power to speak to her without anyone else hearing.

'It doesn't always bring the solace you think it will,' I said, speaking to Beatrice and only her. I thought of Julian, of Jonathan, knowing their deaths did not bring me answers. They did not bring me what I longed for.

'That's for me to find out.'

'What about family, Bea?' I asked.

'Family,' Beatrice scoffed, a tear slipping free of her blood-shot eyes. 'Family is the reason I am doing this. For you, for Simion.'

'For Celia Hawthorn,' Camron added.

'Beatrice, you must fight,' Simion called out. 'He is using you. He is taking your desires and twisting them—that is how it controls. Cut *it* out.'

'She can't,' Camron hissed, flames burning hotter, brighter.

'Then I will do it. I will cut you out myself.'

Simion threw himself into attack.

My mind shuddered with his mental force, knocking me sideways. Beatrice and Camron felt it too, rocking away from one another as Simion debilitated them for a moment. Sword raised, flames glinting off the metal, Simion brought it down towards Camron's back.

But before the sword met flesh, blinding heat exploded out of Camron. Wings of flame smothered Simion, the force sending him careening through the air. His sword tumbled out of his hand, falling pathetically on the floor.

This time, when Simion crashed to the ground, he didn't get up.

I felt the force of the crack as though it was my skull that split.

Everything stilled, the world, the noise, my thoughts. It all went quiet as I held my breath and waited for Simion to move. Time stretched on and still I waited. I thrust my silent pleading into his mind.

Nothing.

'Simion!' Beatrice cried, throwing herself towards her brother. Camron didn't stop her. She gathered her brother into her arms, sobbing fiercely as he looked back to Camron. 'You promised no harm would come to him. You fucking promised!'

'As Maximus would tell you, I am notorious for breaking them. Your brother should have thought twice before attacking me.' Camron radiated with ire. His body trembled, the pale skin of his face stained red. Now, at his back, colossal wings of flame twisted and hissed at the air. Among the twisting, unnatural flames, I saw feathers of gold, ruby and blonde.

Beatrice fussed over Simion's unconscious body; her palms stained with the blood that oozed from the back of his head. The stone step he had crashed into was marred with crimson gore and a chunk of hair and torn flesh.

Tears blinded me as I looked back to Camron, unable to smother the vision of Simion's ashen skin and the wailing screams of Beatrice who held him.

Camron recognised the hate in my eyes. He tutted, the red-gold feathers at his back shaking. 'Please do not make me be like them. Do not make me use your parents as a lesson.'

It was as though Camron spoke with two voices. There was his, but there was another—something feral and boiling. He was possessed. Without taking his eyes from me, he plucked a feather from his wings and held it towards me.

'If you touch them…' I hissed as the room lit up, glowing cords tethering me to the earth. There were too many to choose from. Control may not have been my skill, but, Dryads, I would snap every damn cord until the castle itself fell upon us.

Camron dropped the feather into the sprouting fires beside him; like kindling into a hearth it sparked.

A violent *whooshing* sound filled the room. It tugged me forward, air twisting as flame folded in on itself, before spreading out into a large disc that stood inches taller than Camron and far wider.

'There is so much we can do, Maximus. Together. It is incredible to imagine this single feather is what saved me. It allowed Beatrice to provide me access into Wycombe, straight past their attempts at protection. We do not want destruction, we do not want war. We simply must complete the will put upon us.'

*We.* The two voices overlapped one another as Camron spoke.

'You had me fooled,' I replied, gesturing to the flames that continued to spread. 'It would seem you rather enjoy destruction.'

'When required.'

'Then we share a common interest.' I reached out, threading my mind's fingers into every cord around me.

Magic spoiled the air, thickening and twisting into an unseen force.

'I see you are going to continue to resist me,' Camron continued, his face a mask of pure ferocity. 'It seems you are used to others holding your parents' well-being over your neck. You practically beg me to do the same.'

The spinning disc of fire settled in the centre, becoming as black as the wytchfire. My eyes focused on it, noticing two shapes break away from the light-drinking darkness of the disc's belly. A flash of vivid green eyes; a nest of brown curls set around a soft, freckled face.

'Mother?' I said, unable to fathom what I saw.

My mother steeled her face, jaw tense as the man stepped in from the fire beside her. *Father.* They looked well, better than I had last seen. Bruises haunted the skin around Father's bent nose and tired eyes, but that was it.

Once they both stepped free of the portal, it collapsed back in on itself, casting a bout of scolding air across the room.

My knees buckled as I moved towards them.

'Stand tall, Max,' my father said through a taut exhale, breaking the impossible silence. I looked between his defiant gaze, to my mother's, and saw something shared. Panic. Not for them, but for me.

'Now, darling,' Camron said from his perch inches behind me. I had been so focused on my family I didn't notice him move. Heat crackled in the air as he encased me with his arms and snatched the wand from my fingers. I didn't resist, I couldn't—my energy had been sapped from seeing my parents again. 'Let us finish this, together, so we can all go home.'

Black fire sparked between Camron's fingers, engulfing my wand in a burst of black light. As the wytchfire peeled back, it was to reveal the ash of my amplifier fall between Camron's fingers, coating the ground at my feet in a fine layer of grey.

A resounding agony filled my chest. If it wasn't for Camron's arms, I would've fallen to the ground before him. It was as if his power had cleaved my soul apart—the pain unlike anything I had felt before.

'Do not grieve such oppressive power,' Camron whispered into my ear, his lips brushing my skin. 'The power I will gift you shall be unlike anything you could possibly imagine. It will hurt, it will leave your body scarred as mine is, but the rebirth you will experience on the other side will be unlike anything you could ever imagine. And I will be there, by your side, aiding you through it all.'

Camron couldn't read my mind, it was not a gift he had. But he sensed my passion, he grasped it within me and held it tight. Then he leaned in, lips brushing my ear as he grasped my hand with his and held firm. 'I told you I would give you an army, didn't I?'

My arm burned. I looked down, only to see a mess of melted skin and material blending as one. Fire bled from Camron's hand, spilling freely over my arm.

Where I expected pain, there was nothing but the kiss of ice.

I wrenched away, frantically patting the fire out. The handfast mark could be seen, only faintly, beneath the mess of melted flesh and blood.

Camron stepped back, eyes widening in disbelief. For the first time, I saw the man I had left behind in the South. He looked down to his hands, shaking his head and muttering something beneath his breath. 'I did not mean to.'

'Max,' a voice called out, as the pain rushed over me. It wasn't until they called it again I found the energy to turn and look.

My father stared at me with a heavy gaze.

We had shared a moment like this before. As he had all those years ago, my father now witnessed me in the hands of a dangerous man, someone with the power to harm me. Someone who had harmed me greatly.

I transported back to another time.

The dark of my room, the man, my father stood in the doorway to our home with that very expression glinting in his eyes. A promise of protection, no matter the cost, the glint of instinctual action.

Camron didn't notice, but I did.

And I knew what was to come.

# CHAPTER 52

I buried the pain, threw my head back until my skull smashed into Camron's nose. The muscles across my neck ached as I thrust my head with all my might. All while my father broke away from my mother's side.

Bone cracked against bone; the sound echoing through my head. Camron roared backwards, fumbling for the shattered mess of his nose. Before he could catch himself, I slammed my fist into the side of his head once, then another on his neck. With a final push, Camron stumbled backwards, falling helplessly onto the ground.

Then Father was there, Simion's discarded blade held out in his hand. He swung it, steel blurring in a great arch. Camron raised a hand before him—as if it would stop the sword. Instead, it passed through Camron's flesh and bone, severing the hand that burned me.

Camron screamed on the ground, two voices blending as one. The phoenix and the man.

'No man lays his fingers on my son and gets to keep them.'

The sword's tip pressed between the joint of Camron's

dragon-scaled breastplates, directly over the hard flesh of his chest.

Arms wrapped around me, pulling me back from the scene. 'I'm here, Maximus, I have got you.'

I didn't resist as my mother pulled me away from the two men. Father had his boot on Camron's chest, keeping him down, the blade preventing Camron from moving an inch. But it didn't stop Camron from unleashing a barrage of frantic laughs. Blood splattered out of his mouth, staining his brilliant white teeth black with his gore.

As soon as the pain overwhelmed Camron, he seemed to forget it. Blood splashed from the stub of his wrist. It was as though there was nothing wrong, no hand left on the floor, fingers curled and stiff. 'There is no need to protect your son from me,' Camron said, spitting blood down his chin. 'I am his husband, it is my job now.'

'It will always be my task, in life and death, no matter the cost.'

'Let us test that theory, shall we?'

Father couldn't so much as move before Camron grasped the sharp edges of the sword, smiled and unleashed a pillar of fire out from beneath his remaining hand.

Mother lost her footing and we both tumbled to the ground, screaming out as the conjured flame melted iron and bone. I didn't blink, didn't look away as my father was devoured by Camron's wytchfire. It ate away at him quickly, leaving nothing but charred bone and a puddle of bubbling flesh in the place he had once stood.

'No,' I whispered, my chest cracking open as the vast expanse of darkness overwhelmed my mind. 'No!'

'I warned you,' Camron screamed, frantic in his own disbelief. 'I told you what would happen, I did tell you!'

Pain didn't greet me as I suspected it would. In fact, there was no feeling at all. I was a cavernous, hollow space. Mother held me close, rocking me back and forth on the steps before the burning Heart Oak. Her hands were cold and shaking, her heartbeat a thunderous clash in her chest.

I was vaguely aware of footsteps. I didn't react as Elder Leia flooded into the burning room, a flank of battlemages at her back. For a moment, I wondered what Leia must've thought as she saw the chaos—my mind was no longer protected, could she feel my loss? Did she recognise it?

'Look at me, Maximus,' my mother said, her use of my full name scolding and desperate. It took a moment for the chaos to calm enough for me to make sense of her. 'Don't look at anything but me.'

Beside us, the roots of the Heart Oak flowed out of the stone as though it was a snake, captured and frozen in mid-movement. Mother reached out quickly, wrapped her fingers around the skin of the tree. Her eyes blazoned with the emerald glow of power, the very same hue that radiated from the Heart Oak.

'He is dead,' I spluttered.

Just the thought alone, let alone the admission of it aloud, was enough for me to shatter. I'd been kept from them both, weeks of torture fuelled by my desperate need to see my parents again, only to have Father torn away from me before I could feel the warmth of his embrace.

A gentle wash of calm brushed over me. From beneath my mother's palm, pressed to the sticky skin of my cheek, the emotion expanded. I blinked and the world, the room raging in wytchfire and alive with the sounds of battle, came back to me with complete clarity.

'Camron is possessed,' Mother said firmly. 'The man you think you know is not in control of his actions. He cannot be blamed.'

I shook my head, unable to understand her words. 'He killed him, he did it—'

'Listen to me,' she urged, drawing her thumb over the tacky skin of my cheek. I was crying, but I didn't sense the sadness. It was as though the feeling had been smothered by her.

'Your father died doing the only thing he cared about. Protecting his family.'

'But he isn't my father, is he?'

*He was your father.* The languid song of her voice filled my mind. *The love he had for you was thicker than any blood, it is something that spans far greater than anything else.*

'How are you...'

Perhaps she sensed my confusion and shock because her knuckles paled as she gripped tighter onto the Heart Oak's root.

*Touch the tree, claim your birth right. I kept you from it, I stole you away because I could not bear to allow you to be who you were always supposed to be.* Mother's voice was the calming chime of a bell; it had the power to steady my breathing and focus my thoughts. *Forgive me, Maximus. Do what is required of you.*

There was no hesitation. No pain. No thoughts.

I did as my mother commanded, reaching my fingers towards the rough bark of the Heart Oak's root. Flames of wytchfire hissed like serpents near my fingers, but I kept just out of reach. As I had all those weeks ago, I gave into instinct and intention. When Julian Gathrax had me trapped beneath him, there was no thought or contemplation—only action. But instead of my wand, I now felt the full force of the Heart Oak beneath the tips of my fingers.

Images exploded throughout my mind, racing so quickly I could not make sense of them.

There was a sky covered in flames. Withering life. Piles of

bones. Buildings buried by rolling waves. Ruin. Death. A woman. An army of darkness. Coiling shadows. Birds born from flame. Slithering beasts. Monsters. Darkness. Darkness. Darkness. And a chant, building slowly in a language I did not understand by hearing it, but by *feeling* it.

*Mother is coming. Mother is coming. Mother is coming.*

I threw my eyes open, grasping as I broke free from the vision. I could taste death, hear death, feel the shadows scratch across my skin. But more terrible than everything the Heart Oak had shown me, there was Camron Calzmir.

'Only in death shall we part,' I hissed, as Mother's power failed to hold back the torrent of fury that burned through me. 'He deserves to die for what he has done.'

*For your father, destroy the phoenix that possess Camron Calzmir. Do better, do the right thing.*

Power surged through every vein. It snatched my breath away, filling my body with a weightless light I had never experienced before. With my wand destroyed, I was free to claim a new amplifier. As Mother had spoken in my mind, the Heart Oak was mine to claim. I was born for it, just as the Queen had revealed.

But I was wrong, I didn't claim it. The Heart Oak claimed me.

Far above the ceiling of the castle, thunder rumbled across smoke-stained skies. It shivered over my bones, as the Heart Oak drew out my power and drank it as though it was starved.

'Do you remember our vows?' My voice broke above the roaring rush within me, cresting over Camron like a wave as he continued fighting among the crowd of battlemages at Elder Leia's command.

I didn't know if Camron could even hear me, but I found

comfort in knowing that, if he did, my words would be the last thing he ever heard.

'No?' I spat, eyes narrowing. 'Then I'll remind you.'

The hairs on my arms stood on end as lightning cut down from the skies, through the body of the Heart Oak and into my skin. I channelled it, allowing the breath of godlike power to burn bright as I extended my free arm, flashed my mage-marked palm at Camron and released it entirely.

'Only in death shall we part,' I screamed, as the power filled me entirely.

Light flooded the room in a flash. One sharp inhale and there was nothing but the purple light. There was no room to care for the battlemages who stood in the way. Only in the back of my mind did I hope they felt my draw of power as a warning to move out of my line of sight.

I strained my eyes against the flash of light, refusing to look away. In the last moment, he levelled his eyes with mine and I was certain I witnessed a tear cast down his blood-smeared cheek. Then my power crashed into Camron's chest, breaking his body apart in an explosion of flesh, fire and feather.

Camron vanished.

It was almost as though he had never stood before me at all. In his wake all that was left was the bright golden-red feathers languidly shifting to a resting place on the floor where he'd stood.

My power had torn him apart.

Mother pried my hand from the Heart Oak, one finger at a time. A rush of air hissed throughout the chamber room, a shockwave that spread across every burning pyre of flame. All around me the wytchfire extinguished, blinking out of existence as suddenly as Camron had.

'It is done,' Mother said, cradling me in her arms, rocking me like a child. 'It's over.'

The battlemages looked around in disbelief, metal boots stepping freely over the bed of feathers on the floor.

*Only in death shall you part.* I looked down to my burned arm, searching for proof it was true. All I saw was melted flesh and the scorched remains of clothing stuck to new wounds.

I knew Mother kept the pain away with her power, but there was no stopping her from keeping my eyes open long enough to confirm it.

I could hear Beatrice screaming her innocence, but I couldn't turn my head to find her. My body no longer belonged to me, not as the crackling light I had conjured sparked through my blood.

Mother lowered my head into her lap until I stared at dark sky. Curling ash fell around us like snow. And as the Heart Oak came into view, bark charred, but there was no more fire.

It was over.

# CHAPTER 53

I woke to the languid crash of waves breaking against rock.

In the dark of my mind, I could almost see the crest of dark foam around the base of white stone cliffs. Far off, I thought I heard the roar of dragons. I parted my dry lips and tasted salty air. Attempting to lift my hand to my mouth, I found I couldn't.

Everything came back to me slowly. As I pried my eyes open, wincing at the brightness, it was to find Elder Leia standing at the foot of my bed, Mage Leska hovering just shy of her shoulder. Leia's mane of ivory-white hair had been drawn back into a sleek bun that pulled her striking face into a mask of tight skin. There was no hiding the tension that lingered in her eyes.

'Careful,' Elder Leia said. 'We wouldn't want you ruining my gleamer's hard work.'

I blinked and saw the black curling flames across melted flesh. There was Camron, bathed in them, before he broke apart in a cloud of ash and feather. My mind worked backwards, remembering how Elder Leia had swept in with her formation of battlemages.

My heart cracked in my chest, but not because I beheld grief for Camron.

Father. The pain of loss snuck up on me, a dagger of grief through every wall of my body and mind.

Silent tears sliced down my face, staining the feather-down pillow behind my head. As I gave into the hollowness within, I recognised where I had woken.

I was back in the room within the cottage at the top of the cliffside. The sounds that had encouraged me out of the peaceful sleep were real, slipping in through the open window. The hearth was stone cold, not a single spark to be seen. For a second, I was thankful for the lack of fire. I didn't think I could bear seeing one again.

I looked down the length of me. Bandages wrapped around my fast-marked arm, slightly strained from the spreading stain of yellow beneath. I shifted my fingers, feeling nothing— almost desperate to feel the pain as though it would distract me from my thoughts.

Instead, all the pain of my broken body seemed to linger in my chest, wrapped around my heart like thorned vines.

'It has not been a day since Camron's attack,' Elder Leia confirmed. 'A lot has happened.'

My throat was so dry, speaking was difficult. 'My mother?'

Leia glanced to the closed door of my bedroom. I heard it then, the pottering of gentle feet, the light humming of a voice. She was here. Then a deeper voice resounded through the walls, resonating with me in ways I could never have imagined. Simion.

As the thought of him filled my mind, he stopped talking and the brush of cool breeze caressed the back of my skull.

I didn't let him in. Not yet.

'I want to see her.' I tried to sit up, but my body was weak.

'Deborah can wait, there is something we must first discuss.'

'Nothing is more important than—'

'The Queen is dead,' Leia interrupted. 'That is more important. The injuries she sustained broke her spirit before they broke her body. There was nothing we could do for her in the end but offer her peace as the wytchfire devoured her from the inside.'

I placed a hand over my heart, expecting sorrow but finding nothing. 'I'm sorry for your loss.'

Leia narrowed her eyes and tilted her head slightly. 'Are you?'

I held her eyes, refusing to shy away. 'Yes.'

She rocked back, straightening her spine and rolling back her shoulders. '*Our* Queen thought it important enough, to use her last breath, to provide her Council a final command.' There was an undeniable bitterness about the way Leia spoke to me. 'You, Maximus Oaken, are to be kept North to train and dwell alongside your *remaining* family.'

Discomfort unfurled in me like opening wings. I couldn't help but recognise the jab of her comment; the pain she wished to cause me with her words. Leia paced from the end of my bed to the side, where she towered over me, eyes searching. Before she'd entered the room with Leska, I'd forced the fortress of steel back around my mind, even then Leia prowled my perimeters like a cat stalking a mouse.

'Do I have a choice, in this decision?' I asked, feeling the piercing talons of grief crawl through me.

I dared blink for fear of seeing my father's body disintegrate. Focusing on Leia was enough of a distraction, but how long would that last?

'What makes you so special, Maximus Oaken?' Leia said, ignoring me question. Her refusal was answer enough.

'I don't know what you mean.'

'Before the Queen died, she told us Aldian needs you, that your purpose is far greater than could be imagined. She told us we would rely on you. But, she died before explaining why.'

The Heart Oak glowed in the dark of my mind. I couldn't gleam Leia's thoughts, but it was clear she was not aware I was a product of the Queen. That I could fuel the Heart Oak with my essence. With the Queen dead, the unwanted responsibility rested upon my head like a crown—a crown I'd rather break than wear. The only thing keeping me silent was the knowledge my mother held the answers. I could hear her, pottering around the house beyond the chamber door, whistling the tune of the *run, rabbit, run* nursery rhyme she had long ago used to comfort me.

It no longer had that power over me. Would I always seek to run?

'I'm sorry,' I said, holding her stare with confidence. 'But the answers you seek have nothing to do with me.'

'Then let me *in*,' Leia sneered, lowering her face down to me. 'Allow me to be the judge of that. You are hiding something from me, just like Beatrice had been, I know it.'

I held my smile, even though my body felt exhausted and riddled with discomfort. I knew this feeling had little to do with my exertion of magic, and everything to do with the sapping draw I'd experienced when I touched the Heart Oak and channelled it. If my mother hadn't peeled my fingers from the root, I don't imagine I'd ever have let go. It was like a leech, drawing at my soul.

'My mind is filled with the death of my father,' I spat, numb to the bone. 'Would you care to see his death play over and over? Is that what you wish to see?'

Leia pulled back, defeated, brow furrowed. 'We are sorry for your loss.'

'Are you?' I retorted the same question she had asked me. I knew the sentiment of the answer was the same.

'The Queen may have asked us to keep you, but it is on my authority how we do that. Until you wish to cooperate with me, I will not cooperate with you, Maximus.' Leia turned her back on me and gestured for Leska to step forward. She was dressed in her battlemage armour, silver and bright. A fine layer of ash clung to her obsidian-black hair, and there was evidence of red raw skin across her pale face.

'Leska has been tasked to train you,' Leia announced, which suddenly made me understand Leska's feral grin. 'Once you are provided with a new amplifier, you have years of physical and mental preparation to catch up with. Mage Leska will be your shadow and will be reporting back to me, daily, with news of your cooperation. If I sense you are resisting, our hospitality will not be as open as you would imagine.'

I held Leska's bright eyes, sensing the hate that spilled from her. *Traitor Mage.* She didn't need to say it because I sensed it. I'd been responsible for the death of someone close to her, and now she was responsible for me.

Trepidation spiked as I stared at her.

'And my mother?' I asked, knowing her answer could go one of two ways.

'Deborah has been pardoned for her crime,' Leia said, a frown pulling down at her striking face. 'You will both reside here, build a new home. All I ask of you is you work hard. It is not only me you must prove yourself to, but Wycombe and everyone who resides in it.'

*Build a new home.* 'And what if I don't want that?'

Leia shifted, bed creaking as she pressed two fists into it and leaned forward. 'Have you not learned yet, Mage Oaken?

Desire has little to do with life. It is a selfish want; one I do not have tolerance for. Regardless of my niece's actions, in my eyes you brought this ruin to the city and you will do what you can to help restore it.'

I fought the urge to ask about Beatrice. It lingered on the tip of my tongue, souring in my cheeks.

All I could think about was how Beatrice had caused this— she had allowed Camron into the city, to destroy the Heart Oak and my father.

'Am I allowed time to grieve before I'm to fix *your* city?' I asked, hating how I was losing grip on my body, which began to tremble uncontrollable. Leia hadn't stopped pressing at the boundaries of my mind. I sensed her frustration as her prowling had become a hammering slam of mental fists.

'Once you have healed, Leska will return for you every day come dawn. Do we have an understanding?'

'Clear as day,' I replied curtly. I spared a look to Leska whose sneer only deepened. 'Now, if you don't mind, I would very much like to spend some time with my *remaining* family. I understand the concept of family doesn't register with you, but to me it is all that matters. So, if you both would kindly leave, I have a father to grieve.'

Magic boiled from Leia's skin, accentuated by the widening of her eyes and the lines that framed her pinched mouth.

'You are not the only one to know loss, Maximus, you would do well to remember. The city will soon find out about the death of their Queen and be forced to come to terms with that great loss on top of the many whose lives were taken during the attack on the city. Death is a part of life, it is as unforgiving, it doesn't matter who you are, it comes for us all. And I fear there is more to come in the following days.'

There was something glinting in Leia's eyes which tore

down my restraint and had me asking the single question which haunted me.

'What've you done to Beatrice?' My question hit its mark. Leia grimaced and rocked back a step.

'My niece is in custody,' Leia said plainly, looking down at the sheets of the bed as though they were more interesting. 'She conspired with Camron Calzmir.'

'He used her,' I said, although speaking it aloud didn't mean I completely believe it.

'Regardless, Camron was only able to see her desires and twist them. The ability is like that of a gleamer, except we cannot manipulate wants, only read them. If she did not harbour such deadly thoughts, this would never have happened.'

Would never have happened. My father would still be alive.

'...Camron had given her one of his feathers. It seems he is tied to them, using them as a means to travel great distances in a single moment. Portals. It is a magic we do not yet under-stand, but we will once we can study his...'

There was something else Elder Leia longed to say. Shock at her own loose lip passed over her face, quickly silencing her.

'Needless to say, the phoenix has been dealt with. You, Maximus, saved this city.'

An image of Beatrice sprung to mind, one of her sat before the campfire with a feather in hand. I had thought nothing of it at the time.

'The burns on her arm,' I said, hating how broken my voice sounded. 'It was because she...'

'Beatrice took one of his feathers into the city and cast it into some hearth in one of the city's taverns. It opened a portal for Camron to enter the city, undetected. It's a miracle she made it out with nothing more than the burn on her arm —the tavern is no more than a crate of stone and ash. Thank the Dryads no one else was hurt.'

Leia paused, took a hulking breath in, closing her eyes for a moment as though the light in the room was too much to bear. 'From there, Camron was able to shift through the fires in the city, spreading them one by one.'

My mind raced, piecing together the events that had led up to the attack.

'How did he infiltrate the castle?' I asked, voice barely a whisper. 'All the fires had been extinguished by the time we arrived.'

It was Leska who spoke. 'She made one of her own.'

'From what the gleamers have retrieved from her mind, Beatrice used her power to spark a fire. One small burst of lightning, one small flame, that was all it took. She let him in, and we know what happened next.'

My mind flashed with images of what happened. She never went to help the battlemages protect the castle's boundary. She had lied.

Elder Leia seemed to harden her resolve before my eyes. 'Beatrice will remain in custody until a time the city has returned to some normalcy. Then she will be put on trial.'

'If Camron used her,' I said, hating how emotionless Leia looked when she spoke of Beatrice, 'then surely she is not to blame?'

'Someone has to held accountable,' Leia replied.

There wasn't the chance to ask what she meant before she turned on her heel and shot towards the door. I almost called out for her before my eyes fell to Leska, who stayed back, refusing to look away from me.

'Get some rest,' Leska said, her ash-coated knuckles paled as she gripped the handle of her mace. It hung from her belt, the metal spikes catching the light of the room and winking at me in promise. 'I assure you the discomfort you feel now will pale in comparison to what you will experience in training.'

I sat up straight in the bed, biting my lip to conceal my wince. 'How can I sleep when I'll be so excited to begin?'

Leska's scowl deepened. 'The feeling, Traitor Mage, is mutual.'

# EPILOGUE

The gleamers who healed me had only just left by the time knuckles rapped against the door. Exhaustion was draining, so much that I could hardly keep my eyes open. But I did, long enough to see a face poking around the door. Simion, his broad shoulders blocking out the view beyond. Seeing him made my breath catch in my throat. And suddenly, it was not sleep I was desperate for.

It was him.

'I didn't mean to wake you,' Simion quickly added, retreating.

'Stay,' I croaked, patting the bed beside me. 'Stay with me.'

He didn't need to be told twice. Simion slipped into the room, closing the door behind him. I stared at the back of his head, to the puckered scar that lingered beneath his hairline.

'Have they left?' I asked.

'Only just. I was going to leave with them, but I…'

Silence stretched out between us.

'Say it,' I said.

'I didn't want to leave you.'

I closed my eyes, allowing myself to selfishly devour his words. 'I'm glad.'

He sat on the edge of the bed, shifting his weight until the frame squeaked. 'How are you feeling?'

'Empty.' It was the easiest answer to give.

Simion leaned over, scooped my hand in his and lowered his forehead to it. 'I'm sorry about your father.'

'It isn't your fault,' I replied, surprise at how quickly the anger returned.

*It was Beatrice—* I silenced my thoughts, burying them deep down.

'If there is anything, anything I can offer you.' He could take this grief away. He could bury it until I was strong enough to face it. But I wouldn't give in so easily, not yet.

'I can face it,' I said, gritting my teeth, not quite believing myself.

'Grief is a heavy burden to carry,' Simion replied. 'It doesn't ease in weight as time goes on, we simply become stronger to carry it.'

I took a deep breath, finding it easier to divert my gaze, so I didn't need to see the pinch of his expression.

'Leia told me about Beatrice,' I said. 'Is there anything we can do to help her?'

Is that what I wanted?

Simion's expression hardened, the gold of his eyes glinting with an internal storm. 'That is for me to worry about, not you. You've been through enough.'

I lifted my hand and laid it across Simion's cheek. He melted into my touch, leaning his weight into my hand, which he grasped and held in place. 'When will you learn I do worry? For you. For Beatrice.'

The last I had seen Simion was laid out in Beatrice's lap, blood seeping behind his skull. I longed to reach up and touch him, just to ensure he was real and not a figment of my imagination.

My thoughts may have been closed off to him, but Simion could read my emotions in the lines of my face, as obvious as ink on the page of a book. 'Wycombe has the best healers in the world. I'm fine.'

'Good,' I said quietly.

Simion's gaze dropped to my mouth. It lingered there for a moment. 'Good.'

I almost demanded he acted on his want; Dryads knew I longed for the distraction. Or was it answers? If Simion kissed me, if he opened my emotions up to him, would I feel pain or peace?

Camron spoiled the moment with an unwelcome memory. 'He is dead, isn't he?'

Simion returned his attention to my eyes. For the first time, I noticed how tired he was. Dark smudges were etched into his skin, the whites of his eyes were bloodshot. 'Camron is most certainly dead. A lot of people witnessed what you did. His remains have been swept and scrubbed from the floor. No matter what nightmare he was, there is no coming back from ashes, Max.'

'I'm free,' I muttered, gaze falling back to my bandaged arm. Had the silver marks shattered or broken? Had they faded completely as I cast my bolt of power and tore Camron's body apart?

'You are.'

Then why did Simion look so haunted? His smile had yet to return, his touch was careful as though he held glass and not my hand.

'Something is haunting you,' I said, eyes tracing every detail of his face.

Of course Simion suffered, there were so many things

wrong. Too many to possibly begin to list. The Queen was dead, Beatrice was imprisoned, my father had been killed. Then there was Camron.

Simion lifted my bandaged arm, raised it to his mouth and placed a kiss upon my fingers. It was so tender, so soft, I couldn't help a breathy gasp. 'I can't bear to see you hurt.'

'Oh, how the tables have turned.'

Simion shook his head, full lips pouting. 'If you hadn't destroyed him, there'd be no stopping me from ripping him apart, limb for limb.'

I believed every word; his eyes sang with his dark desire.

'Leia wants me to join Saylam Academy,' I said, directing the conversation away from Camron Calzmir. 'Leska's going to train me.'

Simion's jaw gritted, muscles feathering. 'And do you want that?'

He was the only person to care about my answer. 'I don't know what I want.'

'Well, when you decide, let me know.'

I nudged him, wishing to lean into him until his arms swallowed me whole. 'And what do you want?'

Simion looked at me, truly looked at me. The intensity in his gaze was answer enough. 'Where do I begin?'

'Don't…' I exhaled, closing my eyes. I was weak, so weak I couldn't bear to hear Simion say it. 'Not yet.'

Simion bowed his head.

There would come a time when my heart healed enough to let Simion in. Until then, I couldn't contemplate the budding emotion within me.

'I should go,' Simion said, regretfully looking to the door. 'Your mother is desperate to come and see you.'

I held onto his fingers, gripping harder. 'Thank you. For everything.'

'I wouldn't thank me yet,' Simion said, offering me a smile which melted every defence. 'There is much left to fix.'

'I don't blame Beatrice, you know.' How could I hate her for what she did? She was used by Camron. Her want for revenge was no different to mine.

'Nor do I, but the Council will not see it like that. The people of Wycombe will not...' Simion lost himself to thought, chewing on the inside of his lip. 'I would like to check the burns on your arm before I leave you. I know you've been seen to by the Council's gleamers, but I would rest well knowing you are ok.'

I nodded, glad to offer him my hand again. His touch was mesmerising; his fingers grazed my skin, sending shivers over every inch of me.

Simion never once dropped his eyes from mine as he worked to unravel the bandages. Soft knuckles brushed my skin, snatching my breath. It was a tender, calm moment. Although he restrained from using his power on me, his touch alone was a welcome relief.

Simion looked down to my newly healed flesh and his smile vanished. Before I could follow his gaze, my mind reacted, preparing myself for the onslaught of horror.

My arm was no longer burned, no longer a mess of flesh and agony. I had been healed, so nothing prevented me from seeing the truth. A truth I despised far more than scarred skin. Unbroken and as prominent as it had been the day of my handfasting to Camron, the inked mark across my skin shone proudly in the dull light of the bedroom.

I sat up against the seething pain in every muscle, bone and vein. I pulled my arm from Simion's grip and held it before me.

'But he...'

Simion rubbed his thumb over the silver thorns and vines, but they did not disappear.

'Breathe for me, Maximus.' Simion reclaimed my hand as though it belonged to him.

I was thankful for his cool touch and the ever-present brush of icy fingers. It told me he was lingering in the far reaches of my mind. Even if I had the energy to raise those walls of steel, I wouldn't.

'Take it all away,' I said, pleading with wide eyes full of tears, unable to think past what the markings could mean.

Simion just looked at me, mouth agape, eyes grasped in horror. Then he encased me in his arms, burying his lips into my hair. He didn't let me go, not as my tears stained his tunic. Not as my body trembled violently. I thought the world was breaking apart.

'Camron Calzmir is dead, our bond should've broken.'

*Only in death shall you part.* Then why was my skin still marred by the fast-marks? Why did the silver glow as bright as newly forged steel?

'We will figure this out,' Simion said, words muffled as he held me close. 'I promise, we will make sense of this. Together.'

Fear gave way to anger—scalding, I thought it would eat me from the inside out.

'I don't want to feel,' I snapped, blinded by red. 'Please, take it away. Take it all away.'

If I ever thought Simion had the power to refuse me, he proved in that moment he didn't.

'You are my weakness.' Simion's fingers pressed into my skin, his eyes glowing with magic. I closed mine, exhaling as his power clawed through me, tearing every destructive emotion from my very core. 'For you, Maximus Oaken, I would do anything you asked of me. *Anything.*'

# A LETTER FROM BEN

Dear wonderful reader,

Wow. You made it. What a ride, right?

I want to say a huge thank you for choosing to read my book, *Heir to Thorn and Flame*. This has been a book I have been working on since 2018 and I have never felt more ready for it to be read, devoured and enjoyed. This is only the start of Maximus's story—there is so much more to come. I hope you stick around for more ice-breathing dragons, magical creatures and romance. The heat is being turned up a notch.

*www.secondskybooks.com/ben-alderson*

I hope you loved *Heir to Thorn and Flame* and if you did, I would be very grateful if you could write a review. I'd love to hear what you think, and it makes such a difference helping new readers to discover one of my books for the first time.

I love hearing from my readers—you can get in touch on my Facebook page, through Twitter, Instagram or my website.

All my love,

Ben Alderson

# KEEP IN TOUCH WITH BEN

www.benalderson.com

facebook.com/BenAldersonAuthor
twitter.com/BenAldersonBook
instagram.com/benaldersonauthor

# ACKNOWLEDGEMENTS

I would like to say a massive thank you to my incredible readers. Whether you have been following me since my YouTube days, or if you are from BookTok—this would never have been possible without you.

Jasmine Andrady. BESTIE, I GET TO ADD YOU INTO THE ACKNOWLEDGEMENTS OF A BOOK. Can you believe this is happening? Pinch me. You have been my number-1 fan since we first bumped into each other at school. Without you introducing me to reading—more importantly the incredible library of indie and self-published books—I don't think I would even be here. You willingly spend hours discussing stories. You have read every single word I have ever written. I am so lucky to have you.

Kirsty Bonnick. Well, my egg... This story would never have seen the light of day without your input, encouragement and excitement. I will never forget us spending hours in the coffee shop, coming up with new ways to better torture these poor characters.

Noelle. They say good things happen when the stars align, you must be the hand who moved mine into the right position.

Jack, my wonderful editor. There is no one better to be helping me create this book than you. In the time we have worked together, we have sent hundreds of emails, sharing ideas and concepts. You truly helped breathe life back into the story of my heart. Thank you for saying 'GIVE ME MORE ROMANCE'—Maximus is grateful.

Kellen Graves. Elise Kova. Harry Quinn. Amber Nicole. Kaven Hirning. Merlin Kuwertz. Christine Spoors. Gabriella Lepore, Chloe C. Penaranda, my Discord 'Aldernerds' family —thank you for being my greatest supporters.

And to the team of Second Sky Books. You are truly the best home I could have asked for. I look forward to what incredible adventures we embark on next.

Made in the USA
Monee, IL
15 August 2023